ILARIO:
THE STONE
GOLEM

Also by Mary Gentle

ILARIO: THE STONE GOLEM

A Story of the First History

Book Two

Mary Gentle

An Imprint of HarperCollins*Publishers*

The first part of *Ilario* appeared in a slightly different form as *Under the Penitence*. Copyright © 2004 by Mary Gentle, published by PS Publishing Limited. All rights reserved. An extract titled 'The Logistics of Carthage' was first published in *Worlds that Weren't,* by ROC, in 2002.

This book was originally published in Great Britain in 2006 by Gollancz, an imprint of the Orion Publishing Group, London.

HarperCollins books may be purchased for educational, business, or sales promotional use. For information please write: Special Markets Department, HarperCollins Publishers, 10 East 53rd Street, New York, NY 10022.

FIRST U.S. EDITION

Library of Congress Cataloging-in-Publication Data is available upon request.

ISBN: 978-0-06-134498-5
ISBN-10: 0-06-134498-2

07   08   09   10   11   ❖/RRD   10   9   8   7   6   5   4   3   2   1

Contents

What came before . . .

Ilario: The Lion's Eye

The first story of the first history, in which we met Ilario: painter, scholar, hermaphrodite . . . and unsuspecting catalyst of destinies.

Ilario has served King Rodrigo as the King's Freak, but while surviving the ways of the court, Ilario has yet another lesson to learn: abandonment and betrayal. For Rosamunda, Ilario's birth mother, has arrived—and the secret of Ilario's shameful birth must be kept hidden.

Fleeing a murder attempt, Ilario crosses the sea to Carthage, where the Penitence shrouds the sky in darkness. There, a fateful encounter with the scholar-spy Rekhmire' spawns an adventure that will span continents, from Iberia to Carthage to Venice and beyond, from art to treachery, love to loss, from tenuous alliances to deadly machinations.

And when last we left, Ilario was in childbirth, hidden away in the winding backstreets of Venice. But even there danger and intrigue stalk the would-be painter . . .

Part One

Serenissima

1

Ramiro Carrasco has not seen me as a man!

It was the only thought in my head.

I couldn't breathe. His hands pressed cloth and a bulk of goose-down feathers into my mouth and nose. My vision blacked into sparkles.

My chest hurt as I tried and failed to pull in air.

It can happen just this easily! – because people are busy for a few minutes looking at the baby, because these curtains are drawn—

'Ilario's heart stopped.' Even Physician Bariş will say so. The labour of having the baby. Too much for a hermaphrodite body. Even Rekhmire' will believe it. The midwife will confirm it. Ramiro Carrasco has nothing to do now but wait until my face is blue and then scream out an alarm that I'm not breathing—

And Ramiro Carrasco has never seen me dressed as a man.

The pillow blinded me towards the left field of my vision, but left a sliver of my right eye clear. Carrasco stared down at me, his expression curiously desperate as he bore down with his full weight.

I had time to think *Shouldn't I be the desperate one?* and ceased to claw at the pillow, and at his rock-hard muscles.

I let my arm fall out loosely to the side, over the edge of the bed.

Hard ceramic clipped the tips of my fingers.

My heart thudded hard enough to take the remaining air out of my lungs. My ribs ached with trying to breathe. And— Yes, this is where I saw one of the servants set down a water-jug. A brown-glazed pint jug, with a narrow neck, and two moulded loops for lifting.

My head throbbed under the pressure of his hands. I slid my fingers through the glazed loops at the jug's neck, gripped tightly, and locked my elbow. The weight pulling on tendon and muscle told me it was still completely full.

Lifting pottery and the weight of water together, barely able to see where I aimed past the pillow and his arm, I brought the jug round in a hard arc. And crashed it into the side of Ramiro Carrasco's head.

With all the muscular strength of an arm that, while it isn't male, isn't female either.

Pottery smashed. Water sprayed.

Pressure lifted up off my face.

For a moment I couldn't see – couldn't claw the pillow away from my nose and mouth—

A noise sounded to the side of me. A tremendous crash.

'*Ilario!*'

Clear air hissed into my lungs.

Rekhmire' stood looking down, pillow in his hand; there were the backs of four or five men behind him, low down, on the floor—

Kneeling *on* someone on the floor.

'Ilario!' A knee landed beside me on the other side of the bed; Honorius's lean and chilly hand felt roughly at my neck. Feeling for my heartbeat.

'I'm alive!' I gasped. Pain ached through my entire body. I hitched myself up on my elbows and gazed down past Rekhmire', at where Orazi and Viscardo and Saverico were kneeling on, and punching at, the slumped figure of Ramiro Carrasco de Luis.

'Don't kill him,' I added weakly. '*I* want to.'

Honorius gave out with a deep-bellied laugh, and ruffled my sweat-soaked hair. 'That's my son-daughter!'

'What—?' Federico stepped forward from the thunderstruck family group, boggling down at Carrasco. His shock looked genuine. '*What* did he . . . He can't have tried— There *must* be some mistake—!'

The door banged opened hard enough to bruise the wood panelling, Neferet and her midwife and priest piled into the room, together with those others of Honorius's men within earshot. Tottola and his brother between them completely blocked the doorway.

I felt tension infuse Honorius, through his hand on my scalp.

He looked across, caught Orazi's eye, nodded at Aldra Federico, and then at the door. 'Get them *out* of here!'

Federico blustered, Sunilda burst into tears, Reinalda threw her arms around her sister and led her out through the door. Valdamerca, tall enough to look Orazi in the eye, made a fist and punched at the sergeant's mail-covered chest as he and the two German men-at-arms bodily shoved all of my foster family out of the room.

The slamming two-inch-thick oak cut off Valdamerca's virulent complaints and protestations of innocence.

Still coughing and choking, I got out, 'I don't suppose they *did* know he'd do that!'

'They don't matter.' Honorius spoke with enough habitual authority that I didn't for the moment desire to question him. He beckoned with his free hand. 'Physician. Come and see to this! I want Ilario *thoroughly* checked.'

Rekhmire' stood back as Bariş bent over me.

I reached out one hand to the Egyptian, and one to Honorius on the other side, and squeezed both hard. 'The son of a bitch tried to *kill* me!'

Rekhmire''s severe face was grey, under the ruddy tone of his skin. 'We should not have let him lull us.'

Honorius turned back from confirming with the Turkish physician that, yes, I might have bruises, and yes, I had been constricted as to air, but in fact there was – as I wanted to shout – *nothing wrong with me!*

'Nothing that eighteen hours of labour doesn't put into the shade . . . ' I may have muttered that aloud.

Honorius pulled his hand-and-a-half sword half out of its scabbard, the noise muffled by the loud room. 'Finally. Finally, we don't have to worry about Carrasco any longer!'

Neferet, the Venetian midwife, Physician Bariş, and Father Azadanes all raised their voices, crowding around Honorius, impeding his sword-arm.

He ignored them, looking only at me.

I stared down off the edge of the bed, at Ramiro Carrasco de Luis sprawled supine on the floorboards.

Unconscious, by the trickle of blood staining his chin. Or perhaps he'd just bitten himself while mailed fists were punching him.

His face was bruised, bloody; his lashes fluttered a little and were still. I saw the pulse beating in his throat.

'You can't kill him while he's unconscious.' It was not a rational objection, but I could come up with no greater argument. My hands shook.

Trying to keep control of my voice, I added, 'Denounce him to the Council of Ten. Let them arrest him!'

For all I could see Neferet's face a strained grey, my bitterness spilled out:

'Put Carrasco in a Venetian dungeon! Let my noble stepfather Videric explain to Venice why his spy is in prison! Or let my damn foster father explain why his *secretary* just tried to kill his fosterchild!'

Rekhmire' had not let go of my hand; he must feel how I trembled. His own hand was not completely steady. The Egyptian looked down at me with a warm expression.

'That's my Ilario! Yes. Let's use this to cause as much trouble for the Aldra Videric as we can, shall we? And Aldra Federico, of course. Complaints, lawsuits, public gossip . . . '

By the time I rolled my head over on the bolster to look up at him, Honorius was reluctantly nodding. He shoved his sword into his red leather scabbard with the ease that only comes from long use.

'It's not a bad idea. But, Ilario, if you're hurt . . . If you just *want* me to do this . . . He's a dead man. I have enough influence here that I won't need to answer for it.'

Despite the storm of protests from the Venetians and the Alexandrine, I thought he was probably correct. Apart from anything else, the retired Captain-General of Castile and Leon is a friend of the successful mercenary general Carmagnola, whom the Venetian Council currently employs and won't wish upset.

Years in Rodrigo's court can teach many things.

I have a clear picture in my mind, in the hopes of later making a painting of it. Ramiro Carrasco's face as he held the stifling pillow over me. And his absolute and strange desperation.

'Don't kill Carrasco.' A sudden unannounced fear went through me, jagged as lightning. 'Is the baby— Did the *baby* die?'

That sent the crowd to the cradle.

I slumped back on the mattress, shutting my eyes. So small, born so much before its proper time . . . Likely she will have died when all this violence shattered the atmosphere of peace in the room. For one moment I was completely certain.

It – she – did not feel like my child. I could feel no love, no warmth, no attraction to her. A sheer wave of fear rushed through me; making my head feel as if it was swollen, and my vision black as grief.

'Here.' Honorius placed the carefully-wrapped warm bundle on my chest: it wriggled and thinly whined. 'She's here. She's just hungry.' A confused look went across his sun-burned features. 'I *think* she's hungry.'

His men looked amused, Rekhmire' gave him a look of sympathy, and the unspoken stare that commented 'Ignoramus!' came – I noted as I gazed around – from the midwife, Bariş the physician, the priest, and Neferet. I wondered at that last.

'I,' I said, 'don't know any more than you do.'

Rekhmire' gave a nod, and turned to speak to the midwife.

'Wet-nurse,' he said.

The men-at-arms dragged Ramiro Carrasco de Luis out by the heels of his boots, and I heard his head bang against every tread on the way down the stairs.

2

With a chair moved close to the window, and a blanket about me, I could avoid the worst of the draughts coming in around the cracked wood, and still gain a clear view of the blue sky.

Winter's heavy grey and sharp blue was softening, and the frost whitened the earth only in the early mornings and late evenings.

I kept the room warm for the baby, although the air outside in the middle of the day was temperate enough for me to cast off an over-robe.

While making my own way as far as the Riva was impossible, I heard from my father that ships from other ports already began to dock in the San Marco basin.

'Travel's becoming possible again.' Restless, I abandoned a sketch of my knife and plate – the elipse of the plate defeating me – going to lay on my bed that was now beside the hearth with the child's makeshift cradle. I watched Rekhmire' experimenting with a walking-staff taller than he. 'Messages. Men. We're not cut off. Or, soon won't be.'

The Egyptian finally settled on using just the one crutch, lodged under his right arm. He had abandoned the linen kilt of the Alexandrines for a tunic and trousers in the Turkish style. I suspected this was so that no man could look at his knee, now that the bandages were off it.

A clatter of rapid footsteps sounded. Rekhmire' shifted himself with difficulty to open the room door. The noise resolved itself into Neferet, wearing pattens that tracked mud down the passage past the bedroom. She gave a distracted wave of her hand, not stopping to speak, or pet the new-born.

'No news of Leon Battista,' I speculated.

'Still in the Doge's prison.' Rekhmire' thumped his crutch against the floorboards. 'As is your Ramiro Carrasco de Luis. A man I hope *rots* there.'

I felt no love for the baby – which convinced me I was the monster I had always assumed. A true mother would well up with love, knowing the child as her own.

If I felt anything, it was fear and wonder.

Amazement had me laying with her in the crook of my arm, tracing her perfectly-folded eyelids and dark lashes, and having my stomach jerk whenever her flailing hand intersected mine. I couldn't tell if her fingers closed of their own volition over me.

Fear made me watch like a patient falcon as her skin colour passed from blue-red to red to the normal shade – and panic when her feet stayed the peculiar blue-purple of the new-born. It took Bariş an afternoon to reassure me that this would change in several days, and I blushed at seeing the Turkish doctor after that, feeling a fool.

'I've been asked all questions!' Bariş gave me an aquiline smile as his fingers checked the red fontanelle patches on her skull. 'The fathers, they're the worst. "If it cries when it sees me, does that mean it's not mine?"'

I thought of asking him if he was ever asked that very question by mothers.

But that might lead to disquieting information about his previous Caesarian surgeries, and I had, if I was honest, no desire to know. I merely desired my burning belly to heal.

'She *doesn't* cry,' I said. 'Is she too weak?'

'Some of them don't.' He smiled down at her, lines creasing all his narrow face, and touched his finger to her perfect cheek. 'When she does, you'll be sorry you asked! Now, have I told you how to care for the birth-cord?'

Fear made me lay awake hour after dark hour in the night, waiting for her to wake, and Tottola or Saverico to bring up boiled cow's milk so that one of us might feed her with spoon and cup. After the first few days she turned her head repeatedly from the hired Venetian woman who had more milk than her own son could drink.

But she grows heavier on animal milk, I judged, weighing her in my two hands every day. And she did not have the stolid, lethargic look of those lambs that refuse to thrive. I wondered if I might judge her in the same way that one judges a beast, or whether humankind is different.

After five days, her birth-cord dropped off. It was the last of the landmarks Bariş had charged me to watch for: her bowels and bladder both proved themselves functional earlier, and I learned to pin cloth around her.

She was yellow for a few days, which the Turkish physician also dismissed as a cause for fear.

I felt fear of the darkness; fear of the cold winter nights with the damp blowing in off the lagoon; fear of every gossiping rumour of plague or fever. Her eyes moved under her eyelids as she dreamed. I wondered if she could dream of Torcello, and the sights and smells imprinted on me while she began her birth.

My time passed in small landmarks and the overhanging dread of death.

Days went by. I grew stronger. Neferet lost her womanly plumpness and grew gaunt with worry.

I knew Rekhmire', as well as Neferet, must be contacting all the men a book-buyer would know in this city – but Leon Battista was a son of the Alberti family, it seemed, and the Alberti family had been exiles in Venice these twenty years. If their accumulated interest couldn't move the Doge's mercy, I doubted two Alexandrines could.

Supine in bed, stitches healing, I studied Leon's treatise on vision as if some obscure sympathetic magic would ensure that the more attention I gave it, the more likely Leon Battista would have good fortune.

I blamed the Green priest for superstitious thoughts. Neferet's Father Azadanes claimed the baby's (and my) survival as his own Green Christ's miracle. I found the argument not persuasive.

'Sheer chance!' I said, when Rekhmire' had his prayer-box open, lighting incense to the eight gods within. 'Chance plays far too much of a part in the world for men to be easy thinking of it.'

Rekhmire' finished his ceremony with a bow of his head to the Eight, and clipped the box shut again.

'A man should always be polite . . . ' He dusted incense from the front of his tunic and trousers, and used his crutch to cross the room, putting the prayer-box away in his oak chest. ' . . . Especially to minor gods. The advantage of deities who control small things is that one need never worry about why evil and pain rule so much of this world – minor gods are obviously too weak to prevent it.' He hesitated. 'I don't know what the excuse of Father Azadanes' God is.'

I was inclined to smile at that, but very wryly. 'Heathen! Pagan. Atheist!'

Rekhmire' snorted. 'Make up your mind which!'

The tiny, warm, damp weight of the child on my chest became something I was used to, as I rested in the great bed in the Alexandrine house and regained my strength.

When I complained that I was strong enough, Rekhmire' invited me to move, and I discovered how badly the stitches knitting the walls of my womb could hurt.

I steered clear of Father Azadanes' company, weary as I was of hearing about his 'Green miracle', and how he attributed the baby's survival and mine to the Green Christ. It was difficult to avoid him, since he was much with Neferet.

Once, coming into a room more quietly than I realised, I overheard Neferet asking, 'But can't your God make *my* body mirror what my *ka* is?', and I backed out as silently as I'd come. Her – *his* – desperation hurt me.

The more so because of her jealousy. She watched the baby, in my arms; watched it avidly enough that, if I hadn't had Honorius with me, I would have been half inclined to offer it to her for adoption. Certainly no one would ever get past that lioness-of-Alexandria attitude to harm the child.

Physician Bariş, with a sombre face, came to tell me he doubted his surgery could mend a womb like mine so that it could conceive again. Especially since it had been such a remote chance I should conceive the first time.

I felt a rush of relief, and at the same time terror, looking at the miniature sleeping face and thinking, *This is the only one.*

'Tell you truth,' Barış observed dispassionately, having finished his investigation of my healing surgical wound. 'I'm more surprised to see *you* live than her. Frankly, it's a miracle you survived.'

He looked confused when I muttered, 'Don't *you* start!'

The baby's small size continued to flabbergast me.

She was barely bigger than Honorius's hand when he caressed her in her swaddling bands. Although she didn't wear the tight strips of cloth for long – a day or so later, Rekhmire' muttered something about barbaric customs, and (with Barış's help) overrode the Venetian midwife and my father. The baby girl was allowed to lay on my bedcover, only a swathe of linen around her, in the patches of sunlight that made her dark eyes close and open as slowly as if she were under the sea.

The stitches being painful for longer than I expected, I found myself frustrated in my desire to care for her. Neferet, unsurprisingly, took up every chance to feed or bathe her – somewhat more surprisingly, I had help from not only Honorius himself, but from Saverico and those others of the men-at-arms with younger siblings or their own children at home. Berenguer slid in and out of the room when she was a few weeks old, and left a fish carved out of ash-wood, that she might play with – or at least watch – in the shallow water of her bath.

I wondered much if there might be something wrong with her. But I kept those thoughts to myself.

After a few weeks, as she put on weight by the efforts of cow- and goat-milk, I found that I knew what her name ought to be, even if she still might not live to use it.

I spoke to Honorius one midday, when the rest of the house was still at their meal.

'With your permission – I would like to call her "Onorata".'

My father smiled and wept together, without shame.

'I feel nothing like a mother,' I said to Rekhmire', as the Egyptian handed Onorata back to me after she burped milk over the feeding-cloth on his shoulder. 'I can't put her to my breast . . . '

Looking up, I surprised concern on his face.

'But I feel I should protect her,' I added. 'Perhaps I should think of myself as Onorata's father?'

The Egyptian's brows dipped into a scowl. 'If it comes to it, I would suppose you both, in that sense. But why not a mother?'

Because I would not be Rosamunda if my life depended on it.

The thought of that woman, in Carthage or Taraco, still sends hot sweat down my spine, half the length of the Mediterranean Sea away from her.

Am I not supposed to understand her better, now?

'I have no idea how to be a mother. Valdamerca raised me as a slave.' I shrugged. 'But Honorius is a good father. If Onorata lives, perhaps I can be to her what he would have been to me.'

The Egyptian slowly nodded.

I don't know if Rekhmire' mentioned the conversation to Honorius, but one day after the year's early Easter, when I ventured downstairs, I caught the Captain-General of Castile and Leon drawing up dowry documents for his granddaughter, and another version of his will.

He blushed and put the documents away in his portable wooden writing-desk.

'I leaned to write a reasonable scribe's hand when I didn't have an ensign in camp who could do it for me.' He shrugged, ostensibly casual. 'I want you and Onorata to be wealthy when I die.'

'Now why didn't I think of that?' I nodded towards his sword, where it was wrapped in the scabbard's straps and laying on the window-chest. 'Pass me the sword and I'll be able to afford all the red chalk I could ever need . . . '

Honorius grinned.

'I'll haunt you,' he said cheerfully.

'You do anyway. I can't get away from you. You and the bloody book-buyer!' I raised my voice in case Rekhmire' should be near enough to tease, but there was no response.

And no crying baby, either. He often took her into his lap while he sorted scrolls, so I suspected the one absence answered the other.

Honorius neatly cleaned and wrapped up his quills and wax tablets and paper, stowing them away. He crossed the room and bent over to place another piece of wood on the fire in the hearth.

'I spoke through Carmagnola to Doge Foscari,' he observed. 'Apparently, Messer Leon Battista will come for trial, soon.'

I had wondered why matters would drag on for so long – until I worked out that the Council of Ten would want to know how it was that so very many identical seditious news-letters could be produced within a short amount of time. And since the name of Herr Mainz wasn't being bandied about Venezia, I guessed Leon had not yet spoken.

A slave has always to live under the threat of torture. It is a subject I have given some thought. The idea of Leon Battista having to undergo pain like that, unprepared as he must surely be . . .

Honorius put his lean hand on my shoulder. As if he read my mind in my face, he said, 'Neferet's seen him. She says they're letting darkness and hunger do their work for them. Given the Alberti family's place on the Council, even Foscari won't use outright torture until he can make it seem there's no other option. And by then he'll be out of there. You like Leon Battista,' he finished, with an odd questioning note to his voice.

I nodded. Frankly, I said, 'I think he's a *fool*. But I don't have a city that I care about as he cares for Florence. Perhaps I'd do the same under those circumstances. Slaves don't have homes in that way.'

'No.' Honorius's hand gave my shoulder a final pressure. He looked at me with a smile. 'Have you thought? Onorata is freeborn.'

For my final examination before he departed, the Janissary doctor was visibly not certain whether to request a man or a woman as chaperone.

Bariş seized on Rekhmire''s muttered volunteering with gladness – likely because 'Alexandrine eunuch bureaucrat' trumped both in terms of respectability.

'You should tell the physician if you intend to have sex again,' Rekhmire' mumbled towards the end of an extensive examination, translating some of the medical Greek technicalities.

I raised both eyebrows at him.

A dark flush turned his Egyptian colouring something closer to brick-red than I had imagined possible.

'Whether you intend to fornicate . . . It's not as if you're breast-feeding, to avoid conception. I know he's said, ah . . . that it's all but impossible . . . but . . . You ought not to get pregnant again. That would be very dangerous.'

I grinned at him. 'You're not my master, Rekhmire'.'

Or a mother hen, I reflected, as he looked even more flustered.

Evidently pulling himself together, and ignoring my minor harassment, Rekhmire' faced the Jannissary doctor. '*Is* Ilario capable of conceiving another child?'

I murmured, 'Now there's a question I never wanted to hear . . . '

Bariş looked amused. Rekhmire' failed to.

'Because, you see, if Ilario is capable, then having sex as a woman could be dangerous, if not fatal.' Rekhmire' stuttered. 'Ilario, will you be content to have sex as a man does?'

'Uh.' I felt my cheeks heating; knew I must be red from neck to hairline.

'With – another *man*, that is? I suppose – of course – if you were to have sex as a man does with a woman—' Rekhmire' tucked his arms tightly across his chest and glared down at me. 'Doctor, can Ilario get a woman pregnant?'

'No.' Bariş shook his head. 'Never.'

He glanced from Rekhmire' to me, and back to the Egyptian.

'Because I have never, in my entire professional career, seen such a scarlet shade of embarrassment – I doubt this patient will ever have sex again!'

What concerns I might have had were, by that, and the expression on Rekhmire''s face, exploded completely.

I howled and clutched at my ribs.

Rekhmire' squirmed. 'I hardly meant . . . I had no intention of . . . ! I—'

'Go *away*, Rekhmire'.' I couldn't stop grinning. 'You're not my master, you don't have to force yourself to ask the doctor gynaecological questions! And Physician Bariş is right. At the moment, I'm debating between a monastery and a nunnery! Just so long as it's a celibate order!'

It wouldn't have surprised me had the Egyptian cited some of the more scurrilous rumours about Frankish monasteries and nunneries. Instead, Rekhmire' clattered his crutch against the floor and made a production of lumbering off. I wheezed with the first uninhibited laugh I'd had in months.

Bariş eventually ended his investigations under my skirts.

'You're healing healthily and quickly. Put no stress on that part of your body; avoid heavy exertion for the moment.' He signalled to the giant Balaban to pack up his medical chest. 'Might I have a look at the child? If you don't mind?'

I lifted Onorata out of the oak-chest cot, unwinding the nominal swaddling bands that loosely swathed her. Instead of crying, she beat thin perfect arms against me, and snuggled onto my chest in wide-eyed relaxation, apparently gazing up at the Turk.

'Can you tell? If she's normal,' I clarified.

He ran his finger down the sole of her foot, watching her small toes curl. 'I examined her at the birth.'

'Yes, but – I don't know what there might be on the inside.'

Bariş's ship's-prow nose cast a shadow across Onorata's body as he bent down, peering very closely.

'These things are so rare. Nor do *I* know, to be honest. And most "hermaphrodites" are men born looking in some way like a woman, or women who have what resemble the man's parts. Or nothing changes until they become adult, and then a woman merely coughs and testicles appear . . . I thought the *true* hermaphrodite was only a rumour. A fable.'

I sighed as he lifted Onorata with all gentleness, and laid her back on the wooden chest's bedding.

I put my hands to the hem of my shift. 'You want another look?'

'May I? The last occasions have been a little fraught . . . '

His voice became muffled as he bent down.

The iron instruments were cold, making me flinch.

In accented Alexandrine Egyptian, Bariş observed, 'You have little more than the eunuch has, as testes go! I *wish* I had you for an autopsy, to find out for certain whether this lump is testes or ovary . . . '

'Well, I'm damn glad you don't!'

Bariş gave me something perilously close to a grin, and gestured for me to pull my shift back down. 'A shame I go back to Edirne now my captain has recovered. You could put it in your will that I could have your body.'

Having pulled my shift down, I shrugged my way into the voluminous Venetian over-robe that Honorius had gifted me, and began to lace up the front of it.

'Firstly, I'm not dying! And, secondly, if I *do* die in Venice, not only will my friend Rekhmire' follow you to Edirne and kill you several times, each more horrible than the last . . . I, personally, will *haunt* you.'

The Turkish doctor called for a bowl to bathe his hands. Deadpan, he remarked, 'I begin to see the advantages in the Hippocratic Oath . . . '

Having washed, he took a wax tablet and stylus from an inside pocket of his tunic, and poised the one over the other.

'I may write to Ephesus and Padua with my findings,' he remarked, small bright eyes focusing on me. 'But I have a number of additional questions I wish you will answer, Ilario . . . Which only you can answer. *You* must know which is best – the male orgasm or the female orgasm? So, which? Or is it that you feel you only know what's normal for a hermaphrodite, and not for a man or a woman? How is your sexual appetite? When your man-parts are spent; is it possible to function as a woman until the male refractory period passes? Have you ever dually and simultaneously—'

Honorius walked into the room, perfunctorily rapping on the door.

'Oh thank God!'

Honorius ignored that. 'I need to talk to you. Alone.'

3

'Alone' meant three of us; my father sending one of his men for Rekhmire'. Four, if Onorata counted – blissfully silent, since asleep in her lidless oak chest.

Honorius himself served mulled wine into ceramic bowls. He sat on the joint-stool by the bed, set his own wine down on the stone hearth, and scratched at his hair until it stood up in tufts, giving him the semblance of a fierce, if ruffled, owl.

He broke the silence.

'A letter has arrived. Written to me.'

Fear stabbed under the joining of my ribs.

I ignored Rekhmire''s concerned frown and held out my hand. 'Show me!'

Silently, Honorius fished out creased papers from his sleeve, and held one out between two fingers. I took it.

'From King Rodrigo Sanguerra.'

If my sight blurred with shock, I still recognised Hunulf's penmanship: a particular curve on the 'd' and 'g'. He's long wanted my nominal position as scribe to the Sanguerra family.

I reached for the bowl with my other hand, welcoming the hot taste of spiced wine, and finding my fingers shaking only a little as I read.

'Translated freely,' I observed, 'it appears to say, "Get your arse back here before I sequester your estates *and* put your family under attainder"—'

Rekhmire' snickered, caught Honorius's glare, and glossed it: 'You see why I employed Ilario as a scribe.'

'No.' Honorius kept a perfectly straight face for a moment. He smirked as he took the page back from me and passed it over to the Egyptian. 'I grant you the accuracy of reading between the lines.'

'This isn't like the last one?' I speculated. 'Not a dozen copies sent out to ambassadors or bankers, so that one would get to you sooner or later? This came direct to Venezia?'

Rekhmire' did not even look up to see Honorius's confirming nod.

'It would appear that King Rodrigo knows where the Captain-General is . . . There are other channels by which information could pass, but I will point out that Aldra Federico – and Ramiro Carrasco, when he was at large – are both positioned to have told your King this. Or rather Videric, whom we may assume would tell King Rodrigo.'

Honorius muttered, '*Court politics!*' in tones of deepest disgust

I got up. It eased me to pace the room, despite the pull on my pink and healing stitches.

'This makes twice King Rodrigo's ordered you home.' I paused, bending down to touch the fluff on Onorata's head. 'And as we said in Rome, it's understandable. You retire, rich. You head home for Taraco. No man sees you. The first thing you do is leave again for Carthage—'

'That was to visit you!' Honorius looked mulish.

'I know that! You know that! The King doesn't know that!'

Onorata began grizzling.

Rekhmire' leaned his crutch against the hearth-surround, and lifted Onorata out of her cot into his lap. His arm supported her head with a professional care. I did not know whether to feel pleasure or jealousy that she subsided at once into whining mutters.

Voice soft and even, Rekhmire' said, 'Ilario's correct. King Rodrigo *doesn't* know. He has a foreign general come home – foreign, because twenty-five years in Navarra and Castile means no man knows you. You have the reputation of "the Lion of Castile"—'

The Egyptian pressed on when Honorius would have interrupted:

'—Whatever you think of your reputation, you have it. You return to Taraconensis, you ask your King for nothing, and you go to Carthage. *Exactly* when, as far as he's concerned, Carthage has just robbed him of his First Minister!'

My father spluttered.

I took the opportunity to speak. 'Either Federico will have written, or Videric will have told King Rodrigo himself, that you're my father.'

And if that interview took place between Videric and Rodrigo Sanguerra, I would like to have witnessed it. Between Videric's embarrassment at being cuckolded, and Rodrigo's ferocious temper at not having been told all this before, I thought I would have found it very satisfying.

Rekhmire' handed Onorata up to me and reclaimed his own drinking bowl. 'Which, of course, makes Videric all the more dangerous now. Viler things have been done out of fear than ever stemmed from anger or revenge.'

Honorius sprang to his feet, his fingers white against the green glaze of his wine bowl. 'I can't believe my supposed *King* thinks me disloyal!'

Watching Honorius's stiff back as he stalked over to the window, I doubted he would conceive of anyone believing him that.

I rocked Onorata gently in my arms. 'You didn't return from Rome at his request.'

'I—' Honorius spun on his boot-heel, pointing at Rekhmire'. 'Your messengers caught me up!'

The Egyptian nodded. 'Which is why I thought hard before I wrote. I knew it might look bad.'

Honorius set his jaw. 'I can sort this out ten minutes after I set foot in Taraco harbour – which I *will*, once I have assurances of my son-daughter's and grand-daughter's safety!'

Onorata stretched up her hand and prodded at my chin, although the contact may have been accidental. Judging by the slant of the light, she would be hungry soon.

'If I were Aldra Videric,' I said absently, playing catch-finger with the baby, 'I'd be telling Rodrigo Sanguerra that you came back from Castile with the express intent of talking *his* place as First Minister. I'd tell the King you're in alliance with Carthage. That when Taraconensis gets legions sent in to keep the kingdom safe from crusading Franks, the military governor they put in place of the King will be Aldra Captain-General Honorius.'

Honorius stared at me. Rekhmire' too, I noted.

'Rodrigo will be thinking that you *planned* to work with Carthage, to use me to get rid of Videric.' I shook my head. 'What? I was at court! I learned how all this works so that I could stay out of it!'

'Goddamn!' Honorius muttered in one of the northern Frankish dialects. 'Bloody goddamn . . . I swear you're right. Since the King doesn't merely threaten his anger—'

'What else?' Rekhmire' leaned forward on his stool, wincing at some pain in his knee-joint. 'There's more?'

'Oh, there's more . . . ' Honorius's lean body straightened, his hand closing around the remaining pages. Tendons and cartilege pulled taut under his skin; altered all the planes of light and shadow that made up his face.

'King Rodrigo Sanguerra is generously pleased to write me a *warning*.' Honorius's voice rasped. 'You may read it here, on this second page. He writes to tell me he's taken certain precautions for the safety of my new estates. In my absence.'

Honorius's forefinger tapped a tattoo on the paper.

'He's sent his royal troops in, to protect my lands against bandits – and against land-hungry nobles, who might jump in while I'm away. It seems that four hundred gentlemen and squires in the King's service are billeted on my land, in my castle – for which my estate naturally has to pay bed and board.'

His hand closed up, paper crumpling into a tight ball.

'Four hundred royal men-at-arms eating their bellies full at *my* expense! And I get this favour *because* I'm so loyal to the Crown! Rodrigo Sanguerra's doing me this favour because "is unwise to leave land unprotected in these uncertain times" . . . '

Rekhmire' had the look he wore during mathematical calculation. 'Will your estates support that many men? How many of your own are there?'

Honorius rubbed his brow hard. 'Thirty, thirty-five knights, and their lances? Say six or eight men to a lance . . . Three hundred-odd came home from Castile with me to settle down; act as my stewards, overseers, and the like. Marry local girls. I left most there when I came to Rome. Now – they won't dare disobey the King's orders. And they can't fight off four hundred men without a bloodbath on both sides.'

He stared, for a long silent moment; the flames of the fire were within his view but I doubted he saw them.

'And, no.' Honorius looked up at Rekhmire' as if he had only just remembered what he had been asked. 'My lands can't *support* four hundred extra men! They'll eat their way through the storerooms and the granaries, their horses will empty my stables, my stewards will run the coffers dry attempting to fulfil this responsibility . . . I left no man with the authority to go into debt on my behalf, but I won't be surprised to get back and find they've gone to the Etruscans or the Jews.'

He dropped the ball of paper to the floor and ground it under the heel of his boot.

'If Rodrigo's men-at-arms are anything like mine, they'll be living off the land inside a couple of months! That means the noblemen whose lands border mine won't be friends or allies of mine. Not if their fodder and crops are being raided.'

He glanced at me, with a sour smile containing admiration.

'King Rodrigo notes that, if I were disloyal, he wouldn't gift me this "small contingent" to protect my estates against insurrection from outside. *And* revolt from inside. Which means that if any of my lads protest, they'll find themselves accused of being rebels exploiting *my* absence! And meanwhile the King can go on draining away my resources and making enemies of my neighbours . . . Until I go back to Taraco.'

One of his hands made a fist: I noted how it thickened the tendons in his wrist.

'What I *resent* is that publicly Rodrigo will be seen to be doing something intelligent! In effect, he levies a fine on me that I can't refuse to pay. *He's* not having to support those troops himself, all the while this goes on. And no supporter of mine, if I have any, can point to the King being unfair, because he's *protecting* me!'

I echoed Honorius, quietly for the child in my arms. 'Goddamn!'

Rekhmire' replaced his wine bowl on the chess table. 'I begin to see why it's not merely Aldra Videric who's kept Taraconensis free and peaceful, this past generation and more! In every other man's eyes, King Rodrigo is doing something legal, something moral, to aid you. And meanwhile—'

The Alexandrine lifted one hand and mimicked a twisting motion.

Honorius laughed harshly. 'Meanwhile the bloody screws tighten, until my thumbs begin to bleed!'

My father threw himself down on the wooden settle, stretching out one long leg, and watching as I replaced Onorata in her cot. I hoped her doze would last.

'Ilario.' Honorius spoke quietly. 'There's no need for you to be concerned over this. I didn't come home from Castile poor. It'll take a year or two longer to get the estates in order, that's all. A good harvest next year or the year after and we're set.'

I rubbed my back as I straightened up. 'I can see why you never went in for politics. You're a really bad liar.'

Rekhmire' spluttered.

Honorius, with an unwillingly pleased look, said, 'I can deceive and feint on the field of battle. But you're right: I can't tell lies worth a damn. I see I should tell you the truth in future, you'll find it more reassuring.'

'I suppose that's one word for it . . . '

Honorius added, 'I'm not leaving Venice.'

He barely sounded stubborn about it. Twenty or thirty years of taking and giving orders – especially the giving – and even his common pronouncements tend to sound like statements of irrefutable fact. As for anything he thinks he's made his mind up over . . .

'You are leaving!'

It didn't sound at all impressive in my emphatic tenor. Perhaps because of the alto squeak that crept in, despite my efforts. I glared at the grey-haired soldier.

Not looking up from the page he studied, Rekhmire' observed, 'Going to Taraco might, now, be very advantageous – I know what I would do if I were in Rodrigo Sanguerra's situation. I would offer the post of First Minister to Honorius.'

'*What!*' I turned to face him rapidly enough that I had to bend over, hands pressing against my stitches through my petticoats. I breathed hard. 'You think the King should give Honorius *Videric's* job?'

Honorius exploded into a chuckle and glanced between us, as if we were there for his entertainment.

The Egyptian ticked off points on his fingers. 'It would provide stability for Taraconensis. They would have a First Minister again, and it would be a war hero – twenty-five years of service in the Crusades. King Rodrigo is seen to have a powerful man at his side. *And* it to some degree fixes Honorius under Taraco's standard – how can Captain-General Licinus Honorius sneak off to Carthage and claim to want to be the "strong governor" Taraconensis needs, if he's already King Rodrigo's first adviser?'

Honorius slapped his leg in evident delight.

I snorted. That caught my stitches, too. 'You're forgetting one thing. *Videric wouldn't let him do it!*'

'Possibly. But even Aldra Videric must now be conjecturing that the King gains no current advantage from listening to *him*.' Rekhmire' shot me a sharp gaze. 'I grant you the risk of your father returning to Taraco.

But consider this. Master Honorius was twenty-five years in Castile and Leon.'

Honorius gave me a small, silent shrug.

'And?' I was as bewildered.

'I had some communication with scroll-collectors in Burgos and Salamanca and Avila, before winter set in.' Rekhmire''s rounded features smoothed into a shrewd expression. 'They confirmed what I recall of Castile and Leon – a snake-pit of political alliances and betrayals. All of which, Ilario, your father has steadfastly ignored.'

If Honorius spoke, it would be to snap, *Of course!* I quickly gestured for Rekhmire' to continue.

'King Juan the Second of Castile has one infallibly loyal man,' the Egyptian said. 'Called Alvaro, Count di Luna. Who, because of that position as the King's favourite, is the most powerful single individual in northern Iberia. In more than two decades, Master Honorius never joined any conspiracy against King Juan's favourite. More: he never tried to strike up a partnership with Alvaro di Luna.'

'You think Rodrigo Sanguerra will draw conclusions from that?'

Rekhmire' handed the page of King Rodrigo's letter back towards my father. 'How many Caesars began as successful generals? A man with an army supporting him has always been dangerous. If the soldiers of a kingdom follow one man, tradition and law all make way for him. As far as I can discover, and as far as King Rodrigo Sanguerra's spies in Leon and Castile should be telling *him*, the mercenary commander Licinus Honorius has never given any of his kings one sleepless night.'

Honorius looked plainly embarrassed.

A low hungry whine came from Onorata's cot; Honorius quickly rose and scooped her up, letting her suck on his forefinger, and went over to the door to call for milk.

Rekhmire' directed a look at me that said *I have given him somewhat to think on.*

'He shouldn't go to Taraco!' I attempted to shove hands into breeches-pockets, which in petticoats and a Frankish over-robe is bound to be unsuccessful. 'Not with Videric as his enemy. And you shouldn't be encouraging him!'

'Ilario—'

I rode over Rekhmire''s protest. 'This letter may just be something to get him on the road home! Suppose that's all it is? Suppose it doesn't matter about Taraco, because he's not intended to reach home – Videric will have paid *banditi, masnadiere*, pirates, any kind of thugs!'

'It's possible . . . but Master Honorius is a soldier.' Rekhmire' came to stand at my shoulder, watching my father give orders to one of Neferet's women. 'Have you thought? If King Rodrigo takes his lands, and forbids him to cross the borders of Taraconensis – your father loses everything it's taken him twenty-five years to earn by battle.'

4

I found it impossible to persuade Honorius to leave Venice.

Appealing to emotion, to logic; simply shouting as loudly as I could without breaking my scar open – nothing convinced him.

He sat in silence while I coaxed Onorata to feed. The room's tenseness made her cry and throw her arms about, spattering milk. Eventually I laid her across my lap, to ease her of belly-cramps as the midwife had suggested, but it was an hour or more before she ceased to cry, and fell asleep.

That had proved enough to make Rekhmire' descend the stairs, no matter how awkward he found it, and Honorius joined him. I left Neferet watching over Onorata – since *her* appetite for the bawling, squalling thing seemed inexhaustible – and took refuge in a chalk profile of Rekhmire', while Honorius shuffled through his small company's accounts.

'I won't leave you unprotected,' he remarked, finally. 'I've three lances here. Even if I split them with you, that only leaves each of us inadequately defended.'

'*I* don't need protection!' The proportions of Rekhmire''s eye and nose in no way matched each other. I threw down the slate in disgust. 'You'd be the one going into danger!'

The argument went on for an hour at the least, becoming increasingly mathematical. Rekhmire' joined in, not disputing Honorius's tactical assessments, but digging deeply into the same question – which my father declined to answer: *How many of your men do you need to stay safe from danger on the roads?*

I stopped speaking and let them go at it, treasuring an idea that came into my mind.

When both fell breathlessly silent, I spoke again.

'The answer to "How many men?" is "All of them",' I said. 'It has to be. I'll tell you why. Father, your concern is that when Videric's spies see you and your men leave, they'll kill me—'

'*No*, you can't come with me!' Honorius interrupted. 'I've seen the sewing-work on your belly: there's no way you're riding a horse or being strapped into a litter – *or* puking your guts up by sea! I know how long it takes men to recover from battlefield wounds; you're still weeks from ready, no matter what the Turk said—'

'Yes, but I don't think anyone else knows that.' I walked across the room and rested my hands on his shoulders, standing behind his chair. 'Go with all your men, banners flying. Ensign Saverico is about my height and build, although he's fair-haired. Put him in my green travelling cloak and a skirt. Any spies will report to Videric that I've left Venice.'

'A battle double.' Honorius glanced up, the dawning of amusement in his gaze. 'Well thought of! But not good enough. Am I supposed to leave my son-daughter and Onorata to that whoreson Federico, or any other ruffian who can make his way to Venice?'

'You'll lose your estates!'

He looked away from me. 'My reputation – which you and the Egyptian both seem to think I have – should mean I have no difficulty in earning more money, and buying more land. If it's not in Taraco . . . then it's elsewhere.'

'You are the *worst* liar!'

Honorius grinned, and reached for the seal on a wine bottle.

'Honorius – *Father*—'

It was my first experience of a long and pointless argument as a free individual rather than as a slave.

It was no less aggravating, and I seemed equally powerless. True, no man threatened to whip me when I threw a shoe at Honorius's head. But that was solely because it made him laugh, and then wipe at his eyes as if he were deeply moved.

'Stupid soldier!' I snarled.

He crossed the room and put his arms about my shoulders. As ever, he seemed to have no hesitation in touching me. He wept a little.

'Must have been hanging out with too many damned English mercenaries,' he muttered, wiping his face. 'All the English are far too emotional, always have been!'

I stated it as plainly as I could. 'If you have to fight to be paid again, you might be killed. I don't want that.'

'I am going nowhere until you're safe!' He scowled at me. 'And – what *is* safe? If you and the child could travel, I wouldn't take you with me. You and Videric in the same kingdom? There'd be men waiting at every corner to cut your throat!'

'Then I'll stay in Venice!'

'That's no better!'

The tense silence snapped, broken by a diplomatic cough from Rekhmire'.

'There's Alexandria,' I said, and translated for Honorius: 'Constantinople.'

'"Constantinople." ' Rekhmire' wrinkled his upper lip at the Frankish name for his city. 'I had wondered, if I can find Herr Mainz, or if the Pharaoh-Queen sends a new ambassador for Venice, whether I could wait a month or so until the weather is clearer, and then take a ship down through the Aegean to Alexandria. But, such a long voyage . . . '

Honorius scowled. 'Onorata is still very small. Travel might kill her.'

'Alexandria is far enough from Taraco that Ilario should be out of Videric's reach. And Ilario will have friends and protection there.' Rekhmire' had his chin on his hand, where he sat at the large table; his gaze only glanced across me.

'I won't risk such a young child,' Honorius grumbled.

He looked over at me, but I paid no attention. Fear turned my bowels hot and cold while he spoke to me, and I realised in a flash why.

If, in guilty waking moments, in the early hours of the morning, I held the unvoiced thought that it would be better, kinder, if the sickly child didn't survive – or better if the responsibility weren't left to someone as completely unfitted for it as I – the thought of someone else taking her made the bottom of my stomach drop away with fear.

All the time it was me, alone, there was no concern if I fell into debt and was sold back into slavery. I've lived as a slave before; I can do it again.

But slaves have no say in whether their babies are taken from them. Their children are sold on, and they never see them again.

'You're not rich enough to buy all three of us,' I whispered to Rekhmire', trying for humour and not achieving it.

'If it comes to it, I'm perfectly capable of embezzling the funds of any Alexandrine House,' the Egyptian said, as if it were not only obvious but sensible. 'However. I strongly suggest we don't let it come to that.'

He exchanged a glance with Honorius, as if both of them could come to a conclusion without words.

'Let the weather improve.' Honorius grumbled. 'Give it a few months for the child to thrive. I'll sail to Alexandria with you. Then, when you're safe, Ilario, I'll sort out Rodrigo Sanguerra.'

'Honorius.' Breathing deeply gave me some control. 'I read what Hanulf wrote, and I know what the King dictated to him. I worked for Rodrigo Sanguerra for nearly a decade. I *know* the man. *He won't wait!*'

Honorius smiled, lines spidering his face at the mouth and eyes. 'Let's sit, eat. Discuss this like sensible men. You can protest how you like, Ilario. I won't leave Venice while you need me.'

'Damn it—!'

The rest of the discussion was as fruitless as any I have ever had with a noble of King Rodrigo's court set on going his own way – and being a freed slave rather than the King's Freak did not appear to help me in the slightest.

Gazing at Honorius while he ate delicate flakes of white fish as if they were about to give way to famine, I thought, *Even his affection might fade if acknowledging me ends by robbing him of everything he's earned in his life.*

★

23

My body had returned to as normal a state as I thought it now could achieve, and I was watching Onorata blink sleepily at the spring sunshine from her cradle when Neferet bustled her way into the ground-floor room that looked out into the courtyard, an expostulating Rekhmire' and Honorius in her wake.

'Ilaria!' She had not given up calling me by a female name, as most of the household inhabitants had when not outside in Venice itself. 'Ilaria, I need your help.'

I have been your guest: that imposes obligations. I shot a look at the two men behind Neferet, who were both yelling loudly enough that I could understand what neither was saying. *Obligations, but not without caution.*

'What do you need?' I asked, standing up, my fingers resting on the wooden hood of the cradle.

'The Council of Ten are holding Leon's trial tomorrow.'

Neferet's face was lean, tight, intense. She fixed me with brown-black eyes, and what I thought was a flush under her reddish skin. 'They'll torture him; I *know* he'll be executed, because he won't say . . . anything.'

I wanted to interrupt with some commiseration or sympathy; she didn't permit it.

'His family have disowned him,' she said sharply. 'It's not worth their while to sink with him, is what they mean! I spoke to his father – no matter. We have to do something tomorrow – *I* have to – *you* have to help me!'

The Frankish season of Lent was on the house: I didn't suffer from diet restrictions, since I'd had to regain my health after the birth, but I felt the abstinence going on all around me, and had abandoned wine for the time. That was a mistake, I thought. *I have a feeling I could do with a flask of Falernian right about now.*

'What?' I began.

'He'll be convicted. Sentenced.' Neferet's eyes seemed to gleam in her intense face. 'I can't do anything about that: the gods they know I've tried! But he's bound to be sentenced to execution. I need . . . I would do this myself, but it's the one thing I can't do. I can't do it.'

She shook her head. She looked oddly dignified for a moment, the spring sun showing up every line worry had cut into her soft face over the past weeks.

'I can't think of any plea of leniency they might listen to, except this.' She stepped forward, reached out, took my hand, and closed her other hand over my knuckles. 'I need you to go to the Doge's palace tomorrow, and plead for his life.'

'*Me?*'

Neferet made an impatient sound. In the doorway, Rekhmire' and Honorius fell silent. My father's mouth was a white line. The Egyptian had his arms crossed firmly across his chest.

'You.' Neferet looked down the inch or two of height she had on me, into my face. 'You have to go to them, and plead your belly.'

5

If I stared as incoherently as I felt, it was no wonder she began to speak in slow, plain words, as if to a village idiot.

'Tell them this is *Leon's* child.' She jerked her chin toward the cradle, never taking her eyes off my face. 'Tell them he visited Tommaso Cassai in Rome. And seduced you, while he was there. You followed him here, pretending to be a widow. It's *why* you're here. You need a father for your child. You need them to commute the sentence from execution. It doesn't matter to what. Anything, so long as he lives! We can aid him later. But you have to go there and do this for him; it's the thing that *I can't do*.'

Rekhmire' came up behind her and put his hands on her shoulders. She didn't let go of my hand.

I could see the man under her disguise – or the false pale body that held her female *ka*, as she would say. She stood with a kind of exhausted, humiliated dignity, gazing down at me.

If I didn't much like her, still, pain for her wrenched through my belly.

'Of course I will.'

'I won't have you put yourself into danger!'

Honorius and I spoke at the same time.

Rekhmire''s great hand tightened on the shoulder of Neferet's long Alexandrine robe. His grave dark gaze met mine.

'You can take your father's armed escort,' Rekhmire' said. 'No man would think the less of you, not after you were attacked by a madman.'

The last few words let me know what story had been given out about Ramiro Carrasco's attempt to murder me.

Honorius glared. 'I don't like it! The boy Leon – nice enough boy – wouldn't have him in a company of mine, and the world doesn't need more lawyers – but I'm not risking my son-daughter for him!'

His protectiveness made me smile. It's frightening, because I'm not used to it, and what one learns to value, it may pain one to lose. But it still made me warm.

Freeing my hands, I bent over the cradle and picked up Onorata. She had grown, but she was still smaller than any new-born should be. I slid my finger over her palm, and she made an infinitesimally tiny sound and closed her small perfect fingers on me.

'I haven't taken her out of the house,' I said.

Honorius erupted into a fine amount of oratory, Rekhmire' speculated about what Alexandrine physicians might advise, and Neferet said nothing at all. She continued to look at me.

I have seen the expression before, on slaves' faces, before they break down and beg.

Hurriedly, I said, 'We'll take the midwife. And ... your Father Azadanes?' Who, privately, I thought would be of more use to Neferet as a friend than to me as a Green priest. 'And the wet-nurse. And the soldiers.'

My father gave me a furious look.

Knowing him, I knew that Neferet's distress had already lost him the argument he would still have with me.

I looked from Honorius to Rekhmire' – the Egyptian's expression heavy with thoughts I shared – and then at Neferet. 'You do know how small a chance this is, don't you?'

The Alexandrine eunuch dressed as a woman gave me that inclination of the head that, outside of Frankish lands, passes as a bow.

'I know,' Neferet said. 'Nonetheless.'

The great medieval palace of the Doges was in the process of being demolished – rather, demolished and re-built – so I spent my time leading us between scaffolding-covered walls, and treading close enough to the heels of the Doge's soldier that I wouldn't lose him as he led us inside. Every so often I looked inside the fold of my cloak to find Onorata still breathing.

No love connected us, but I would wake two or three times in the night, convinced she had died as she slept, and must crawl to the foot of my bed and look at her in her chest-cot, and feel her breath against my finger, before I could go back to sleep.

The Council guards escorted us into the main chamber of the Doge.
They will see through me.

The thought echoed through my head clearly enough to down out the ringing footsteps on the flagstones, and the echoes that came back from the Gothic vaults. I had no time to look at the ducal splendour of Foscari's half-rebuilt palace, in the new Classical style. I could only think *I will join Leon Battista Alberti in prison!*

I thought sardonically that I ought to have been barefoot, with my skirt hems worn to frays, and the baby in my arms wrapped in faded linen. That would make them believe the poor seduced woman come to get justice from her ravisher . . .

Looking up, past the semi-circle of white-faced old men under Phrygian caps, all identical to me in this state of fear, I caught Leon Battista's eye where he stood between four armed guards.

His eyes bugged out of his head.

'He'll give it away!' I muttered.

Honorius gave me the same look he gave disobedient young recruits. 'Steady.'

On my other side – and I was beginning to wonder when they had constituted themselves my bookends – Rekhmire' leaned on his crutch and suggested, 'Will you take the baby?'

Honorius spoke across me. 'Not for a moment. Let them see us.'

I might not be a grubby-faced ex-whore with snow on my feet and a baby in my arms, I reflected, wondering if I could paint that in any way that these rich fat men would believe.

What they must see in front of them in this dark and torch-lit hall was a young woman in silks and satins, clearly of good family, her father in knight's armour, her Egyptian scribe at her elbow, her armed escort clattering across the stone floor behind us, and the nursemaid with the child two formal paces to my rear.

Like it or not, this stands more of a chance of presenting them a picture they'll buy.

'This is my daughter—' Honorius stuttered over the word, in a way I'd never heard him stutter over 'son-daughter'. '—Ilaria. I demand compensation for her! I demand justice!'

All of the ten men at the council table looked at Honorius, except for the middle-aged man with alert brown eyes who took in my appearance in an instant, and slightly lifted a brow.

'Messer Captain-General Honorius.' It was the keen-eyed man who spoke: I realised this must be Foscari. 'We have read the evidence you put before us. What claim have you on this man's estate, except the testimony of this woman?'

Onorata was wrapped up with swaddling bands, very loosely, for the look of the thing. Being fed, I had every hope she'd sleep and look sweet. With her arranged in the crook of my arm, I stepped forward and waited until Honorius finished repeating verbally what he had dictated to any number of the Doge's secretaries.

'Lords, seigniors, illustrious *Duca*.' I let my Iberian accent come out, and caught Leon Battista's eye as I looked up as modestly as I could. 'If the late Tommaso Cassai, artist in Rome, could speak to you, he would tell you about the truth of this—'

Yes: he'd tell you I'm lying in my teeth!

'—If you wish, I will swear an oath that Messer Alberti promised me marriage before he seduced me, and I therefore considered us betrothed—'

I said I would swear it. Not that it would be true.

Because I will swear myself black in the face if it helps. And if court life teaches you anything, it is how to lie with the greatest innocence.

'—I don't beg you not to punish him, illustrious sirs. Only to have mercy on my child. Who needs her father!'

And that may be true – or she may already be overburdened with a mother-father.

The man to Foscari's right said, 'We could order some settlement made out of the prisoner's estate?'

Honorius's hand closed around my elbow and gently pulled me back – but I had no chance of breaking his grip. He glanced down as he let me go, and stroked a fingertip over the baby's fine fluffy hair where it protruded from under her linen cap. I saw Doge Foscari register his smile.

That's useful: he sees that the baby's grandfather is willing to acknowledge her—

My thoughts were interrupted by a burst of deep-throated laughter from the councillor on the Doge's left hand:

'That is poetic!'

He was overweight, with the high colour fat men in middle age get. I stared at him, not knowing whether to wish him dead of a heart spasm on the spot. Foscari lifted his eyebrow again, as if he wished to seem slightly disconcerted; the other men on the council followed his lead by frowning.

'Poetic justice, perhaps.' Doge Foscari linked his fingers together on the polished dark table. The cabochon-cut rings he wore reflected in the shine, in dark incarnations of their colours: emerald, ruby, sapphire. I wondered which, if any, was the ring with which the Doge of The Most Serene Republic weds the sea every Easter-tide. The council put their heads together again and I couldn't hear anything they said.

Rekhmire' touched my shoulder, and Saverico took the baby out of my arm, returning her to another wet-nurse brought for the look of the thing. I dabbed at a damp spot on the silk brocade bodice Neferet had loaned me, and saw my fingertips shaking.

Not the time to be holding a child. Nightmare visions of her fragility assailed me, and I blinked them away, staring across the room at Leon Battista. At this distance I could see little enough – only that he seemed well-dressed, grubby, pale with his time in prison; but had evidently been kept in locked apartments, rather than down below us in the dungeons.

That will not stop them hanging him now, if they decide to.

We would look like a normal aristocrat family gathered in this justice hall. Even an Alexandrine secretary would not be so unusual. I wondered how many of the councillors were looking and wondering where the other representative of Alexandria was this morning. *Do they know she's his lover? Do they know 'she' should be here in place of me?*

Hot sweat gathered, and rolled down my back between my shoulder-blades. The canvas straps of the corset chafed under the sleeves of my bodice. For the first time in a number of years, I wished for a sword, and the memory of my knightly training.

'You paint, Donna Ilaria,' Foscari remarked, leaning forward and speaking plainly and clearly to me.

It may have been how he spoke to foreigners uncertain of the Venetian language. It felt as if he spoke to a child of eight or ten winters.

'I was studying the New Art in the studio of Tommaso Cassai.' Some truth must have rung in my tone, since that was the case. I saw two of the councillors speak to each other behind the chair of a third. 'Messer Leon Battista Alberti presented me with his treatise on the eye, and vision in painting. It is here.'

Rekhmire' walked forward and placed *De Pictura* on the table before the Doge, bowed, and returned to his place behind me.

Foscari shot a look at Leon Battista. 'The writing of this took you some time?'

'Yes, messire.' His voice sounded dry.

'And the copying, also, to have a copy that Donna Ilaria might have read to her?'

Leon Battista nodded, not speaking.

The Doge Foscari leaned back in his carved chair. 'Clearly, Donna Ilaria's father, Lord Honorius, supposed there to be a betrothal, all that time. Or you would not have been permitted to give such a gift. You do not deny this?'

Leon's chin came up. 'I say nothing.'

. . . And therefore, so far, not one of us has lied.

'I understand there has been legislation passed in Florence of late.' The Doge ignored a choked-off laugh from the fat man, and looked further down the table. 'Simon?'

The sleek man he addressed leaned his hands on the table. 'Indeed, seignior. They have passed laws legitimising prostitution. Messer Alberti will have heard.'

'They have done this,' the Doge Foscari looked blandly at Leon Battista Alberti, 'so that the young men of the city should become less interested in, shall we say, exclusively male pursuits.'

I fixed my eyes on a tile on the floor, following the ochre and red glaze's repeating geometric pattern. *I will not look at my father, I will not look at Rekhmire'!* 'Exclusively male.' Let Doge Foscari think the young woman is modestly pretending not to understand what is referred to.

Under my skirts, I have a womb and (as I ascertained privately once I was sufficiently healed) a functioning penis. 'Exclusively male' is considerably outside my experience.

' . . . And to further eradicate the sin of Sodom,' the Doge was saying. He had risen to his feet at some point; a ripple of light from the torches shot back colour from his jewel-encrusted brocade robes. Drawing him would be easy, painting the effect of that light and shadow unbelievably difficult. He held out his hands, plainly giving judgement.

'This is the sentence on Messer Leon Battista Alberti. Because of his family's good name, and because of the lineage of the Captain-General of Castile and Leon,' a bow towards my father, 'it is considered just that the penalty of execution be commuted to exile. Messer Leon Battista Alberti shall have a month to leave our territories of the Italian Peninsula. But in the interests of holding up a good example, and discouraging that sin of Sodom which in Florence is so prevalent, and which threatens us everywhere, Messer Leon Battista Alberti shall hold to his promise of betrothal.'

Rekhmire''s arm quivered, where he had stepped close and now pressed against me. I felt his shock as clearly as I felt mine. Honorius frowned and opened his mouth. Out of sight, I dug my fingers into the palm of his hand, cutting myself against the edge of his plate gauntlet.

Foscari turned his head away and fixed an unrelenting gaze on Leon Battista.

'Because we will see justice done, you will be married in the presence of a priest. Before you depart from Venezia! I will call for a confessor now, and you shall be shriven clean so that you can marry. This child will have a father's name. This shamed maiden shall be made into a wife.'

Silence echoed through the chamber.

The Doge turned towards Honorius. 'It has been forty days: your daughter has been churched.'

Honorius took no notice of my nails digging into the thin leather glove he wore under his gauntlet. He bowed with the skill of a courtier, and spoke with the bluntness of a soldier. 'Yes, lord. She can wed whenever you desire.'

There is nothing else he *can* say, I admitted to myself. Anything else will smack of trying to win concessions, either from the Alberti family or the Doge himself, and this Foscari is likely to find some way to remove Leon again if he thinks his decision is being used for advantage.

The Doge looked across the vast chamber at me. 'As soon as you are wed and able to bear the journey, you will leave Venice and join your husband in Florence.'

Leon Battista choked. 'Florence!'

'You may join your family there,' Foscari said amiably. 'Other members of your family are also returning, I understand. We will miss them, after so many years in our Republic.'

The candlelight showed his face all innocence as he taunted Leon Battista.

'As I understand,' Foscari concluded, 'the ban against your family in Florence has been lifted. Your exile is over. There are already moves to make your father one of Duke Ludovico's councillors. Of course, the agitation and rabble-rousing will stop; it doesn't become the Alberti to act against their own Duke. As I'm sure your family will tell you.'

It was clear enough to me: the Alberti family have been given a place in Florence again – on the condition that they keep their insurrectionary son under control.

Leon was close enough between his guards that I read the realisation in his face. No more pamphlets, no attacking the Republic of Florence for its injustices, because the Albertis have a stake in the city again – as it stands. No more talk that might lead to revolution. The poor will stay poor, and at the mercy of the powerful.

Leon's expression closed. He bowed.

He might continue to think his family had sold him out. Or he might tell himself that ideals of good government are a naive man's illusions. I didn't know him well enough to know which way he would go.

Once again, I thought. I'm marrying someone – and I have no true idea of who they are.

6

'It's arranged.' Honorius threw off his cloak, and came to stand by the hearth. 'The banns will be read thrice, and then you'll be married.'

I sank further down on the settle, easing my shoes off. My toes were hot and cold at the same time, and I wriggled them in my stocking-hose, presenting them to the fire. 'Good! Tell Neferet she and Leon can leave as soon as we're done.'

Honorius nodded soberly. Rekhmire' shot me a questioning look.

Dear god, I thought.

He wants to know if I've told Honorius what happened in Rome—

'It won't be legal,' I blurted out.

Honorius turned his back to the fire, hitching up the skirt of his doublet and warming his backside. 'How could it be? I'll be honest, Ilario, I don't know if you *can* marry. As a man-woman—'

'I can marry.'

'What?' He suddenly frowned.

'This gets Leon safely out of Venice,' I said. 'But you should know . . . I went through a Christian marriage ceremony in Rome. To an Etruscan woman, Sulva. I was married: that time as the groom. This time, it will be the bride.'

I have rarely seen such an expression.

'Groom?' Honorius stared at me. 'Bride.'

'You should reassure Leon it's in name only,' I emphasised dryly. And then, as the thought occurred to me: 'Although it may not bother him: he's with Neferet, after all.'

His face made me itch to reach for my chalks, in the same way as I had wanted to in the Doge's hall. The difference being that Honorius, unlike Foscari, made me want to smile.

Rekhmire' crossed the room in answer to a soft knock at the door. Tired enough to watch without seeing, I barely registered one of the house servants pass a note to the Egyptian.

'Life.' Rekhmire' observed as he came back from the door.

'What?'

'Our assassin – Secretary Ramiro Carrasco de Luis. The Doge's Council have committed him to prison for life. I suspect he'll end up on one of those islands.'

The Egyptian's nod towards the unshuttered windows made me

follow his gaze. A small patch of blue sky showed between the buildings opposite. The canal reflecting the sky's light back to it. I thought how brilliant it would be out on the lagoon.

In which are isolated small islands, covered in cypresses, which they call lazaretto: quarantined islands for sufferers from leprosy, or prisoners who will never be released. Sometimes both on the same island.

If that made me shudder, I had only to remember the moments of not being able – because of another's physical force – to breath in air. Nothing kills human sympathy so fast.

'We won't be rid of him.' Honorius spoke without moving away from the fire.

'A life sentence,' Rekhmire' began irritably.

'Not *Carrasco*.' Honorius glanced down apologetically, evidently realising he robbed me of heat. He sat, beside me, his back nearly as upright as the oak settle's. 'Videric! Or, some other man, or men, *sent* by Aldra Videric. Videric *will* send more spies. More murderers.'

The tone admitted of no doubt. I glanced automatically towards the cradle in the corner of the room, to reassure myself that Onorata slept.

No matter that a child doesn't understand, I think she hears the tone of a man's voice . . .

'You're right.' I rubbed at gritty eyes. 'I saw them drag Carrasco off and was glad – that lasted, oh, a quarter of an hour. And then I realised that as soon as Videric stops getting what reports Carrasco was sending him, he'll send other men, to replace the ones who attacked us on Torcello.'

In my mind I have the flare of a striped cotton robe as a man turns, the clack of his war-sandals on tiles as he walks away, leaving me with a woman who he fully expects to murder me. *That's the last time I saw him,* I realised suddenly.

I ran for a ship immediately after my mother – after *Rosamunda* – tried to kill me.

I know he sent her after me. I know he will have sent others. But that's the last I saw: his face concerned with worry for his wife – and all of it a flat-out lie, to get me into the same room with her so that she could put a dagger into me.

It is more than three quarters of a year now. I wonder if that fair hair, that burly profile, look any different. If exile back to his estates at Rodrigo's order has made him look old. Or whether he merely bides his time, knowing that sooner or later one of the murderers he sends *will* kill me. And then the scandal may have the chance to die, too, and he may in the future come back to court . . .

'Carrasco's arrest solves nothing.' Restless, I rose to walk about the room, careful not to tread the hem of my petticoats underfoot. 'If no one else tells Videric, Federico will – because God forbid my foster father shouldn't be scrambling to be in favour with every faction he can find!'

Honorius seemed surprised at my bitterness. 'You know him better than I do. This Federico, I mean. Videric I remember as Rodrigo's Chancellor, before I went north for the Crusades.'

He looked a little bitter himself, and I wondered if his expression mirrored mine – or mine his.

'Ilario, you can't expect me to be unbiased. Videric blackmailed Rosamunda into staying with him instead of leaving with me.'

Much as I like the idea that Honorius is my father, it still jolts me that Rosamunda remains my mother.

And that that is irrevocable, no matter that the man I thought my father is only a stepfather – my mother's husband.

And a man who will send other men to kill me. I have considered this, wide awake in the Venetian darkness, while the campanile lets me know it is three, four, five in the morning.

Rekhmire''s crutch struck the floor with a hollow sound as he came to peer out of the window, at the narrow view afforded of the Campo S. Barnaba from this room. 'I'm told the Council's dungeons aren't good for the health. It's possible Master Carrasco won't be transported to the lazarettos.'

A breath of chill touched me that was not this winter cold. *If there were other Alexandrines here, I would suspect that was an offer . . .*

'All the while Carrasco was here,' I speculated, 'Videric evidently felt he *would* kill me. He either doubted, or he sent the men who attacked me on Torcello to assist Carrasco. Now . . . I have no idea how many men he can hire who would murder me for money, or where they'll be, or how long it'll take them to get to Venice – if he didn't give up on Ramiro Carrasco and send them weeks ago.'

I intercepted a look between the two men.

'You're right,' Honorius agreed as if the Egyptian had spoken. 'It's even more unsettling when that happens in petticoats.'

'What, when I prove I have more wit than a firefly?' I glared at both of them. 'Remind me *never* to dress up as a woman again, once I'm out of Venice.'

Rekhmire' gave me a crooked smile. 'Breeches or petticoats, you are still in need of a good beating. I regret I never took my opportunity as your master.'

Such jokes are a lot easier for the master to make. But, free, I can afford to smile at them, and I did.

His expression becoming serious, Rekhmire' stated, 'Aldra Videric will send more men: he cannot afford not to. More hired men who won't think twice about killing. Sooner or later, there will be a slip – even among your men, Master Honorius.'

I miss Rekhmire''s presence at the wedding, I realised, looking around the cold and gloomy Frankish church. He had been a rock of comfort when I went to Sulva, however much he may have disagreed with my reasons for that marriage.

'Man and wife,' Honorius murmured in my ear, as we walked down the aisle to the altar-rail, his baritone surprisingly quiet for a man used to shouting across battlefields. He proceeded to prove himself far too much in the Egyptian's company of late by adding, with black humour, 'Which one would *you* like to be?'

I clapped my hand up to my mouth, hiding a splutter of horrified amusement. I bowed my head, and hoped the looming members of the Alberti family would take it as feminine shyness. 'The Lion of Castile is about to come to a horrible end in the Most Serene Republic, I hope you realise?'

'Ah, what it is to have a dutiful daughter . . . '

He squeezed my arm with quite genuine encouragement and stepped forward to consult with the group of middle-aged men in dark velvet and miniver fur. I caught sight of Leon Battista at the back, his Roman nose all the more prominent for the gaunt lines of starvation in his face.

And that would be how they convinced him . . .

I wished again that I had Rekhmire' at my shoulder, to exchange looks of realisation, and to discuss, *sotto voce*, whether it would be wise to go through with this, despite Neferet's pleas.

A persistent wail echoed into the high Gothic beams.

Honorius took Onorata out of Attila's arms, displaying her in her swaddling clothes to the Alberti men. Unused to it, she found the bindings uncomfortable, and her crying had a determined edge. I bit my lip and stayed where I had been left.

'A girl?' The older Alberti sounded displeased. 'Well, there is no need to worry about dowries, she can always be put in a convent. There's time for a son later. At least this proves my grandson capable of siring a child.'

The significant look he shot over his shoulder at Leon led me to suppose he had made aspersions to the contrary. Leon's mouth set in a thin line: he did not look towards me.

I thought it was I who was making the sacrifice here. But I have no lover to object to my name being coupled with another's.

Honorius handed my baby back to the large Germanic man-at-arms, and Attila took a longer way down the church so that he might pass me, heels ringing on the flagstones, and let me look at Onorata as he passed. Her face was scarlet, her eyes screwed up and hot with tears. He touched a forefinger to the swaddling bands and gave me a significant look – by which I knew him off to remove them.

I have marked the sympathy between soldiers and small children before now, in Taraco; I had not ever thought I would be grateful to it when it provided me with at least six persistent and efficient nursemaids. Even if they are not half so enthusiastic during the small hours of the night, or when it came to changing breech-clouts.

'Madonna Ilaria.' The priest beckoned me forward to stand at Leon Battista's side.

S. Barnaba had nothing worth the looking at, its altar-piece was third-rate, and the Green priest – evidently hired by the Alberti family – rattled through the ceremony so fast that it reached the moment of commitment before I was ready for it.

Leon had no shred of prison dirt on him now, even the stench being eradicated in favour of soap and civet, but I could recognise the expression on his face. That of a slave who has been punished by dark and isolation, and found it full of unexpected monsters.

'Yes.' My mouth formed the appropriate words before I was aware I had made my decision. Consenting to wed this man, in name only, is nothing more than words to me. It is freedom to him.

I walked out of the church married for the second time in half a year. This time as the bride.

'We understand your daughter and the child cannot travel as yet.' The Alberti patriarch spoke to Honorius, without even a glance towards me. 'We will send our son from Florence to collect her, as soon as she may.'

The proper things were said, the Alberti men departed in a splendidly-decorated oared boat, and I noted Leon Battista slipping quietly off into the Alexandrine embassy ahead of us.

It took me a time to settle Onorata, she being too disturbed to sleep – eventually conceding only when Attila fetched a bowl of milk and a spoon from the kitchens, and sat by the fire to feed her with infinite patience.

I recall those hands, so much larger than my child's head, loosing the bolt that tore the Carthaginian agent apart. It will not be the first or last man that he has killed.

I made a sketch with coal and chalk, that was only broad shapes except for the features, but caught the difference between the two faces: one still unmarked and with deep clear eyes, the other with half a lifetime worn into skin creased with staring through sunlight.

Coming downstairs, I walked into Rekhmire' as he left the main room, and clutched at him to keep both of us on our feet.

A fragile Venetian glass hurtled through the door and smashed on the opposite wall.

Rekhmire' wouldn't be able to bend down with his crutch; therefore called for one of the Egyptian's servants to sweep up the fragments. I nodded towards the open door, hearing loud raised voices beyond.

'What is it?'

Rekhmire' finished steadying himself with a grip on my shoulder, and brushed himself down. 'It's Master Leon Battista. He says he cannot travel to Alexandria, it appears.'

Alexandria would be a good refuge for him – for us all, I thought. It was too cold to stand in this passageway, spring or not, and besides, I was curious as to the actions of my husband. I strode through the open door, Rekhmire' behind me, the cloth-padded end of his crutch stomping down on the floorboards.

Neferet instantly flung away from Leon Battista, where the dark man stood silhouetted at the window, and glared at me. '*Here* she is. The happy bride! No wonder you won't leave Venice!'

Slave or free, I can recognise when someone desires a mere target for their temper. Without venom, I reminded, 'You asked me to do this.'

She stalked out of the room, pulling the door behind her with a shattering crash.

Rekhmire' took some moments to arrange himself in the armed chair by the hearth; I took the settle, and after a moment Leon Battista walked to sit beside me.

'That's poor thanks for saving my life.' He spoke firmly, holding my gaze. 'I've told Neferet the marriage will remain in name only: she has no need for concern. Please don't take that as an insult – if I were not hers, I could seek for no better woman than you for my wife.'

Rekhmire''s luminous dark eyes caught mine. Whatever else Neferet might have said in her rage, I perceived that 'hermaphrodite' was not one of those words.

'I don't take offence,' I said, and attempted to sound as if I only changed the subject out of feminine embarrassment. 'I had expected you and Neferet to be on the first ship out for Alexandria-Constantinople?'

Leon Battista looked down at his hands. The knuckles were more prominent than they should be. He rubbed his fingers together.

'My family's exile is ended, on condition they rein in their rabble-rousing son.' His expression turned sour. He looked up, without lifting his head, and met my gaze through his long, dark lashes. 'Therefore, I have to be seen in Florence. *With* my family, carrying on the family's affairs, and not fomenting rebellion against the Duke.'

Rekhmire' leaned forward and prodded the coal with one of the fire-irons. He sat back with a grunt. 'The Alberti family expect Master Leon Battista to be in *your* company, Ilario, as soon as you may travel. Not Neferet's.'

The short walk from church had given me enough time to solve that problem. 'Tell them I *died*! Plague. Cholera. Anything! It happens all the time. You can safely tell anyone that, just as soon as I can leave Venice.'

Not before. I would be very surprised if the Alberti didn't have men watching their son's wife. And, by his expression, I had no need to spell that out.

Leon's mouth quirked. 'There's no need to condemn you to an early grave. When it becomes possible, I can prove our marriage void.'

'You can?' All the banns and church offices had been what I understand the Frankish marriage ceremonies to be. I could not help looking at him in surprise. 'How?'

Leon Battista took a deep breath. 'I married Neferet six months ago, in the autumn.'

My mouth was open, but I could make no sound come out.

'Although,' he added, 'for obvious reasons, I can't take Neferet to Florence as my wife – the family would insist on having a council of midwives to examine her, to confirm that she was a virgin before she married me, and capable of child-bearing. And that . . . '

'Yes, I can see that would present problems.'

The door opened; Neferet's women servants came in, followed by Neferet herself – she looked taken aback to see me still present, and she glared at Rekhmire', but since neither of us moved, she gestured for wine to be served.

After a warming sip of the wine, I had courage enough to look her in the face. 'Couldn't you go to Florence as Leon's mistress?'

The lines of her face spoke, *I don't know what business this is of yours!* more clearly than any word could have.

She nevertheless seated herself gracefully on one of the window-embrasures, reclining on cushions embroidered in the Alexandrine style. 'Think, Madonna Ilaria! Leon arrives *without* his new wife and infant child, but *with* a mistress – and a foreign mistress at that! How long before the family demands he be respectable?'

Something under a quarter of an hour after passing Florence's walled gate, I suspected, but didn't desire to say. Neferet's long-fingered large hands still faintly trembled with anger. No need to draw the lightning down on myself.

'If I go as a cook or servant,' she said, her graceful reclining pose stiffening with her neck, 'or anything else an unmarried woman may do, I will be assumed as a matter of course to be Leon's whore.'

Her head turned: she fixed Leon with a desolate stare.

'And I am *your wife.*'

Leon Battista sprang up, went to the window, and knelt down beside her. I thought it tactful to turn away and converse with Rekhmire' while Leon comforted her.

I drained my wine glass. 'No one would care in Alexandria, would they?'

'That they are man and man, not man and wife? Likely not; why should they? If they want to live as man and woman, and are discreet, Ty-ameny would permit it. Given Master Leon's interest in the arts and architecture, and the Classical writings, I think she would even forgive him being a Frank.'

There was a very faint teasing air about that last. I smiled briefly at him.

'But still,' Rekhmire' murmured, the amusement leaving his expression, 'Neferet didn't expect to return to Alexandria without him. That will hurt her.'

'*I would take you with me!*' Leon's voice rose. 'I swear by Christ on the Tree! If there was any way it could be managed—'

Perhaps the matter had been enough on my mind recently that I saw through it, in that instant, to an answer. As if I reached up and caught the tail of the lightning-bolt, and was instantly gifted with illumination.

Yes: this will work!

But she will not like it, I realised. It may work, but she will hate it and me . . .

I stood up, finding by that I drew Rekhmire''s and Leon's attention. Leon had one arm about Neferet's waist, where he knelt at her side. Neferet's large fingers were interlocked with his.

'You said it yourself,' I remarked, meeting Neferet's gaze. 'There's no role for an unmarried woman in a house in Florence. Or for one married to a *different* man, or to a widow, unless you could produce visible evidence of a husband. You wouldn't be trusted because you're a foreigner.'

Leon scowled, looking as if he would interrupt.

'*I* found Venice far more confining than Rome or Carthage,' I said, 'and in Carthage I was a slave! But leaving that aside: in Venice, I've been a woman. In Rome, I was,' remembering Leon's presence, I stumbled over, 'dressed as – a man.'

Rekhmire' gestured with an open demanding palm. 'And?'

I turned to the other Alexandrine. 'Neferet, couldn't you go to Florence—'

Some friendly deity moved me to add a phrase:

'—disguised as a man?'

She stared.

I added hastily, 'Nobody would think anything of Leon taking on an Alexandrine scribe as a secretary—'

'*Disguised as a man?*'

Neferet shrieked loudly enough that I had time to think I would, if I had simply said *go to Florence as a man*, either now be deaf, or have had something injurious thrown at me. And likely deserve it.

I snapped out, 'If I can disguise myself as a man, you can!'

I saw her turn the matter over in her mind. She knows, from gossip with Honorius's men-at-arms, that I was a thoroughly convincing young man in Rome. She has been telling me, all the while I've been here, that truly I am a woman. If I can pass as a man, therefore – why not she?

'I won't do it!' She stood up, trembling. 'It's undignified! And you—' She swung around, pointing a finger at Rekhmire'. 'You've never believed me anything but Jahar pa-sheri! You see me as a monster, don't you?'

Rekhmire', pale under his reddish skin, sat bolt upright. 'No more than I do Ilario!'

Frustration sealed her lips: she glared at Rekhmire', and at me, and turned on her heel to shout at Leon Battista.

The Florentine was still kneeling on the floor beside the window-seat. He looked up, without rising.

'Neferet – I really don't mind.'

Her hand made a fist, in the folds of her dress. She stared so intensely at him, her glance would have made glass catch fire and burn.

'What do you mean?'

He put a hand on the window embrasure and pushed himself up, making a face as his knees evidently pained him. The wet cold in the Doge's prison takes a long time to leave a man's bones.

'I don't care.' He walked over and took each of Neferet's hands in his own. 'Whether you're a man or a woman, whether you *dress* as a man or a woman – none of that has any importance. It's you I love.'

Neferet began to cry.

I had my arm under Rekhmire''s other armpit, acting as an additional crutch, and tactfully removed us from the room. I signalled as I left for one of the men-at-arms to guard the door – since there is an obvious method by which Leon could convince Neferet of his love, and if I were Leon, I wouldn't even waste so much time as it would take to reach the bedrooms.

Heading by common consent for the kitchen, where it would be warm, Rekhmire' shook his head as he walked, still gripping lightly at my arm.

'I haven't seen Neferet in a scribe's kilt in fifteen years. And then only when court formalities wouldn't let her get away with anything else.' He steered us towards the kitchen inglenook, with a wave to the cooks. 'Better send up the wine in wooden bowls – it's not like the house has much Venetian glass left!'

'You're glad for her.'

'Am I?' He busied himself with being seated, tucking his crutch beside him, and easing that leg into a stretch towards the fire. The heat of the fire, perhaps, cast a flush onto his cheek.

'She's your friend. You're happy that she's happy.' I winced at a dimly heard crash from the depths of the house. 'Or at least, if not happy, that she can be with Leon.'

'The Florentines will find her a trifle feminine, I think.' He gave me a sudden grin. 'But then, all we Alexandrine eunuchs are feminine males, according to common talk!'

I grinned back. 'I don't think you'd suit a Frankish skirt and bodice . . .'

In the hours following, Neferet's quarrel broke out from time to time, like an unquenched brush-fire – but it had little enough true heat, given that she would break off from her ranting to look in wonder at Leon, and her demeanour invariably softened after that. Since the Alberti were due to depart in two days, she had perforce to make a decision and pack.

41

I woke early on that morning, to feed Onorata, and to bid Neferet farewell. I found her in the atrium of the house – and for a moment truly did not recognise Neferet in this slim and straight-shouldered man, dressed in the short linen jacket and white kilt of an Alexandrine scribe.

'Ilaria.' She spoke with the pitch of her voice lower, a little husky.

Her skin showed smooth, under the linen. Her face looked curiously bare with only a line of kohl above each row of eyelashes. She had her hair cut short, falling to touch her shoulders, as one of the Alexandrine customs is, and a narrow braided reed-band holding it back from her eyes.

Honorius's men-at-arms, at the house door, could be heard greeting Leon Battista.

'Good fortune,' I said, a little hurriedly, not able to put all I thought into words.

'You too.' She – he – smiled.

It was a morning cool and damp enough for fog, rolling in with the smell of the sea about it, clinging to Venice's brick walls and Roman-tiles roofs, and filtering the sunlight to diffuse glory. At the gate of the Alexandrine house, Leon Battista awaited us. He greeted Neferet with no more than a companionable nod – something neither his servants nor the oarsmen of his boat would be surprised to see, in a man collecting a new officer for his household.

Their eyes linked. It was a different enough story that I thought *I hope they can be discreet.*

'This is a custom among my people.' Neferet opened a small folded cloth that she carried. I saw a glint of reddish black. She held up a braided loop, handing one to Leon Battista, and one to Rekhmire', and – after a fractional hesitation – one to me.

A bracelet, I found, clasped with gold, and made with braided shining hair. Neferet's hair, now that she had dropped her hair to man's length.

'Thank you.' Bereft of words, I could say nothing else.

Neferet, or Jahar, gave me a look with humour in the depths of it, and murmured, 'Think of it as a wedding gift . . . '

I stumbled though Leon's formal farewells, and watched as Rekhmire' limped forward on his crutch to give last departing words to both apparent men, all the while my thumb caressing the braided bracelet, and the damp fog pearling on my velvet over-gown.

I turned and went back into the embassy.

A few moments later, Rekhmire' stamped back inside – as well as a man walking with a crutch may stamp – blowing on his fingers against the damp cold, and swearing.

'What?' I asked.

'—Holy dung that hatched the cosmos-egg!' he concluded. 'Damn that woman!'

Having seen the boat depart, and Rekhmire''s salute to it, I'd thought all well.

'She still won't tell me where Herr Mainz is!' He made a fist, his face scarlet. 'Nor will Master Alberti. And they wait until *now* to tell me this!'

'Why won't they?'

'Some nonsense that the Florentine Duke will demand Herr Mainz, if he appears openly in Venice, and that at the moment, La Serenissima would probably keep Florence quiet by handing the man over. If they don't imprison him on their own behalf, and try to beat the secret of this printing-*machina* out of him!'

I shrugged, following the Egyptian towards the kitchens. 'If I were Herr Mainz, *I'd* certainly want to stay out of sight.'

'Sacred Eight, I want to *help* the man!' The padded end of the crutch thwacked the short, wide floorboards. 'Ty-ameny needs him; I want to invite him to Alexandria—'

'—Which, until the weather's better, is inaccessible by road, and no ship will risk these seas. So he can't leave Venice.'

'Sun god's *egg*!'

'You would have said precisely the same thing, if you were in Neferet's place.'

While true, it was not tactful; I was not in the least surprised when he stomped away towards the stairs, muttering under his breath. 'I could have hidden him *here*! Sent him to Edirne with the Turk! *Something!*'

I heard him calling for fresh ink as he vanished into his room, and guessed he intended a ciphered message to follow Neferet, and say this and more.

I reflected: If I were her, I'd make sure to drop the paper in a canal – or in the Arno, if it reaches her in Florence.

Florence, I belated realised.

My wife and my husband will end up living within the walls of the same city.

The man-at-arms Berenguer grinned at me, the following morning.

'Get your cloak, Mistress Ilario. You're being abducted.'

7

It said something for the state of mind to which constant threat had reduced me that I wore a dagger on my belt about the house – though the dress's hanging sleeves might have made drawing it quickly impractical.

One look at Berenguer convinced me I had no need.

'Abducted?'

'Sold,' he corrected himself, picking my winter cloak up from where it lay across the back of the wooden settle. He held it up, as a gentleman does for a lady. 'Betrayed by the faithless mercenaries employed by the foreign captain Lord Honorius . . . '

Berenguer might not have liked a hermaphrodite when he met me in Rome. He might from time to time still give me wary looks when the two of us chanced to be in a room alone together, as if I might leap on him, and seduce and rape him simultaneously. *But as for not trusting him to be faithful to my father . . .*

I walked across the room to stand with my back to the black-haired man-at-arms, letting him settle the woollen cloak around my shoulders.

'Who's buying me?' I inquired.

Berenguer somewhat automatically tied my cloak-ties for me and then stood back a little awkwardly and permitted me to raise the silk-lined and fur-trimmed hood myself. His sharp glance assessed me.

'The weasel-lord,' he announced. 'What's-name? The one with the horse-faced wife.'

'Federico. That's my foster father you're insulting,' I added, settling the folds of the green cloak about me. 'Accurately, I may say. Although Valdamerca has her charitable moments.'

Berenguer chuckled, at least partly with relief that his lord's son-daughter hadn't chosen to take offence when treated like a woman and spoken to like a man.

'Her husband's about to be *very* charitable!' He held the room door open for me, hand on the hilt of his bastard sword. 'Do you think you could look frightened for us?'

'Us', it transpired, were fifteen of my father's soldiers – Attila and Tottola without smiles, and therefore at their most intimidating; every man else in brigandine or breastplate, with swords or maces; even Saverico with his polished sallet under his arm, a red and gold silk sash tied from shoulder to waist.

A tall, thin soldier with his cloak hood raised proved, on lifting the edge of it, to be Honorius.

'Help,' I observed gravely. 'Oh, oh, I am being stolen away! Will nobody help a poor defenceless—'

'"Defenceless"', my backside!' Honorius brushed his knuckles against my cheek with open affection. 'I told Berenguer when he brought me this story – if we just take the money and hand you over, not only will we be rich, *I'll* have some peace and quiet!'

Under the cover of general amusement, and donning of cloaks over armour, intended to disguise the immediate passage of armed mercenaries through Venice's alleys, I asked Honorius, 'What in Christ-the-Emperor's name does he think he's *doing*!'

'Lord Videric? Sending your foster father to buy off my soldiers. After all, they're only common mercenaries.'

Over the less-than-sincere thanks offered by his men at that point, I managed to amend my question. 'Truly, I meant Federico.'

'Being desperate! That's what *he's* doing.' My father produced a short length of rope, wrapped it about my wrists in a false knot, and gave me the two ends to grip in my hands so that I looked sufficiently bound. 'I spoke to the Egyptian about this. He suggests that, if messages and travellers are getting through from the Peninsula, Federico will have heard directly from Videric. I think he's right. Whether or not Videric knows we disposed of Carrasco, he's clearly told Federico to move his arse.'

I nodded. 'Something was going to happen, now. It's inevitable.'

The sky above me was the colour of lapis lazuli ashes. The warm air shifted, bringing me the scents of cooking, canal water, and the lagoon. However cold it may still be, and how wet, the world is beginning to move again. If long sea voyages are still unsafe, there are the coastal routes. And some of the better-maintained roads, the Via Augusta included, will be open.

'Is Rekhmire' coming to make sure I'm properly sold?'

Honorius shook his head. 'He'd be recognised. I've requested him to stay here with the rest of the guard, and protect my granddaughter.'

I ignored a stab of disappointment. Because, injured leg or no, I will trust Rekhmire''s determination to protect Onorata above most men's.

'Videric will send more men to kill me,' I observed as we walked across the Campo S. Barnaba. 'True, the more men he hires, the more gossip, the more danger people will hear what he's doing – but I think he'll be willing to risk that, now.'

'Bandits. Pirates. Thugs.' Honorius grunted. He pulled the front of his hood forward. Dressed as a plain soldier, there was nothing to mark him out from the other cloaked mercenaries. 'Knew I should have brought more than three lances . . . '

'We're worth six!' Saverico grinned. Tottola slapped him on the shoulder, which all but sent the slight ensign staggering.

I expected a boat to be waiting, but we instead walked on into the mass of lanes and small squares, until we had left the Dorsodura quarter, and finally approached the Grand Canal. We emerged on the edge of that wide thoroughfare at the foot of the Rialto Bridge.

Berenguer glanced at Honorius for permission, and fell in beside me as we walked in under the wooden roof that capped the bridge.

'We've arranged a public place for the exchange.' Berenguer's grin showed two teeth missing, far back on the left side. 'Less chance of anybody cheating . . . '

The sides of the bridge were also walled with solid planks, but no man could see that except from the outside. Inside, too many shop-booths blocked the line of sight; goods piled up clear to the bridge's roof. We picked a way up the wide stone steps, between merchants and gossiping servants; groups of men purchasing goods or changing money; woman accompanied by male relatives or armed servants.

I shook my head, amazed. 'Federico approached you directly?'

Berenguer gave that kind of shrug that invites discrete admiration. 'Sent one of his servants. But I'd seen the man at that palazzo, when you went after the secretary. Told him I wouldn't talk to anybody but his master.'

'And Federico *agreed*?'

If that's the case, Honorius will not be so far from the mark if he describes my foster father as desperate.

'Yeah. Next time, sure enough, there's Lord Weasel – beg pardon, Lord Federico – muffled up to the eyes, and telling me that he knows we're mercenaries, we're for hire, and he can offer us a better contract than Captain-General Honorius—' Berenguer put up his hand, as if to say *you've heard nothing!*, and added, 'His *first* offer is, every man who comes in on this can get a place in Lord Carmagnola's Venetian army, and have a share of the plunder of Milan, along with Lord Weasel's hefty bribe—'

Attila stepped up on Berenguer's other side, towering a full head above us. He had braided his beard, but left his mane of hair loose; any man could believe him an eater of babies and easily hired murderer. He snorted. 'The General and Lord Carmagnola fought together, up north, so he'd have our arses skinned if we even *thought* about this!'

Berenguer grinned. 'Lord Weasel thinks we're too dumb to know that. So I ask: what will Lord Federico pay in cold cash? And he says: every man can have a safeguarded voyage to the mainland, a saddlebag of gold, and a horse to ride away on. All we have to do is bring him the General's son-daughter, so she can be put away in a convent, safe and sound!'

Ahead, at the top of the steps, I could see light. The open drawbridge section of the Rialto, that is winched up to let tall-masted boats through on their way up the Canal Grande.

'Kidnapped and put in a convent.' I glanced at Honorius, but he had already fallen back into the crowd of armed men, indistinguishable as their captain. Tottola moved in on my flank, a mirror-image of Attila's Germanic wildness.

Berenguer gave me an apologetic glance and took hold of my elbow. 'Lord Weasel, he sounded like he believed it. But if he's your foster dad, he'd want to, wouldn't he? This Lord back in Taraco, this Aldra Videric, he didn't mind sending men to kill us. I don't reckon you'd ever see the inside of any convent.'

'No.' My pulse jolted, chest feeling hollow. The muscles and tendons at the back of my knees pulled, walking up the steps, after so long recovering from Physician Bariş's surgery.

Berenguer scanned the crowds blocking the steps. 'Anyhow, I told Lord Weasel as how he'd have to give us gold. *And* a ship to get off this island. He bargained a bit, but he agreed. Normally, I'd reckon he'd tell the Doge we stole his money and have us taken up and hanged for theft, but he can't risk us talking. Not that it matters . . . '

The crowds became no thinner at the high arch of the Rialto Bridge. I found myself in the midst of cloaked men who might be conspicuous in their number. *But then, Federico will have brought household men-at-arms, too . . .*

Looking above the heads of the Venetians, I saw a mast and sails gliding past.

The creak of the winch and clatter of chains indicated the drawbridge was being wound down into place again.

'Deal is, half the gold when we hand you over; half when we reach the mainland.' Berenguer surveyed me, head to foot. 'Could you maybe look frightened now?'

I have over a dozen armed soldiers around me, and my father.

'No.' I shrugged. 'It would look unconvincing. He'd see that. I can manage "sullen".'

Berenguer's hand went up, tilting his sallet's visor to shield his eyes against the spring sun. 'We don't want him to run before we get the money . . . He's here!'

Gathered in the small open space between the sheltered Rialto and the drawbridge itself, we were not quite enough to block the general way. I saw Federico instantly, his white face visible under a brown felt hat as he approached from the Rialto's other side.

One man in his livery colours walked behind him, a middling-sized iron-bound chest clasped in both arms.

I bit my lip, preventing myself with difficulty from pointing this out to Berenguer or Tottola. *They see it too – and they are besides supposed to have betrayed you!*

Berenguer pulled at my elbow, striding forward onto the drawbridge itself. 'Come on, you!'

The planks did not shift underfoot, but I could see the green waters of the Grand Canal between them.

Only Berenguer and Tottola came forward. The dozen others remained on that side of the Rialto Bridge; I supposed by prior agreement. The urge to break out laughing almost overwhelmed me. If I could not manage fear or recalcitrance, I contrived to look exasperated – by way of thinking of my silverpoint drawing of Onorata back at the embassy, which I had spent three days on, and ruined with four unwise strokes just before the midday meal.

I looked across the short distance at Federico, and greeted him with a glare of hate. *He will expect me to have deduced himself behind this: who else is there in Venice now who can act on Videric's behalf?*

It may not be true in a week or two's time – but for now, there is only my foster father.

'Lord Federico.' I spoke before either he or Berenguer could, and heard my voice shake. With excitement, but I hoped he did not recognise that. 'You were never a father to me. But I didn't think even you could hand me over to be butchered like a hog!'

Tottola's immense arm wrapped around my upper chest, squeezing my tender breasts painfully if (I thought) accidentally. His other hand clapped over my mouth.

It was less violent than it looked, by far, but the sensation that he need only move the upper edge of his hand to stifle me made it easy to struggle. The German soldier's grip locked solidly around me.

Federico pulled off his brimless hat, ran his hands through disordered wispy hair, and pulled the hat on again. His skin was pale, dotted with sweat across his wide brow. He hissed, 'You will not be butchered! I have a promise of that! It is no more than giving you up to the life of a devout religious!'

Imprisoned in some cold stone nunnery or monastery, woken every three hours through the night to pray, and fed only on what we might grow – nothing of this appeals to me, whether in God's name or man's. But no need to argue the matter.

I took a long look at Federico, wondering if it could be marked on his face: this man that raised me, sold me, benefited by me – is he also willing to help murder me? Or does he genuinely force himself into a belief that this is no more than kidnapping?

In the dialect of Taraconensis – which I thought he might suppose these mercenaries not to speak – I asked, 'What hold *is* it that Videric has over you?'

Federico laughed.

He spoke in the same local variant of Iberian Latin, while he fondly shook his head. 'He has no hold over me! On the contrary, he values me.

He has for many years taken my advice on investing his gold – I have a nose for where the trade will go, and what items are best bought and sold, and when. The Aldra Videric would hardly be half so wealthy if not for my aid—'

'Why not make *yourself* rich?' I cut in, holding his gaze. 'Foster father, you forget. I know what the estate is really like. I know that Valdamerca keeps hens and sells the eggs for pennies when she's at home. I know how long it took you to save up Matasuntha's dowry.'

Federico waved an impatient hand. 'It will come – gold clings to gold! Do you think me rich enough to invest on my own? At least at first? Ridiculous! But Aldra Videric has the funds to invest, and I benefit, also.'

I wondered what tiny percentage Videric doled out to him – remembered I must seem to be scared of abduction – and decided I could risk no more questions.

He and Berenguer spoke rapidly in one of the Frankish tongues. I turned my head so that my hood drooped concealingly over my face.

More quietly than I had ever heard him speak, Tottola murmured, 'Not long now . . . '

Federico snapped his fingers briskly, and folded his arms where he stood. The serving man staggered out onto the Rialto drawbridge, iron-bound chest clasped in both arms. Berenguer stepped forward, taking a key from Federico's hand, and thrust it in the lock and twisted.

I caught the merest glimmer.

The reflection of light from true gold is unmistakable.

'Looks about right.' Berenguer slammed the lid down and turned the key again, and hitched the chest over onto his hip as if it weighed no more than Onorata.

Federico, turning away, reached out and grasped my arm just below the shoulder. 'Ilario, come with me.'

''Fraid not.' Berenguer pulled sword and scabbard together out of the straps of his belt, and lay the still-undrawn weapon flat across Federico's chest.

With one hand to the sword-hilt and the other gripping the mouth of the scabbard, he could have edged steel free in a moment. But because he did not, because no sword was actually drawn, no man looked at us or interfered.

Federico stared down at the red leather of the scabbard in pure astonishment. 'You have your first half of the gold! Three thousand ducats! You get no more until you set foot on the Veneto!'

'She's – he's—' Berenguer stumbled. 'Ilario's not going anywhere with you.'

'We have a *contract!*'

Berenguer showed his teeth. 'Yeah. We did. Sorry about that – we changed our minds.'

It will not be so easy, I thought. And caught the moment that the skin

49

folded and creased at the corners of Federico's eyes. In his narrowed gaze I saw anger and fear. *The latter is far more dangerous!*

Berenguer jerked his head, the polished finished of his helmet blazing back the sun. The dozen and more cloaked men strode forward onto the bridge itself, surrounding us.

Something nudged my shoulder.

I glanced back – just sufficiently less tall that I could glimpse Honorius's features, under the drooping edge of his hood.

'Contemptible!' Federico's jaw came up: he glared at Berenguer. 'You may attempt to cheat me. But what of when I go to your master Licinus Honorius, and say how you were willing to betray him for money?'

A cloaked figure brushed past my shoulder. Lifting his hands, putting his hood back, my father remarked cheerfully, 'Licinus Honorius already knows.'

With another company, it might have been possible to deceive Federico into thinking that the Captain-General had merely discovered the betrayal, and averted it.

These men have fought too long together: there's no mistaking their comradeship.

Which means my foster father is aware he has been taken, lock, stock, and arquebus-barrel.

Federico drew himself up, remarkably unafraid for a man with one servant at his back.

'How unfortunate to find you engaged in something so dishonest, Captain Honorius. But all the same, I believe you won't stop me taking my foster child away from here.'

'You think?' Honorius cocked a brow, and nodded towards the railing of the drawbridge. 'Think again.'

Honorius had clearly not left all twenty of his remaining men at the Alexandrine embassy. Ten of them, I saw, occupied two boats moored to slanting posts just at the side of the Rialto Bridge.

Seated in the bottom of the wide-bottomed boats, hands manacled behind them, were twice their number of men – a mixture of household servants without their livery badges, hired bravos, and that kind of man who is a petty criminal or a mercenary soldier according to the season of the year. More than half had ears cropped, or 'T' for 'thief' branded on their foreheads.

Honorius called an order. The men-at-arms rowed back into the side canal from which I deduced they must have come.

I turned to Federico. He seemed self-possessed – except for the colour of his complexion. A man might have blown plaster-dust across his skin and got that same aghast white.

All the rage is gone out of him.

He might have been furious at the trick, as well as a raid of consequences – Honorius's men-at-arms being unnerving *en masse* – but there was no anger to be drawn from his expression.

Federico looked about – for his servant, I realised. When I too looked, I couldn't see the man. Honorius's soldiers must have permitted him to run. He could go nowhere that would harm us.

'Keep the money.' Federico spoke abruptly. 'I'm done.'

There was more than satisfaction in Honorius's smile.

Of course, I thought. Now Honorius has three thousand ducats: he need not betray his location by going to any banker in any city.

Except that he *must* go back to Taraco! I made a grim note to bring this to my father's attention, yet again. *Before Videric robs him of all he has!*

Federico moved almost unconsciously back, feet shifting on the heavy planks.

I stepped forward and caught the velvet of his doublet sleeve. 'You may give Videric a message from me—'

'Videric? No!' Federico laughed harshly. He looked down at my hand, not pulling out of my grip, and then back at me. A scarlet flush covered the pallor of his cheeks: he looked unhealthy, and feverish. 'That's it: I'm *done*. I have Valdamerca and my girls with me – Matasuntha's husband will have to take care of her. Let the King confiscate that pitiable shack of an estate! I'm not returning to Taraconensis now.'

I found my hand holding the fabric tighter, as if I could keep him from escape. 'What do you mean, not going back to Taraco now? When *will* you go back?'

Federico laughed.

I heard bitterness in it, but a surprising amount of relief, too.

'Not ever.' He spoke almost gently, and stiffened his shoulders as he looked around at our mercenary soldiers. 'Never. This is what comes of trying to improve on my orders. Aldra Videric suggested I bribe your soldiers merely to desert, and then permit the men he will send to deal with you. I thought, if I had you in my hands to bring to him . . . '

His gaze was directed at the green water below, stippled and criss-crossed with gold light where wavelets caught the sun. I thought he saw none of that.

His tight, controlled voice quivered. 'And he will expect me to pay it back out of my own pocket! He will call me a fool for failing, and ask me for three thousand ducats. Dear Lord!'

Federico shook his head, and took a kerchief from his doublet sleeve to wipe across his forehead.

Things will not have changed so much in the eight months I have been gone, I thought, and said, 'You don't have three thousand ducats in gold.'

'Nor if I sold the estate!' Federico wiped his forehead again, and opened his hand. The white cloth spiralled down, spreading on the canal water below as it landed, and gradually sinking. He stared until the whiteness entirely vanished.

'I'm done!' he repeated. Straightening up off the drawbridge's railing, he snorted – a sardonic sound, that might have been a laugh – and looked at me. 'No need for concern. I have a nose for business, and I've made enough business contacts while making my lord Videric rich. I won't starve. The Alpine passes in northern Italy will be open by the time I reach the mainland. I think that Flanders and all of north Burgundy have it in them to be even richer than they are now . . . And I'm done with playing lapdog for my Lord Pirro Videric Galindo!'

Federico rolled out Videric's given name and matronymic with relish.

More than taken aback, I could only say, 'I thought you were his man.'

'And what is the use of supporting a man permanently out of power? Yes, he has wealth; he can buy men to do his bidding. But he's not a power in the land now, and he never will be – Videric becoming King Rodrigo's First Minister again: what are the chances of that?'

The scorn in his voice was hard, dry, and, I judged, perfectly genuine. It left me blinking at him in shock.

Federico patted my hand, where my fingers were still clenched in his sleeve. '*You* may give Aldra Videric a message from me, Ilario, since I hope devoutly never to see the man again.'

'I'm hardly so keen myself!'

Federico surprised me by laughing out loud.

'Nevertheless, if you do, convey him my regards. Tell him, I hope his miserly testicles wither and drop off. That, when he dies, I shall dance on his grave. And that, if I had known a quarter – an eighth part! – of the trouble waiting for me when he sent me after *you*, I would have thrown myself down on the Via Augusta and let the mule-train trample me to death!'

The soldiers chuckled, behind me. I heard Berenguer choke back an outright guffaw.

Federico clasped my hand in his and turned it over. I did not resist him. His thumb brushed the scribe's calluses, and those left by sword-use, still not gone after months without training. He regarded the smear of black charcoal that came off on his skin with seeming amusement.

'Aldra Videric knows you well enough to know you won't abandon the New Art. Just a word of warning.'

He patted my fingers with his other hand, and released me.

Looking up at the hooded figure of Honorius at my side, he said, 'Satisfy my curiosity, Aldra. Is she your son-and-daughter? Or did some son of yours father him? Or is it coincidence?'

Honorius took the iron-bound chest as Berenguer passed it to him and patted the lid. 'It would take more than three thousand ducats to buy those answers.'

'Indeed – I suspect them not for sale.' My foster father regarded my father for a long moment, looking almost jaunty. 'I also suspect you aren't a man to shoot someone in the back. Do let me know if I'm incorrect.'

Federico nodded politely, caught my eye as he turned away, and shot me a look so complex I could not unravel in it all the old loyalty, old grudges, despair, joy, and risk. His boots rang on the planks of the drawbridge, and then were muffled on the stone of the Rialto steps.

His back would not stop prickling until he reached his own palazzo, I guessed.

Perhaps not until he's out of Venice and across the Alps.

And it is not we who he fears.

The men he will send to deal with you. I heard Federico's voice in memory as he shoved his way into the Rialto crowds.

'He won't be the only man watching his back, now,' I said.

And it is not only here we face danger.

I looked at Honorius as we turned to retreat under the covered steps of the Rialto. It is weeks, if not more than a month, since my father received his letter from King Rodrigo. And, apart from the likelihood that Rodrigo's men have eaten Honorius's estate bare, now, and raided the others nearest to it . . . it is never wise to have a ruling king as an enemy.

8

Winter has not ever been my favourite season – at Federico's old estate, it meant feet continually numb in freezing mud; at Rodrigo's court, if fires burned in great brick hearths big enough to stable a horse, and I had boots, still, there was more venomous gossip around the Yule fireside than at any of her time.

Now I watched for spring's signs with terror.

If they come for me, and this family I have here, who will look after my child?

Even if she survives, she'll become a foundling in turn.

Trees, such as they are in Venezia, remained reassuringly bare of branch. But close inspection showed buds on every twig of the hazel beside S. Barnaba, thick and swelling, even if with no green at the tips yet. Travellers crossing the S. Marco square wore the clothes of Greece, Turkish Tyre and Sidon, Malta, and every other port from which further ships daily arrived. The Merceria was piled high with goods of all kinds, the scarcities and excuses of past weeks forgotten as if unspoken. People walked with heads up, their backs not stooped over into biting winds, although the sea-cold still drove into our bones.

Rekhmire' was out every day, rowed up and down this canal and that, trying for news on whether seas to Constantinople were traversible yet. Or whether any man had seen a Herr Mainz, late of the Germanies. Attila taught him a phrase or two to speak to the few northern men in Venice. Travelling by gondola or other boat kept Rekhmire' from putting his weight on his injured knee. He still came back to the embassy swearing – although whether physical pain occasioned this, or frustration, I couldn't say with certainty.

'Just when I could do with Neferet's salons,' he grumbled, one day without cloud, when I noted it stayed light into the early evening. 'Your father can provide me with an introduction to Captain Carmagnola, but outside of the military world ... I have never known a man so uninterested in politics!'

That was frustration. I grinned. 'Can I draft a reference from you? Rodrigo would like to know his throne's safe, I'm sure.'

'Safe from your father!' Rekhmire' grunted, and dug the tips of his fingers hard into the misshapen muscle about his right knee. He still wore Turkish trousers, on the excuse of cold; I had come to the conclusion that it was he who didn't wish to see his healing injury. The Egyptian added, 'He may be distracted from that – it's conceivable that King Rodrigo Sanguerra may have foreign troops on the Via Augusta before July . . . '

Even when I set foot in Carthage first, under the hissing naphtha lights, I was obscurely comforted by the thought that Taraconensis lay behind me in all its familiarity. I might desire not to be in that kingdom, but it was reassuring to know my past lay untouched behind me. The thought that it might change – all of it – and the men of Carthage march north and take control . . .

'Nothing may happen until next year,' Rekhmire' murmured. I knew he saw me concerned.

'Assuming we see next year.' I shrugged. 'There's no arguing against geography – it will be possible to take a ship from Taraconensis to Italy before it's safe to sail from Italy to Constantinople. If Videric sends another Carrasco, or more men like those on Torcello island . . . how long before they can get here?'

Rekhmire' frowned, recognising the rhetorical question. 'You could persuade nothing out of Lord Federico before he departed?'

Two of Honorius's more disreputable-looking men-at-arms had followed Federico and Valdamerca and my foster-sisters to the mainland, undetected as far as it was possible to judge. Whether Federico was indeed planning to head over the Alpine passes when they opened, or whether he would go elsewhere, he was not seen to take any road that led in the direction of Iberia.

'I think he was telling the truth – he *is* done with this.' I looked about for my roll of cloth with charcoal wrapped in it. 'I wish I might say the same.'

My fingers desired to draw. There was a thought in my mind, but I could not see the shape of it. I went for my sketchbook, to study Onorata again while she was blessedly asleep in her cot beside the fire, and see if my mind would work while my fingers were occupied. Rekhmire' talked while I looked into the tiny face, transferring the shadows to paper

It could be twelve or thirteen years before I know. Before *we* know. Whether she gets her menses, or not. Whether she changes, and becomes like me – although I was always both. But fear hangs over her, nonetheless, with me for an inheritance. What *is* she?

I reached down, adjusting her woollen blanket, and pictured Neferet and Leon sailing to the mainland. The long road they would have to travel. And at the end of it, there are Masaccio's friends: Brunelleschi, Donatello, other names he often mentioned while I sat as St Gaius and listened to him detail their work in sculpture and architecture.

I carefully drew the line of my child's lip – and by the end of it, an idea appeared full-blown in my head.

★

Refusing Honorius's company in a way that he would accept was not easy. Likewise that of Rekhmire', despite his difficulty walking. On the excuse of shopping for a better quality of chalks, I managed to get their agreement that I would go accompanied by the two largest men of the guard: Attila and Tottola, of course.

Honorius reminded me, in their hearing, as I walked down with him to the gondola at the landing stage. 'That weasel-eyed bastard Federico may still change his mind and come back! He may think his quickest way to favour is to travel back to Taraco with your pickled corpse in a barrel.'

'Thank you.' I blinked. 'A charming image!'

Attila lumbered down into the blue-painted wide gondola, gripping each side in hands the size of hams. His brother paused – and offered me a helping hand down onto the stern bench.

I waved, eyes tearing up in the cold wind, and the gondola crept out of the Dorsodura quarter, and into the busyness of the Grand Canal.

9

With Tottola and Attila at my shoulder, I followed the guard down into the lower rooms and dungeons of the ducal palace.

It was clear why the Doge Foscari wanted to rebuild the palace. The lower we went down, the more the stone steps glistened with water and the walls with white nitrous deposits. A damp cold crept into my bones. I pulled my fur-lined cloak more securely around my shoulders.

There was a reason why I was wearing silk and brocade and was evidently warm – Honorius's soldiers might think it a desire to aspire above my social station, but it was not.

'Here,' the jailer said, unlooking a tiny iron-barred wooden door, with a squeal of ungreased metal. I put coins into his hand, and ducked low to enter. Attila muttered something at my back – he had not liked their swords being kept at the guardhouse before we were allowed into the dungeons.

'You're lucky this one's still here,' the jailer added. He was a plump man, with laughter-lines about his eyes; I could imagine him patiently playing with grandchildren, or explaining duties to a slow apprentice. The complete blank failure to register the men chained to the walls, I suppose one develops as a consequence of such work.

'Lucky,' he repeated, thumbing the small coins in his palm, and holding the door to with his other hand. 'When he come in, his head was all swole up; then he had a fever.'

Head swollen.

The sounds came back to me with hallucinatory clarity: Honorius's men striking him in righteous anger, dragging him down the stairs.

I am not the only one to have struck him on the skull, and that jug was heavy enough to crack bone.

I do not feel guilty.

The jailer stressed, 'Hot as anything, he was. If I hadn't taken pity and brought him water . . . That's why he's still here, see? No man wants to move him when he's got jail-fever, it's the risk *they* might get it.'

I stepped forward, towards the door. Another ducat made its way from my fingers to the middle-aged man's hand.

More cheerfully, he said, 'Tough little bugger, though! He was dizzy and falling over and raving for a week; it would have killed another man. Here.'

The jailer swung the oak door open, and I saw it as thick through as a man's hand is wide.

Muttering, the jailor felt in his pockets for flint and tinder-box, and set about lighting the torches in the cell. A curve emerged from the darkness: became a man's back, where the man slumped on straw on the floor. For several minutes I watched.

Ramiro Carrasco de Luis did not raise his head.

'I know what it's like,' I said.

He turned over, at last. I saw comprehension on his face.

Hoarsely, he said, 'Ilaria . . . You were a slave. You know what it's like to be chained up like a dog.'

'And now you know, too.'

The torchlight showed me his face clearly enough. His bruises were mostly healed. Fading scabs still covered the cuts; the swelling had finished going down over his right eye. Under his prison-filthy clothes, I suspected there would be other injuries; a cracked or broken rib or two, now probably healed.

Ramiro Carrasco rasped, 'Not so pretty to draw, now?'

'You'd be more interesting to draw now,' I said truthfully.

He flinched as I stepped near to him.

I wondered: Have you begun to learn what can happen to a man in a prison?

' . . . Although I don't know if I could use you for the beaten Christus Imperator in the same panel as St Gaius.'

Another flicker of expression that was almost a flinch. Painfully, slowly, he got to his feet. As he straightened up, I thought he might be doing it simply to stand taller than I was, and not be intimidated.

He blinked at me. I saw him realise that we were much of a height.

'I thought you'd come for a look.' He attempted a glare of moral superiority. 'Poke a stick through the bars.'

He spoke with his gaze on me, ignoring the jailer and Attila and Tottola as if they were not present. I admired that attempt at dignity.

'You think I'm petty enough to want to see the man who tried to kill me chained up in his own filth?'

That wasn't quite accurate: the cell had basic facilities of straw and a chamber-pot. But Ramiro Carrasco coloured up all the same; I saw that clearly in the torchlight. To paint a blush in that light would require skill.

'*I* would.' Carrasco shrugged. 'Why wouldn't you?'

'I didn't say I wouldn't. I'm as petty as the next . . . woman,' I specified, remembering the jailer behind me. 'You put a pillow over my face. I was terrified. I don't much mind seeing you here, terrified yourself.'

'I'm not afraid!'

He might be speaking the truth. What I saw, if I looked as close as an artist can, was not necessarily fear. It was very like the desperation I had seen in his eyes as he pushed me back against the bed. But mixed with hopelessness, now.

'Why did you want to kill me?'

He scrubbed his fingers through his curly hair, each as filthy as the other. 'I didn't *want* to!'

And that is the truth.

The realisation surprised me. I caught Ramiro Carrasco's eye, and the half-sardonic and half-frightened look there.

A smugness, at having told me a truth he thinks I will dismiss out of hand.

And something that isn't fear of execution, or exile, or dying in jail.

'Why did you try?' I ticked it off on upraised fingers just protruding from the fur of the cloak, wrapped warm around me in this freezing prison cell. 'Near to the Riva degli Schiavona. In the gondola. Across the lagoon, on Torcello. You *tried*, certainly.'

Temper slashed in his tone. 'I've been convicted! What more do you *want*?'

'I want to know why.'

I turned away for a moment, guiding the jailer aside, speaking quietly enough that I knew Carrasco couldn't hear me. The man nodded and left.

Turning back, I found Ramiro Carrasco with a face that stress and helplessness made white and drawn.

I held his gaze.

'Are you a man who can kill because he's promised money? I talk to my father about that. When he has peasant levies to train . . . it takes time to make a man kill another man. You have to brutalise him. Convince him that the man he's killing isn't human. You can make professional soldiers out of some men. Most of them still vomit their stomachs empty, after a battle. But . . . some men have no knowledge *here*,' I put my palm against my abdomen, 'that any other man is real. So they can kill without thinking about it. Sometimes they look like kind grandfathers.'

I didn't look to see if the jailer had returned. And was quietly glad that Onorata's grandfather has never become inured enough to the sight of a battlefield that he doesn't, even now, spend some nights not daring to go back to sleep.

Ramiro Carrasco stared away from me, into the darker corners of the cell. I reached out and turned his head towards me. He appeared surprised at the force I could exert.

I said, '*You* haven't that capacity. Which, for an assassin, is perhaps unfortunate.'

He only shivered. I thought he might protest against 'assassin', but he merely gave me a look as full of hot hate and rage as any I've seen. Behind me, Tottola stretched himself in unsubtle warning.

I asked, 'Why did you do what Videric told you?'

At the name of my father – my mother's husband – he first flinched and then laughed.

'Get out of here.' His voice had a harsh undertone in its whisper. 'You'll get nothing out of me.'

'I don't need to. I know Videric wants me dead. I know *why*. I know it was Videric who sent you with Federico so that you could get close to me. I know there was more than one man with you, and I know they didn't get further than Genoa. I know Videric will send other men, now you're out of it, because he really *does* need me dead. No, I don't need you to tell me any of that.'

Ramiro Carrasco de Luis blinked in the light of the torches. He wiped his wrist across his mouth. Sweat, smeared away, left whiter skin displayed. A waft of unwashed body smell came to me when he lifted his arm.

'I don't understand.' He was careful not to phrase anything as agreement with me. 'If you don't want to know anything, why are you asking me? What are you asking me?'

'Why you'd try to do it. Try to kill me. Why you feel you *have* to.'

I saw decision on his face.

He spoke again, in a dialect common in the hill close to the Pyrenees, which was unlikely to be understood much outside of Taraconensis, and his bright eyes watched me to see that I comprehended:

'It was a choice between you and my family.'

The simplicity of his statement was at odds with the ferocious contained emotion behind his eyes.

'I'm the first of my family to go to university.' He spread his hands, mocking himself. 'I have a lawyer's degree! My mother and father, my brothers, my cousins and *their* parents, they'll all serfs, still. Tied to the land. Owned by the man who owns the estates.'

No need to ask his name.

'You will think it very little of an excuse.' Ramiro Carrasco spoke sardonically. 'Nor would I, in your place – what are twenty people you don't know, compared to your own life? But *I* know. I know my mother Acibella de Luis Gatonez; Berig Carrasco Pelayo, my father; my brothers Aoric and Gaton, and my sister Muniadomna . . . my uncle Thorismund . . . my grandmother Sancha . . . And I don't know you. Why should I care about some *freak*?'

He spat the last word. I looked at him.

The hatred comes from helplessness. From being arrested, charged, imprisoned; locked away from being able to kill one Ilario Honorius. And knowing that, because of that . . .

'Blackmail's very like being a slave,' I said, into the cold silence of the dungeon. 'They can kill your parent or your child, or sell them away from where you are. There are never as many slave revolts as you'd think

60

there would be. That's one of the reasons why. Do you know how long he'll wait without hearing from you?'

The question caught him by surprise. Carrasco shook his head before he realised. 'It's not – there's *not*—!'

I ignored the stuttered denials of something it was too late to deny.

The same odd feeling of fellowship came back to me. It is no wonder I could never hate this man. I nodded, absently, thinking, Perhaps this will not be so unpleasant to you – or perhaps you will find it unbearable.

I heard the jailer returning, grunting as he carried a weight down the passage. The torch showed him with tools in his hand, and a small block of steel-topped wood under his arm.

I took a leather bag of coins out of my cloak's inner pocket and passed them over.

'Do it here,' I said.

The jailer looked a little uncertain. I signalled to Attila and Tottola. Having spoken to them on the way, they knew what I wanted. Of all of us in the cell, I saw an expression of surprise only on the face of Ramiro Carrasco.

The two soldiers picked up Carrasco and held him down, bent over the anvil. Hands in Carrasco's hair held him stretched rigid. The jailer slid a slave's collar around Ramiro Carrasco's neck and cold-hammered a rivet home.

'This isn't legal!'

'You'd think so, wouldn't you?' I watched, arms folded, the cloak warmly wrapped about me. 'But Venice has always been able to put prisoners and captives of war into her galleys as slaves. It's legal to buy a prisoner as a slave in Venice. Provided you don't stay on Frankish territory. Perhaps they didn't mention that when you studied law? It's true all the same.'

He couldn't struggle in the two men's grip, but it didn't stop him trying. 'Why do you want me enslaved? What *use* am I as a slave?'

He hasn't realised what has happened to him, even though the collar is now around his neck.

Some don't. I have seen men whipped until the blood runs before they realise that their freedom has gone. That they're property. I wondered what it would take to make it clear to Ramiro Carrasco de Luis.

In Iberian I said, 'You'll know one thing about the law of slavery, I don't doubt. What happens when the owner of a slave is murdered?'

The chime of the hammer fixing the second rivet all but drowned his words:

'The household slaves are tortured—'

'Tortured. Why? Why not questioned?'

'Because it's assumed all slaves lie; it's a legal assumption—'

I saw it hit him.

If Ilario dies, I am a household slave; I will be tortured.

61

Not even because they assume a slave committed the murder, but simply that a slave will not be trusted to be honest *because* they're a slave.

Ramiro Carrasco looked up at me with wide dark eyes.

I watched him as I spoke. 'If something were to happen to me, if I were to die – even if it was merely from a sickness . . . Then, my slaves will be turned over to the authorities, and tortured to find out what they know. And Ramiro Carrasco the slave won't know anything about what killed me. But – interrogated men talk about everything they know, if they're subjected to enough pain. Everything.'

There was no need to say it aloud, in front of the jailor; I saw the understanding in Ramiro Carrasco's expression.

Everything. Including every order Aldro Videric ever gave you, when he told you to murder me.

10

Outside the Doge's palace, Tottola went to the Riva degli Schiavoni to summon a gondola. Attila crossed his arms, the end of the slave's chain-leash held in one hand.

Ramiro Carrasco blinked against the sunlight, weak as it was.

It was clear enough to show up the filth caking him. He did not, for all he wore the same clothes, appear much to resemble the sardonic secretary of my sister Sunilda.

Tears ran down his face, and he lifted both hands to wipe them, since his wrists were manacled together. I wondered if it was the brightness of the light.

He shot a dazzled look at me. 'My family—'

I gazed back coolly. 'As an owner, I can always *volunteer* my own slave for interrogation.'

He took a step forward and Attila jerked the links of the chain through his fingers. The iron collar came up hard against Carrasco's windpipe. I couldn't help wincing in sympathy; I know how that feels.

'Declared your slave . . . ' There was a degree of wonder in his tone. *No, he hasn't realised the truth of it yet.*

'You have to stay with me now,' I said, gently enough. 'What we're going to do with you, God knows. But you have to live with me, as my slave, so that if anything happens to me, all Videric's dirty little facts get spilled out into the open. It's a balance, a set of scales: if he kills me, everything comes out into the open.'

Videric may know me well enough to know I only want to be left alone. But whether he believes it – whether he fears having knowledge at large, in my head, not safely in a hole in the ground . . .

'You're my precaution,' I said. 'And since you have to be a slave for it to work – then you *are* a slave. You don't understand that yet, but I suppose you will.'

Attila rumbled a brief, 'Let me belt the cheeky bastard.'

Ramiro Carrasco opened his mouth. And shut it again.

'That's right.' I shrugged. 'If I tell Attila here to beat you until your bones break – and if he was the kind of man to do it – I could order it right here, and no one could stop it happening. *You have to understand this.* You don't have the legal protection of being a serf. You're no more human than a horse or a chair.'

It was not my words that had the effect on him, I thought, but the sombre lack of surprise from Honorius's soldier – a man whom Ramiro Carrasco would probably know, from his visits to Neferet's house.

'You . . . ' Ramiro Carrasco turned his head and looked at me. His back straightened. Even under the filth, he had a certain amount of dignity. I wondered how much experience of slavery it would take to curve his spine, and make him – as I sometimes still do – lower my head automatically in the presence of the free.

Ramiro Carrasco said, 'You may have stopped him killing my mother and father.'

'Yes.'

Because if that news were to reach him, he would turn traitor to Videric freely; any man would.

'But you had no way of knowing that I – that it was because . . . You couldn't know!'

I flicked back in the small hand-sewn pages of my sketchbook, abandoning an effort to draw the standing gondolier steering his craft in towards the steps. I found the page I wanted, and turned it towards Carrasco.

He looked down at his own face, in a preliminary sketch for Gaius.

'Look at that, Ramiro. Tell me that I *didn't* know you weren't doing this of your own accord.'

His collared neck straightened; he stared at me with fierce affront. '*Drawing* me? You couldn't know anything about me!'

Studying and reproducing the planes and features of a face, time after time, seeing how it subtly alters with each emotion . . . Once, I stopped midway through a charcoal drawing of Ramiro Carrasco, when I had put in the tone of his face, and only an outline of his hair. It made him look white-haired. I had thought, *This is how Carrasco will look when he's fifty.*

I stated, 'You've never killed a man.'

I saw the shock on his face.

'If you can fight with a sword, it's because you saw an arms master for a few weeks while you were at your university, and any new recruit would kill you inside two minutes. You were planning to stick a knife into me, because anybody can do *that*, surely? You've been delaying, delaying all the time, terrified that the Aldra would carry out his threats – I don't know what reports you've been sending back to him, but I know you wanted to convince him you were just about to succeed. All the time, just on the verge of success.'

The muscles that surround the jaw bone relax under shock. His mouth hung very slightly open. It wasn't fair that it gave him a look that was faintly comic. Under these circumstances, that could move one to pity.

'Yes, you could kill a man in self-defence,' I hazarded. 'No, you're not an assassin. And Videric wouldn't care what being a murderer would do to you. Why would he? Here you were – educated, so capable of taking a place with Federico; capable of being blackmailed, therefore controllable; capable of getting close to the man-woman Ilario. You were perfect. But just . . . not a natural assassin.'

Carrasco's voice cracked with desperation. 'Let me go back to Taraco! I don't even know if they're alive, if my father—'

'They're better protected from the Aldra while you're here.'

Videric would calmly and coldly work out that his weapon had turned in his hand, I knew. And would I put it past Videric to go into a white rage, and order his serfs slaughtered out of rage? It would be stupidity. But . . .

Carrasco stared at me. I read the same knowledge in him. Yes, he knows Videric well. And wishes he didn't.

'I can't guarantee anything,' I said. 'I'm sorry. I wish I could.'

'You're sorry?' Ramiro Carrasco's voice went up an octave.

By his side, Attila looked thoughtfully at the chain-leash's end. I shook my head. The exchange went right past Ramiro.

Carrasco spluttered, 'You're *sorry*? I tried to smother you!'

'Yes. I do remember.'

The caustic remark was very much in his own vein. It stopped him dead.

'Ilaria . . . You can do . . . whatever you like to me, can't you? If you want revenge for me frightening you . . . '

He didn't say *for hurting you*; he was perceptive enough to know which I would resent the more.

I shrugged. 'That's one of the things about being a slave.'

'And I can't . . . ' His dark eyes blinked against the spring sun, running clear water after the jail's permanent dimness. 'I can't thank you for perhaps saving my family's lives, either. Because you'll just think I'm trying to escape a punishment.'

'That's another of the things about being a slave.' I moved forward as the gondola came in to the steps. Looking back as I took Tottola's extended hand, I said, 'With slavery as you find it in Iberia, nothing honest can be said between slave and master.'

Attila thrust Ramiro Carrasco into the boat behind me, the chain drawn up tight enough that he had the secretary-assassin by the neck, iron biting into the secretary's prison-filthy flesh.

Honorius and Rekhmire' appeared on the Alexandrine house's jetty before we got within fifty yards of the landing stage. They watched in silence, one standing beside the other, as the gondola glided up and we disembarked.

'What?' Honorius pointed at the stinking and wet figure crouching in the bottom of the boat – wet because Ramiro Carrasco de Luis had not entirely believed Tottola wouldn't let go if he jumped over the side of the gondola.

Ramiro Carrasco coughed, shivered, and spat over the side, wiping his running nose.

The royal book-buyer chimed in, '*Why?*'

'I bought him,' I said – and watched comprehension spread over their faces.

11

'You're a wonder!' the Captain-General of Castile and Leon grinned, pulling me up out of the gondola and into his arms, and swinging me around in such a way that my scars pulled painfully – which I would not have told him for the world.

'Well done!' Rekhmire' gave me a pat on the shoulder, when he might reach me. 'Ilario – that was almost *clever*.'

'Why, thank you!' I mimed being offended, and gasped a little, under the impression my ribs might crack. Honorius released me. I added, 'All I need to do now is get word back to Videric, to tell him.'

A thought made me grin.

'A shame Federico decided not to go back to Taraco – I would like to have seen his face, when I asked him to carry the message . . . '

Rekhmire' openly snickered.

'Shall we go in?' I added.

'What about him?' Honorius jerked a thumb at my purchase.

'He's a slave, he has to be seen to be treated like one.' I glanced at Rekhmire'. 'I was thinking – along the lines of the Alexandrine model. Once we get out of Venice.'

The book-buyer smiled, and inclined his head.

Honorius continued loud congratulations while I introduced Carrasco to the kitchens and the soldiers, with stern words that the man should not be injured because valuable. I thought one or two of them entirely likely to give him more than a brain-fever, if left unwarned; attempting to murder a woman in child-bed is comfortably different enough from a soldier's killing that they can safely feel the utmost contempt.

Even if the woman is not wholly a woman.

The late frost bit at my fingers as I returned from the courtyard, having shown Ramiro Carrasco the iron bars on the gate. I sent him off to Sergeant Orazi to be found a place to sleep. Rekhmire' came up with me on my way to the main room, his steps more uneven now because of his less-than-successful attempts to use a walking-stick instead of his crutch.

'Out with it!' I directed, when we had reached the room and he had not yet spoken.

Honorius looked up curiously from a joint-stool by the fire, evidently equally desirous of hearing the answer.

'I admire your initiative.' Rekhmire' racketed over to the room's only armed chair, lurching like a town drunk at midday. 'To conceive of buying Carrasco – and to put the plan into operation—' He gave a faint smile. 'It's admirable. It's worthy of a book-buyer.'

'Spy!' Honorius rubbed his fingers hard under his nose, preventing himself from laughing. He had ceased to be entirely clean-shaven in the last few days, and was growing a moustache. I assumed he thought it would disguise him, at least to be less recognisable at a distance. It came out a little greyer than the hair of his head.

Having an ear for nuance, at least where the Egyptian is concerned, I smiled at my father, and turned back to Rekhmire'.

'But? "It's admirable" – and I hear a *but*.'

Rekhmire' sighed. 'But it won't work.'

29

The four words dropped into the room and brought about complete silence.

'*What do you mean, it won't work?*'

I checked the door and window by reflexive action. No Ramiro Carrasco; no guards or servants other than Honorius's trusted men.

'How can it not work?'

'Consider.' Rekhmire' steepled his fingers in the old way he had had in Rome. 'If you die, Carrasco is legally tortured, and Videric's secrets come out. If *Carrasco* dies – nothing.'

I stared at him. Able only to echo. 'If Carrasco dies . . . '

'Dies *first*. All you've done,' Rekhmire' observed, 'is given Videric a motive to have Carrasco assassinated before he kills you.'

Into the stunned quiet, Honorius's voice intoned, 'Shite.'

'I—' The inescapability of it flooded in on me.

'I wondered why he had been left alive,' Rekhmire' added, shifting uncomfortably on the hard chair. 'It wouldn't have been difficult to get a man into the prison to silence him. Evidently Videric didn't consider him a danger. If you've made him into one . . . '

The Egyptian shrugged.

' . . . You ensure he will kill both of you.'

'*No.*' I slammed one fist into my other hand. 'I thought it out, every step of it! It *will* work. It's a stand-off. All the while I have Ramiro Carrasco, Aldra Videric can't touch me!'

'All the while you *have* Carrasco,' the Egyptian emphasised softly. 'I grant you, it works while you do. But what you've done now is given Aldra Videric a reason to kill the slave before he kills you. And the easiest way to be sure of that, is to kill both you and he together.'

To come so close to safety – *so close*—

Despair went through me. I pushed it down, out of sight, so that the two men should not see it when I turned back to them.

Honorius clearly forced himself to sound encouraging. 'It's a good plan, while it works.'

Rekhmire' very briefly smiled. Knowing him as I did, I thought it was an appreciation of the irony of the assassin Carrasco now become the target.

Frustration washed through me. I thought it no metaphor, now, that men's vision goes red when they hate.

'It doesn't matter what I do!' I snarled. 'He'll never get back into power, the King will never take him as First Minister again, but Videric is just going to keep on sending more men! He'll send soldiers, he'll – I don't know – bribe a ship's captain to maroon me – send a proper murderer who's efficient enough to sneak through a military guard – *something*. Aldra Videric, he'll just ... keep on coming. Keep. On. Coming.'

30

There has to be an answer.

I can't see it.

Venice, which had seemed safe enough while I knew the freeman Ramiro Carrasco's location and temper, seemed dangerous now.

I thought there might also be an outside chance that, as a slave, he could still be able to hire men to kill me. But given the risk to his extended family back in Taraconensis; I doubted he would attempt that.

But . . . I have no idea who else is here from Taraconensis. Who may be on the road here, of docking on a ship this minute . . .

No one knocked on my door. Honorius and Rekhmire' both knew me better than to think I would want companions. I curled up in the window embrasure, taking charcoal to a wooden board, and rubbing out everything I drew that I was unsatisfied with. Which was everything. Proportion, value, perspective: all eluded me.

Some time towards the evening, when the dusk came swiftly down, a servant brought a plate of food and a jug and cup. Not until I caught his individual way of moving in peripheral vision did I realise it was not a servant, but Ramiro Carrasco de Luis.

Not a servant but a slave.

I put the drawing-board down and stretched my legs, uncurling out of my seated position with spine to the wall. The secretary-assassin stood by the table, food abandoned, his expression awkward. I wondered why he was so ill at ease; whether I should be suspicious.

'I'll take it back.' Carrasco's resigned voice broke the silence. 'I'll get someone else to bring you a meal.'

Poisoning me will keep his family alive, at least, provided Videric keeps his word – even if it'll get Carrasco handed over for a judicial burning as a poisoner.

Unless they flay him, as a slave who has killed his master.

Ramiro Carrasco's face showed a faint pink colour that was not reflected warmth from the hearth fire. 'You ought to eat.'

He abruptly reached down to pick up the wooden plate. It had dark bread and pale cheese on it, and I could smell that what was in the jug was honey ale. All of which can be sabotaged, I suppose, if a man sets his mind and ingenuity to it. But then, what can't be?

Crossing the room, I caught hold of Ramiro Carrasco's wrist, took the plate out of his hand, and set it back on the table. He appeared surprised that I would be strong enough to arrest his movement.

'I'll eat,' I said. His skin felt cool in my grip. I released him. 'Who sent you? My father? The Egyptian?'

Ramiro Carrasco de Luis looked down at the floorboards.

There was enough light from the window and the hearth-fire to let me see he ferociously blushed.

I could scent him sweating, too, but there wasn't the cold sweat of fear.

'You got this for me.' I couldn't help smiling at his evident embarrassment.

'It's not – tampered with!'

'You got this for me. Because . . . '

He was not in the dark Italian doublet and hose that he had worn as Sunilda's secretary, and naturally enough he had no stiletto at his belt. I'd bought him, but who clothed him?

Honorius, probably, from the household guards' baggage. The rumpled woollen hose, and doublet with darned point-holes, both looked as if they might have been discarded by some soldier after long service.

Carrasco had enough of the freeman still in him that he stood as if the scruffy clothes were a humiliation rather than a fortunate gift.

'Because?' I prompted.

Some man in the house had cut his hair back to the scalp, presumably to rid it of prison mites. Under his leather coif, he was quite bald. The same long-lashed black eyes looked back at me that I had spent weeks drawing.

I doubt he really needed to have his head shaved rather than washed – but someone will have found it amusing.

Ramiro Carrasco looked down at the table top, and blushed painfully red over his neck and ears, that I could see where the coif was cut high. He muttered, 'You're right, you can't say anything honest between master and slave. I just wanted . . . You . . . I do *know* I'd be dead of sickness by now!'

I picked up the crust of dark bread and bit a corner off. It was yesterday's. Dry enough that anything would soak into it.

What? some part of my mind scoffed. You think he has a chest full of poisons in his bedroll, all ready to play the assassin again?

Although he only has to have had access to my painting gear. The poisonous paints will kill any artist, if a painter is foolish enough to lick their brush.

'If I were in your position,' I said, 'I wouldn't poison the first plate of food. *Or* the second. I'd wait until I was trusted, until people were used to me, until I wasn't noticed. Then I could be certain the food would be consumed . . . What? You think I was never sold to any man I didn't dream of killing?'

Carrasco flushed. 'I forgot you've been a slave.'

It would have taken counting on my fingers to get the right of it. 'I think I've spent more of my life formally as a slave than formally free. I know all the tricks. And it's not like I've forgotten how many times you tried to have me killed. Even if I do understand why.'

The look Ramiro Carrasco de Luis gave me was something to treasure, if one is not immune to normal human vindictiveness.

He stood with his balance on the balls of his feet, shoulders hunched a little. I thought he would have liked to brawl with me. He glanced at my hand, where I bit at the dark bread again, and looked remarkably uncomfortable.

'You will not allow me even to thank you, for keeping me alive—'

'You don't want to thank me. You just feel you ought to. I *have* saved your life.' I couldn't help grinning, momentarily.

'Ilaria—'

'You're another one who's going to have to be beaten into remembering "master".' I put the bread down, drank from the jug – watching him and seeing no reaction other than a flushed anger. 'Listen. You call *everybody* master or mistress. They call you . . . whatever they like. It's like a dog or a horse. If I don't like the name "Ramiro" I can change it.'

That brought his head up. His dark eyes glared at me. Names are important.

'As for thanking me,' I said. 'You're glad to be alive, but you don't desire to thank me for keeping you that way. You hate the fact that I rescued you. I'd guess you spend half your time wishing I was dead, and half the time wishing *you* were. And you don't wish to thank me for making you a slave – you find it humiliating, because you have more pride than any man *ought* to have. Certainly more than you have sense. Travelling with Federico and his wife and daughters, being Videric's man covertly, knowing what was really going on . . . that suited you. Being property, being a shield between Videric and the man-woman . . . No, that sticks in your throat.'

I watched Carrasco go as white as he had been red.

'She-male!' he spat out finally, intending it for insult, not description.

'Ramiro, I spent enough time drawing you to know you.'

He knocked the wooden plate off the table, stalked out of the room, and his footsteps died away while the plate still spun and clattered on the floorboards.

How many times is he going to be whipped or starved before he realises what he is, now?

One word could have started that process. I felt more sympathy than I wanted to admit with his position. Am I to be the first to cause weals on his back?

A shield.

Yes, I thought. And I must finally admit it: Rekhmire' and my father are right. It merely puts Ramiro Carrasco where *he* has to be killed before I can be.

There must be a solution.

I can't see it!

The night came; I slept deeply, aware of no dreams; and opened my eyes with a snap in the morning, mind suddenly awake and aware, everything instantaneously laid out before me as the light and shadow of a drawing sometimes is.

I hauled a man's doublet on over my night-gown and clattered down the stairs.

The smell of cooking permeated the house from the kitchens to the main room downstairs, overlooking the still-bald garden of the embassy. Evidently I had slept through men breaking their fast. Walking in, I found that the long oak table was cleared – of knives and plates, at least.

My father and Rekhmire' sat with opened boxes and crates about their feet. Some of the smaller crates occupied the table top, surrounded by heaps of straw. The window's light caught shining curves.

I recognised glass goblets, lantern-shields, beads, jugs; all such as I had seen on the lagoon-islands of Murano and Burano.

'Old mercenary habit,' Honorius murmured, as he had in Rome; studying the pattern of a blue glass goblet he held up. 'Venetian glass will make excellent export goods . . . '

The room's far door closed behind Ramiro Carrasco.

Rekhmire' and my father, at the bench at the long table, smiled their individual smiles.

'I know another slave who was impossible to train,' the Egyptian remarked, blithely provoking.

I met his gaze.

Rekhmire' stopped and looked closely up at me. 'What is it?'

Honorius hooked a joint-stool up to the table, in invitation to sit, his gaze narrowed expectantly.

'I have the answer.' I slide a crate towards me, picking one of the glass goblets out of the straw. 'I doubt you'll like or approve of it.'

Rekhmire''s dark eyes fixed on me, intent and intense. Characteristically, he said nothing, only waiting for me to speak.

I tilted the goblet, watching the spiral of coloured glass in the stem catch the light. 'I don't like it either . . . But I can see no other way.'

Honorius reached and took the glass out of my hand, and set it firmly on the table. '*Well?*'

'Videric isn't going to stop—'

Old habits coming back to me, I sprang up, striding to open the room's far door. No man was listening. I checked the door I had come in by, and left both open – since it's harder to eavesdrop at an open door.

'Bear with me, and listen.' I paced back, resting my palms on the table as I leaned and looked at them, across the crates and packing.

Honorius nodded. Rekhmire' remained motionless.

'And tell me where I may be wrong,' I added. 'Ramiro Carrasco is some protection to us, because he will implicate Videric thoroughly, should he come to be tortured. And I suspect, if Videric harms his family out of pique, Carrasco would turn into a willing witness for us. But – if Videric can send a man who kills Ramiro Carrasco before he kills me, that doesn't matter.'

'Masterly,' Rekhmire' murmured under his breath, and held his large hands up defensively as I glared at him. 'No, Ilario, please. Continue. I'm sure this has a point . . . '

The waspishness reassured me. Rekhmire''s temper only verges on inadvertent rudeness when he is under great stress.

And that means the situation is as dangerous as I say it is.

Leaning with my hip against the edge of the table, I picked fragments of the straw packing out of one of the boxes, and looked across at Honorius.

'Tell me why you first went to Castile and Leon.'

Honorius looked as if he flushed, under the sun-browned skin. 'Your mother—'

'No.' I stood up straight. 'No, I understand *that*. Rosamunda didn't want to leave a rich man for a poor man.'

The bluntness must have hurt him, but he only nodded.

'You were a soldier. Why did you go *north*?'

Honorius's brows came down. 'Because that's where the war was! Still is, for that matter.'

I reprised the history of it, even though I could see a light of knowledge come into his eye. 'You couldn't have succeeded as well as you have in Taraco?'

Honorius shrugged. 'There wasn't going to be war in Taraconensis, I thought. I was right: there hasn't been a war on the Frankish border with Taraconensis for twenty-five years, to my certain knowledge. I knew if I went north to the crusades—'

I nodded, interrupting him, and set off pacing around the long table again, too restless to stay still. Rekhmire' leaned his head back as I passed him, intent dark gaze on me.

I said, 'We've both listened to the gossip in the salons. Every man seems to think Taraconensis so weak now, that Carthage might send legions in. So that the Franks can't press down from the north, take Taraco, and threaten North Africa.'

Honorius merely nodded. His frown was thoughtful. He had spent more than a little time talking over this with Carmagnola, I knew from my own observation.

'Ask yourself: what changed?' I held up my hand, stopping him speaking. 'And we know, of course. It started half a year ago, when Carthage sent their ambassador over and caused a scandal—'

Honorius scowled. 'You're saying *Videric* is the reason why—'

'Rodrigo had Videric as his adviser, his First Minister, all the time I was growing up at the court.' I ended at the head of the dark oak table, resting my weight on my hands. 'I *know* Rodrigo Sanguerra. Yes, he's a good king. But if you force me to admit it, I have to say – he would have been less good without Videric.'

I went on swiftly, before either staring man could interrupt me:

'Others think the same thing. How *true* it is – hardly matters. Politics is a matter of belief. And men believe that Taraconensis is weak because the First Minister has been banished from court.'

In the silence, I heard servants' voices distant in the kitchens, and Saverico out in the embassy courtyard, laughing like a much younger boy at some remark Berenguer made.

Honorius's scowl did not lighten. 'Ilario – what is this?'

'It's inescapable.'

I straightened up, facing both of them: the Iberian soldier and the Egyptian book-buyer.

'Aldra Videric needs me dead. If I'm dead, the scandal starts to die, and eventually Rodrigo can recall him to court. Videric's a rich man, a powerful man. He can afford to pay to send any number of thugs and murderers after me. And to arrange for any witnesses to be killed, after.'

I saw Honorius and Rekhmire' swap glances. Clearly, this is not a new thought to them.

I pulled one of the smaller crates towards me, running my finger across the grain of the beech wood. That soothed me enough to get words out:

'I know that Aldra Videric will not run out of money. And he's well enough guarded at his estates that it would not be possible to attack or ambush *him*. Nor will he forget this matter – the only thing Videric has ever had is his place at the King's side. He won't forgive losing it. He won't cease wanting it back.'

I took a breath, feeling an odd combination of confidence and swimming dizziness,

'I remain the obstacle. What Ramiro Carrasco can say might give Videric a moment's pause. But as far as that goes – as you say – he can probably arrange an attack by bandits that wipes out an entire party of travellers, just as soon as we leave Venice. He's rich enough to crew a ship and send men after me that way. I've thought of this backwards, forwards, and sideways. The answer remains: Videric's not going to stop coming after me.'

Honorius put war-worn hands down on the table. 'Ilario . . . naturally this must worry you. I can defend you—'

'Not indefinitely. And it puts you in danger.'

I circumvented Honorius's further words by pointing at the Egyptian. 'You too, Rekhmire'. You're a witness.'

With an unexpectedly hard note in his voice, Rekhmire' stated, '*I* am a representative of Alexandria-in-Exile and the Pharaoh-Queen.'

'Then go back there and be safe,' Honorius rapped out. 'This isn't your fight—'

The temperature in the room dropped ten degrees. Expression rigid, Rekhmire' said, 'Is it not?'

'Damn it, man, you know what I mean! You *can* leave, and so you should—'

'If I had not *interfered* at Carthage,' the Egyptian's voice bit down, cutting Honorius short. 'If I had not thought it so *wise* to go spilling Aldra Videric's secrets – your son-daughter might not be in such complete danger of being killed! Yes, you have every right to blame me for that—'

'I don't blame you!' Honorius jumped to his feet, waving his hands wildly. 'Ilario doesn't blame you!'

'It never *occurred* to me to— Will you two *be quiet*!' I yelled. 'And just for once *listen*!'

The silent room echoed to a tiny sharp snap.

I looked down. The serpentine stem of the goblet I had picked up had snapped neatly into two.

Gently, I put the parts of the glass down in the straw-lined crate.

'I have the answer,' I said, 'if you will *listen*.'

Honorius seated himself again on the bench, one hand resting on the table. As I watched, it curled into a white-knuckled fist. Rekhmire' steepled his fingers and gazed at me over his clean spade-cut nails.

'Videric will not stop,' I repeated. 'And I can see only one way to stop him eventually killing me. Killing *us*, I should say – he won't leave witnesses. And that one way is . . . We have to see that Videric gets what he wants.'

Honorius blinked in total bewilderment. 'But he wants you dead!'

I snorted a laugh, and wiped at my face.

'Apologies! No. Think. He wants me dead, but only as the means to something else. He desires to be summoned back from exile. He wants to be Rodrigo's adviser again. Videric wants to be the King's First Minister of Taraconensis.'

Rekhmire' stared at me with as blank an expression as I had ever seen on his face. 'And . . . '

'And – that's what we have to do.'

I looked from the Egyptian to my father, and from Honorius back to Rekhmire'.

'That's what will stop these attempts at murder. That's what will make us safe. I have to *help* my greatest enemy.'

Rage boiled up through me with the suddenness of thunder in

summer. I seized up the wooden crate of export glass, and hurled it two-handed and bodily towards the room's further wall.

It struck home with a vibrant, world-shattering crash.

'I have to *help* the man who's trying to kill me. And the only way to help Videric . . . I have to help him get what he wants. I have to put him back in power.'

Part Two
Alexandria-in-Exile

1

'*That* means . . . ' I broke the silence with some deliberation. ' . . . that I go back to Taraconensis, now, and negotiate this with Videric. Face to face.'

Rekhmire', bent awkwardly over on his crutches, and surveying the remains of the crate of export glass, shot a startled look at me. 'You do not!'

'Is it necessary to point out that you freed me in Rome?'

The Egyptian straightened up, monumentally prepared to rebuke me.

Honorius rose to his feet, knocking his own glass over. Spilled wine spread in a pool of reflection that I wished I might paint.

The Lion of Castile snapped, 'You may be of age, but as your father—'

I stopped pacing and completed his words: '—You've learned to recognise a losing battle when you see one?'

'Don't you be cheeky with me, young Ilario!'

I swung around, striding back up the room, ignoring the pull of healing stitches. Low as the beams were, and cramped as these small quarters might be, movement was the only thing that eased my mind. Wearing one of Neferet's Alexandrine housecoats and a doublet is not like wearing Frankish petticoats. *I begin to feel more myself than I have since I came to Venice.*

I pushed open the panelled shutters, letting in cold spring air, and gazed down at the canal at the rear of the embassy. Brickwork reflected in the water. The sun stood high enough overhead to strike down between the tall buildings. Symmetrical ripples spidered off the water, too bright to look at directly.

'Tell me that there's *any* other way to do this!' Dazzled, I turned about; resting my back against the windowsill. I stared into a room now completely black to my eyes. 'Videric lost his place at the King's side because people won't allow Rodrigo to have a would-be murderer there. You know Carthage will have said Videric tried to kill me, no matter how much of it was Rosamunda!'

In the brilliance of the water outside, I see the Court of Fountains in Taraco, regardless of the heat there and the chill here.

'Videric will be devising plans to get back into favour. Which all depend on having me dead and forgotten. He'll send more men like

Carrasco. If we're in Frankish territory, he's long used to dealing with the banking firms and all the major merchants for King Rodrigo – he can pick up gossip about hermaphrodites, about painters . . . With Federico's reports, he knows as much about what I'm doing as *you* do.'

Honorius frankly scowled, I saw, as my eyes adapted back to light and shadow. He desired to contradict me. Clearly, he couldn't.

Rekhmire' seated himself on the bench with a grunt, and a clatter of crutches. 'It's true: Aldra Videric *would* be better returned to court as your King's minister. Carthage is under the Penitence, and Iberia is the grain-basket of the empire. Any excuse to take over more of its kingdoms . . . It seems there are too many people with confidence in First Minister Videric as a politician, and King Rodrigo's right hand.'

Which made me desire to spit out something bitter. Why hearing confirmation of my thoughts should create such revulsion, when I had been brought to admit the truth of the argument through long hours spent feeding Onorata and brooding, I did not know.

I stared both of them down: the sitting spy, and the standing General, whom I cannot afford at this moment to think of as friend and father. 'Who else can sort this out but me? If I go back to Taraco, persuade Videric that I'm not interested in having Rosamunda arrested for my attempted murder—'

Honorius interrupted by lifting his head and bellowing, 'Carrasco!'

While my ears still rang, Ramiro Carrasco came in, and shut the door behind him on the sound of a crying baby. He shot a frightened look around the room. The slave's look, which I know well: *What have I done?* And: *It doesn't matter if I did anything or not, am I going to suffer for it?*

He does learn fast.

'You.' Honorius seemed reluctant to call the assassin by his name again. 'Tell me something. How long might you live, if you stepped off a ship in Taraconensis now?'

They speak of men going white. It would be more accurate, I thought, feeling the shape of it in my fingers that itched to draw, to say that their faces go sunken. It wasn't possible to tell if Ramiro Carrasco the slave looked pale in this dim room. He did instantly look ten years older.

He snorted unsteadily. 'Minutes if I'm lucky! As long as it'll take the Aldra to send out his household men disguised as bandits. On territory he *knows*.'

Carrasco swung about, unslavelike, and shot me a look of appeal.

'My family – they'll be dead too! He'd leave nothing! You can't be thinking of—'

Honorius, apparently unmoved by Carrasco's disrespect in not addressing him as 'master', leaned his hand on the table, tapping a finger on the wood. 'Ilario's thinking of travelling back to Taraco. What about it, Ilario, would you take your slave?'

Honorius didn't take his eyes off Carrasco as he spoke.

That will be part of his continuing investigation into whether the man speaks the truth, I thought. As well as pointing out to Ilario what an idiot Ilario is . . .

Stubborn, I said, 'Ramiro Carrasco will stay with you.'

Rekhmire' leaned his elbows on the table, beside Honorius; his weight making the wood groan. 'So much for the slave Carrasco as your shield against Aldra Videric . . . '

'He can be that out of my company.'

I doubted the truth of it even as I said it. And kicked a joint-stool out of the way as I paced back down the length of the room.

Ramiro Carrasco blinked at me with the bewildered look of a slave realising that none of the decisions which will affect him are taken with any reference to what he thinks.

I could read nothing on Rekhmire''s impassive countenance. An unexpected pang went through me. *Who knows*, I thought, *what orders he'll receive from Alexandria, when ships can safely travel here from Constantinople?*

Orders that take precedence over this.

'And my granddaughter?' Honorius demanded, behind me. 'Do I sit in some place as yet undecided, with your slave and your baby? While you venture back to Taraco, walk up to Videric, and – watch your head go bouncing across the ground, because it won't take ten heartbeats for one of his men to "protect" him! He needs you dead, Ilario! What better excuse for instant execution than "Ilario wanted revenge and I had to defend myself"? You won't get a chance to speak to the King. Nor to any other man. Videric's informers will tell him what ship you're on, and some thug will hit you behind the ear with a cudgel and tip you over the quay-side before you get a foot off the gang-plank!'

I swung around. 'Then tell me some other way to do this!'

The shout bounced back flatly off the plaster and beams, silencing Honorius.

I leaned on the other side of the table, both fists against the wood, staring down at the retired soldier, my father. 'Videric must listen when I speak to him. How can I know, here, what it will take to get him back in favour? I don't know how King Rodrigo will ever be able to say, *Here's Videric, he's my First Minister* again. And if I don't go and ask Videric, face to face, I never *will* know!'

Rekhmire' raised his clear low tenor voice. 'If you will stop charging full-tilt into things—!'

Honorius interrupted, a burning look in his eye. 'I forbid this.'

Rekhmire' smacked one large palm against the side of his forehead. 'Amun and Amunet! The donkey can be led but not driven!'

Honorius snorted down his nose and glared at me. 'In my experience, the donkey can't be led *or* driven!'

My fingernails drove painfully into my palms.

83

A faint sound of Onorata's crying reached through the ill-shut door and clawed down the tendons and muscles of my neck, stiffening them. With an effort, I pushed away my urge to rush to her.

'You,' I said quietly, 'need not look after the child: I will. I may be no mother at all to her—'

And that's as well, when you think of Rosamunda!

'—But at least I know now how to be a father.'

I inclined my head in thanks to Honorius. He looked taken aback in the extreme.

To Rekhmire', I added, 'I know you have business for Constantinople; I can't ask you to go out of your way. I do thank you for what you've done for me. If you're going to Constantinople – to Alexandria – it would help me if you'd take Ramiro Carrasco with you as your slave. Probably Videric will have a harder time getting him murdered if he's there.'

Rekhmire''s mouth looked as if he'd eaten fresh lemon.

He turned his head, not to look at Carrasco, as I expected, but to exchange glances with Honorius.

'Fucking idiot!' The retired Captain-General of Leon and Castile waved an expressive hand. 'My son-daughter; not you.'

'Ah.' Rekhmire''s smile was that familiar all-but-imperceptible one that meant he was truly amused. 'Well, it is more generally applicable, after all.'

'Oh, ay.' Honorius nodded, hit himself on the chest with his fist, and then pointed a sword-callused hand at Ramiro Carrasco. 'Ilario's father, slave, and . . . '

'"Book-buyer"?' Rekhmire' suggested.

You could have scraped paint off acacia wood with Honorius's look of scepticism.

'Book. Buyer.' The soldier paced down the room and planted himself in front of me, with the light of the window in his face. His eyes narrowed, either against the brightness or his thoughts. He glared down the few inches difference between our heights.

'If you go marching back into Taraconensis, Videric will kill you! Yes, I'll agree: you're right that Videric needs to be put back at Rodrigo's side – with a collar on him, so he can't do too much damage! But this is not the way to go about it!'

The Egyptian snorted. 'You'll never tell him – her – Ilario! – that.'

Rekhmire' was being chronological, I thought, rather than mistaken in his gender.

I could see in his expression that same emotion I'd seen when he asked me how long it was after Rosamunda attempted to stab me that I fled Taraco.

How long was it after I met Sulva that I asked her to wed me?

Anger set me to pacing the room again. 'No, Taraconensis isn't safe. Nowhere else is more safe! Father, you said it yourself – Videric's had

Federico looking for me in Rome, and Florence, and Venice. If I looked for a local mastro in Bologna or Ravenna or Milan, now, Videric would find me. And none of that—' I glanced aside, taking in Rekhmire''s glare. 'None of it, no matter where I hide, will get me closer to putting Videric back into power!'

The silence after my words rang in the low-ceilinged room.

Honorius folded his arms. In the same moment, Rekhmire' also folded his. In another mood it would have made me burst out laughing – both of them scowling like pediment sculptures in Green cathedrals. As it was, it snapped what little temper remained to me.

'I bought that man!' I flung out one arm to point at Carrasco. He visibly startled. 'Because he is protection. Because all I want to do is be left alone to paint.'

The floorboards creaked under me as I restlessly shifted, gripping my hands together to deny that urge to frantic pacing.

'Because I have a child that, if it doesn't die of some childhood disease, or merely *die*, I need to protect. And now the sole and only way I can see to achieve that – is to go back and sort things out with my stepfather—'

Rekhmire' interrupted. 'Say if you leave Venice, take sanctuary in Alexandria—'

'There is no sanctuary!' I found myself making fists again, nails leaving white crescents against my skin. 'None that's more than temporary. Videric's been the King's councillor for more than twenty years. I know how courts work. Videric knows men in every major city in the Mediterranean and Frankish lands, and if he's out of favour now, he can still find some men who think that won't last. So they'll do him favours. Look out for travellers. Pass word back to him. He found me here; he'll find me again. If he can't kill me because of Ramiro here, then he'll kill both of us, and the only way I can see to stop this is to go back to Taraco!'

'But,' Rekhmire' protested.

The reasonable tone of his voice triggered my vision to a blur of rage. 'No, I won't hear more!'

Honorius drew himself up a little, at the table's end, inclining his head. He rested his hands flat on the wood.

If I painted him, I thought, it would be just so, with campaign maps under his fingers, and lanterns behind, illuminating the dark interior of a military commander's tent.

'Yes, this has to be done.' He fixed me with a direct look. 'But there is least of all any sanctuary for you in *Taraco*! I at least have an excuse, a need, to go home to my King. And I'll use that chance to talk to him; convince Rodrigo Coverrubias that I'd far rather see First Minister Videric than First Minister Honorius. But you – you have no reason to go home except to be murdered, and I won't allow it.'

There was no blustering father in his voice now. It was all confident

Captain-General; the commander who knows he will be obeyed because there is no other reasonable option.

More quietly, he added, 'Constantinople is still the safest destination – for you *and* that rat's testicle Carrasco.'

Honorius continued over Rekhmire''s splutter of amusement, and Ramiro Carrasco's glare.

'Let the spy take you to his city, until we can begin to solve this.'

Rekhmire', having looked sour as an early plum at *spy*, broke his silence with a sigh. 'Regrettably, I might need to send, rather than take.' He glanced up at Honorius. 'If I don't find Herr Mainz by the time ships can sail for Alexandria, then I suspect my orders will send me to Florence, to shake the information of his whereabouts out of Neferet. And Ilario is hardly welcome in Florence.'

Without ever having been there, I reflected.

Honorius gave the Egyptian a sceptical look. 'You won't be riding or walking to Florence until that knee's healed up. But in any case, when I leave for Taraco, I desire some man to look out for my son-daughter's interests—'

I pounced on my father's admission. 'You'll go back, now? Persuade Rodrigo to take his troops off your estate? Convince him you're loyal?'

Licinus Honorius gave me somewhat of an old-fashioned look. He sighed, shoulders appearing to relax their stiffness. 'Say I agree with you. That returning Aldra Videric to the position of First Minister is the only way to both end this and keep Taraconensis safe. Which of us, alone, is in a position to begin this? Not the spy—'

Rekhmire' snorted.

'—since King Rodrigo doesn't know the Alexandrine well enough to trust him as I do.'

I caught a fleeting look of embarrassed pleasure on Rekhmire''s face. The trust of the Lion of Castile is not given lightly, or hurriedly. Evidently he appreciated this.

'And not *you*,' Honorius snapped bluntly, glaring at me. 'Videric would show you your liver inside two days. That only leaves me.'

I could find no ready answer.

Turning aside, I directed Ramiro Carrasco to clear up the broken glass, and stood tearing at my mind for ideas while he did so and departed. Nothing came to me.

Honorius's hand rested on my shoulder with a sudden pressure that was startling.

'I'll go,' he repeated. 'As soon I have a safe refuge for you and Onorata. I'll go back to King Rodrigo – I knew that I would have to.'

I found myself torn between grief and joy. Joy that he could reconcile himself with the King; that he will not lose everything he ever earned – with his own blood – because of me. And grief, I reflected, because I will badly miss his presence, and because he may be going into more danger than we know.

Honorius turned his face to the window for a moment, as if he could pierce the buildings and the haze of aerial perspective, and see westwards all the way over the Italies, and the Middle Sea, clear to Iberia. His eyes slitted.

Turning back, my father shot me a look that, even in that dim panelled room, I could not mistake for anything but wry humour.

'To be fair ... ' Honorius sighed, and put his arm around my shoulder. 'You realise, I hope? That this is the only way I might go home – and not kill Aldra Pirro Videric a quarter-hour after I set foot on Taraco dock?'

2

'*Kill*—' Breath left me. *I have not thought of this!*

Under the smile of Honorius's much-creased face, I saw frank amorality, that if I had to guess, I would attribute to stratagems on the field of battle.

'Ask yourself, Ilario. This man persecutes my son-daughter. Apparently he won't stop. What's the best way to ensure he will? A foot of steel through his ribs, and make mince-meat of his heart and lungs. The dead have no friends or allies.'

Honorius had the flat of his hand resting against his thigh, where his sword would hang were he not in the house.

A little weakly, I said, 'You won't kill him? Because – apart from needing the whoreson bastard as First Minister – they'd hang you for murdering a noble! Lion of Castile or not.'

'"Lion of Castile" would get me hanged with a silken rope,' Honorius mused, somewhat over-gravely. 'Or at least the charity of an efficient headsman at the block. I once saw an execution take twenty blows of the axe, and the man's head was still on—'

'*Father!*'

'—just,' he completed gruesomely, with an open, loving grin. 'No: I won't kill Pirro Videric. Much as the little shite deserves it. No: I won't get myself executed. Or even arrested. Yes: I'll talk as persuasively to His Grace King Rodrigo as I can. Are you content with that?'

'More or less,' I grumbled, with the intention of seeing if I could provoke a laugh out of him. It did.

'Very well.' He sobered, fixing me with a bright gaze. 'And now we must make plans for you and my granddaughter.'

I continued to pass nights broken by feeding Onorata. That would have given me time to think deeply on my father's proposed departure, and how long I might be safe in Venice, if I had not ended all but delirious with sleeplessness, and unable to think at all.

Seeing this, Honorius took it on himself to take at least one of the night feeds ('What, you think me not capable of feeding my own grandchild? How many brats do you think a mercenary baggage-train *has*?'), although he drew the line at changing her soiled cloths.

Rekhmire', while content to nurse a sleeping child as he wrote his correspondence ready for sending east, lost his fascination for her as often as she puked or burped over him. Although I did find her in his company surprisingly often for a man who claimed to have no idea of what eunuchs and babies might have in common.

'The ability to bawl their heads off when they don't get their own way?' was not the politest remark I ever allowed to unwisely escape me.

Rekhmire' merely sniffed.

'*I* am not as sentimental as those great oafs of soldiers,' he observed, and then pinched at the bridge of his nose as if to ease a headache brought on by writing. Eyes still closed, he added, 'You have a dozen "uncles" for the child, who would take more care of her than an egg made of diamond – if only because they know Master Honorius would unravel their guts if they damaged his precious grandchild.'

He opened his eyes and glared at me.

'For the Eight's sake, take advantage of that while you can!'

'I will.' I nodded at the portable writing-slope on his lap. 'If you've correspondence I can help write, I will. Meantime, since I've forgotten the outside world exists, I'm going out to the Merceria.'

'Only if you—'

'—take half of Honorius's company with me,' I finished, ahead of the Egyptian, and found myself with a grin. 'I will. Can I run any errands for you while I'm out?'

Rekhmire' snorted, in a less than dignified manner, and rummaged among the scrolls and documents on the table beside him. '"Run"? I doubt you'll run anywhere until those stitches heal! But if you care to waddle about the city for a while, see if you can discover any more of these put up on walls?'

I took the paper he handed me. It was instantly recognisable: one of Leon's seditious hand-bills.

'You think Herr Mainz might be still here, and printing for someone else?'

'I hope so. I have no great desire to go to Florence . . . '

Despite walking about considerable areas of Venezia, with various of Honorius's guard, I saw no similar hand-bills. The following day, I conceived of asking among the scriptoria, on the pretence of looking again for work, but found no one familiar with the overly-precise lettering of the supposed printing-*machina*.

The following day brought sleet, slanting and chill, and took off every appearance Venice might have had of being in early spring.

My healed stitches itched, and still pulled when I walked, I found. Those of the soldiers I privately consulted assured me this was normal for edged-weapon wounds – which I supposed Caesar's cut at the base of the womb might best resemble.

I refused to wear wooden pattens, and that at least made walking easier, without trying to balance several inches above the mud.

Ramiro Carrasco can clean my shoes for me, I reflected, as I plodded over a high hump-backed bridge, treading in Attila's footsteps through the mire. *Ah, the evils of slavery . . .*

The thought that it might be a true evil took the smile from my face. *True evil, if I only think that slavery's bad when I am the one sold and enslaved.*

Leon Battista's hand-bill crumpled up in my hand as I clenched my fist.

I tugged off my leather gloves to smooth out the thick paper.

'Holy Eight!' I stopped suddenly enough that Tottola walked into me from behind, and I felt him grab my biceps with hands like iron, so as not to send me flying.

'What?' He looked down at my belly, under the long cloak, as he released me. 'You took ill?'

'No. But I realise I've been looking in the wrong places!'

I held up the printed paper illustratively as Attila strode back to us, his hand on his sword.

'Master Leon Battista had enough of these printed . . . It doesn't matter if no man recognises the print.' I rubbed my thumb over the rag-made surface. 'What I should have been looking for is the man who sold him this *paper*.'

'This the last workshop?' Tottola rumbled behind me.

'For today.' I pointed. A tabarra stood a few doors down the narrow street, torchlight reflecting into the mucky grey daylight and the half-frozen canal. 'You can wait for me . . . '

'We'll come with you.' Tottola didn't have the hint of a sigh in his voice. 'Both of us.'

I recalled Sergeant Orazi's advice, passed on to me at one point: that his troopers should be made far more scared of him than they were of any conceivable enemy. Between that and loyalty to Honorius, there was no chance the two Germanic mercenaries would leave me unguarded.

We entered the fifth warehouse that day; I took a half-hour choosing three variant colours of green earth pigment, and discussing with the workshop-master the advantages and disadvantages of various mixtures of size for wood and canvas.

'I need to buy more paper,' I finally observed. Attila and Tottola had become bored enough to amuse themselves by looming over the shopkeeper's apprentices and watching them pale – doubtless having been raised on Tacitus's *History of the Huns*.

'What kind of paper?' The workshop master stretched out his hand as I put a torn-edged sample into it. 'Ah.'

I fully expected to be told it wasn't familiar, or wasn't made by this workshop, or sold here – or else that they had only small quantities available in stock. Two of the parcels Tottola carried contained unavoidable purchases of paper.

The Venetian workmaster put the torn scrap of paper down by the edge of the terre verte pigment tub. 'Yes. Whoever recommended you here was correct: this is our make – I'd know that drying-lattice pattern anywhere.'

He straightened up, and spoke again before I managed to collect myself:

'I'd like to help, but we're out of stock. A customer came in at the beginning of Lent, bought up the whole stock; it'll still be a week or two before we have any more of that particular kind pressed. When do you need it by? Or can I offer you this other—'

'I need it now,' I interrupted, mouth unaccountably dry. *Whatever Rekhmire' can do as a book-buyer, I can do.* It's nothing but pretence and asking questions.

With what I hoped resembled genuine rich-man's petulance, I whined, 'Are you sure you don't have any left? Just a small piece?'

The man shook his head, as one will do when wondering at the vagaries of customers. 'He bought up all the sheets. Don't forget a sale like that.'

I looked brightly at him, as if the thought had just struck me, instead of being painstakingly constructed between Attila and myself in the gondola that brought us here.

'Where did you have the paper delivered to? If I could go and ask him if he has any left . . . even a quarter sheet . . . '

My heart thudded in my chest.

Here's where he says the man had it collected, they didn't deliver.

The works master reached down for a ledger, thumbed through it with agonising slowness – and halted his finger halfway down a page. 'You'd tell him we sent you? Like his custom again, if I can get it.'

'I'll make certain he knows.' I offered the carefully saved end-sheet of paper, and watched him write down an address.

Once outside, I took a deep breath of wet, freezing air – and realised Attila and Tottola were looking down at me with identical expressions.

'Escort me there,' I directed, with a look that plainly informed them I did not expect to come to harm in their company. 'But you'll have to wait outside. If this Herr Mainz knows Leon Battista got thrown into prison, I imagine he's somewhat nervous.'

'So I am!' Tottola muttered, as we set off towards the churches the master had used as landmarks while telling me directions. 'The General will have my balls!'

'And that Egyptian bastard will have *my* balls to go with yours – and his!' Attila muttered.

Tottola made no reply, but he looked worried. On a bearded Hun a head taller than any man in the streets of Venice, that is suitably impressive.

'Honorius expects you to guard me,' I said, the cold air welcome in my lungs after what seemed like weeks indoors. I stepped out more briskly. 'And "that Egyptian bastard" will be too busy being pleased, if this comes off, to even think about how we did this – *or* about your balls, Attila. Which, let's be honest, no one wants to think about . . . '

I said it much in the same manner as the young ensign Saverico might have. The large German soldier snickered. I thought Attila was more comfortable with the part of me that was young man than young woman.

Attila continued my arguing for me with Tottola as we trudged across campo, bridge, canal-path, and more bridges.

The address turned out to be a small shed at the back of a closed-up house. The house looked to have no occupants; the shed had two shutters propped open to let in the light.

I left the two mercenaries at the head of the alley.

There being nothing to be lost by a direct approach, I knocked on the shed door and opened it without waiting for an answer.

In the dim natural light that was all the illumination, a lean man with rough-cropped black hair turned away from a bench and towards me, both his hands laden down with long thin metal teeth that I thought Leon Battista would have recognised as type.

I spoke in the clearest Frankish Latin I could manage.

'You'll be the German Guildsman, Herr Mainz.'

I added rapidly, as I saw consternation on his face:

'The Alexandrine embassy would like to speak with you.'

3

At *Alexandrine*, a flood of emotions passed over his face. He stepped forward, into the better light. The lines of his face spoke of hunger and distrust, and of hope.

Irritably, he muttered, 'You ignoramuses still have it wrong! "*Master of Mainz*", not "Herr Mainz"! "The Master of Mainz" is still my title, even if expelled from the guild!'

'Ilario Honorius,' I introduced myself. Something in the shadows at the back looked very like a wine-press, if a great carved wooden screw might be combined with trays and racks, rather than a grape-tub. 'If I have your name wrong, how should I say it? It was Messer Leon Battista who called you "Herr Mainz".'

'Chicken-hearted Florentine!' The German came almost up to the door. With the dying light from outside, I could see his robe and hose were patched and worn. 'My name is Johannes Gutenberg, of the *city* of Mainz. Where is Herr Alberti? I have not seen him these many weeks.'

'Prison. Florence. Exile.' I gave the knowledge in chronological order, and briskly – what a man who has been lied to needs is the truth, blunt as it may be. 'Why didn't you come to the Alexandrine embassy?'

The German printer seized at his hair, knocking his black felt hat off the back of his head, and yanking his short crop up into hedgehog-spikes. '*You* ask me that! You, one of Alberti's lackeys! I could be in Constantinople!' Gutenberg choked out. 'With a patron! I could work with the best materials – the finest resources – and *you*—'

He spat on the dirt floor at my feet.

'Your petty little republic! Who is Duke? Who cares! Honest men can't work, or are killed, and then another nobleman, same as the last!'

I moved my foot. 'I don't disagree. But a clear explanation and less public noise might be of more use than a political discussion. Florence isn't my republic, and I'm not a servant of Leon Battista Alberti.'

And Herr Mainz must take me for a man, I realised, with my back to the open door's light, and cloaked as I am. Since he doesn't treat me as a woman.

'I'm from the Alexandrine embassy,' I persisted.

'The woman said, no messages; that she would not take even letters from me!'

93

That confirmed every suspicion. *Damn Neferet!* I wondered which of the sacred Eight one appeals to in such circumstances.

Honesty still remaining my best option, I said, 'Madonna Neferet was a conspirator along with Leon Battista; they both had their reasons for wanting you to stay here in Venice. They've both been sent into exile, now. The representative of Alexandria has been looking for you.'

He snorted derisively.

I brought out the hand-bill, hoping it would act as my credentials.

Tilting the paper to catch the grey light, I observed, 'I've seen nothing like this before. The edges of the letters are sharp as if they'd been cut.'

'They are.' Herr Mainz sounded smug.

I nodded at long metal stylus-shapes in his hands. 'But if your type is made from lead – I know lead—'

My mind clearly sees a silver-grey smear on the masonry of a bridge. Saverico's brigandine; Rekhmire''s leg. *This may be an even more dangerous use for lead.*

'I'm not ignorant,' I offered. 'Men have been talking about the dangers of a mechanical scribe, and if one could be built, since I was a child. Lead's soft. It deforms. The type would be crushed after printing a few sheets, the edges of the letters smeared.'

He gave me an abrasively close-mouthed smile, confirming himself secretive as other German Guildsmen, and no fool.

I took a breath, and pressed the limits of my authority.

'Alexandria wants you and your printing-*machina* in Constantinople, if you'll come. The Pharaoh-Queen may be willing to become your patron, if the printing works.'

The light gave Mainz – Gutenberg – oddly silver eyes. He looked stunned. 'I have not dared to go out, to search . . . The Doge's officers, here . . . '

I took a swift glance around the shabby workshop. 'What do you need to bring with you, to replicate this device in Alexandria?'

Herr Mainz looked at me for a long moment, turned his back, and emptied his handful of long metal type into a large canvas bag.

The contents of a rattling shallow tray followed.

'What I need? All of it!' Gutenberg freed one hand to tap the side of his head, without turning round. 'But all is here, safe, I do not forget!'

'No, but accidents happen to any man.'

He shrugged, as much as a man may who is rapidly tying up the neck of a sack. 'What, you'd have me tell my Guild secrets? The ratio of antimony and tin to lead, so that the edges of these letters stay sharp? Then what is stopping your theft of that?'

I could find no quick answer that I thought would convince him.

I squinted through the gloom. The *machina's* screw was turned by wooden shafts, thick through as a gondola's oar.

'We can send men back to dismantle the printing-*machina* and bring it.'

I glanced around, uneasy for no reason I could pin down, and wished for the first time in many months that I had a sword, and a more recent memory of my knight's training in Taraco.

'If I may, I'll call my father's guards, and we can go to the embassy now.'

I found myself glad of the grey cloud and sleet, that brought twilight in ahead of its time.

A gondola took us as far as the Canal Grande, and then another boat over to the Dorsodura quarter, where we reverted to foot. In a maze of small alleys and waterways that bemused my sense of direction, Tottola took one long stride and caught up, dipping his head to murmur:

'There are men behind us. Somewhere between ten and twelve, lightly armed, no armour except breastplates.'

Dread twisted cold in my belly. 'The Venetians were having his workshop watched!'

Attila, as closely attached to Herr Mainz's side as he might be without rope binding them together, spoke something in one of the Germanic tongues of the Holy Roman Empire, to which the printer responded.

Reverting to Visigothic Latin, Attila said, 'Council of Ten.'

Increasing my pace put a line of pain across my lower abdomen.

'I can't run,' I confessed, feeling my face burn hot against the cold wind. '*Get him to the embassy.* Don't wait for me. Once you're there, they can't touch him.'

The Germanic brothers exchanged a look over my head.

Tottola grunted. '*I'm* not waiting to see what the captain would do if we left you!'

He moved swiftly enough that it took me by surprise. As Attila and Herr Mainz burst into a run, Tottola scooped his arms under my shoulders and knees, and lifted me clear off the cobbles.

Abandoning the parcels of paper, and the ceramic pots of green earth pigment that shattered as they fell, Tottola clutched me against his chest and began to run.

'Bar the gates!' Attila bawled as he hustled Herr Mainz ahead of me. '*Turn out the guard!*'

Berenguer and Saverico hauled the iron trellis of the Alexandrine gate open, stood ready, and slammed it on the heels of our passing through.

The bare garden of the Alexandrine house filled with running men, Sergeant Orazi at their head. Tottola breasted the flood – and failed to put me down, despite urgent request. The house door banged open; we entered from cold to warmth.

Rekhmire', balanced on crutches in the entrance hall, shouted at me immediately he saw me. 'How could you leave this house where you're safe!'

Pointing out that I am most safe wherever Honorius's Hunnish soldiers are, I thought would not help me.

'I'm back here safely,' I snapped, as Tottola set me down on my feet like a child in the entrance hall. 'Even if the Venetians *are* on our heels!'

That turned out not to be a wise thing to say: Rekhmire' broke into a flood of Alexandrine Latin – much of which I understood, although I would rather not – and then into Pharaonic Egyptian.

A glance at Honorius as he stomped in from the gate showed him unlikely to help me with translation.

Not that I need it, I reflected, watching Rekhmire' balance his two crutches precariously in his armpits, so he could windmill his arms while he shouted at me. It all amounts to 'You can walk around Venice, I can't, and this gives rise to fear.'

'We have the officers of Foscari's council on our doorstep,' Honorius announced matter-of-factly. He surveyed the man from Mainz, where the German stood dishevelled and panting, and then turned his attention to me. 'And *you* found him, why?'

'Because I engaged in a paper chase!' I rearranged my cloak, that had been rucked up in the chase. In peripheral vision I saw Gutenberg blink as he caught a glimpse of my skirts. 'As to the Doge's men – I thought they had no idea of where he was.'

It had seemed reasonable, as we were rowed back, to suppose that the Council of Ten must be hunting for a large facility, a factory or a large scriptorium, or a workshop where woodcuts had somehow been made able to cut small letters. Not one man in a shed.

The Egyptian got out hoarsely, 'They surely must have failed to find him while Alberti was here, or they would have stopped him.'

Talking to Gutenberg in the gondola had given me somewhat of his background; I summarised it.

'He was setting three or four pamphlets a week. As fast as Leon could write them. They went off in bales on mule-back, to Florence. After Leon and Neferet left, he didn't have business contacts, and he heard the Doge's council wanted to speak to him and went into hiding.' I cocked my head, listening to raised voices at the outer gate. 'They must have found him and been watching him, hoping to pick up other conspirators.'

'Instead, they found us.' Honorius scowled. Noise rose louder from the gate. Evidently the Council of Ten weren't used to being defied by armed foreigners.

Honorius's household guard are not a large number of men, I realised, compared to how many soldiers the Doge of Venice might call to arms. *Suppose we end with Carmagnola outside the Alexandria House?*

Rekhmire' abruptly closed a hand over my shoulder. His eyes shone bright in the lantern-light. 'Listen.'

I could pick out nothing among the voices, strain as I might.

Honorius, when I caught his eye, shook his head bemusedly.

Rekhmire' secured his grasp on his crutches and swung himself awkwardly and rapidly out into the late afternoon twilight, seeming oblivious to the cold sleet landing on his bare head.

I barely caught Honorius's signal to Attila, to stay with Gutenberg, and then my father strode with me as I stumbled outside again in the Egyptian's wake.

Lanterns illuminated the gate area, but made the desolate garden even darker. The scent of canal-water pervaded the air. Voices lifted in screaming confrontation at the iron grille of the Alexandrine house, where iron bars had been dropped into sockets across the gate.

Words rang like brazen trumpets in the language of the lagoon, and in Visigothic and Frankish Latin – and in another tongue that I only recognised as I caught it for the second time.

'*Listen!*' I echoed, seizing Honorius's arm. 'That's Pharaonic Egyptian, I swear it!'

The mercenary soldiers made way automatically for my father, their faces grim under the lanterns, helmets and pole-axes and swords catching the light.

The circle of torches and lanterns beyond the gate was wider, and the Council of Ten's officers more numerous, but I hardly spared the Venetians a look.

In chiaroscuro, their reddish-brown flesh covered by lamellar leather armour, and with spears in their hands, a squad of some fifty or so men in Alexandrine clothing formed a double line towards the gate.

Down the path between them, across the S. Barnaba campo, a well-padded male figure strolled, not shivering despite his linen kilt and bare legs. His scarlet cloak flowed out behind him, light sparking from the fabric where droplets of rain lodged in the weave.

He stopped before the iron of the gate, a yard or two of space separating us.

His features took me back instantly to another city and another embassy. I found myself rubbing my hands one against the other, as if my skin felt still sticky from trying to pry stone fingers out of Mastro Masaccio's throat.

The Alexandrine cast a leisurely eye around, the uproar from the Doge's soldiers quietening as he did so, and ended with a nod of greeting to Rekhmire'.

'I'm sorry,' Lord Menmet-Ra remarked. 'Am I interrupting something?'

4

He seemed so consciously pleased with his pose that a man could hardly resent it.

Inadvertently, I broke the silence. 'You're not in Rome!'

Heads turned. I blushed. *That sounded foolish!*

I had thought that, having drawn so many sketches now of Masaccio in ink or silverpoint or charcoal, I had begun to have difficulty in remembering Masaccio himself. This tall round eunuch in Alexandrine kilt and lapis-lazuli collar returned Masaccio's dead features intensely to my mind.

'Ilario.' He nodded to me.

'Lord Menmet-Ra,' I apologised.

The last time I saw the Alexandrine, he had been dishevelled and in a night-robe, Masaccio's blood staining the hem. The torchlight gave him stature, although he was still clearly fleshy. He carried an air of authority that he had barely seemed to in Rome.

He added, 'I was hoping to speak with you, Messer Ilario. I have a message for you, from the Pharaoh-Queen Ty-ameny.'

It may have been anticipation or dread, or only the icy wind, that made my eyes water and my throat ache.

Menmet-Ra turned back, raising his high tenor voice that rang over the darkening square.

'Go home, men of Venezia! This is Alexandrine soil – as much so as the ambassadorial warship in San Marco basin, that has brought me to your city. Go ask your superiors if they wish to offend the Pharaoh-Queen through her newest ambassador, before you rashly act here!'

Heads bowed together in the dusk; I heard whispered consultation.

The officers and men of the Council of Ten faded into the darkness, only boots echoing between the high brick walls to mark their departure.

The gate being unbarred with a clash, Menmet-Ra signalled his men to follow, and swept through with some gravitas, despite his body having the smoothness of fat rather than muscle. I did not truly note what words he and my father exchanged, but I stumbled dumbly in their wake, back into the house.

Established in a carved chair by the great hearth in the main room, the

Alexandrine looked unhappily at Rekhmire''s crutches, and then lifted his kohl-lined eyes.

'Ty-ameny says you must bring the German. As to the other matter . . . '

'Carrasco.' Rekhmire' spoke brusquely. 'Fetch wine.'

Ramiro Carrasco went out, wordless. Lord Menmet-Ra extended his hands to the fire. There were goose-bumps on his arms, despite the oncoming spring, I saw. The waters of Venice make anywhere cold, no matter if you're used to Taraco or Constantinople.

'Well, our cousin got me at last . . . ' He looked up ruefully at Rekhmire'. 'You see before you the newest appointee to the position of Ambassador in Venezia.'

'So I gathered,' Rekhmire' remarked dryly, seating himself on the oak settle by the fire. I took a place silently beside him, as quiet as slaves are when hoping not to be noticed.

'With a warship?' Rekhmire' added, one brow raised.

'Trireme,' the older man's light voice said. 'I believe the Queen, all praise to her ten thousand ancestors, thinks the Doge of Venice needs a reminder who rules the eastern seas, and not merely some few fathoms of the Adriatic . . . '

They exchanged looks that I thought in less professional men would have been broad grins.

' . . . And so no making my way here on hired boats,' the new ambassador concluded. 'I come with flags, banners, arbalests, a company of marines, and all to impress. Ah—' Menmet-Ra rose to his feet with the grace of a much thinner man. 'Lord Honorius.'

My father pulled the door closed behind him and Ramiro Carrasco, stepping forward, and giving the impression he ignored Carrasco as the younger man served wine into Venetian goblets.

'I've got my sergeant sorting your men into quarters. Just as well I'm leaving, or we'd be sleeping six in each bed!'

Honorius had discarded sallet and sword, and was in nothing more martial than a pleated doublet and hose. Nonetheless, as he crossed to the hearth and planted himself with his back to the fire, no man could have taken him for anything else but a soldier.

I knew my father well enough, now, to realise this entirely deliberate.

'I hear you want to speak with my son-daughter,' he added bluntly, flipping up the back of his doublet-skirts to take best advantage of the heat on his arse.

If the subject had not put a thrill of fear through me, I might have snickered at the Lion of Castile playing the blunt mercenary commander.

All but inaudibly, Rekhmire' murmured at my ear, '*How* long do you suppose it will take to house-train the man?'

His fellow Alexandrine heard, as I thought he had been intended to. Encourage him to underestimate the Iberian barbarian . . .

Menmet-Ra seated himself again, and spoke with deliberation. 'If you are aware of an incident in Rome, at which Ilario was present—'

Honorius nodded curtly. I chose it as my moment to interrupt.

'Lord Menmet-Ra.' I leaned forward on the settle, my gaze on him. 'The . . . statue. Golem. Did it go to Alexandria? Did anyone finish painting it? Is it still in Rome?'

Honorius's brows went down as if someone had pinched a thumb and finger full of flesh over his nose. 'Ilario, you will not go anywhere near that monstrosity!'

I had described Masaccio's death; I could not make him feel or smell what the reality had been like. Meeting Menmet-Ra's gaze, I saw under his self-possession, an identical fear to mine.

'The gift of Carthage,' the Egyptian ambassador emphasised slightly, 'is in Alexandria, now. The painting of it remains unfinished. I escorted the gift from Rome to Alexandria myself.' He paused. 'Not on the same ship with it.'

I might have laughed if I had not been moved to shudder.

Rekhmire' looked across and curtly signalled Carrasco to leave. I rose and took the wine glasses around myself. Not that it will make a difference to have Ramiro Carrasco hear anything – but I understand why Rekhmire' prefers his absence.

Lord Menmet-Ra nodded thanks and sipped at wine from a sea-blue glass. He looked up.

'I see you're made free now.'

He thus neatly avoided using the terms *freeman* or *freewoman* to me.

'In which case, I can now extend the request of the Pharaoh-Queen in person, to you, that you come to Alexandria—'

'No prodding!'

The words fell out of my mouth without my expecting it.

Rekhmire' put his hand lightly over his eyes. Honorius grinned.

'I mean,' I managed, 'that I have no wish to end with the doctors of Alexandria examining me.'

Menmet-Ra smiled across at Rekhmire' with the ease of long friendship.

'I've had too much of that kind of interest before,' I said levelly. 'Being hermaphrodite.'

Menmet-Ra's kohl-darkened brows went up. 'Ah! No. Although I dare say there are many of our scientists who would like to examine you. But my business with you is not to do with that.'

My business with you.

The golem's fingers a joint deep into Masaccio's larynx as he and I both tore with useless human hands at motionless stone.

No . . . I suppose that business was not going to be done with so easily.

The large, fat Alexandrine put the tips of his fingers together. With all the appearance of good humour, he said, 'The Pharaoh-Queen Ty-ameny has no hold over you, not being the slave of one of her people now. Nonetheless, she requests, if you can, that you come to Alexandria, and tell how it was that Masaccio died. There was no one but you and he alive in that room with the stone engine when it killed him. If you could bear witness . . . '

He left an encouraging gap into which I could speak my agreement. I looked at Rekhmire'.

The book-buyer shifted where he sat on the wooden settle. 'Ilario, you will understand that this "gift of Carthage" is partly an encumbrance, partly a dare – and, I imagine, the Queen's advisers are now afraid, partly a trap.'

'I understand.' It was too much to resist. I moved to lean on the back of the settle, and looked equably at Menmet-Ra. 'I *understand* that Carthage is giving this one of their golems to Alexandria because the thing can be used as a weapon – even if it hasn't yet – and the Lords-Amir are showing off. Daring you to discover how it walks and moves and obeys. Because they're convinced you won't be able to.'

The skin around Menmet-Ra's eyes crinkled. 'Masaccio hired no stupid apprentices, I note.'

It made me grin, until what occurred in Rome crashed down on me again.

'I'll be frank.' The Alexandrine ambassador glanced at Honorius. 'Since Rekhmire' reports you and your father trustworthy.'

Oh, does he?

The book-buyer was none too eager to meet my eye.

Menmet-Ra continued. 'Any gift from Carthage to Alexandria is likely to be a poisoned chalice – Lord Honorius, as a military man, you will understand this.'

Honorius inclined his head in the Iberian fashion, said nothing, but appeared to listen willingly enough.

'It is a concealed threat. Yes, they show us this one of their weapons, and leave us to guess at what else they might have devised. They show they're certain enough of no other man investigating the golem's secrets by giving us the gift of one. And the more our scientist-philosophers baffle themselves examining this golem, the more powerful Carthage grows in our minds . . . and the more fearful of them Alexandria is.'

Menmet-Ra looked up, addressing me directly.

'After the events in Rome, I made my report from your eye-witness statement. But it is still only my report. You were the one that saw. There are those at home who would have the Pharaoh-Queen turn down this "golem" – I think rightly so. Suppose it were to run amuck one day in the courts of Alexandria? How many could it kill, before it was overwhelmed? And, most importantly, if it has hidden orders that send it against Ty-ameny herself . . . '

I opened my mouth to speak the obvious suggestion.

'No.' Rekhmire' raised a brow at me. 'The Pharaoh-Queen – all worship to her ten thousand God-ancestors – is very nearly as stubborn as you are. There is no chance of dropping the thing into Alexandria's harbour!'

Menmet-Ra gave Rekhmire' a look I couldn't identify. 'The Pharaoh-Queen, all praise to her ten thousand God-ancestors, does not desire to look frightened in front of Carthage! Which if she refuses the gift, or sends it away, or visibly incapacitates it, she will. But it is *not* safe to have near her.'

The truth would not greatly benefit me, but I spoke it all the same. 'I don't know what else I can add to what I told you in Rome.'

'Nevertheless. She very much desires to speak with you,' Menmet-Ra said. 'As soon as you feel you might come to Alexandria-in-exile.'

'Thank you,' I got in, before Rekhmire' or Honorius could speak. 'But, obviously, I'll need to talk this over with my family.'

'Of course.' Menmet-Ra stirred himself, finishing his wine. 'I shall hope to speak to you again. Before I completely immerse myself in opening this embassy for business.'

His smile was amiable, but the sensation was odd: to hear that what has felt like my house belongs to this stranger.

Menmet-Ra added, 'And on that subject – I should speak to Neferet.'

'Ah.' Rekhmire' blinked, with the expression of an amiable lizard. 'I believe I also have matters I should discuss with you.'

Honorius spoke gracefully-extricating farewells, grabbed me firmly by the elbow, and I followed his lead in leaving the room.

'We'll talk it over,' Honorius muttered, 'but not near my export glass!'

'Sorry.'

He patted my shoulder, with a wry smile.

Glancing back as we mounted the stairs to his rooms, he added, 'This is no opportunity to miss – if Master Rekhmire' can persuade his ambassador into it, you might make your way to Alexandria on one of their warships. That would greatly ease my mind about your safety.'

I closed the shutters against the chill early evening, and plumped down on a linen chest, wincing as my stitches twinged. 'I imagine Rekhmire' will be escorting Herr Gutenberg and his mechanical copyist on that ship. Before the Doge decides he *can* search the embassy.'

'Well, then. It never hurts to have a highly-placed man in court, to introduce you to his sovereign.'

It took me a moment to realise that my father meant Rekhmire'.

But, yes, he is more than a book-buyer.

I watched Honorius put a taper to the oil lanterns. Swelling yellow light limned his hair and cheekbone.

'Alexandria is half a world from Taraco,' Honorius said thoughtfully. His eyes were lucid in the soft shadows. 'Outside Frankish territories, too. The Pharaoh-Queen won't need Videric's influence or friendship, even if he had any to give. And you're intelligent enough to answer her questions about that stone blasphemy and still avoid going into the same room with it. Of all the places for you to be, while I return home . . .' He smiled at me. 'You may even learn something!'

'I've seen Alexandrine art. It's all toes-pointing-down. And chests face-on and faces in profile. The New Art's here, in the Italian cities!'

'So are Videric's informants,' Honorius said dryly. 'You know, I wonder if my estates at Taraco ought not to have some Alexandrine work, as well as Italian? I hear they make faïence tiles, and amazing enamel-work.'

I gave him a look. 'What would you know about enamel work unless it was on the pommel of your sword?'

Honorius grinned. 'I can learn.'

He brought bread and cheese, and another bottle of his better wine, and set them on a bench by us, reaching out for a braided-stem glass and tilting it against the light.

'I don't like dragging a youngling all around the middle sea,' he observed, and shot me a keen glance. 'Better she's with you, though.'

I am by no means so sure.

'And you need have no concern for money, or worry that you'll find yourself dependent on the book-buyer's charity.'

In another mood, that would have made me bristle. 'I'd sooner not be dependent on any other source – but I doubt I can keep myself and Onorata on encaustic wax funeral portraits in Alexandria!'

Honorius snorted. 'I intend to leave you half the household men-at-arms,' he added.

'We had this quarrel in Rome!' I chewed at the dark gritty bread. 'You'll make me noticeable—'

'That hardly matters now!'

'—and you'll rob *yourself* of men you need to have with you.' I met his pale eyes, and held his gaze. 'If you go to Taraco with only a small number of soldiers, Aldra Videric or Rodrigo Sanguerra will think the best solution to the problem you pose is a quick death, or quietly vanishing into one of the King's prisons. You must know this!'

'I want you to be safe! I should have bought you when you were still a slave. You'd have been so much less trouble!'

'I wouldn't count on it!' Rekhmire''s voice came from the doorway. At Honorius's beckoning gesture, he took the armed chair nearest the hearth.

Putting his crutches down, and allowing his forearms to rest along the arms of the wooden chair, he for a moment resembled one of the

Pharaoh-Kings of Old Alexandria, heir to a thousand generations of history. The lantern-light made sculpture of his face.

With an entirely irreverent-to-history gleam in his eyes, he murmured, 'I've given Pamiu much to think on, while he arranges this household to his satisfaction! Ilario, are you inclined to risk another sea-voyage?'

'To Constantinople?' I shrugged. 'I can tell your Queen Ty-ameny what I saw. I doubt it will help. It will tell her nothing except that the golem . . . obeys orders. And I suspect they know *that*.'

'You don't know what her philosopher-scientists will discover from what you saw.' Rekhmire' spoke in an eminently reasonable tone.

'I still say I should go back to Taraco and have it out with Videric!'

Honorius made a growling noise beside me, and I found myself in receipt of his 'you-lower-than-dirt-new-recruit' glare.

'Alexandria is your best choice.' Rekhmire' spoke unusually abruptly. 'If only as a shelter. A place to rest. To give you time to think, to plan, to—'

'—be prodded by every one of the Pharaoh-Queen's philosophers because they've never seen a true hermaphrodite before!'

Rekhmire''s brows went up. 'Oh, I wouldn't say *never*. You're not unique, you know.'

My temper was uncertain, but I managed to avoid that particular inviting trap, and grin at the book-buyer. Which, although less satisfying than throwing breakable objects, still pleased me greatly when I saw his startled look.

More because I desired to bait him than by way of serious argument, I said, 'You should let me send word to Videric, and meet him, and settle the matter.'

Rekhmire' snapped like a bad-tempered mastiff. 'Certainly, if you met, it would settle the matter – with a freshly-dug grave! Ilario, come to Alexandria.'

I grinned at him to let him know he'd been provoked. 'Maybe I should have left Venice with my husband.'

Honorius rested his chin on his sun-darkened fist. 'If Madam Neferet sees you in Master Leon's company he'll probably flay the skin off your face before you reach the Arno!'

I found the reference to Neferet as *he* unexpectedly jolting.

Rekhmire' drained his glass of the dark wine. 'Neferet had sufficient trouble before leaving Venice.' He caught my puzzled look. 'You heard none of the gossip? I suppose not. It was widely said of your wedding that Master Leon Battista had thrown Neferet over in favour of a "real woman".'

My father and I looked at each other for a long moment. He hit his thigh with the flat of his hand several times, straining to breathe. I bit down hard on the root of my thumb, not knowing whether I desired to laugh or cry.

'If they *knew*.' I shook my head.

'It would be additional danger,' Honorius said mildly. 'As if you needed it! The longer you stay in Venice, the more likely it is some rumour will be spread by the midwife or priest – although God He knows we bribed them well enough! Or a story will come north that you got married in Rome, and not to Messer Leon.'

Rekhmire' repeated, 'Come to Alexandria.'

Nothing but being contrary moved me to say, 'Give me one good reason why!'

He pushed himself to his feet. For all he stood like an Egyptian monolith, I thought he seemed oddly uncertain.

'I can protect you there.'

'Oh, you can?' I caught, out of the corner of my eye, a smile on Honorius's face. 'Why can you protect me in Alexandria? Why would you want to?'

Rekhmire' looked surprisingly pained.

'I think of you as a friend, not a master,' I said hastily. 'But shouldn't you be, I don't know, off buying more scrolls?' I gave him a slant look. 'Or finding more mechanical copyists for the Pharaoh-Queen?'

Rekhmire''s lips made a compressed line that spoke much of irritation, to one who knows the man. His gaze, when it met mine, was in part amused, and in part annoyed.

'I do have to escort Master Mainz back to the city—'

For Egyptians, I think, there is only one city in all the world. Without qualification, the words mean Alexandria-in-Exile.

'—and it is the weather for sea travel.'

I wondered momentarily whether the voyage from Ostia Antica had been dogged with sickness because I was with child. *If not, I swear never to set foot off land again!*

'Come to Alexandria,' Rekhmire' repeated, as if he would go on tirelessly repeating it like water wearing down granite. 'I can protect you.'

I looked him in the eyes. 'Why?'

Sounding momentarily confused, Rekhmire' said, 'What?'

'Why can a book-buyer for the Royal Library protect me?' I jerked a thumb at Honorius. 'I can understand it with the Captain-General here, and his thugs in livery—'

'Thanks!' Honorius grinned, as I intended him to.

'—but why do you say you can protect me?'

The monumental face smoothed out into complete immobility. It was possible to read nothing from him. I might have painted that face, or rendered it in marble, and no man could have got any clue as to his thoughts.

The Egyptian wiped his hands down his linen kilt and looked up from his chair.

'This may come as a shock,' he said sardonically, 'but I have certain resources I can call on. Menmet-Ra will help with the voyage. You would travel under a pass-port of the Pharaoh-Queen's protection, which I would provide.'

'And you can do that because . . . '

Rekhmire' began to look cornered.

I folded my arms and gave him a recalcitrant stare.

'Why should I trust you to get me – and my daughter – to Alexandria? What makes a buyer of scrolls so capable of that?'

'Ilario—' He bit off whatever he had been going to say, glared back at me, and snapped, 'Because I'm a spy!'

The room poised, full of silence.

'Ah.' I didn't look away from his gaze. 'Good. I did wonder when you might tell me . . . '

Rekhmire' positively snarled at me. '*What!*'

Honorius slid down a little on the bench beside me, hammering at his thigh with his fist. Small tears easing out of the corners of his screwed-shut eyes. I couldn't make out what he wheezed.

'Father?'

The Captain-General reached for the bottle and glasses, tipping a fair amount of wine from one into the other. He pushed a glass at me, and held one out to Rekhmire', ridiculously delicate in his warrior's fingers, never mind the Egyptian's large hand.

Honorius lifted his own glass, as in a toast. He remarked cheerfully, 'I bet you don't get a lot of *that*.'

5

At Rekhmire''s suggestion, Honorius broke off from packing long enough to send ten men, inconspicuously, to pack up and bring back Herr Mainz's printing-*machina* from his workshop.

They found the anonymous shed stripped bare.

I supposed the Venetians might gain some knowledge from the construction of the *machina* itself, but the German Guildsman's satisfied smile confirmed that the metal type was key.

Since mercenaries must be expert at moving their habitation, and Rekhmire' I knew to be more than used to packing up as a book-buyer, I left the household to their skills.

Ramiro Carrasco entered the room I had come to think of as mine, just as I completed packing what art supplies I judged worthy into a chest for transport, and throwing out what paper I had wasted on unsuccessful rendering.

'You can take these down.' I indicated the ash-wood chests. It disquieted me how easy I found it to give plain orders.

Although some of that is the influence of men-at-arms, and not merely experience of slavery.

A faint fuzz of black hair showed under Carrasco's coif, growing back in. A blue mark under his eye was a bruise, and new. No great wonder if he didn't mourn the departure of my father's company for Taraconensis.

'I feel strange at leaving this room.' I looked about me, touching the green velvet hangings of the bed, and continued without forethought: 'After all, I gave birth to a child here.'

Ramiro Carrasco coloured from the skin at the neck of his shirt, clear up to his ears and scalp; a glowing scarlet translucency of the flesh that might as well have been a brand.

I refuse to be embarrassed that this man tried to kill me!

'I'll take these,' he muttered, squatting to lift one chest. He did not add 'master' or 'mistress'. I was willing to bet he owed his black eye to another such omission.

Shooting an apologetic glance, he added, 'Will I come back and help with the child?'

Onorata's blankets, clothing, and feeding gear still occupied the bed in sprawled heaps. She herself, in her lidless oaken chest, was beginning that restless shifting of her face that meant she would wake soon and be hungry.

'*Lord Christ Emperor on the Tree.*' I sat bonelessly and suddenly on the edge of the bed, hard enough to jolt my teeth, and found myself staring up at Carrasco as the only other adult present.

He put down the box, stepping forward. 'Is she ill? Should I fetch a physician?'

'What? No.' My knuckles were white, where my hands made fists quite without my own volition. 'I realised – I haven't taken her out of the city before. A *sea* voyage! Suppose it kills her? She's so small!'

Carrasco gave me a bright-eyed and unguarded smile, still a little russet from his previous embarrassment. 'You put me in mind of my youngest sister and *her* first.'

At *sister* he blinked uncertainly, evidently registering that I had dressed in doublet and hose for travelling.

'She's a small one, but she's thriving.' Carrasco squatted down by the oak chest, not touching my child, but looking at her with unselfconscious approval.

'How can you *tell*?' The Turkish physician had been extensive in his description of stools, rashes, fontanels, birth-marks, crusts on her eyes, and illnesses in general – but seemed to think I must know what constituted good health.

Carrasco lifted his head and looked at me, amazed. On the bed and its dais, I sat considerably higher than him; I felt it failed to give me any moral authority. He seemed momentarily entirely confident.

'She's growing. After the first couple of weeks, provided they grow and they don't get sick, they're all right.'

'Certainly she eats enough!' I might sound frustrated, I thought. 'Eats, sleeps, shits – I swear you could set a monastery clock by her! Every Vespers, Matins, Lauds . . . She doesn't do anything *else*. Do you think there's something wrong with her?'

Seriously, Carrasco observed, 'Your father should have hired you a nurse.'

He stood, and I saw him glance at the bed again, his flush reasserting itself.

'If I remember, madonna, she's two months old or a little less. She'll do more when she's older. They say she was early?'

Reckoning up weeks, it came to me that if she had gone full term, it would be now that she would have been born. Looking at her in that light, her minute hands and ears and eyes did not seem so undersized for a newborn.

I made to stand and found my knees still weak. 'How in Christ-the-Emperor's name will I manage when she starts moving about! Talking!'

If they were not my blood-kin, nevertheless, Honorius's most trusted men-at-arms had filled the place of family these last months. But without her grandfather, and with all the responsibility falling to me . . .

I wondered if the attempt to hire another wet-nurse would be worth my child's frantic roaring and screaming and obdurate refusal to feed.

My child.

'I can make you a sling, for the babe.' Carrasco shifted his weight from one foot to the other as I looked at him, and shrugged. 'Madonna. My mother used to carry the little ones that way. Left her hands free.'

The blush was not quite gone from his skin. The involuntary colouring spoke of shame. And if 'madonna' is not 'mistress' or 'master', it is still a respectful form of address for the women of the Italies.

If I didn't think Carrasco a man forced into violence by desperation – if I hadn't thought him capable of feeling guilt for attempting to kill a new mother – he would not be under the same roof as Onorata.

I managed to unclench my hands. 'Thank you. Yes. How warmly should I dress her, if I carry her in this sling?'

My erstwhile assassin stepped up onto the dais, sorting with quick efficiency through the piles of clothes, and laying out thin shawls, and a tiny fur-lined hood.

'If there's anything more odd than this day in my life—' I caught Ramiro Carrasco's gaze. '—I'm going to need to be better rested to meet it!'

He made a movement that was part shrug, part slave's duck of the head, and all amazingly awkward. To my surprise, he followed that with a smile.

'Shall I help you with her feed, madonna?'

'I can do that. You carry the boxes: I can't . . . '

He nodded, and took up the packed chests, and in the quietness of his departure, I began to ready the pottery vessel with a glazed spout that had proved the best thing for Onorata to suckle and feed from.

A scrape of wood on wood made me look up. Rekhmire', crutch lodged securely under his arm, had evidently just stopped at the open doorway. He smiled and came in, awkwardly dumping the scrolls under his free arm onto the bed.

'Are you ready?' He peered intently at Onorata in my lap, as she suckled at the pottery spout, but directed the question at me.

'Yes. No.'

Panic returned in a flood.

I did not let it alter my cradling of the tiny child.

'How am I to feed her on the *ship*! We can't be forever putting into ports to buy milk—'

Briskly, Rekhmire' said, 'It's a *galley*, Ilario!'

At my bemused look, he added, 'Built much on Venetian lines, I must admit, even if it is out of an Alexandrine dockyard. Three rowers to every oar, a full complement of marines, the captain and navigator and his officers, and I don't doubt a passenger or two beside you and I and Herr Mainz! With a crew of two hundred men, we'll be calling in at coastal ports for water and food every other day – the pilot's knowledge of that, and the headlands, currents, and landmarks, is what will take us to each port on the way through the Aegean to Alexandria . . . '

'Calling into a port every other day?' I had thought only of the deep seas the *Iskander* survived, in the autumn storms, not this coastal hopping from harbour to harbour.

Rekhmire' nodded. 'And even if not – you'll find, down towards the port side of the captain's cabin, the enclosure where they pen up the animals for slaughter during the voyage. The galley carries several goats in kid, and three nursing nannies, for the milk, and your father has added several more to that contingent.'

A smile touched his solemn face.

'I think Master Honorius would turn the galley into a livestock cargo ship, rather than think of the child going hungry.'

Evidently he would rather turn a joke than put into my mind the dangers of the whole ship sinking, should we encounter bad storms.

There are banker's scrips in my purse.

'I can't support her on my own.' The reality of that failure biting deep, I could hear an edge to my voice. 'Lord Emperor Christ knows what I'd be doing if I hadn't found you and Honorius this year!'

'Children should be raised by the whole family.' Rekhmire' brushed his thumb over her forehead, and down to her flared lips, that had latched onto the pottery spout with no apparent indication of ever letting go.

I snorted. 'Without all her soldier-uncles, I'll be hard put enough to feed her properly all day and all night!'

Rekhmire' turned his head, looking mildly at me. 'Does being no man-at-arms disqualify me from assisting?'

My face was a little hot. I satisfied myself that Onorata had done with sucking, and sat her upright to burp her, wiping off the resulting gob of milk.

'You have responsibilities . . . '

I detected something like pique in Rekhmire''s expression, I thought.

Experimentally, I added, 'But you know she falls asleep fastest when you read her old Aramaic . . . '

He put his ruddy-coloured finger to her palm, and her pale tiny hand clenched over his nail. 'You know very well she's working on a translation. Aren't you, Little Wise One?'

A slave is ill-advised to roll their eyes or be sarcastic; I was under no such restriction. 'Yes, *master*.'

A thought came into my mind on the heels of that.

'Do you realise – if she'd been born in Rome, you'd have owned her too?'

110

'Dear holy Eight!' Rekhmire' closed his eyes devoutly, and somewhat spoiled the effect by peeking out under his long eyelashes. 'Two of you. It hardly bears thinking of.'

Onorata burped again.

That, and Rekhmire''s expression, made me laugh, as he evidently desired. Taking my mind from the lives of slaves and their children when not free.

'The *Sekhmet* leaves at dawn tomorrow,' he added, retrieving his hand as Onorata abandoned interest in his finger. 'Are you ready?'

'No.' As ever, I found it more than easy to give him the truth. 'It terrifies me, to think of such a small baby on a long voyage across the sea. How can she ever survive it?'

If I expected baseless reassurance, I was mistaken. Rekhmire' thoughtfully nodded agreement.

'But,' he said, 'you're as far from Taraco, here, as you are from Alexandria-in-exile. So it would be no better for her to travel to your home country. If you could stay here, that would be best – but Venice is full of fever in the hot weather, and in any case, I doubt you can stay here in safety from your enemies. This is not the best choice, but I can think of no better.'

He softened nothing, but he did not lie.

I held the tiny solid weight of Onorata, marvelling at her dark lashes and scant feather-light hair. Like Herr Mainz – Herr Gutenberg – I have a need for truth, no matter how little varnish men put on it.

6

The dawn was not even grey in the east when the household stirred again for our departure.

Licinus Honorius I found in the makeshift Alexandrine bath room, when I came to tackle him on the final details of a military guard; two of his men-at-arms bringing in jugs of heated water to fill the porphyry tub.

Naked, he was thin and muscular, with white scars crossing every area of his body, in particular below the knees and elbows.

'Shins and hands. Targets.' He wiped himself down with a wash-cloth, as dignified as if he were clothed in more than soap-opaque water. 'You need not nag. I'll leave only two men with you – one as bodyguard for you, one for the child.'

In the last instance, when all else has failed, a bodyguard's duty is to interpose their flesh between mine and a weapon. I thought I could have refused it for myself. Not for Onorata.

'Who?'

'Tottola and Attila.' He stood, receiving the towel I handed him with equanimity. I wished I had ever thought to ask for a nude study of him: he would be ideal, I thought, for one of the more martial Prophets.

'They have the advantage,' he added, 'of looking nothing in the least like Iberian soldiers. I've told them to take off my livery badges.'

'You'll take all the rest?' I fixed Honorius with as beady a gaze as I might manage. Difficult to exert authority over a man older than I am, and besides my father. 'And take the Via Augusta?'

The skies will be clear, the stars able to be seen for navigation at sea, but not yet as reliably as in the summer months.

'*Yes.*' His exasperation was more reassuring than promises. 'Hand me my shirt. Besides, I have a surprise for you – you will *appear* to be travelling with me . . . '

The importance of secrecy regarding my whereabouts and destination was not lost on me; I could not, however, guess at his meaning. Honorius, dressed, grinned and led me through to the Alexandrine House's warm kitchens.

'No!' the Ensign Saverico's voice whined. 'I won't wear women's dress; I'd sooner be flayed alive!'

Honorius shot the boy a look that seemed to promise just that, and he subsided.

Saverico, in a dark wig – purchased from one of the local whores – and a gown I had borrowed from Neferet, was, it seemed, ordered to make himself visible on the short voyage to the mainland, and as they rode across the Veneto. He folded his arms across his bodice and blushed at me.

'Be cheerful,' I advised him. 'By definition, you need not make the most convincing woman . . . '

This time Saverico joined in the laughter.

'*You'll* travel cloaked,' my father directed me, with similarly no apparent expectation of being disobeyed. 'I don't want to be able to tell if you're woman or man!'

I thought it was Saverico who muttered 'Nothing new there!', but he was smiling, and I let him escape without retribution.

Honorius would have taken us by way of the S. Marco quay for a farewell, I knew, but the importance of my seeming anonymous argued a less public rendezvous with the Alexandrine galley. Honorius and I therefore parted in the bare garden of the Alexandria House, behind high walls, with only just enough grey light to see each other's faces.

'Let me say goodbye to my grandchild.' He took a whining Onorata into his arms. 'I'll miss her first walking and speaking.'

'Just as well, or her first words would be military curses!'

Honorius grinned like a boy. He pushed his ungloved hand into Onorata's tiny fingers. She shoved his thumb against her lips, making gnawing motions, the crying forgotten.

'I do wish,' I observed, 'that you might come as far as Alexandria and keep doing that!'

'She's biddable enough with her grandfather.' He smirked, sounding very smug, and ended with a sigh. 'If I trusted her in the borders of the same kingdom as Pirro Videric, I'd ask to take her home with me. I've raised no children from this age . . . Constantinople will be safer.'

Files of Alexandrine sailors and slaves moved past us, down to the other boats, whose oarsmen began to spider them out into the canal. I had a panicked urge to step back and leave the breathing, living child in Honorius's arms.

If I felt no rush of affection when I looked at her, I could still be taken by surprise by the intensity of my desire to protect her.

The same fear that drove me to think of rockfalls, floods, butchering free-company bandits, and thunderstorms, on the road to Taraco, and made me fear that this was the last time I would see Honorius, paradoxically argued that my daughter would be far safer with him than with me.

'I know nothing of children!' I muttered, staring at her darkening blue eyes. 'I'm not even a proper mother.'

Honorius's fingertip traced the amazing clarity of her skin, where he must feel the faintest fuzz, and moved to the whorl of her ear. I had drawn that shell often enough (before permanent exhaustion overtook me) to know every curve and kink of it. Sometimes I had drawn it by candle-light, when I sat awake, filled with fear, watching her breathe and praying I would not see her stop.

'If I hadn't seen before how soldiers are sentimental over children,' Honorius observed sourly, 'I'd wonder why I scarcely had a chance to hold my own grandchild!'

That was so much hyperbole that I couldn't help smiling.

Honorius continued, 'As for Attila and Tottola, the further advantage of those two is that they both have families at home. Young brothers, cousins; maybe a bastard or two. Between them they can likely change the babe's shit-rag if you fall for sea-sickness on the voyage . . . '

'That's good to hear. Although I was thinking of leaving the task for Master Rekhmire'.'

My father looked across the bare earth to the Egyptian, where he stood in close and rapid conversation with one of Menmet-Ra's slaves. All Rekhmire''s weight leaned onto his stick, although unobtrusively enough that only drawing it had let me know, through my fingers, how much he relied on that support.

'Can't think of a man better suited,' Honorius said urbanely. 'I owe the man too great a debt not to want to see him disconcerted from time to time . . . '

I grinned. Then, 'Debt?'

'He wrote to me to come to Carthage. He gave me you.' Honorius looked openly moved. 'And he's sworn that if, Christ the Emperor forbid it, you should die while in the East, he'll bring Onorata to me.'

That thought sobered me.

Most things that could be responsible for killing me would kill her too. I did not say it. *Honorius will know this.*

My father scowled reflexively in the book-buyer's direction. 'If he fails to look after you both in Constantinople, I'll show him the colour of his own spleen!'

I wondered briefly what colour a spleen was, and whether Galen had written anything on the subject. And realised that Honorius, if asked, might give me an answer based on far more empirical observation.

I didn't ask.

'It's time,' I said.

Honorius put Onorata into my arms, and held us both in an embrace.

'As soon as it's safe to come to Taraco, I'll send word.' He reluctantly released me. 'Trust no one who doesn't come with my authority. Any messenger of mine will inquire of the progress of an altar panel to St Stephen, and then correct to St Gaius if you query that.'

Wordless myself because of the constriction in my throat, I could only nod.

'And I want to see some drawings of your Gaius Judas,' Honorius observed, as cheerfully as he could pretend to. 'Give you something to do when you're lazing about in Constantinople.'

'Lazing.'

'Of course.' He unbuttoned the purse at his belt, and took out a bag of softer leather. 'You should be able to trust my banker, but just in case. These are all my rings. If you need money, sell them; it's why I give them to you. If you're afraid of robbery, don't hide them in the child's cradle, or your hair, or your cunny. It's the first place any pirate or bandit will look.'

I felt my cheeks hot. 'For a respectable military man, you know far too much about how to steal!'

'Used to taking precautions . . . ' His amused tone dared me to doubt it. 'Most often from being robbed by the men I was commanding!'

The men in his livery grumbled mock-outrage.

'There are three bracelets in here that look like cheap brass,' Honorius added. 'Which they are, on the surface, but scratch below and you'll find solid gold. Wear those at all times. And as I said, you may use my name for credit, whatever you need; you have letters to every banker I've had dealings with over the years. I'm good for sufficient funds to keep you safe and get you home. Understand?'

He fretted like a horse with a harness that galls.

'I understand,' I said, 'that you'd like to lock us both up in a Tower of Ladies at the estate, and perhaps let Onorata out when she turns thirty!'

I understand him to be as afraid as I am of those things in the world that threaten what we love.

Honorius cupped his hands over my shoulders, surprisingly gentle even though he must still find them too narrow for a son and too wide for a daughter.

'I know I can't stand between you and every danger. I know you can cope with all hazards. I merely . . . *wish* I might protect you from all ills and accidents, no matter how foolish that is.'

I shrugged, lightly enough to not disturb the baby. 'I understand: I feel the same way about you. And how old are *you*, Lion of Castile?'

Honorius laughed out loud.

'We'll both of us protect the babe, then.' He held her hand between the thumb and forefinger of his own.

The wind came up from the lagoon, heavy with the scent of silt and rot, and at the same time a warm and a chill breeze. Spring, and I am at last leaving this city: I feel as if a cell-door opens.

Honorius embraced us both again, and I turned away to carry out of Venice the child that had not existed as a fully-human living soul when I entered it.

The light in the east was the colour of Naples Yellow as we climbed into the boat that would take us through the canals of the Dorsodura quarter, and out into the basin where lord Menmet-Ra's *Sekhmet* was moored. My feet left dark marks in the dew on the canal-side flagstones. I had my hood up, and pulled well forward, and Onorata tied into a buckram and linen sling under my cloak. *I doubt any man might recognise us unless he stands next to me.*

The creaking of oars all but lulled me asleep, since I had slept so little before. A dim lantern let me see the baggage boat ahead, and from time to time a candle-lit window permitted me a view into some Venetian's daily life. I could not help but look back when I witnessed a woman pacing with her baby against her shoulder, the raw screaming audible through half-closed shutters.

Clouds bulked up before the sun could rise, keeping the small boat inconspicuous. I heard the water lap and drip. The turn of raised oar-blades just caught the light, letting me know the other boats still accompanied us. Wind in my face brought more than the scent of the lagoon – brought the open sea.

I only realised that we had rowed under the stern of the moored Alexandrine galley as it blocked the dawn like a mountain of darkness above us.

There was a pervasive strong odour of tar. And tar adhered to my hands when I climbed up the steps on the side of the ship, and onto the galley's stern deck.

On this high deck, I could not help a glance back towards the Riva degli Schiavoni. I saw lights enough that I knew men were working; loading cargo, unloading early fishing-boats. I heard no clash of arms. Saw no reflections of torches from armour.

If the Council of Ten has the Venetian soldiery there, certainly I don't see them.

Herr Mainz scrambled up the steps to the deck, the German men-at-arms behind him assisting Rekhmire'. Attila and Tottola wore identical fixed frowns, visible by the galley's lanterns – which might have been taken to indicate intense devotion to their duty, but I thought had more to do with the send-off the rest of the company had given them, a scant few hours before. Tottola failed to hide a wince when Onorata, impossibly hungry again, or else disturbed by the stink of the tar on ropes and deck-planks, began to cry.

The galley's captain showed every disposition to put me in a low cabin, close to the water-line, at the stern of the ship. Despite its prestigious and secure nature – it was, after all, where the captain kept treasure and valuable small cargo – I balked, after discovering I would have no light except through the hatch from the cabin above.

By the time I had argued strongly enough to secure the higher cabin, I felt an all but imperceptible life in the wood of the ship.

'I'm going up on deck,' I told Rekhmire'.

I had missed seeing the *Sekhmet* as we approached, so that I had no clear idea how a hundred and twenty feet of galley appears to the naked eye; I did not desire to miss our casting-off for Constantinople.

Rekhmire' followed me to the deck, jerking the padded crutch and shifting his weight with rapid efficiency. I kept Onorata with us in her sling, not simply because I thought she would otherwise wake, but because I did not feel safe leaving her without the German men-at-arms being over their temporary inconvenience.

Pale cool light flooded the arch of the sky. Venice lay spread out behind us.

'Ilario—'

The ferrule of Rekhmire''s crutch slipped on the deck.

His hand came down hard on my shoulder, and his fingers dug into the muscle there. I heard him curse under his breath, raggedly and with no restraint.

I stood perfectly still, Onorata clasped to my chest, until he caught his balance again.

'You'll be glad to get rid of that.' I nodded at the crutch as he straightened up.

Rekhmire' shut his eyes, as if he did no more than listen to the heave and grunt of the oarsmen, and the yells of the deck crew raising the main lateen sail above our heads. I saw one of his hands creep down to push at the muscle of his thigh. He still wore the Turkish fashion in trousers; I had thought it because of the cold.

'I was not about to say in front of Pamiu or your father.' Rekhmire' opened his eyes, focusing on the distant campanile of S. Marco behind us. 'But – if the Turk's diagnosis was correct, and if the physicians in Alexandria have no better treatment . . . Then it's unlikely I will ever walk again without this help.'

7

I am lost on this ship! I realised.

I signalled to one of Menmet-Ra's linen-kilted servants, requesting briskly that he take us to our cabin. Rekhmire' stomped in my wake. I said nothing while any man was within earshot.

The cabin's thick wooden door closed. The noise of running feet, men casting off ropes, and creaking oars drowned out anything a listener might have overheard.

'Why didn't you tell me?'

Rekhmire' blinked at me in his most feline manner.

'What should I have said? That I'll be lame?' His expression altered significantly. 'Does it concern you that I won't be able to act in defence of you, or Onorata?'

Frustration and some nameless emotion stifled any reply I might have formed.

A brisk knock sounded on the cabin door. Onorata jolted and began to grizzle. *Hunger,* I thought, although it might have been wind or heat. She did not feel wet enough to change.

'Come!'

At my summons, Attila walked in with a straw palliasse over his shoulder. He threw it down inside the door.

'One of us will be awake at all times,' he said brusquely. 'The other one will sleep across your door. We know you're the Lion's *son-daughter*—' He emphasised the first term. '—but we've got orders to keep you safe.'

His eyes were a remarkable pale blue, this Germanic mercenary, and he could not stand in this galley cabin without bending his head. I wondered at the change between Venice and his attitude here on ship. A matter of sole responsibility, perhaps, now there is only him and his brother?

'I'll agree to any defence, within reason. Consult with me first.' I waited until the tall German nodded. 'Do we have Carrasco?'

'In the hold, in chains, until you want him.'

Conscience might have pricked me. But I think Ramiro Carrasco quite capable of jumping into the S. Marco basin, as volatile as he seems now.

This cabin would belong to some junior officer, I guessed. For all my own protests, Rekhmire''s influence with Menmet-Ra had gained it; and you might sleep six men in it, if four of them lay head-to-toe on the floor, leaving the wooden box-beds for two others.

The Egyptian swung himself over to the far bed and sat down, wedging the crutch in a niche between bed and deck.

I do not know what to say to you. Except that, without me, you would not be injured.

Cherry-flower might be over-ripe and dropping from saplings hardy enough to root in the Adriatic ports we visited, and the day warm enough to go without a cloak at midday, but spring is still a dangerous season for travel.

I saw little enough of the ports myself, and little enough of the Pharaoh-Queen's trireme. One instance of being shown the higher stern cabins above me, where the captain bunked, and the helmsman followed the track of the lodestone in its binnacle, was interrupted by a frantic summons to feed Onorata, since she had apparently decided to take the pottery bottle from no hand but mine.

I likewise had little enough time to admire the breath-taking regularity of the sweeps, the oarsman not standing at their benches as the Venetians do, but sitting by threes, and drawing the long oars when the lateen sails were not sufficient, or we had spent too many hours tacking. There were arbalests set at weapons ports between every bench. And at the prow, where a Venetian war-galley would have the iron beak that served as a ram, I saw a sparkle of sun on bronze.

Herr Gutenberg came back with tar marking every item of clothing he owned, raving about a siphon and dragon's-head spout that would shoot Greek Fire at any enemy of Alexandria. I fell asleep upright on my bunk listening to him.

'Three month colic,' Attila muttered, when he woke bleary-eyed before his shift guarding the cabin door was due, and looked with some dislike at my child.

I sat with her face-down over my lap, rubbing at her back, in the hope that her wide-mouthed screaming might stem from a frustrated desire to fart.

I was appalled. 'It lasts three months?'

'It usually ends when they're three months old.' He dug a dirty fist into his eye as if he would grind it out of the socket, and yawned. 'Usually.'

That there was another part of the ship, I didn't realise until I wondered just where Rekhmire' had stowed Ramiro Carrasco.

Brief inquiry gained me the knowledge that, below the rower's benches and the line of cargo between them (on which the officers walked up and down to supervise), there was another hold. This took cargo or pilgrims, a man from Dalmatia on his way south informed me, and showed me down the steps to the galley's dark interior. They likewise had no light except what came in the hatches – but this hold ran the length of the ship from stem to stern, running off into darkness either side of me; pilgrims and other passengers sleeping with their heads to the hull and their feet to the middle, where their luggage lay as a central barrier.

White sand ballast filled the ship to the level of this deck, as the Dalmatian showed me when he took up a plank and unearthed his bottle of wine and his eggs, which he had stored there to keep cool.

The stench of the bilges, combined with the idea of food, sent me rapidly up to daylight before I had a chance to look for Carrasco.

If not for Honorius, I would be travelling there. I doubt Onorata would survive it.

In the cabin, Onorata was screaming again.

I put her into the sling and took her up on deck.

The buckram and linen sling encompassed Onorata, supporting her body and head, although I kept my arm under her until I should grow used to it. I brought my cloak around her, to shield her from the ripe brisk wind blowing from the pine headlands of the coast. Her tiny screwed-up features showed dwarfed in her fur-lined hood. I wriggled my finger in to touch her neck, and judged her neither too warm nor too cold.

Rekhmire' stomped to stand beside me at the ship's rail, in that open middle area around the mainmast that they call 'the market-place of the galley'. The crutch's ferrule scraped on the deck. He cocked an interrogative brow at the sling.

'Well thought of,' he approved.

'Ramiro Carrasco made it for me,' I said, taking the opportunity for truth.

The Egyptian scowled.

'It's perfectly harmless!' I protested. 'Safe. One of the things you learn in a large family, it appears.'

'If he were not a necessary shield to you—' Rekhmire' broke off, took a visible effort to collect himself, and gave it up. 'Have you lost your mind? Taking help from him? The man tried to murder you!'

His words brought the memory of Ramiro Carrasco in prison sharply to my mind's eye. '*I* came nearer to killing him. I cracked his skull.'

Rekhmire' snorted.

'Besides which,' I added, 'you need not either trust nor like him, but – *I need a servant!* And since he had to come with us, it might as well be Messer Carrasco.'

'Plain Carrasco the slave!' Rekhmire' corrected with a snort.

He stomped off down the deck before I could add more.

This voyage would be infinitely easier if those two men co-operated.

Watching Rekhmire's rigid back, I thought, *It won't happen.*

'Say what you like!' Exhaustion made me stubborn. 'I haven't slept in

120

twenty hours – *again!* – and you neither. Attila has to be on guard and Tottola asleep. There is no one else!'

'You'd trust Carrasco with your *child?*'

The note in Rekhmire''s voice was far closer to pique than to concern, I thought.

His heavy lids hooded his eyes. Had things been right between us, he would have made some joke regarding the necessity of strangling the bawling brat in any case.

'I don't *care* how trustworthy he is!' I raised my voice over Onorata's roaring. 'I have to sleep!'

The same went for Attila – curled up on his pallet, all of his clothing and blankets pulled over his head and wrapped about his ears – and for Rekhmire' himself. Spattered ink showed his failure to compose report-scrolls away up on the deck in a brisk wind. The cabin seemed full of something tangible, as if you could touch Onorata's hopeless wailing.

Blue patches marked Rekhmire''s eyes that were nothing to do with kohl. 'You *trust* that—'

Evidently an epithet escaped him.

'"Spy"?' I suggested sweetly.

'"Would-be murderer"!' Rekhmire' snapped.

'I just want him to sit here for an hour and watch her! Then I'll walk her on the deck again.' I thought my muscles might easily recover from their weakness after the Caesarean, given the amount of exercise I gained walking and crooning to the baby. 'I don't believe he'd hurt her.'

Rekhmire' threw down a stoppered ink-horn. 'You *cannot* propose to put your child into that man's care!'

He said considerably more, but tiredness blurred the edges of it. At this moment, I thought, *I* am a greater danger. If I sleep now, I'll roll over and suffocate the child; at least if Ramiro Carrasco has her for an hour, I'll be less exhausted.

'Besides,' I added, 'Tottola can watch him for an hour, instead of the door.'

I sent Attila to unchain Videric's spy and my slave.

Ramiro Carrasco had not benefited from his week in the hold, I saw, with those Alexandrine slaves not involved in rowing or sailing the trireme. He stumbled into the cabin half-awake and fearful, hair in spikes.

'You're looking after Onorata,' I said bluntly. 'Nurse her. Feed her if she carries on crying. You know how to do that?'

'Yes.' He looked stunned.

I did not dare not stand up to pass her over, dizzy as I felt. Carrasco squatted, not meeting my eye, gently taking Onorata from my arms into his.

I strung words together. 'If she sleeps, and Attila's awake by the next

121

ship's bell, get him to help you make her feed. Wake me if anything is wrong, or if you even *think* there is. Understand?'

Carrasco didn't rise. He unwittingly echoed Rekhmire', in a hoarse whisper. 'You'd trust me with your child?'

'If I thought you were a man even *capable* of harming my child . . . I would have sent a lying message to Videric, telling him I'd bought you,' I said. 'And I would have paid the Venetian jailer to cut your carotid artery while I stood and watched, to make sure.'

There was no threat in what I said. What threat could ensure the safety of Onorata? I saw him take in the reality of the situation, however, before I lay down and wrapped my cloak over my ears, and sleep came over me as black and dark as the sea beneath the galley's hull.

Before the *Sekhmet*, I would have thought it only possible to fear storms, sea-thieves, clouds that obscure the stars, and pestilence-banners flying from harbours we desired to put in to, for just so long.

Had I been travelling alone, this might have been the case.

As it was, I fretted from the Adriatic to the Aegean, week on week, and I missed the company of the book-buyer.

If Rekhmire' was much absent in conversation with the captain – a man originally from Rhodes, or Cyprus, or some such island – Tottola and Attila attended to their guard duty with considerably more attentiveness than when they had comrades to take responsibility from their shoulders. One always slept, one always woke; and they assumed a demeanour that made Menmet-Ra's returning slaves (when I could strike up a conversation) regard them as the worst kind of cannibal Franks.

The Master of Mainz never slept, or not in our cabin. I felt no inclination to blame him: *I* would have slept elsewhere if I could. Gutenberg busied himself with every aspect of the trireme he could investigate, from the Greek Fire weapon at the prow to the *bussola nautica* that indicates the position of the magnetic poles. I changed Onorata's shit-rags.

Onorata bawled.

Ramiro Carrasco sung her a lullaby that, after final frustrated inquiry, I discovered to be only the rose of the compass sung to a tune of his own devising. *Tramontana, Griego, Levante, Sirocho,* and so on to include all eight winds.

If it had not granted me sleep, I would have resented my daughter for attending more to the man who would have killed her than to her mother-father.

'"Ostro, Garbin, Ponente, Maistro" . . . ' Since she appeared soothed by only that lullaby, I learned the song by default.

Being in constant attendance on the child, I found myself taken for a woman, for all I dressed in hose. Attila pointed out that I might be a woman dressed in male clothing for travelling, as many do. That gave me pause to think of where I was going. If I had been on better terms with Rekhmire', I might have asked to borrow Alexandrine clothing.

For all I had been thinking of it league after league, the arrival at Constantinople nonetheless took me by surprise.

8

Harsh light blazed up off the water, and the land to either side.

'I dreamed of bears last night.' I blinked, surprised to hear myself sound morose.

Tottola glanced down from where he leaned on the ship's rail, at my right hand. 'That only counts if you dream *before* you embark.'

Attila's massive elbows came to rest on the sun-baked wooden rail at my other side. He murmured, 'Just don't sneeze, now . . . '

I managed a sneer at him, for his superstition, as well as I might for the jumping frogs of nervousness in my guts.

Other than leaving Rome – when I had other matters in my mind – I always observe the politenesses of travel that I was taught along with court behaviour. Step on board a ship with the right foot, never with the left. Avoid sneezing or coughing as one comes on board. Sailors have been known to tip a supposed bad-luck passenger overboard before now. But they're only ancient delusions: certainly I wouldn't go so far as to delay a voyage if I dreamed of bears or boars or any other Heraldic beast on the night before sailing.

'Besides,' I said aloud. 'That's the harbour: we're here now. If we sink, I'm sure somebody can fish us out . . . '

'Assuming they'd bother,' Rekhmire''s voice remarked, more amiably than he had for some weeks. He directed a shame-faced smile in my direction. 'Are you certain you wish to associate with us so closely?'

He claimed this land to be no further south than Taraconensis, merely much further east. I, having sweated the more as the ship sailed south past each Greek island, doubted him. Confronting him a week ago, I had borrowed what garments of an Alexandrine bureaucrat might fit me.

'I look like one of your people,' I said mildly, hitching at the wraparound linen kilt that I wore. Over it I'd belted a sleeved robe – made from a single thickness of linen fabric, light enough to bear the heat of the morning but enough to keep my skin from burning.

And enough to hide my bare chest.

Rekhmire' didn't need to hide his. He had his braided cloth and reed headband tied around his forehead, this time over a voluminous hood or veil of flax linen, which held it so that his shaven head and his neck were protected against the sun.

'Pireaus and the last three Greek ports, they took me for an Alexandrine eunuch,' I added, smugly.

'That,' he observed, 'is why no one will bother to fish you out of the harbour. Far too many of us here as it is. Place is swarming.'

I failed to stifle a snicker. And thought myself regrettably comfortable in his company, for a man with whom I had not settled a quarrel. If we *had* quarrelled. And if I was certain over what.

Ramiro Carrasco shot me a puzzled look, standing holding Onorata among the baby's luggage. Which, if you leave out of the calculation any sketchbooks I may have brought on the voyage, or any Greek scrolls that found their way into Rekhmire''s hands, was the largest single amount of baggage in our expedition.

The crop-haired Herr 'Mainz' strolled past Carrasco, his gaze going between me and Rekhmire'. 'This. This is Constantinople?'

Rekhmire' murmured a phrase in Alexandrine Greek, and then added, 'Franks still call it that. We call it the cities of the Pharaohs of exile. Or New Alexandria, if that's easier for you, Master Johannes.'

The German guild-man nodded absently, his gaze still fixed on rocking water, packed hulls and bare masts, and the massive and monumental stone walls of the city.

I thought, I have seen nothing like it since Carthage, and Carthage's walls are no longer seen in daylight!

My hands itched to be at chalk and paper.

Rekhmire' was still talking to the German. 'How would you prefer to be introduced to the Pharaoh-Queen Ty-ameny? As Master Mainz?'

'It may be best.' The German didn't shift his gaze from the bright waters. 'The Guild in Mainz dismissed many of us when they threw out the patricians. If your Pharaoh-Queen will not think it odd?'

The German is as nervous as I, I realised.

Thoughts of Videric, deliberately pushed into the background all this month we sailed south, intruded back into my mind. Between that and the vista rising from the water beyond the *Sekhmet*'s prow – great walls decorated with painted bands and enamel, the ochre-coloured domes, the temples and the obelisks lining the skyline – I felt amazingly small.

And I have essentially come here – to ask for help.

I must be mad.

That thought was purely honest.

No one here will have any reason to help me, no matter what I can testify about the Empty Chair and Masaccio's death.

And here I may see again the thing that murdered him.

My fingers shook, cold despite the heat. I thrust one hand up each opposite sleeve, folding my arms, and leaned on the rail again. One of Menmet-Ra's slaves, by name Asru, giggled in a high-pitched voice, and I glanced aside from the magnificence of Alexandria to see her flirting unsubtly with Attila. She had one of her hands clasping at his arm, trying to run her fingers through the thick fair hair that, unbound, fell to his waist.

Beyond her, Ramiro Carrasco de Luis, with the baby's baggage piled up in a mountain about his knees, cradled Onorata up against his shoulder. His hand, huge against her tiny cloth-wrapped body, rubbed at her shoulder-blades with two fingers. In an undertone, he murmured, 'There we go . . . '

Onorata's face screwed up. She jerked, and made a sound like a kitten sneezing.

A gobbet of something white and half-digested hit Carrasco's neck and doublet-collar about equally.

The baby's unfocused blue eyes returned to gazing out at sunlight fracturing off the water. The assassin, still supporting her by one hand and the sling, scooped at his neck with his fingers, dragging the mess out from between his linen doublet and his steel collar. He wiped his hand down his hose. I heard him heave a half-exasperated and half-satisfied sigh as I got to within a pace of him, and he placidly went back to stroking Onorata's shoulders, humming under his breath.

'Where did *you* learn to do that?' I demanded, since it was in no way the way I burped her.

He leaped as if I'd stuck a sword point in him. My daughter began to howl. Tottola and Attila put hands to weapons as one – assessed the situation instantly – and took an automatic pace away across the ship's desk. Away from a disturbed baby.

Red-faced, I muttered, 'Shit . . . '

'She's done that. I changed her.'

I glared.

Between distracting her and petting her, Carrasco and I persuaded Onorata that she desired to sleep more than she desired to scream like the fabled steam-ball of the Alexandrine philosopher Heron. I found it difficult to be soothing when I wished to strangle the man beside me.

I shot him a glance, and met harassed dark eyes. And snorted. 'Maybe I should light another candle to Rekhmire''s Hermopolitan Ogdoad. It seems to work.'

'Or it was colic, and now she's older . . . ' He rocked her a little, in her linen wrappings. She settled curled up onto his breast, nosing momentarily for something she would not get from him.

Or from me. I was momentarily bleak.

'Amazing,' Rekhmire' remarked, at my shoulder, 'how "wet-nurse" comes in the list of required talents for an assassin.'

The dark-haired Iberian immediately lowered his gaze.

He's picked up some slave habits, I realised. Among which is the necessity of hiding your thoughts from your owner.

'Give her to me.'

The solid, warm bundle in my hands felt so breakable that, even with the sling, and Onorata tucked into the crook of my arm and with my other hand supporting her head, I couldn't convince myself that she was safe in my arms.

Ramiro Carrasco muttered something, and I looked up and raised a prompting brow.

He moved his shoulders under the patched doublet. His iron collar gleamed dully in the sunlight. 'Like I said, I'm the next-to-eldest in my family. I used to have to look after the young ones a lot, before the priest took me off to teach me my letters.'

Anger stung me. I have not paid enough attention to this before – or, I have, but the necessity of having more than one set of hands to look after Onorata made me wilfully ignore it. 'How long do you think I'm going to have an assassin near my baby?'

Ramiro Carrasco de Luis blushed like the schoolboy he would have been when his local priest singled him out as worth teaching his letters.

'You can kill me. Torture me.' He looked down at his dirty bare feet. 'Without needing to think whether anyone will ask why. They won't. Under these circumstances, do you think I'd take a step out of line?'

I thought him a long way from the sharply-dressed secretary who'd waited on Aldra Federico and Sunilda. The sun had bleached his doublet, and the foot-less Frankish hose. He went bare-headed as slaves do, his hair growing out short and shaggy. The labour the captain had also co-opted him into on the *Sekhmet* had hardened his muscles, as well as his palms and the soles of his feet.

I waited until he looked up, rubbing my thumb in small circles on Onorata's chest since she seemed to like the rhythm. 'I've known slaves who decided they had nothing to lose. Who felt it didn't matter if they were tortured to death, so long as they had that one strike back at the master they hated. You might wait your moment, and drop my baby over the side of the ship. Or just pinch her nostrils together. After all, it isn't a season yet since you tried to kill me.'

Shame made me hot even as I spoke.

This is gratuitous cruelty. Since I am ashamed of having not been sufficient for my child. Ashamed of trusting Carrasco out of sheer convenience.

Onorata stirred, whimpered at tension she must feel through my arms and chest. She reached out with one wavering starfish-hand.

With the automatic reaction that meant this must have happened a hundred times before, Ramiro Carrasco absently reached down and put his forefinger close to the baby now cradled in another's arms.

Onorata's hand closed around his finger, lifted her head a little as she pulled it to her mouth, and lay back mumbling his nail as she subsided into dreamless squirming.

'She's advanced,' Ramiro murmured absently, 'for three months. She holds her head up well—'

He glanced up.

Tethered by the infant's grip, wide-eyed, the Iberian assassin gave me a look of slave's terror.

'I didn't mean anything . . . Mistress!' Carrasco added rapidly. His gaze skidded up and down me, like a water-insect on a canal. 'Master!'

He grew used enough to seeing me in gowns in Venice to think of me as female. The eastern robe and kilt, which is male clothing in Alexandria, is enough like Frankish women's gowns to confuse him further. His eyes widened enough to show white at top and bottom.

I frowned, in sudden realisation. 'Have the ship's other slaves been telling you stories?'

He nodded.

That will go a long way to explain why he looks more ready to soil himself than Onorata does.

'It's not all lies,' I said. 'But Alexandrine slavery's different. I've been trying to follow Rekhmire''s model. It was the one I preferred to live under when he bought me.'

Ramiro Carrasco de Luis looked as thoroughly miserable as I have ever seen a man.

'You're right.' He managed to achieve looking me directly in the eye. 'Nothing honest can pass between a slave and a master. Anything I say, you'll think I'm ingratiating myself through fear of punishment. I wouldn't harm a child—'

Anger momentarily broke through, to be succeeded by despair.

'—but you'll think I say that for the same reason.'

I knew the secretary-assassin had not had particularly comfortable treatment in Venice; Honorius's men, who would have treated a slave with some decency, set out to make the life of the man who had threatened their commander's family a complete and total misery. The smallest things do it. A kick here, a spit in one's dish there; an accidental knock into a canal, after telling tales of monster- or plague-infested waters. They might have done worse if Honorius had not had a quiet word with them. The old skills of slavehood led me to be in a place to overhear my father order that they should not maim or bugger or kill the man.

But that was all he ordered.

I studied the peeling red and callused finger that Onorata firmly gripped. No great wonder if the university-taught lawyer had sunk into himself; kept himself to menial duties with his eyes always cast down. But . . .

'I saw you with Federico and Sunilda.' I spoke quietly enough that I wouldn't wake the baby. 'I'd say you were an expert at ingratiating yourself with people.'

The frustration and despair on Ramiro Carrasco's face was something I couldn't sketch with my arms full of Onorata, and that was a shame.

How have I become so vindictive? I wondered.

Am I so jealous, if my child appears to love him better than she does me?

I wanted to claw at my chest through the thin linen; claw at the small breasts that – ache as they might – would give not even one drop of milk.

'If I trusted you, I'd be a fool,' I said.

'So you would,' a powerful tenor voice interrupted.

I looked up to see Rekhmire' looming over Ramiro Carrasco. The Egyptian nodded to me. His gaze went to the finger that Onorata suckled on.

'Get the rest of the baggage ready for disembarking,' Rekhmire' added.

The secretary-assassin removed his hand from Onorata with a gentleness that did speak of younger brothers and sisters. He instantly slid off through the crowd of sailors and soldiers without another word.

If he had his shirt and tunic off, I wondered, how many weals would I see on his back?

'You can't trust that man.' Rekhmire' gazed, not at me, but at the massive masonry walls of Constantinople harbour gliding past. They dwarfed the other ships anchored here in the Golden Horn.

His expression would have seemed impassive to someone who didn't know him well.

Oddly enough, his overt bad temper reassured me. 'You got out of the bunk the wrong side this morning . . . '

Rekhmire' suddenly smiled at me. 'It's always a little nerve racking to see one's superiors again. Who knows what I've failed to report back in the last half year or so?'

The idea of the large Egyptian being dressed down by his spymasters here in Constantinople . . . I smiled. 'I'd like to hear *that* conversation.'

A sudden change came in the tone of talk around us. Rekhmire' frowned. I glanced around. Attila and half the ship's crew were looking over the port side of the boat—

No, every man looks in that direction.

Clasping Onorata, I elbowed my way back to Tottola's side at the rail, the book-buyer in his familiar place beside me.

Ships lined the quays at the foot of Constantinople's massive walls. The larger vessels anchored further out in the harbour. More of them moored here than there had been ships in Venice. Every kind of ship: cogs, dhows, bireme galleys. Warships.

At Venice, I missed the full-distance sight of the *Sekhmet* moored in St Mark's basin. At Alexandria, now – I found it brought home to me that the Alexandrine navy consists of more than one trireme.

'Six,' I counted, and took unfair advantage of Tottola's presence to tie Onorata's sling firmly around his chest. I hauled prepared paper and silverpoint out of my linen purse, to sketch everything from the high sterncastle of the nearest trireme to its triangular prow sail.

Yes, it came from the same dockyard as the *Sekhmet*. But to see the ship all at once, whole . . .

Six – no, seven – of the narrow vessels rocked on the gentle swell in the harbour. Twenty-three paces from prow to stern, if they matched ours: better than a hundred and twenty feet. And a mere seventeen or eighteen feet wide. Narrow, knife-hulled vessels, with bronze nozzles pointing out of the dragon's mouths at their prows. Oars spidering rhythmically into the sea . . .

Hand and eye moving between ships and paper, it took me a minute to notice that the smaller sails were set. On most of the triremes, a crew of oarsman was in evidence.

'They're not moored—' I caught the line of one galley's stern as she turned away from us: a heartbreaking beautiful swell up from the water, past the cabin ports, to the central stock of the rudder.

A few lines put in cargo cogs in the background, for the scale.

'Do they patrol the harbour here?'

Rekhmire' did not answer. I sketched the tracery of rope and sail against the sky, angry that I could not – because I did not know the use of each – draw it properly. If I had Mainz's freedom about the ship, I would know every function.

I hatched horizontal lines for the hull's reflection in the harbour and abandoned the page, turning to the next empty sheet, and the trireme that carried the lion-head of the Pharaoh-Queen on its mainsail. 'That's one *big* ship . . . '

At my ear, Rekhmire''s voice sounded oddly.

'No – no, it's really not . . . '

I lifted my head from the page, and saw what he must be looking at. 'That's an interesting trick of perspective.'

Close at hand, a hull with a rack of masts rose up against the background of Constantinople's walls as if it were a mountainside. A ship whose designation I didn't know – not a galley, not a cargo-ship – but which some trick of distance and light made ten times the size of every other ship here.

Unimaginably huge . . .

I watched as one of the Alexandrine navy triremes rowed to pass far behind the evidently foreign craft.

Attila swore. '*Christ Emperor!*'

I leaned out, ship's rail hard against my belly, healed wound forgotten. I stared into the light blazing up from the water.

Distantly I could hear the trireme's drum beating the pace. The oars lifted, dipped, flashed drops of sea water—

And the trireme did not slide out of sight behind the close-at-hand ship.

It glided *between* us and it.

Not something that is small, close at hand, seeming large. Something large, far off, that is vast.

'Not a trick.' Rekhmire' sounded stifled. His face showed blank shock.

As the ranked oars sent the trireme curving towards the stern of the foreign ship, I stared at the top of the trireme's mainmast.

The very top of the mast did not reach as high as the foreign ship's stern deck.

I judged a man standing in the crow's-nest of the trireme would still find himself the height of a house below the foreign ship's taffrail.

'I – wait!' I gripped Onorata almost too hard, finding myself with both arms wrapped protectively about her sling. 'I *remember*—'

Memory came back with instant clarity. Cannon-metal grey skies. Storm-lightning and rain shining all but purple on the heaving Adriatic swell. And seen from the deck of the *Iskander* . . .

'I've seen this before!'

Beating up against storm after storm in the Adriatic. And the sailors telling hushed rumours of . . .

'Ghost ships.' I breathed out. 'That's . . . '

'Not a ghost,' Rekhmire' completed, his hand coming down warm on my shoulder.

'But it is a ship.'

My eyes no longer lied to me. The ghost ship was moored far out from the quays, almost in the centre of the harbour. Each of the Alexandrine navy galleys patrolled around it: around the great walls of wood that rose from the water. A blue-glass shadow echoed it, as deep again.

Now I saw it again as it was – and how I had seen it at sea. That vast assembly of bare wood, ranked stark as a winter forest against the sky, would hold lateen sails. Sails piled higher and higher, one row on top of another, each bellied out in a tight curve against the wind. I had seen rank upon rank of them, rising up against the storm.

In this clear morning light of Constantinople's harbour, each spar showed the irregular edges that meant sails bundled and furled.

Below the masts was a great broad hull, with a flat prow. A hull that my eyes told me stood ten times longer, and five times higher, than any other ship in the harbour. The deck swarmed with men so tiny at this distance that I must believe the size of their ship.

As we inched past the ghost ship, I saw painted on the prow, in green and gold and red paint, a great spiked serpentine beast. Eyes were flat black-on-white discs, staring out across the Alexandrine waters and at us.

With shaking fingers, I made notes too rough to be of use. But copying the drawing of the serpent told me one thing.

Not in Iberia. Not in Carthage. Nor Rome. Nor Venice.

'Not the Turks, either,' I found myself murmuring aloud, thinking of the patterns woven into Bariş's tunic. 'I've seen much while searching out the New Art. That – that is nothing like any style of painting I've ever seen.'

9

Identical shock showed on each face. Honorius's two men-at-arms, the ship's sailors, Asru, Carrasco, Johannes Gutenberg. Rekhmire'.

Attila snorted out a protest. 'They don't *build* ships that big!'

Rekhmire' frowned and muttered words which I finally distinguished as a list of shipyards. 'Cyprus, Sidon, Tyre, Venice, Carthage, La Rochelle . . . '

He glanced up at the trireme's captain, on the sterncastle. I could see the man shaking his head.

'No. None of them.' Rekhmire' narrowed his eyes against the sun glittering off the water. 'Menmet-Ra said nothing of this. It must have arrived recently, therefore. Within the last few weeks.'

'Arrived here? You're likely right—' Onorata whined and mumbled. I stroked her cheek, hypnotised by the sight of the immense ship. '—but I think it's been in the Middle Sea longer than that.'

My drawing had gone, destroyed by weather, but I could recognise what I had taken for delirium and *trompe l'oeil*, in the Adriatic sea.

Rekhmire' tilted his head back. At this distance it was possible to pick out small figures of men on that impossibly high rail. Not possible to see any detail. He mused aloud, 'It will be – interesting – to know how it came to be here.'

'And if anybody can find out, you can!'

He gave me the same abrupt and undignified grin that he had sometimes gifted me with in Carthage.

It stayed quiet enough that I could hear ropes creaking overhead, and the sweeps groaning as the oars brought us steadily on towards our mooring place. The captain bellowed something obscene as our wake wavered, the rowers' attention being all on the huge ship. I realised we were listing, every man who could lining the rail on this side of the ship.

I shaded my eyes with my free hand. 'How many men would it take to crew something that size?'

'It's . . . remarkable.' Lines creased Rekhmire''s forehead; I could see them where his hand lifted his cloth veil as he tried to cut out the ambient light from sky and flashing wavelets. He looked back at me. 'But, if I may say so – not our first concern. We have matters to take up with the Pharaoh-Queen. Although it might be useful, perhaps, to mention to her that you've seen this vessel months ago.'

Our ship drove on steadily towards the mountainous masonry of Constantinople. I realised I had the jumping frogs in my belly again.

The ghost ship. Yes. But . . .

Sooner or later, the Pharaoh-Queen will call me in to bear witness to what I saw in Rome.

When this city had been built by the Romans and Carthaginians, it was called Byzantium. The Franks called it 'Constantinople' after one of their emperors, and added monumental grandeur to the place. But it was the last of dynastic Egypt that had taken the city and changed it to New Alexandria, long centuries in the past, after the Turks overran the Egyptian homeland.

It looked nothing like the harbours of Frankish ports, or Iberia, or even Carthage. I stared out at the squares of the city, lined with great inscribed obelisks; temples with masses of clustered pillars under great roofs; and the bas-reliefs that ornamented buildings – painted bas-reliefs, bright as enamel—

I could do nothing but stare as we docked and were greeted. A bevy of bureaucrats stood by, awaiting the galley's small boats. It occurred to me that if Menmet-Ra had sent messages indicating his success in finding the printer and the hermaphrodite, his messengers might have had better sailing than ours, and arrived here before us.

'Come.' Rekhmire' touched my shoulder. 'We'll go up to the palace.'

The Pharaoh-Queen Ty-ameny, otherwise Ty-Amenhotep, Lord of the Two Lost Rivers and Ruler of the Five Great Names, stood around four foot six in her bare feet, and wore a beard.

She *was* barefoot, I saw; a pair of gilded sandals having been kicked off across the rush matting on the faïence-tiled floor, and she reached up and unhooked the false beard from her ears as the mute slaves showed us into her bedchamber. Sunlight streaming in through the linen-draped windows spot-lit the small, black-haired figure as she turned and beamed.

'Rekhmire'! You're back.'

'Great Queen.' Rekhmire' lurched only slightly as he stepped forward, aided by his crutch. He bowed almost double, and put his free arm very gently around Ty-ameny, embracing her as one does a relative or close friend. 'I've brought you Ilario, son-daughter of Licinus Honorius, who is lately Captain-General of the Frankish thrones of Leon and Castile.'

Ty-ameny nodded briefly, with a quick and bird-like movement. Her arms were thin but muscled, and showed ruddy under the half-sleeved white linen tunic she wore. A heap of brocade and cloth-of-gold on the bed, spilling down the sides of the dais, had the look of formal clothing – and the braided beard hit the top of the heap with some force.

'I can do without one more formal audience!' Ty-ameny dusted her hands, and put small fists on her hips. In a tunic that came down to her knees, and with matt-black hair cut in a curtain that fell below her waist, she looked something between the beggar children and fisher-girls down on the dock, and – because of the quality of the cloth – a great lady. She strode across the mats to where a sunken area of the floor was lined with marble benches, padded with silk cushions. She waved one arm at her slaves.

'Good day to you, Freeborn Ilario.' This in halting Iberian. 'Please, sit. You should drink.' She met my gaze with eyes that were black as sloes, and smiled. 'Foreigners don't drink enough in New Alexandria, and then we have to treat them for heat-stroke.' Back in the Alexandrine Latin lingua franca of the eastern Mediterranean Sea, she added, 'Cousin Rekhmire', Pamiu tells me you've had my witness with you for *months.*'

She used the familiar for 'cousin', rather than the formal. I raised an eyebrow at the Egyptian book-buyer, taking a seat on the low couch as I did so.

Rekhmire' looked back at me, as innocently as any man might.

I wonder if Ty-ameny of the Five Great Names would mind if I kicked him on the ankle?

But I felt oddly cheered that he would tease me again, after the tension between us on the *Sekhmet.*

Slaves poured watered wine into golden cups, that were circled with cabochon-cut sapphires in the pattern called Horus-Eye. Rekhmire' offered his hand to the Pharaoh-Queen, and with surprising grace led her to an individual small couch. She curled her bare feet up under her as she sat down.

He shot me a glance as he thumped down onto the padded bench beside me, and smiled. 'Fourth cousin; nine hundred and seventh in line to the throne of the Ptolemies. Were you wondering?'

Ty-ameny made a sound that, had she not been in her thirties and the ruler of a great city, I should have described as a snicker. 'Has he been playing the humble scroll-purchaser again?'

'Oh yes.' I mentally rummaged through the rapid briefing he had dumped on me on the way up the Thousand Steps to the palace, while I was still more concerned with leaving my daughter yelling at Tottola. 'Yes, Divine Daughter of Ra.'

She had all of her teeth still, and they showed white in the pale-vaulted room as she smiled. 'What would it be in Iberia? "Aldra" – lord? "Altezza" – "Highness"? And every man in this room is higher than I am!'

Ty-ameny leaned forward, both her hands cupping one of the golden bowls, looking keenly interested.

'A man-woman – what do you call yourself? Hermaphrodite? If you'd consent to it, there are natural philosophers here who would dearly like to speak to you, after this matter of Carthage's gift is dealt with.'

Rekhmire' spoke before I could get a word out.

'No prodding!'

The Pharaoh-Queen's kohl-lined brows shot up into her straight-cut fringe.

With an effort of will I kept *I told you so* out of my glare.

Ty-ameny loosed her cup with one hand, and slapped her knee. 'Rekhmire', *what* have you been telling her! Him. I'm sorry—' She swivelled back to me. 'Which do you prefer?'

'Usually I go with what I'm dressed as, Altezza.'

She nodded thoughtfully. 'I suppose "he"; you're most like our eunuchs, after all.'

Rekhmire' said firmly, 'No.'

'No?' Her brows went up again, and came down. There were a few minuscule golden spots on the reddish skin of her cheeks, I saw; like freckles. She bit at a thumbnail, and looked at me with a curiosity that was so frank I found it difficult to be offended. 'I suppose not. You have both? And—'

'And you,' Rekhmire' put in smoothly, 'were far too curious back when I was made eunuch, never mind now, Ty-ameny of the Five Great Names.'

His face was monumentally solemn.

The Pharaoh-Queen gazed up at him where he sat, pursed her lips in a silent whistle, and gave him a surprisingly gamin grin. 'I'm in trouble if I'm "of the Five Great Names" . . . '

'Ilario didn't come here to be put in a specimen cabinet in your secret museum!' Rekhmire' spoke mildly, but anyone who knew him could see he was amused now. 'Kek and Keket!, but I wonder what Pamiu wrote in his report from Rome. Great Queen of the Five Names, this is a painter, Ilario, whose account of the gift of King-Caliph Ammianus of Carthage you should hear. What any of us have under our robes is nothing to do with the matter.'

The black gaze of the small woman switched back to me.

'No prodding,' she said meekly.

I thought Rekhmire', if he hadn't the control of a lifetime, would have been quaking; I could feel his arm quiver where it rested against mine.

I managed to say, 'Thank you, Queen Ty-ameny.'

She grinned, and signalled for slaves to pour more wine. Two men and two women came in. I noted that they took a reasonable pride in serving deftly, and didn't seem to be always on the watch against being hit.

'You're already in possession of delicate information.' Ty-ameny smoothed her tunic over her knees, and directed a keen black stare at me. 'I suppose the Carthaginians ordered their gift painted at Rome so that rumours would spread out among the Franks. I understand that Menmet-Ra allowed the Italian's apprentice – you – to come in and work since things were progressing so slowly?'

'I wasn't told why.' The memory of hours spent carefully laying on coat after coat of colour and tint brought me back Masaccio's face, laughing as he told me stories while he painted with intent genius.

'According to Menmet-Ra, your late master took so long, and kept breaking off to do so much other work, that Menmet-Ra feared he would run over the deadline Carthage had ordered. It would never do to insult the King-Caliph unintentionally ... ' The Pharaoh-Queen's eyes narrowed.

I couldn't think of Carthage.

The warm wind blew in scents of the Alexandrine harbour and the palace gardens, and linen curtains streamed in the breeze.

He didn't break off to do other work, I thought. Even if they assumed so. He drew the job out so he could study the golem. He died simply because he wanted an amazing thing for himself. He didn't want it to come here ...

The chamber was silent, I realised. I looked up from my wine cup.

'I understand that you were fond of your master.' Ty-ameny smiled sadly.

'He was painting things in a way no other man could. Maybe never will.' I felt the muscles tight between my shoulder-blades. 'Is the golem here?'

'The golem is in my throne room,' Ty-ameny said, suddenly tight-lipped. 'So that Carthage isn't offended at a rejection of their gift. That thing stands there – by my throne – already has blood on its hands – and I have no idea if it waits for some signal to run riot, kill everyone around it!'

'Couldn't you drop it in the harbour?'

She raised a brow at me, in a way that very much reminded me of Rekhmire' himself. 'You put much work into it, I understand.'

'Some of the best statue work I've ever done.' I steadily regarded Ty-ameny. 'If you can't push it into your harbour, I can lift a sledge-hammer.'

Her mouth quirked up at one corner, in a very distinctively sardonic smile. 'I understand why you might feel that way. It isn't possible, because of the situation between nations, to destroy it. We study it. And, as Carthage designed, we have not the slightest idea how it works! Months it's been here, and none of my philosophers can tell me how it moves, even. Not with all the resources of the Library. Someone in Carthage has made a breakthrough – House Barbas, my counsellors suspect. And Carthage won't share the secret ... '

Because of Rodrigo's purchase, I am both used to courts and great nobles, and used to being present at the discussion of policy. If Ty-ameny was treating me in the same way, it might be because she knew how long I had been a slave. Or else Menmet-Ra's report had been specific about my silence as regards what happened in the Roman embassy.

'I'll tell you everything I know.' I shrugged. 'It won't help you.'

'I shall still be grateful.' She inclined her head with a movement so suddenly graceful that I had no doubt that this woman had been on the throne of Alexandria since the age of four.

She shot a glance across to Rekhmire'. 'But you will have seen our problem? In the harbour? I thank the Gods you're home today! Now I have a man I can trust to deal with this. No—'

As he rose, she gestured to him to sit. Rekhmire' only steadied his balance on his crutch, shot her a silent intense look, and made an apologetic indication of both the crutch and – now he was in the formal Egyptian linen kilt – his visibly scarred knee.

'Oh, pah!' Ty-ameny said lightly.

I did not desire to be jealous of how bright his face grew at her words. Or resent that he never reacted so to any encouragement of mine.

But then, I am neither his employer nor his sovereign.

Ty-ameny bent almost double with her hands on her own knees for support. The scars were still inflamed, I saw; ridges of pink and purple flesh that stood up twistedly about the cap and side of his knee. Some patches of flesh seemed to have healed white and hairless.

'I'll have my physicians look at it.' She straightened, seeming almost apologetic. 'May I send you on work, first? You can see it's urgent.'

My stomach turned suddenly unaccountably cold.

Of course, he is her agent, she can send him where she pleases—

Suppose she sends him away, out of Alexandria?

For some reason I had not envisaged being on my own here, in charge of a baby and Aldra Videric's return to power.

My court manners abruptly returning to me, I stood up and bowed, preparing to leave.

Ty-ameny held out an arresting hand. 'No, this concerns you – you particularly, Messer Ilario, if you would consent.'

On my feet, it was just possible, from the window of this great fortress tower, to see down to the harbour. And to see the top masts of one ship. One ship only. No other is tall enough to be visible. I sat down again.

'Cousin.' Ty-ameny faced Rekhmire'. 'You will go aboard and talk to these foreigners. No delegation has been successful so far, but I have every confidence in you.'

It was not what she said, I realised, but the casual competency with which she said it. She really does trust 'cousin' Rekhmire' the humble book-buyer . . .

'I take it your injury will not prevent this?'

He shook his head.

'And if you would agree.' She turned towards me, speaking with the utmost directness. 'I would like you to go aboard as one of the delegation. Posing as Cousin Rekhmire''s scribe, perhaps.'

Rekhmire' snorted. 'Ilario will go! Especially if it involves getting closer to some new painting or fresco or inlay!'

He has just informed the Pharaoh-Queen that she may offer me whatever terms she likes and still see me fight tooth-and-nail to get near the foreign ship.

I caught Rekhmire''s eye, and found the amusement I expected.

Ty-ameny leaned forward, addressing me. 'But you have a child, with you?'

Between Menmet-Ra and Rekhmire', no matter how discreet the latter might have been, I doubted there would be anything the Pharaoh-Queen didn't know about my private life. Privacy had not been possible for a slave in Taraco either.

That doesn't mean I have to like it.

I went on the attack. 'My daughter Onorata will be safe and guarded, Great Queen. But I have to admit, I don't understand – I was Rekhmire''s scribe in Carthage, and I did reasonable work. Good work, even.'

I avoided Rekhmire''s eye, suspecting I might find even more amusement there now.

'But I don't see why you want me to be his scribe aboard this ship. Rather than one of your own people.'

Almost absently, Ty-ameny stood and padded over to the window. She had to come much closer to the sill, short as she was, to glimpse the high masts down in the harbour. The sunlight glimmered on the straight black hair that fell in a cape over her shoulders and back. Her small hands clenched into fists at her sides.

'They've been here three days now ... My diplomats and philosophers have discovered nothing of these foreigners – not their name, not what weapons that vessel carries, nor the intention of its captain. I have every confidence that Rekhmire' will open negotiations in a manner that I can trust.'

She turned around, silhouetted against the bright light outside. I couldn't see her expression when she spoke:

'They will allow very few men aboard. I am told I could not risk myself in any case. But I desire to see what that ship is like – and have my Royal Mathematicians see it, also. Ilario, I understand from Menmet-Ra and from Rekhmire' here that you follow what the Franks call the "New Art". If you'll agree, I wish you to go aboard the ship with Rekhmire''s servants – and draw for me exactly what it is that you see there.'

10

Attila nodded a greeting, standing guard at the door of our assigned palace rooms.

Inside the chambers, I found his brother. Tottola might not wear his breastplate in this climate, but even in the palace he wore mail. He carried his gauntlets hooked by their buckled straps over the hilt of his bastard sword, banging at his hip. His polished steel helm – very like Honorius's sallet – sat upturned in his lap, with Onorata laying propped up in it as if it were a very odd cradle.

She followed his moving finger with her dark blue eyes, and cooed in a serious and attentive way.

Tottola had her naked, in the heat, and Ramiro Carrasco scurried out of our vast quarters with the jug and bowl he had evidently used to bathe her. She had been fed again, I realised, and felt a twinge at having missed it.

Onorata kicked her bare feet. Tottola sang under his breath, and continued with verses that she was thankfully too young to understand. Half her lullabies were marching songs. Lengths of linen padded the metal of his sallet, and protected Tottola's helmet-lining against anything unfortunate.

It was a habit he had picked up from my father, who delighted to find his grandchild small enough to cradle in his sallet. Every man, from Sergeant Orazi down to Ensign Saverico, seemed to think it was permissible to joke with their lord about the likelihood of baby-shit next time he put the visored helmet on . . . And soon, now, she'll be too big.

I took the opportunity to unstopper my ink bottle and quickly sketch tones on the rough paper to show her with Tottola's curving protective arm. 'I'll never understand soldiers . . . '

Rekhmire' offered Onorata his finger, which she batted away. He turned back to me. 'The child will be safe enough with them while we go aboard.'

It was not until I started drawing her that Onorata looked to me like an individual child. I had worried, in Venice and on the voyage: if you put her down among a dozen other babies, would I know mine? A mother is supposed to know her child. There is instinct – which I clearly did not have.

But I know the slope of her upper lip, and her grave, extraordinary stare.

There were sufficient drawings of Onorata in my sketchbooks that Queen Ty-ameny was convinced using me as her eye was sound. One could see how Onorata had grown since we left the Most Serene city of Venice.

'She'd be safer with Honorius,' I grumbled. 'Back home.'

Hot countries, plagues, the bowel-flux, flies, itches, irritations, rashes – if I sat down, I dare say I could come up with a list of similar discomforts in cold countries, too. Nowhere is as safe for her as I could wish. But here . . .

'Ty-ameny hasn't let any of them come ashore.' I nodded towards the window, nominally in the direction of the harbour.

'Her advisers were very keen on quarantine.'

'So no man's seen these strangers.'

'Except to say they're not Franks, or North Africans; they perhaps look like Turks or Persians, but then again, *not* like them . . .' Rekhmire' repeated rumours frustratedly. 'They arrived three days ago: if it was a plague ship, the doctors who went aboard the first day would probably have sickened by now.'

The way I heard the rumour from Attila, who had been gossiping in the palace kitchen and barracks, Queen Ty-ameny had only got doctors aboard the foreign ship by threatening to raise the vast iron chain and keep the monstrous vessel out of the shelter of Alexandria's harbour.

If that ship had *to arrive here, it might have waited until we'd come and gone!*

I put a finishing smudge of shadow onto the drawing of Onorata, abandoned it, and walked out onto the balcony beside Rekhmire'.

He leaned heavily on the yellow stone balustrade, gazing down – very far down – at the glimmering blue of the harbour.

'Even if it weren't so large,' I said, 'that's a style of ship I've never seen.'

The Egyptian inclined his head.

'And she just . . . expects you to go and talk to these people?'

'It would be some other man, if I hadn't returned at the right moment.' Rekhmire''s eyes might have been narrowed against the sunlight. 'Ty-ameny feels she can trust me. If I fail, I shall only fail. I won't be a part of one or other of the court conspiracies, with my own ideas of who should be sitting on the Lion-throne.'

'And there was me thinking all this monumental grandeur meant a different kind of court to Taraco . . .' Sometimes directness is the only way to knowledge. 'Why does she trust you? Because you're her cousin? Which, by the way, you never told me!'

'A fourth cousin is one of the very many.' Rekhmire' blinked mild eyes, apparently amused to be withholding information. He sharpened his gaze, and smiled outright. 'No, you have it right; she feels she has good reason. I had a hand in preventing one of the early assassination attempts, back when she was coming of age and taking power from the Regency Council. She knows I won't lie to her.'

'Given most courts I've visited, that would be invaluable.' I suspected there was more to it, that he'd done more than 'had a hand in preventing' whatever had happened – probably discovered the whole thing, I reflected. But if the Queen had so much confidence in her wandering book-buyer . . .

I was still holding a half-inch stub of red chalk. I held it up demonstrably. 'Will she regard this as constituting a debt?'

'For you to ask for help with the situation in Taraconensis?'

Frustrated, I shrugged. 'I'm thinking of asking somebody – anybody! – just how I get Videric accepted as the King Rodrigo's chief counsellor again. Because, worry at it as I may, I have no idea!'

The hour passed noon; the hot sun was too much for me. I turned and walked back inside, taking refuge in the stone room's coolness and shade.

Rekhmire' followed me in, sandals soundless on the floor.

A fan made of fine woven fibres, and hanging from a frame, moved two and fro in a leisurely stirring of the air. I opened my mouth to castigate the German men-at-arms for letting in a palace slave – and saw, in time, that Ramiro Carrasco sat bemusedly pulling on the fan's cord.

Rekhmire' went to the door, exchanging words with a servant there, and came back after a short time with a clear drink made of herbs, and with hacked-small chunks of ice floating in the jug. I realised myself thirsty in the extreme – which argued that we all must be, and I requested he find more, especially for the men wearing mail-shirts.

By the time Rekhmire' returned, I had experimented with stroking Onorata's palms and the soles of her feet with quick strokes of melting lump of ice. Feeling the skin of her belly, she no longer tended to the overheated.

'It couldn't hurt to have the Pharaoh-Queen in our debt,' I suggested.

The Egyptian smiled, levering himself across the floor and into the sunken area. He thumped down, took the baby from Tottola's hands as the German soldier proffered her, and put her into the crook of his elbow. Tottola made thankfully for the iced drink.

'She sends further word,' Rekhmire' added.

My traitorous child ignored me, even as I sat down next to the Egyptian. She waved her hands at him. He broke off to answer her in some nonsense-tongue.

'*What* did the Queen say?'

'How carefully we need to tread. They apparently don't desire too many men on board at one time.'

Tottola lowered the jug and wiped his mouth. 'Damned if I can see why not, sir. That thing's the size of a city! What can they be frightened of?'

Since they had evidently been allowed to advise Honorius, both the German brothers thought they should continue that habit with me – and, by extension, the book-buyer.

'The Queen will want to send as few people as possible,' I put in, stroking Onorata's scurfy curls. 'In case they take hostages. I'd expect a balancing act between men with enough rank to honour the visitors, and people who wouldn't be missed.'

Rekhmire' inclined his head. 'She's reluctant to risk her witness to the golem. But since you're the only practitioner of the New Art here, that leaves her no choice.'

Tottola made a noise like a horse snorting, and glared at Rekhmire'. 'I know the Lion of Castile – if you let Ilario come to harm on that thing, sir, don't bother coming ashore!'

At his raised voice, the baby stopped waving her arms, poised for a moment between bubbling with amusement and screaming in fear. Rekhmire' slid a large hand under the baby's arse, supported her head, and thrust her instantly towards me. 'She's hungry.'

It was a guess. I took her in my arms, heavy for the small size of her, and warm and faintly damp as she was.

'Ramiro.' I signalled him to leave the fan. 'Help me feed her. She might just sleep through until I come back.'

Rekhmire' was in the process of giving Tottola his impermeable bureaucrat expression. 'I refuse to take responsibility for Ilario – since Ilario doesn't just draw trouble like a lode-stone, but goes out specifically to invite it home with him – her—'

I might have protested at that, but my bodyguard was far too busy agreeing with the Egyptian.

'When you two have finished bickering like an old married couple,' I remarked, 'you'll be disappointed to know I plan to *ask* if I may draw things on the strangers' ship. *And* where I can safely draw. Nothing like being taken for a spy to make life interesting. Right, Rekhmire'?'

Under his ruddy skin, I could swear he went a darker red. 'I knew I should regret telling you that!'

'As if you had to *tell* me!'

I broke off, since Tottola was in the process of making a remark entirely similar in meaning, but more restrained by military discipline.

I was still snickering intermittently, and holding Onorata while Carrasco fed her, when two or three of the Pharaoh-Queen's eunuch bureaucrats were shown into the room by Attila.

If I heard anything of the hours of intense briefing, it fell back out of my head instantly. I was too busy reckoning up every item I could put in a scribe's leather satchel, that I could carry over my shoulder. All tools for drawing, since I doubted any man would let me heat the bronze

143

pallet-box for encaustic wax painting. The leather snapsack to protect paper and papyrus from splashes as we were rowed out into the harbour. Silverpoint stylus, reed pen, ink, chalk, charcoal-sticks, and perhaps it would be worth taking a wax tablet: stylus-lines can be incised into the soft surface as well as the more normal letters and words . . .

'Ready?' Rekhmire' inquired. 'I tell you now: if you choose not to risk yourself because of the child, Ty-ameny will understand that.'

Much as I hate being any man's to beat or fondle, the life of a slave is at least easier in that one is ordered, not asked to decide.

I glanced around the great high-ceilinged rooms, beyond whose windows the white furnace of afternoon was cooling to early evening. 'I'm ready.'

The noise of the city rose up about us as Ty-ameny's soldiers escorted us down towards the quay. The sound was different to Venice, although I saw the trade was no less intense. *Different and familiar*, I felt. More like the Turkish cities along the Old Egyptian coast, and Malta, and Taraco, and Carthage.

One of the war-galleys sent in a boat. I sat upright, cooled by the occasional spray. The oarsmen rowed us through the encircling ring of triremes. I watched the touch of the sweeps, that kept each oared vessel with its Greek Fire siphon pointed at the massive foreign ship.

Hunched in the rocking stern, I practised a quick charcoal sketch of the serpent-decorated ship, to shake the stiffness out of my hand.

In a few minutes we, also, will be at the centre of that circle of potential Greek Fire.

I have barely been in Constantinople four hours, I thought, as my sandal touched the deck of the vast foreign ship.

My body was still adjusted to the motion of the sea under my feet. Every step up to the palace and down to the harbour again had felt as if I were slamming the soles of my feet into granite. The consciousness of the shift and dip of a moored ship would feel reassuring to me.

But there was no sensation of the sea on this colossus. I might have been standing on a wooden fortress in the harbour.

Two other eunuch bureaucrats accompanied Rekhmire'; one in my former job as clerk. They stood by his shoulders now as he spoke for a long time to the guards who surrounded us. I glanced briefly over the monolith's side at the plank and rope ladder, bobbing down an incredible distance to the ferry boat, and gave up that route of escape.

The ship's crew crowded close.

Freaks surrounded me.

No. Men.

But flat-faced men; men almost with the faces of village idiots. I have been, from time to time in Taraco, put in company with those born

144

witless, or with no voices; only the ability to lumber about, grinning and groaning. Some of them can be remarkably gentle, given kind treatment.

The ones surrounding me now were barefoot, wearing high-collared belted robes. They held long thin-bladed spears, and carried short swords.

A ship of the mad, the witless. I recognised those odd, folded eyelids; the emotionless features. Shuddering and cold despite the evening's heat, I wanted desperately to tell Rekhmire' what I saw. *But no, it can't be; madmen couldn't sail a ship!*

Rekhmire' stood very upright, his back to me, speaking in a normal tone; trying as many languages as he could think of.

I knew what he must be saying: Hello, may we come aboard, who is your captain?

Did Ty-ameny's eunuchs get us this permission by the equivalent of point-and-mime!

Rekhmire' spoke again, with considerably more confidence.

I recognised the language, if not the words. Occasionally, I'd heard it in Venice, from traders come in not by sea, but over the long land routes from the lapis mines in Afghanistan and the east. A dialect something like that spoken by the Turks and Persians. I understood one word in five, if that.

The larger of the black-eyed men broke into a broad grin, looked up at Rekhmire' – just looked up: he was almost of a height with the book-buyer – and laughed out loud.

'*Gaxıng jiandào nî!*' he exclaimed, in a completely different-sounding language, and began to rattle off the Persian or Turkish dialect at an amazing rate. He gestured towards the stern of the ship.

The way to the captain's quarters? I wondered.

As respectfully as if he were still my master, I murmured to Rekhmire', 'Will you ask permission if I can draw as I go? Those spears look sharp.'

Cautiously, the Egyptian spoke to the broad man in belted robes that, now I could look at them closely, were not Persian at all. The fabric shimmered. Silk.

Absorbed in the play of light and shade in the fabric's folds, and what a difference it made to the colours of the blue dye, it was a minute before I became aware of Rekhmire'. He waved a broad hand, and gazed equably down at me.

'Draw something for this gentleman, if you please.'

I unfolded my drawing book, showed the stub of red chalk on an outstretched hand, and then – as well as I could with fingers that were shaking from the climb – managed line and tone that encompassed the shape of the ship's flat prow.

The foreign man scowled.

Or I thought he did; I realised I could read none of his thoughts for certain from his expression.

The man smeared his forefinger across one sheet of paper, smearing the chalk, and lifted it to his finger to taste.

His head snapped around; he rattled off something very quick, very emphatic.

Rekhmire' bowed, in the Turkish fashion, and replied. As well as that unknown language, I recognised some of the versions of Carthaginian Latin from the western coast of Africa. Evidently everything was having to be said two or three times, three or four different ways.

'He wants you to show his captain, I believe.' Rekhmire' shifted a gaze that took in all the Golden Horn, and the great fortress city – in which, now I thought about it, he must have been born or grown up. And now to find this huge, dangerous vessel and its unknown crew here, right here in the harbour . . .

Rekhmire' inclined his head to the stout man in silk robes, gestured his eunuch clerks to precede him, tucked his crutch neatly under his arm, and took hold of my sleeve with his other hand.

I whispered, 'They look like—'

'Yes, but they speak like men. Like you or I.'

Rekhmire' paused for a moment after that last remark, gave me a smile that only he and I would ever comprehend, and ducked his way under the wood and silk awning that protected the doorway into the poop deck cabin.

The ship's captain was no different to his officers and crew, I thought at first glance, except for his size; he stood well over six feet tall. His broad face shone sallow in the light through the ports. Looking up at us from a table full of maps and charts, his heavy brows dipped down; he had the same small eyes as every other man on the ship. And it was almost as if he had been facing into a desert wind, dehydrating; or had been hit in the face: the flesh of his eyelids swollen up and only narrow slits of sloe-coloured eyes visible.

A close-fitting black cap covered his hair, and his thin black beard was shaven at the sides, but fell down to touch his belt at the front. As he turned I saw his robes were slit at the side, and that under the plain ochre over-robes, immensely-patterned blue and red and gold thread shone. I could not have begun to guess at his age.

I leaned over toward Rekhmire''s ear. 'Ask him if he'll sit for me to paint him!'

With perfect aplomb, Rekhmire' remarked, 'Shut up, Ilario,' and bowed deeply in the Turkish fashion to the man evidently in command of this vast vessel.

The squarish man who had greeted us rattled off something, nodding at me, and the tall captain held out his hand.

Looking at the square-set officer for confirmation, I put the leather snapsack into the captain's hand.

He upended it on his desk, turning over sized parchment and tinted paper. Before I could warn him, he opened a stoppered ink-horn and spilled oak-gall ink over his fingers. He prodded messily and suspiciously at the sharp point of a stylus, until I warily showed him how it sketched palest grey lines on a paper prepared with fine-ground bone dust. I had no idea if he gained any idea of the connection between that and the older silverpoint lines in my sketchbook that had turned brown.

He flicked through the sewn-together pad of sketch paper with nothing I could read in his expression. It was not a new book, I realised, embarrassed, as he stopped momentarily at a few lines that held something of Onorata's sleeping face.

'Eh.' He beckoned, took my sleeve, and led me round the immense map table.

There were papers and brushes neatly spread out on his desk, and shallow white dishes. He tipped water onto a flat slate and took up a black stick, grinding one end on the surface as if he ground pigments. The brush he used to take up the wet blackness was not of familiar animal hair. I bent close, observing how he divided his pigment among pots with great or little amounts of water.

The scent was unfamiliar but distinctive.

He felt my sketchbook with his thumb, shook his head, and drew up a sheet of his own very fine, light paper. With a look of intense concentration, he dipped his brush first in water, and then less deeply in liquid pigment, and less deeply still in the deepest black. The curve of his wrist was very quick with that last: I just caught that he touched not the whole of his brush, but either side, in turn, very lightly.

Two, three, four strokes. No more than six at most, black, the brush held at different angles—

A shape glistened on the paper. Differential pigment made it miraculous: pale and dark lines drawn with the same swirl of a brush. Graduating from ink-black through pale grey to grey pearl.

Recognition snapped into my mind.

'Horse!' My voice squeaked embarrassingly.

As solid as if it lived, the mane and tail of a galloping horse shaped the wind. All its hooves raised off the earth, except for one – and that one, I saw as I peered closely, was not on the ground, but on the back of a flying bird.

It was as if he painted darkness and used it to carve light out of the page. A horse in such living movement that I almost felt it.

Rekhmire', his clerks, and this captain's officer all watched me.

There were other sketchbooks tumbled out of my snapsack; I fumbled one up, and thumbed through until I found what I wanted.

'There! Horse!'

Done months ago in Rome: carts setting off with Honorius's luggage. Here, a cart-horse with every muscle bunched and clenched as it began to shift the dead weight of the vehicle . . . Done in red chalk, or at least half-done; unfinished, but the study of the forequarters had some virtue to it, so I had not thrown it away.

The captain exclaimed loudly.

I suspected I'd learned the word *horse*, when I could get my ear around it.

He beamed down at me. I realised I was grinning back at him like an idiot.

Behind me, Rekhmire' respectfully spoke in the Turkish dialect, and the large foreign captain frowned thoughtfully. After a moment he jerked his head; I wasn't sure whether it was assent or negation.

'Cheng Ho.' He leaned down, looking into my face intensely. He spoke again: this time I might have represented it as 'Zheng He.'

Guessing, I copied Rekhmire''s bow. 'Ilario Honorius.'

He couldn't fit his tongue around the words. He planted one large hand flat on the page of my sketchbook. More exchange of words in a number of different languages took place between him and Rekhmire', while Zheng He – if that was a name, and not a rank – paged through my book of drawings.

Rekhmire' finally said smoothly, in Iberian, 'Zheng He, the Admiral of the Ocean Seas, desires you to show him what you draw before you leave the ship. I suspect he'll destroy anything that he doesn't want known about.'

A trickle of cold permeated my belly. 'Don't let him get any ideas about putting out the artist's eyes, along with the preliminary sketches.'

Rekhmire' muttered something. For a second I saw him look genuinely appalled, before a diplomatic blandness reasserted itself.

In that Iberian dialect which it was unlikely his clerks spoke, never mind these foreigners, he asked, 'Is that what you were threatened with in Taraco?'

'And it could have been done. Easily. Could you tell him I'm not a slave? Make sure you tell him that!'

Rekhmire' reverted to Turkish, in which I could pick out the word for slave and not much else. Then Carthaginian Latin, in an odd accent. After two or three exchanges with the large foreigner, Rekhmire' bowed, looked momentarily puzzled, and gestured for me to take back my book.

'The Admiral Zheng says every man is a slave. He himself is the humble slave of Emperor – "Zhu Di", I think. Zhu Di of the Chin. Or *of* Chin. He, ah . . . '

Rekhmire''s brows rose as the foreign admiral added something.

'He says, this is the first civilised country he's found in two years of sailing. Because the bureaucrats sent to meet him are slaves and eunuchs, as they should be.'

148

11

If we hadn't been in a foreign ship's cabin, surrounded by clerks and Zheng He's armed sailors, I thought Rekhmire' would have howled with laughter. When something hits his sense of humour, it affects him strongly.

'You can tell the Pharaoh-Queen she did something right, then.' I barely managed not to grin myself. 'Should I go draw things before he realises I'm – not exactly what he thinks?'

'That might be wise.' Rekhmire' bowed to the Admiral, and murmured, aside, 'Do try not to get killed while we're aboard.'

'This ship has more arbalests on its deck than your entire navy; if these people didn't *want* something, they'd be using them!'

His brow rose again. Why he would think – with Honorius for a father; with King Rodrigo's training – that I wouldn't take automatic notice of armaments?

The Admiral rattled off something in the oddly-toned language. He wiped his fingers on a cloth, surveyed his desk, swept up a small box and tipped the contents into his hand. Small gold-marked sticks, oval in cross-section, black and red – belatedly I recognised his ink-sticks. He let them slide and click back into the box, and thrust it into my hand.

He wants *me to draw!* I all but shouted aloud.

He spoke urgently again, and finished by pointing at the squarely-built officer, and then at me.

'*Dong ma?*'

That was *do you understand?* as plainly as I had ever heard it. I bowed. 'Thank you, Admiral Zheng He.'

I went out in the company of my minder.

An hour later, I had the smart idea of sending in to Rekhmire''s scribes to borrow more of their paper, since I'd run out.

I persuaded Jian (my guess at the pronunciation of the squarely-built officer's name) that this would do no harm. Talking to each other, each in our own languages, I'd added what I thought were 'yes' – *shìde* or *hâo de* – and an all-purpose apology, *duìbùqî*, 'sorry', to my vocabulary. If I hadn't found the word for 'no', that was because I found he didn't often like to use it. Jian would distract me, or misunderstand me, or carefully not hear me, if anything requiring a refusal arose. I wondered if that was him, or the Chin in general.

There was also *hùndàn*, but I suspected I hadn't been intended to hear that one. Certainly Jian hustled me away from the lower deck tiers where one of the anonymous oarsmen threw it after me. I stored it away for a useful insult, when I could find out whether it was on the order of friendly abuse, or something certain to start a fight to the death. It pays to find that out beforehand.

I smiled, thinking of Honorius; he'd appreciate another foreign oath. The ship was a marvel.

What I took to be other officers muttered, seeing me draw the outlines of sails and hull, and broke out into outright complaint when I sketched the swivel-based arbalests they had mounted on the decks, and the exact number of masts and cross-trees.

Jian screeched at them, highly-pitched as a hawk.

What he said, I didn't know: I suspect it was *Our captain sees no sense in hiding what any man in this city can see if they sail a dhow past our moorings!* Although that was not true of the interior cabins, with their great Turkish-style pillows on the mats instead of Frankish or North African furniture; or of the interminable storerooms and holds, that carried food and water enough to allow Ty-ameny's generals to make a guess at what crew the ship carried.

If it's under five thousand men, I'll eat my chalk, I reflected, and yelped and shot up into the air as a hand went up my linen tunic from the rear.

Whoever it was behind went over with a scream. The old reflexes of slavehood either keep one perfectly still under assault, because it may be a master, or lash out, because it may be another slave. My reflexes evidently didn't think I had a master on this ship.

I swung around to face a gang of twenty or thirty of the foreigners, as well as the one writhing on the deck and clutching his knee.

Before I could speak, the officer Jian beat his way through the crowd with the use of a short wooden stick. Thankfully, I saw he had a clutch of paper in his other fist. I stepped forward to take the sheets from him, and, as he yelled at me, to mime what had happened.

The deck around us sounded like a mews when the falcons have been disturbed; all high screeches that set the nerves and blood on edge. I slid my hand into my satchel, putting my hand on my pen knife – a blade less than an inch long, but made of such quality metal, and taking such an edge, that it would go through any man's jugular if I merely brushed his throat.

Jian thwacked two of the nearer sailors with his staff, kicked the man on the deck, and over his loud screaming, evidently ordered the others to drag him away. Whether to punishment or medical treatment was unclear. Jian swung on his heel, exclaimed '*Duìbùqî!*' as clearly as he evidently could, and scratched at his tied-back hair, plainly puzzled at how to get through to me.

With as much of what I could remember of Turkish, Carthaginian Latin, and the Venetian trade patois, I attempted to describe the assault.

Jian finally beamed, and nodded. He tried several languages, before a combination allowed him to make himself almost understood. 'You are not a masterless slave?'

I opened my mouth to try every word for 'freeman' I could remember, thought of Rekhmire' repeating *we are all eunuch slaves here*, and settled for pointing at the main cabin. 'Master Rekhmire'.'

The Egyptian name puzzled him until I mimed someone taller, broader, and – with a chop of the edge of my hand, down at kilt-level – eunuch. Jian grinned.

I pointed at the steps leading up to the rear poop deck, gestured for Jian to sit, and tapped my chalk against the new paper.

I was still sitting there, drawing yet another of the surrounding crowd of sailors, when Rekhmire' came out to find me.

The sun stood further down the sky. The tide smelled of weed. Jian cleared the audience and I stood up, brushing fruitlessly at the chalk and charcoal that marked the front of my linen robe, and handed the latest sketch off to the remaining Chin sailor. He bowed, repetitively, and ran off. He might have been holding the paper upside down – I wasn't sure if these people could see, in any real sense, how I put things down on paper, but their desire for a souvenir from the mad foreign slave evidently overcame their lack of understanding.

'Are we leaving?' Buckling my leather case, and slinging it over my shoulder, I glanced hurriedly around.

Even if not allowed back on board, I have enough to keep the Pharaoh-Queen's philosophers happy. But – there is so much more—!

'For the moment, we leave.' Rekhmire' beckoned his clerks, and swung himself on his crutch with the appearance of calm, towards the side of the great ship.

Falling back on the Iberian no man would understand but us, I asked, 'Did you find out why they're here? Are they a threat? Did the Admiral tell you what they want here?'

The Egyptian reached out and rested his arm across my shoulders, letting me take a substantial amount of his weight. I was momentarily startled. Clearly he found this physically wearing.

But to Jian, it will hardly hurt to have us appear master and slave again. And that is how he will take this.

Rekhmire' gave me a brief smile all friendship and relief. I concluded myself not the only one glad to be leaving. He reached for the ropes of the cradle in which, it was evident, they intended to lower us to our own vessel.

Looking over the heads of the Chin sailors, he murmured, 'I *can* tell you why this ship is here in Alexandria.'

'You can?'

I let them tie us in to the leather sling like luggage, closing my eyes against the distance from deck to sea.

Rekhmire"'s voice spoke Iberian in my darkness, as the ropes jolted and lifted.

'The Admiral was clear enough about that. Although other things are less clear. But I think I believe him as regards this. This ship is here, in this port – because they are lost.'

12

'Lost?'

The Pharaoh-Queen Ty-ameny gave Rekhmire' a look that could have melted Venetian glass, never mind smashed it.

My drawings lay spread out over the pink marble tiles of this one of her private chambers. She had questioned me extensively about each sketch. And now, when Rekhmire' answered her question . . .

'Lost,' she repeated flatly.

'Yes. And seeking a route back to this empire of theirs,' Rekhmire' said equably. 'Which, as far as I can make out, is called "Chin". Thousands of leagues to the east. Past Tana—'

That name was one I recognised, having often heard the Venetians mention it: a port in the north-eastern part of the Black Sea.

'—at the end of wherever the Silk Road goes.'

I think Ty-ameny and I stared at him with precisely the same expression.

'As for why they're here . . . They became lost during a storm; I'm uncertain where. But they can at least navigate well enough to sail towards the sunrise, and sailing east has finally brought them to Alexandria. It's clear to them that there's more sea beyond here.' Rekhmire''s nod indicated the vast window, and the eastern horizon beyond the Golden Horn. 'They think they can sail to Chin on the Black Sea waters. They have no idea that it's a closed sea. And that there's nothing but land beyond the easternmost Turkish ports.'

'And you . . . '

'I have said nothing of that, as yet.'

It would be strange, I thought, to have no idea of what the Middle Sea looks like.

True, no two charts I'd ever seen in a shop had ever got the shape of the lands the same – or put them in quite the same place, come to that – but the names of ports, the number of leagues and days' sailing between them, the knowledge of rocks and reefs and pirates . . . All these were, if not precisely known, still capable of making a shape in my mind's eye.

I imagined Zheng He and his great ship creeping along from headland to headland, as the trireme had, but with no pilot. Sometimes lost out of sight of land . . . losing his course if a storm made his lodestone useless . . .

As to where they might have sailed before they got here, what seas there may be between the Middle Sea and the place where the Silk Road ends – for that, I have no shape in my mind at all.

I thought of the Admiral's horse. Four or five curves and strokes of a brush. Like nothing I have ever seen.

Aloud, I stated, 'They're not lying if they say they come from very far away.'

The small Egyptian woman pulled her feet up onto the cushions on the marble ledge, tucking her legs under her. She leaned her chin on her hand. Ty-ameny of the Five Great Names might have been a robin's egg, with her freckles spattered across her nose. Certainly her eyes had the same lively bird-like look to them.

'They're lost.' She made the admission with clear reluctance.

Rekhmire' shrugged, in a way that made it clear that the magnitude of it didn't escape him. 'He and the interpreters and I aren't always in accord, but if I'm understanding Admiral Zheng He, his ship was driven through what I would guess are the Gates of the Hesperides, past Gades, some time last winter. Since then, he's been sailing about the Middle Sea.'

Including the Adriatic. The memory of what I had thought an optical illusion was strong. I wondered if Leon would add more in *De Pictura* on how you can have something directly under your eye and still be unable to see what it truly is.

'Looking for a way out.' Ty-ameny corrected herself. 'A way *east*.'

She frowned up at Rekhmire', who prodded with the ferrule of his crutch among the spread-out papers.

'Is it as simple as that?'

'Possibly.' The book-buyer glanced at the Pharaoh-Queen, a frown indenting his brows. 'Look at what Ilario's drawn. It's more than possible this Zheng He's been at sea as long as he says he has, given the clear evidence of wear on the ship. He has trade goods from Africa in his hold. *And* goods from the far southern coasts of the Persians. It would take a strong sea to sink that ship. He naturally wouldn't show me his charts, but it's possible he's come by sea from the land where the Silk Road ends.'

Since there was an obvious one unspoken, I appended, 'But?'

'But . . . He may be lying. Or exaggerating for threat's sake. Or – well.' Without asking permission, the tall Egyptian shuffled himself along the bench, settling ultimately on the cushions within an arm's reach of the Pharaoh-Queen.

She put her tiny hand on his arm. 'Well?'

Rekhmire' looked down at my spread-out papers, his brow creased with more than worry. 'Well, there is nothing here to confirm or deny it . . . but what the Admiral Zheng He claims is that when he was driven before the great storm, he was separated from the rest of his fleet.'

Ty-ameny did precisely what I did, I noticed a moment later: stared at the palace window overlooking the harbour, as if she could see through the city's massive walls, and the darkening evening, into the heart and mind of the foreign man aboard the foreign ship.

'"Fleet",' she echoed, a little derisively.

Rekhmire' linked his broad, large fingers, and looked down at his hands. 'Which he claims is made up of ships the same or similar tonnage to this one we have out there. He exaggerates, of course, because that is what a man will do. But—'

Ty-ameny slapped his shoulder, as if she were no more than a younger sister to him.

'How *many*?'

'His lost fleet,' Rekhmire' said, 'he claims to consist of two hundred ships.'

A silence filled the royal chambers.

Ty-amenhotep of the Five Great Names snorted, the sound remarkably like any camel's bad temper down in Constantinople's marketplaces.

'Two *hundred*? Oh, he might at least tell a convincing lie!'

She sprang up, absently turned on her heel, and paced with that control of the space about her that I have grown used to seeing among powerful men. Seeing the same gestures in a woman—

As I also rose to my feet out of respect, I realised, *Now I know how disconcerted men and women feel, when they lay eyes on me.*

'Two dozen would be bad enough!' she grumbled. 'And even two would pose a danger. Is it significant that this foreign admiral feels he must boast?'

One wall of this particular room was carved with bas-reliefs and cartouches in red and blue. At least some of the sculptors, I saw, had chosen to depict Old Alexandria falling to that Turk who had kept his defeated enemies in iron cages. Constantinople would never need, behind its vast walls, to be concerned with similar enemies. But more than one ship like Zheng He's . . .

Rekhmire' reached for his crutch, but sank back at her gesture. He confirmed my thoughts. 'Not only is Zheng He lost, but lost among men not at all like him. I think he lies and exaggerates no more than any other commander.' The book-buyer shrugged. 'But then, we have hardly been allowed to see everything on the ship.'

I had been permitted to bring only one thing away, apart from my drawings for Ty-ameny – a tiny cup, no larger than a child's hand, in which Jian had served me a colourless and fairly insipid wine. Showing it to the Pharaoh-Queen had gathered some admiration. The ceramic was light and translucent enough that when, as now, I put my finger inside the empty cup, I could see its shadow through the side.

Ty-amenhotep raised her voice to call for more servants to light sweet-smelling oil lamps; she and Rekhmire' spoke of court politics; and I sat regretting the terre verte pigment lost in Venice – using egg tempera on a gesso ground, I might have begun to make an attempt at capturing the glaze's pearlescent shine, along with its transparency. Although that is a task for a master, which as yet I am not.

Masaccio, making colour value into mass and form . . .

The master that should see this is dead.

I wondered, then, the word in my mind, whether the Master of Mainz would also be housed with us. Or whether the Pharaoh-Queen's 'Royal Mathematicians' – as she named her natural philosophers – would have him all night explaining his printing-*machina*.

Standing wearied me, but Ty-ameny continued her pacing. I rubbed my hand across my eyes, the darkness behind my eyelids welcome.

The familiar drag and click of Rekhmire''s crutches let me know he had risen.

I opened my eyes to see him join Ty-ameny at her window, overlooking the vast city.

'Sidon?' he suggested, naming a port that I thought somewhere west and south of us. 'They might leave their ship and march home along the Silk Road.'

'I wish they might leave their ship here!' Ty-ameny gave her cousin her gamin grin. 'But if I were the captain, I wouldn't be parted from it. Besides, can you imagine sailors asked to turn soldier and march all those thousands of leagues? Never mind what they carry as cargo.'

The lamp-lit chamber was comfortable, even if it dwarfed the book-buyer and the Pharaoh-Queen with its high ceiling and vast blocks of masonry that made up the walls. I felt not only at ease, I realised, but as if it were familiar.

Because neither Ty-amenhotep nor Rekhmire' take exception to my presence?

As Rodrigo's King's Freak, it never surprised me to be involved in court business in Taraco, although I steered clear of factions. That I could fall into the same pattern here, as Rekhmire''s scribe and Queen Ty-ameny's artist, felt similarly comfortable.

'Great Queen,' I suggested, into the perfumed silence, that was broken only by the noise of voices and vehicles in the city below. 'I think the Admiral desires charts. His officer Jian was speaking of them.'

She nodded, receiving the suggestion equably. 'Not to give too much aid at first – Rekhmire', if I send you with maps of the coast here, and the waters to the east; let him see land-maps that show the road to Aleppo and other Turkish cities. I think it's well this Zheng He begins to believe they're at the other end of their trade route with us.'

'Us barbarians.' Rekhmire' made the addendum gravely.

The Pharaoh-Queen gave him a look.

'That's what he calls us.' Rekhmire' smiled down at Ty-ameny. 'The Admiral Zheng He says their empire has lasted five thousand years. Older than Carthage.'

'Five thousand years of emperors? And two hundred giant ships?' The Pharaoh-Queen craned to look around the carved stone frame of the window, at pale light behind the gathering clouds. 'I suppose they have a trading colony on the moon, too!'

I risked mimicking Rekhmire''s equable look. 'That would explain why they don't look like anyone else, Great Queen. Or draw or paint like anyone else.'

Ty-amenhotep of the Five Great Names glanced from me to Rekhmire', and stalked past us, back into the room to flop down on the nearest seat. 'Cousin, either you've been too much in Ilario's company, or Ilario has been too much in yours!'

The book-buyer gave me a more relaxed smile than I had seen since we boarded the trireme in Venice.

He seated himself again on the marble bench, collecting silk pillows with his free hand and stuffing them behind his back. I joined him. He beckoned for my drawings, and ink and chalk-work, and the two of them bent over my efforts again.

Jian had taken some of the Admiral's scrolls out for me to look at. Delicate, as if the colour had been put on with spring water, or spring light. Language didn't allow him to explain how.

As well as sketching all aspects that I could see of their great cistern-shaped hull, I'd paced out the distances across the deck and made a quiet note of the measurements. Looking at the Pharaoh-Queen Ty-ameny as she scribbled furiously on a wax tablet, I thought her as capable as her Alexandrine 'philosopher-scientists' of working out the exact tonnage of Zheng He's ship. And the offensive power of the ship's cannon (cast out of recognisable bronze), and their engines that shot great long iron bolts (if I could judge by the ammunition stores).

Among the scattered papers I saw my drawings of two-handed ceramic containers, that might have been pots for oil or wine, but – from Jian's ardent keenness to remove me from their vicinity – I knew must be weapons as well. They looked as if they could be fused. Some parts of the hull stores had the distinctive scent of gunpowder.

Still, I thought, hauling my ankles up to sit cross-legged among the cushions beside Rekhmire'. Magnificent as it is, it's only one ship. It can't threaten to take on the navy here and bombard Constantinople's walls down . . .

Unless the rest of the hypothetical fleet turn up.

And then even Carthage and Venice will be pushed to hold on to sea-power in the Middle Sea.

By the window, a patch of moonlight progressed across the shining stone floor.

I watched it, in silence unbroken except by the rustling of paper. My hands felt oddly empty, since they held neither a stylus nor Onorata.

There has been little enough time, I thought, rubbing at the gravel that seemed to be collecting in my eyes. Little enough time since we landed, and all of it taken up by the Admiral of the Ocean Seas, but—

Sooner or later I must ask her.

Must ask the Pharaoh-Queen of New Alexandria, *How do I make the Aldra Pirro Videric into the First Minister of Taraconensis again?*

'—Ilario?'

The Pharaoh-Queen was turning back from dismissing a beardless fat man who I took to be a eunuch servant. By the sound of her voice, it was not the first time she had asked.

I straightened myself up beside Rekhmire', piqued that he had not used the elbow I was leaning against to nudge me into greater attention. 'Yes, Great Queen?'

'The hour's late.' Her eyes shone darkly in the many lamps' light. 'And it's a poor reward for you helping me with the foreigners' ship. But I need, urgently, to speak to you. Will you tell me everything that you experienced with Carthage's stone golem?'

13

We left Rekhmire' with a dozen of the Queen's Royal Mathematicians, checking calculations and speculations regarding the ghost ship.

A tall and unusually thin eunuch mathematician by the name of Ahhotep joined Ty-ameny at her signal, walking the palace's corridors quickly enough beside me that his linen robe flicked against my bare ankles. Two slaves took lamps ahead, light shading from terracotta to burnt-earth colours up the carved walls.

If I had been paying closer attention, I could have overheard what Ty-ameny and her black-haired adviser spoke of. Weariness and fear kept me concentrating on putting one foot before the other and falling over neither.

I wondered if Tottola had needed to call Ramiro Carrasco to feed Onorata, and whether she was asleep or screaming.

Cool air touched my forehead. It was not until I saw sky above a wide courtyard that I realised we had left the main palace. Obelisks blotted out stars and moon.

Ahhotep glanced back at me with a friendly smile. The moonlight caught the fine silver chain about his neck, that all the bureaucrats wore symbolic of their slavery. He pointed to one side and a dimly-seen frontage. 'The Royal Library.'

It might have been part of the palace or separate; I would not be able to see unless by daylight.

The pressure of air at my right hand was suddenly less; I guessed at an empty outdoor area, perhaps a larger public square. Our footsteps came clicking back from a nearer wall – except for Ty-ameny, barefoot and noiseless.

What caught my interest, through the ache in my muscles, was that Ty-ameny stopped by the vast doors of a final building, and dismissed her slaves, taking one of the lamps into her own hands.

The Pharaoh-Queen of the Lion-Throne can walk around at night without guards . . .

Either that argues a devout respect for the Queen, unlike that in other kingdoms, or – it belatedly occurred – her guards might merely be very good at keeping themselves out of sight.

Ahhotep opened a postern gate, bowing Ty-ameny and myself through. Inside, the lamp's inadequate light showed the curves of vast pillars, set close together. I could not see their tops. The eunuch mathematician took the lamp from the Queen and led the way forward, out across an open space tiled in red and blue and gold.

'Throne room,' Ty-ameny murmured, as if she too were reluctant to disturb the silence.

Ahhotep suddenly held up the oil-lamp.

I found myself facing the Carthaginian golem.

'*Ilario!*'

The female voice sounded sharp, but with concern. I fought to throw dizziness off and move in response.

Mosaic tiles were hard under my hands and knees.

I sat back, falling heavily to one side. Ty-ameny thrust a cloth at me. The eunuch Ahhotep returned out of the darkness with a bucket, and began spilling sand over something on the floor that the lamplight did not clearly show.

My throat felt raw. The taste of vomit was disgusting in my mouth.

'I ought to have realised!' Ahhotep sounded as if he were repeating himself. 'Great Queen, I'm so sorry! Master Ilario, how can I apologise!'

I dimly remember Rekhmire' once mentioning that the Royal Library kept fire-buckets of sand in every room. Evidently it was a practice throughout the palace complex.

I doubt he ever imagined them being used to cover up sick.

I pushed my heels against the tiny ridges of the mosaic, edging back. Wiping the cloth over my mouth took away some of the taste.

Only yards away from me, at the edge of the lamplight, stood feet too large for life-size – but skilfully painted in the colours of flesh.

The stone feet of the Carthaginian golem rested immovably against the floor. The shadows hid its height, but I glimpsed a curve of reflected light on its fingers, where its hands hung by its sides.

'I should have realised!' Ahhotep moaned again.

My own realisation was closer to *I wish to hit Ahhotep.*

The golem stood, half-painted, beside the Queen's ancient stone throne. Under other circumstances, the carved porphyry block would have been impressive in itself: a dark purple stone, the seat worn down into a deep dip by dynasty upon dynasty of Pharaohs. But the crystalline glitter in the rock could not take my eye from the painted golem.

Like a Venetian harlequin.

I'd forgotten we hadn't finished the face.

In the gold lamp-light, one blind stone eye looked at me. The other was painted to have the brilliance of life. Lustrous and brown and my stomach rose again, threateningly, as I recognised it – the evident model for the painted stonework was Masaccio's eyes, where he had begun to give its face some touches of a self-portrait.

I wiped the cloth hard across my lips.

160

If I'd thought anything, after Menmet-Ra's arrival at the Alexandrine house, it was that Ty-ameny must have had one of her craftsmen finish off the painting here. I'd even imagined asking, with insouciant gallows humour, 'What butcher did you get to finish this paint job?'

Instead I throw up, like a child.

'You know that it killed the master I was apprenticed to?'

Ty-ameny moved her bird-boned shoulders in a shrug. 'Yes. I regret that. *You* know, that if I had a choice, I'd wrap in anchor-chain and dump it in the Bosphorus!'

Ahhotep fumbled in the sleeves of his robes, bringing out a stylus and wax tablets. 'The diplomatic representatives of Carthage would notice, Great Queen, and we dare not seem afraid of anything they offer us. Master Ilario, anything you can tell us will be helpful. Don't worry what Lord Menmet-Ra may have reported before. Just begin at the start, in your own words.'

Climbing to my feet, I realised I recognised the gleam in the skinny eunuch's eye. *It is Masaccio's.*

I thought of Rome; the chill of early autumn. If Tommaso Cassai had had the chance to hear about this golem, would he have cared if it had killed a man before?

In all truth – no, he would not.

And this Ahhotep, black hair cut at jaw-level and wearing formal Alexandrine robes, might have been the Florentine painter's blood brother in that respect.

All my muscles tensed, every tendon; every nerve on edge.

If that thing moves, I will be out of this throne room so fast—

I thought it not impossible it might have connected itself to me, somehow, in the embassy at Rome; that my presence might move it to act.

Fear moved me to recklessness. I picked the lamp up from where Ahhotep had stood it on the dais of the throne, and held it close to the golem. This close, the light showed me every scratch on the bronze and brass metalwork of the joints.

The nobles of Carthage being what they are, Ty-ameny will have been put in possession of the words to make it move.

Even if she will not use them.

'The paint looks absurd.' Mimic skin and veins and hair as it might, you may as well put a ribbon on a boulder. 'This is nothing more nor less than a weapon, no matter what shape it is.'

Ty-ameny stepped lightly up the carved porphyry steps and sat on the throne, a yard from the golem. The lamp cast shadows in the sockets of her eyes.

'If we're very lucky,' she observed flatly, 'whatever madman wrought this in Carthage can only make a few of them. A handful. Not dozens.

Because if you see these on the field of battle, in numbers . . . If I see them outside this city's walls . . . '

Honorius had seen my one partial rendering of the stone golem (done out of memory), and instantly remarked, *A man armoured invulnerably at every point!* And after a pause, had added, *Who can't be stopped by wounds. Only hacked to pieces.*

I repeated this aloud.

Ahhotep looked as if he had suffered six weeks with a fever. Stress drew dark lines down from his nose to the corners of his mouth.

'I fear it badly enough, Master Ilario.' He put his hand on the edge of the purple throne, glancing at Ty-ameny. 'As her Great Name knows, I fear seeing this thing come to life and kill the Queen. Tell us what you know.'

I told him everything.

What I thought I could not remember, his questions prodded out of me. The night turned on, oil in the lamp guttering, until at last I was telling my story in the dark. I couldn't shut my eyes hard enough to prevent hot tears leaking out from under the lids. *Masaccio. Sulva.* And where is her bride-piece statue, now?

Ty-ameny became gradually silent.

I fretted. *I am telling her nothing she does not already know.*

An urgent need for sleep weighed me down, but I felt an unexpected sympathy for the Pharaoh-Queen – I, at least, need not ever see the monstrous thing again; she must have the golem beside her throne whenever she gives audience.

'Could it not have sunk on the ship coming from Rome?' I finally blurted out.

A new oil-lamp flared to light under Ahhotep's hands. By it, I saw that Ty-ameny smiled. She shook her head. 'Too many spies and gossips have seen it here.'

The gleam of light on stone disturbed me.

'It needs painting, Great Queen. Could it not be in a workshop, instead of standing beside the throne?'

Ahhotep came forward, one hand fiddling with his neck-chain. 'The Carthaginian envoy is expected. He will expect to see the gift where protocol demands it should be.'

'For the same reason,' Ty-ameny put it, with a gloomy cheerfulness that reminded me much of Rekhmire', 'we can neither set it in Roman concrete nor forge chains around it.'

'Can't you—' I waved a hand, frustrated. 'Restrain it secretly, in some way?'

'If there is such a way, none of my Royal Mathematicians have advised me of it.'

Silence fell. It had been quiet some time when I heard Ahhotep's sandals on the mosaic, diminishing away from us. Before I could

162

formulate a question, I heard the creak of a door opening. A larger postern door, by the faint light that streamed in from it, wet and chill with dew. The sun has risen.

'From what you tell me,' Ty-ameny observed quietly, '*any* man may have the word that orders the stone man to act. I need not go to the trouble of banning all Carthaginians from the court, because they might send anyone. One of their own, or not.'

Raw-throated from speech, now, I nodded my agreement.

'I need to stay alive.' The woman pushed herself up, weight on her wrists, and stepped stiffly down from the throne. Unselfconsciously, she reached up to link her arm in mine, walking us both towards the door.

The flagstones outside were dry of dew already. The sky was a perfect infinite blue, and the sun not yet risen.

'I don't mean that I don't want to die.' She made a small smile, evidently a strain. 'Although I don't. But I need to live out this generation, and I need my daughter to rule the next one. And not just for Alexandria's sake.'

She looked at me with some concern.

'You need to sleep. But we'll go back by way of the Library – Ahhotep, go tell them we're coming – because there are things I need to discuss with you.'

Passing the building last night had given me no idea of its size. The lemon-coloured light of the dawn illuminated roof on roof, storey on storey, of the Royal Library; and I suspected that the obelisk-fronted door we entered by was only one of many opening into a library complex.

Inside, the stone of walls and floor shone pale, echoing daylight through the corridors and halls. Stepping over the threshold, I was hit by the scent of parchment, papyrus, scrolls . . . Plunged into memory of the scriptorium in Rodrigo Sanguerra's castle.

Our steps echoed. I followed Ty-ameny's small figure through gallery after gallery of leather scroll-cases, lost among squat pillars and vast square-lintelled archways. The rooms grew smaller and scruffier after a while, and the Queen called greetings to eunuch clerks already at their desks, doing reconstruction work on old papyruses. Cheerful voices called out from one chamber to the next.

About the time I thought we'd run out of building – and owned myself completely lost – Ty-ameny turned sharply right and loped up a flight of sandstone steps, that were less surprisingly worn away into a dip in the middle.

The arch at the top opened into a bright gallery. Carved windows opened into a piazza below us.

No books. No scrolls. *Because the light would fade them.* They want good light for . . .

'The printing-*machina*.'

The Pharaoh-Queen's subjects must have been working through the night. Herr Mainz – Herr Gutenberg – stood beside a wooden frame, gesturing expansively, and broke off to grin like a badger at Ty-ameny.

'Great Queen! We should have it finished before the end of today. Or at least the prototype.'

Ty-ameny strode up to stand beside him, not even as high as his shoulder. Her eyes glittered as she appeared to follow his report of his progress.

'You also know how this works?' she demanded of me.

Gutenberg stroked blunted fingers over a tray of metal type. 'Messer Ilario does not. No man but I, not even in my Guild.'

Storms on the voyage through the Aegean might have robbed Ty-ameny of her printing-*machina*; likewise the cholera and plague endemic to large cities. I thought perhaps Ty-ameny might persuade him to write his plans down, where I had failed.

Ty-ameny smiled at him. Her tiny ruddy-skinned hand stroked the printing-*machina*'s frame as if it were a blood-horse.

'Not the details. The meaning. That in the time the scriptorium takes to copy a scroll once, I can have you set the type to print the same words. And in the time it takes to copy a scroll *twice* – I can have five hundred copies, printed and ready!'

She wiped her fingers down her plain linen robes, seemingly unaware of the black grease.

Gutenberg very precisely explained, in a mixture of German and bad Carthaginian Latin, how it would take longer to set up his lead letters the first time than to copy them on paper, but after that . . . Ty-ameny clearly wasn't listening. As Gutenberg went back to his machine, she took my arm, gazing up into my face, and pointed.

'You see that?'

I stared into an empty corner of the gallery.

'A bucket.' Embarrassed by memory of what happened in the throne room, I added, 'Master Rekhmire' told me – you have them in every room here, because of the fear of fire.'

I thought of Masaccio's cluttered workshop, full of wooden frames, canvas, pigments, oils, buckets of sand and water. The same principle, even if he had appeared to work in chaos.

Ty-ameny released my arm.

'Yes. We have buckets. Water and sand. And all the walls are masonry. And there are courtyards between various buildings in the complex, to act as firebreaks, and cellars below, insulated from one another by the living rock. Because these walls are piled high and stuffed full with papyrus, vellum, paper . . . Everything flammable. Even our shelves are carved out of stone.'

Her gaze searched out Gutenberg's tray of lead letters.

'There have been minor fires before. We've lost scrolls. Scrolls that were the last copies of their work. And it doesn't matter how many clerks I put into the scriptorium, they won't catch up the copying of four thousand years of collecting. And one day, one day . . . One day everything we have will burn.'

Finding myself close enough to the wall to touch it, I ran a finger down a seamless masonry join. 'You can't know that—'

Ty-ameny's head jerked up, as if she woke from a deep sleep or vision. 'I can!'

Ahhotep muttered something; she chopped her tiny hand down in a surprisingly fierce gesture. She turned sloe-dark eyes on me, and I was not conscious of her small stature.

'If there's no great fire, still, we're not as great a power as we once were. Conquerors will pass through with fire and sword. It will be Carthage or the Turks,' she added, with a flat pragmatic certainty.

I was unsure that Gutenberg understood her Alexandrine Latin; he straightened and frowned at her.

Ty-ameny paced to the window, and it did not change her dignity in the least that she must stand up on her toes to stare out at the city below.

'Cousin Rekhmire' could have told you this, but I see he has been circumspect. Still, it's not a secret among my advisers. We were a great empire – once. Now we have only one city, with no hinterland. The Turks have taken our old lands, and nibble away at our borders here. And Carthage is jealous of any sea-power not hers.'

Her hand gripped the sculpted frame possessively.

'I'd counted on having my reign and my daughter's before someone takes this city and burns it. Time enough to copy the most valuable volumes here – or at least some of them. I no longer believe we have two generations. I may be the last of the line of Pharaohs. But now I have *this*—'

She turned about, her gaze hungry on Gutenberg and the *machina*.

'Now – we can turn out a flood of knowledge! Copies of every scroll and book and document in the Royal Library – many copies. I'll send them as royal gifts to the kings of Francia and Persia and Carthage if I have to. I'll sell them cheap through Venice. This city will send out so many copies that no fire or war or shipwreck or disaster can ever destroy every copy of a work. This knowledge will *not* be lost.'

Between the Egyptian Ahhotep and Gutenberg, Ty-ameny appeared the size of a child. Speaking, there was enough desperate energy in her to make someone three times her size.

I should ask if I can paint her!

Hard on the heels of that came another realisation.

'You don't mean that Alexandria will fall some day in the far-off future, do you, Great Queen? You expect it in our lifetime.'

In her lifetime.

In mine.

In Onorata's . . .

'Soon,' Ty-amenhotep said. 'But I'll sell printed scrolls to the Franks, to North Africa, to Persia and the Silk Road. Pages for pennies. If not for the fact that men don't value what they don't pay for, I'd give them away! But every ducat that they earn, I swear I'll turn to hiring more scribes, and building more of Herr Mainz's machines!'

I grew up hearing stories of Constantinople as a city great beyond all cities of the earth, last home of Pharaonic Egypt, repository of occult knowledge, free market of traders from every country in Europe and Africa, and from impossibly distant Turkey and Hind . . .

Hearing a very little of the hollowness of that image in her tone, a shiver went down my spine. I thought of Alexandrine Constantinople's thick walls reduced to rubble and dust – but their inheritance, a river of knowledge, flowing out first to all the quarters of the earth.

Ty-ameny beamed at the German.

'We'll need many of these machinae. I think I can persuade my council to give you whatever funds you need. How long will it take you to train apprentices?'

'Herr Mainz' was reduced to a burbling, beaming mess in the next few minutes. I moved to stand aside with Ahhotep by the vast masonry windows, and smiled. It's pleasing to see someone get their heart's desire.

'Master Ilario.' Ahhotep had his elbows on the window-ledge, the dawn's brightness falling on his soft skin.

I followed his gaze. In that direction, I saw there was indeed an open square of sorts; a public plaza. Great wide steps led down to the city below – which made me conclude the squat black building that we faced, now, was that throne room of Ty-ameny's where the golem stood.

'Suppose,' the tall eunuch muttered, 'he has no time to set up printing machinae, because the stone monster has turned on the Pharaoh-Queen and killed her?'

I need not turn to look at Ty-amenhotep to remember how small she is, barely coming up to my breast.

All of us are that small in front of the stone golem.

'Would Carthage dare kill your queen? Other kingdoms would condemn them—'

Ahhotep shrugged. 'Evidently, if they *can* do it, they *may* do it.'

I protested, 'And you won't dispose of it, you won't chain it up—'

Ahhotep indicated the direction of the harbour with one long clean finger. 'Show ourselves afraid, and you'd see the Carthaginian fleet in the Bosphorus in a month!'

Frustration boiled up in me. I waved a hand at the library complex about us. 'Old Egypt was always supposed to be the heart of occult knowledge. Don't you have – I don't know – ancient Egyptian magic! Can't you bind the golem with invisible chains?'

Ahhotep looked at me as if I were a child. '"Magic"?'

Somewhat defensively, I muttered, 'My child was born by Caesarean in Venice; there was a priest there who swore *that* was magic—'

'Miracle,' Ahhotep interrupted. 'If I know Green priests. Miracle, not magic. Yes. The Franks do show a distressing capacity, on occasion, for circumventing what is possible.'

The eunuch stared thoughtfully at my lower abdomen, in the manner of a man pondering autopsies.

'I suppose,' he said diffidently, 'you would not be willing to let me see your scar?'

Once here, with Rekhmire''s favour keeping a roof over my head – and faced with a plain curiosity from Ahhotep that I must recognise from the mirror – matters seemed different.

'Prod away,' I offered, resignedly reaching for the fastening of my linen robe.

Ahhotep took me into one of the side-chambers of the gallery, making copious notes and little cries of excitement. I listened to Ty-amenhotep and Master Gutenberg, outside, discussing which manuscripts might best be set in type first.

I continued to worry obsessively at the matter of the stone golem.

14

I woke, finally, to Attila pacing the length of the immense chamber, soothing Onorata, singing some obscene song that he and his brother had concocted about 'Admiral Black-Eyes'.

I can only pray for her to remember none of this when she grows up!

He supported my baby's head well, but he walked up and down more roughly than I would have done. Every so often he stopped to show her bas-reliefs, and cartouches painted in red and blue on the walls. I was unsure she could see so far yet.

'I'll feed her,' I offered, staggering up and seizing a robe.

Her body was warmly solid in my arms; it was no hardship to sit on a couch by the wide windows, with a towel thrown over me, and let her coo and slurp over the sloppy gruel that Carrasco thought should be her introduction to anything other than goat's milk. Had we been going by the clock, it would have been an early evening meal.

The familiar drag and click of Rekhmire''s crutches let me know he had come into the room. He paused beside me to brush his fingers over Onorata's forehead.

Her translucent eyelids closed, hiding the blue of her eyes. They had begun to remind me of Honorius's eyes, though not as pale and wind-washed as the man who had sat around far too many military camp-fires.

'Ty-ameny would like you aboard the Admiral's ship at least once more.' He wiped his sticky hand on my towel, and smiled down at me. 'If you'll draw for her.'

'Oh, I'll draw.'

Rekhmire' thudded down onto the marble bench edging the room, and unexpectedly held out his arms for Onorata. I put her into his lap, and began to clean up myself and my surroundings, while he sat among embroidered cushions telling her stories of Lion-Headed Sekhmet (who apparently punishes evil-doers), and Ra Son-of-the-Sun, and the steersman on the Boat of the Dead.

'You don't need to draw,' he remarked. 'The Queen would consider any request about Taraconensis from you on its own merits.'

'I hope the brat pees on you,' I observed. 'And do you really think I *don't* want to go back on Zheng He's ship?'

'I was unsure.' He beamed up at me. 'But at least, while I'm holding your child, you can neither hit me nor throw things at me!'

I considered the bowl holding remnants of Onorata's food, narrowly dismissed the temptation, and by way of pointing out certain errors in the book-buyer's reasoning, threw a cushion that missed my baby and caught him neatly on the ear.

Anyone who lives at court – King's Freak, or merely in attendance on the ruling powers – knows the necessity for every least adviser to have his say. I watched Ty-ameny recede into a crowd of Constantinople's eunuch bureaucrats over the next few days, on occasion taking Rekhmire' with her. I confined myself to drawing on board Admiral Zheng He's 'war-junk', as I understood him to call it, and left others to study the sketches.

I spent considerable time, when it was not too hot, on the city walls, and at the gates leading down onto the quays. Drawing gate-guards while I talked with them, and merchants; children playing complicated games with pebbles, musicians crouching in corners and playing for coins, sailors coming and going from the moored vessels. Onorata, under her cradle's sail-cloth awning, seemed to take notice of the movement, I thought.

Neither Attila nor Tottola seemed adverse to duties involving sitting down. On occasion, both the German men-at-arms would accompany me. Attila sloped off to see the Alexandrine slave from the *Sekhmet*, Asru. Tottola, on his off-hours, seemed to be working his way through the palace kitchens.

Something over a week later, we walked back to the palace in time to sleep through the scarifyingly hot hours between one and five in the afternoon, and I found Rekhmire' usefully present for conversation. He fell in beside me in the corridor, not having been out to Zheng He's ship for two days, and consequently rested enough that he used a silver-handled stout stick instead of crutches.

'Those twelve ships.' I nodded in what would have been the direction of the harbour, if cartouche-strewn corridors and bright paintings of Ra and Horus and Sekhmet hadn't got me turned around. 'The Greek-fire ships. That's all the Alexandrine navy, isn't it?'

The Egyptian opened our chambers' doors for me, and looked on while I put Onorata down to sleep. 'I believe there are two the other side of the Bosphorus, patrolling Turkish shores.'

I crossed the room almost on tiptoe, so she would not wake and grizzle. Sprawling down onto the sunken bench beside Rekhmire', I showed him a page of my sketchbook.

'Some of your old cannon on the city walls are bound with leather.'

When barrels are cast, not poured, they soak leather and wrap it around the muzzle-loading brass cannon-barrels, so that they won't burst with the first shot. I'd seen more than a few at old fortresses in the Taraconensis hills.

I hated to think what Honorius would say if anyone expected him to fight without iron cannon.

'You do realise?' Rekhmire' reached for the jug and glass standing beside him on the sunken seat. 'That most visitors aren't allowed to go where you go?'

'I realise that either Ty-ameny implicitly trusts your opinion of me, or someone is going to put my eyes out with hot irons before I leave. In case I should draw images again, once I'm far from Alexandrine Constantinople.'

'Ilario—' He halted, Venetian glass of watered wine halfway to his lips. 'She trusts my opinion.'

'And now you can tell me why.'

'I have long been loyal—'

'*No.*'

On such occasions, mere reassurance in words won't do; I saw him read that in me.

'I won't risk judicial mutilation just because you *think* your Queen trusts you, and by extension me. *Why* does she trust you?'

Rekhmire' put his glass down. He reached for his stick, pushing himself up onto his feet. Before I could complain at his leaving, he laid the stick back down on the bench, and tugged at the belt holding up his linen kilt. He folded the cloth down before I could speak.

Against his ruddy skin, I saw an ancient white scar, as wide as three fingers, just above his hip.

'Come here.' He beckoned, and reached around to his back.

Half-turned away from me, he looked over his shoulder, and eased down the pale cotton.

I saw he had a corresponding scar on his back, a little larger and more jagged. Frighteningly close to his kidney.

'I was big at fourteen.' He didn't readjust his linen wrap around his hips yet. 'And Ty-ameny had just reached the size she is now, though we are the same age. She trusts me because the sword only went through me far enough to give her a purely decorative scar.'

Cold sweat dampened my tunic between my shoulders and under my arms.

'You put yourself between her and a sword.' A wide enough blade, by the injury. He would need an Egyptian physician to survive that! 'It went *through* you . . . '

Rekhmire' turned back around, facing me, and traced the white irregularity in his skin. 'Some lord had very carefully chosen a number of the Royal Egyptian Guard who could be persuaded to revolt against their young Queen. I passed that information on, but didn't trust the minister who said it would be dealt with. Ty-ameny . . . '

'Decided you needed a career as a book-buyer?'

'Something very like that.'

'Well.' I shrugged. 'I suppose my eyes are safe enough, then.'

The cold sweat didn't go from my spine. Even jokes don't make that thought easier.

I looked up at the large Egyptian. 'I can see why Ty-ameny trusts you as she does.'

Rekhmire' smiled sardonically. 'I tell her it's foolish. Just because a man takes a wound for you once, you can't trust him the rest of his life! But she refuses to listen. I am . . . therefore careful about who I tell her *I* trust.'

That made me feel unaccountably warm.

Onorata interrupted from her cradle with a cough. I listened until I heard her even breathing resume.

'She could die.' I gave Rekhmire' my hand to clasp, so he could sit down again with more ease. 'That's what wakes me up sweating at nights. Fever. Cold. Anything. Nothing.'

'True enough. But she can also live.' Rekhmire' nodded towards the bench on the opposite side of the sunken area, at the failed egg tempera painting of Zheng He's porcelain cup and those other drawings that littered the area – and would do until more of Ty-ameny's bureaucrats came to remove them for study. 'Remember your family is building up a debt. The Queen owes you much.'

I may have looked irritated.

Rekhmire' sounded faintly apologetic. 'You were in King Rodrigo Sanguerra's court: I need not tell you any of this. When the moment comes, then you ask.'

'*What* do I ask for? "Would Constantinople like to step in and sort out the court of Taraco?" No! Would King Rodrigo like that? Frankly—' I bit my lip as Onorata grumbled in her sleep, and added, much more quietly, 'Frankly, *no*! And it would be a direct provocation to Carthage.'

Rekhmire' nodded, and ground the heel of one large hand against his eye and socket.

He surveyed the resulting smudge of kohl on his skin with disapprobation.

'First things first. You may come to the next council,' he added, not very much as though it were a suggestion.

'How long before Queen Ty-ameny deals with the Admiral and his ship?'

I did not add, *And can listen to pleas for help from book-buyers' assistants?* since the renewed accord between Rekhmire' and I seemed to make that redundant.

'A week or so. Certainly before the end of this lunar month.'

15

The smell hung heavy in the air, rich in the back of my throat where I couldn't choke it away.

It was a hot climate, for all the stone walls about us. Necessity put us on the Library's upper floors, to get the natural light. But that made this hotter than the earth-insulated cellars.

'Shall I turn that over for you?' The philosopher Bakennefi nodded down.

It is hardly the first dead body I've seen.

Not even the first body cut to pieces. I once managed to attend a public dissection in the university at Barcelona, along with two hundred other students, in the hopes of discovering what those lumps and bumps one sees while drawing the human body actually are, under the skin – and what they look like when there is no such surface.

Perhaps, I thought, it's that this small old man was obviously a slave.

Masaccio said that in the same way one can't draw robes without knowledge of the body underneath, it's not possible to draw skin without knowledge of muscle, tendon, ligament, bones.

'Yes: turn him.' I managed to get the words out without bringing up the bile at the back of my throat.

Bakennefi carefully turned over the dead man's skinned hand.

I set about drawing the uncovered tendons and muscles of the palm.

This Bakennefi was Bakennefi Aa, 'eldest', out of the three brother Royal Mathematicians who ran this department, along with Bakennefi Hery-ib ('he who is in the middle') and Bakennefi Nedjes ('small'). He had a watercolour of the autopsy in progress on the vast stone slab beside him. He painted it as delicately as if the dead body were a book opened for his enjoyment. There seemed to me to be little connection between the carefully-labelled bright organs and the slithery mass in the opened belly. But that may have been because I deliberately avoided looking closely.

I swatted at one of the ever-present flies.

The hum of the swarm was loud enough that a man had actually to raise his voice to be heard, despite the twenty or so slaves with fans waving the air above the stone slab clear.

Bakennefi Aa gave a last prod at the opened palm with his iron-hafted pen. 'Do you know, I think this one's done with? He's a little more past his time than I imagined.'

Sheer cowardice made me turn away and set about putting brushes, reeds, scrapers and paints away with my chalk in the leather snapsack. If I had to hear the sounds of the cloth being wrapped around the dissection body, and smell the sudden wash of stink as slaves lifted it, at least I need not look.

And the worst thing is that these drawings will be invaluable to me.

'You are good.' Queen Ty-ameny's light voice spoke behind me. I startled hard enough to drop a brush.

'I wonder you don't ask me for a commission,' she added.

Scrabbling hurriedly on the Library's marble floor, I stood up again, clutching the brush, flushed. Ty-ameny was standing on her toes looking at my painting. She glanced at me for an answer to her implied question.

'Why not?' She wore a simple linen tunic edged with purple, and her black eyes looked brightly at me. 'Why wouldn't you ask? I might agree.'

I stuttered, 'I grew up in a court, Aldro.'

No matter how small and provincial it might have been.

'There are always factions in a court,' I added, packing the brush away in its wooden box, and slipping that into my bag. 'Aldro Ty-amenhotep, I've been used to being next to a King, most of my adult life. Not that I had any power in Taraco. But even a Fool who has the King's ear gets courted.'

'Perhaps even more so.' Ty-ameny grinned, and tilted her head up, watching me. As if it were a familiar story, she murmured, 'Pay attention to any one man, and before you know it, you're on one side, and there are other sides, all of whom have reason to hate you. And whoever you listened to first, they don't trust you. I wondered,' she added, 'why you've stood so much in my cousin's shadow while you were here.'

I couldn't help a smile in response to hers. Rekhmire' wasn't liable to give his loyalty to a stupid ruler.

'I'm too used to being a King's—' *pet*. I chose a better word. '— associate. Kings don't awe me. That's sometimes unfortunate. Other lords have found me disrespectful in the past, because of what I'm used to. And any court faction you like to mention thinks I can be bribed or threatened. I find it better to stay in the background, where I can't give offence.'

The buzz of flies diminished, most of them giving up now and circling to find the open stone windows. Two slaves remained, waving fans made out of huge white feathers, and concealing the kind of relieved boredom that comes with not being ordered to any dirty or difficult task.

Ty-ameny walked over to the window, her thin arms folded across her chest. Gold bracelets flashed back points of light that left dots across my vision. She gazed out at the blue sky – at the sun she gravitated towards, I suddenly realised, at any moment she might.

'Divine Father Ra!' she muttered, either in prayer or exasperation. 'Ilario . . . You've done good work for me with Zheng He. As one of my court painters, here, you could afford to keep your daughter.'

Having occasionally had an oak door slammed in my face, I recognise that feeling of shock. Even if this is from a door opening.

'But . . . Master Rekhmire' will have told you my business in Iberia.'

'In broad detail.' The Pharaoh-Queen Ty-ameny rested her elbows on the stone sill.

The spreading gardens below had the air of something Roman. A stone maze beyond a hedge looked darker, a mass of obelisks and pyramids that I thought must be monuments or graves. Momentarily I pictured the ancient junipers growing in the dark, in Carthage's tophet. If I painted Baal's face now, could I get it right? Now there's Onorata?

Ty-ameny shifted herself around, looking a considerable way up to see my face. Under that study, I reached out to the silver basin on the sill, water warmed by the sun, and began to wash blood and paint from my hands.

The Pharaoh-Queen said, 'And what are your intentions towards Rekhmire'?'

A slave thrust a towel into my hands and I dropped it.

What?

The slave passed me another cloth. Mute through bewilderment, I dried my hands and returned it. Not that the droplets wouldn't have been sucked up by the sun in a few minutes.

'Intentions?' I forced myself to calmness. 'To help him wherever I can, Highness.'

She put her hand up on my forearm. Her fingers were as small as a twelve-year-old girl's, and her palm sandy and hot.

'It would displease me personally if Rekhmire' were deliberately hurt.'

Bakennefi had also examined me, at Ahhotep's request; both of them had found something to criticise and cluck over in the stitches removed from my lower belly. I will always bear the marks. Now I thought I heard Honorius and Rekhmire''s voices spontaneously chiming together: *Save the mother.*

Ty-ameny's clear small voice said, 'Suppose his duties take him to a different land, now? Suppose he were to leave Alexandria tomorrow? With the foreign ship?'

There was a sharp pain in the pit of my stomach, keen enough to make me wonder if Alexandrine food might not be suited to it.

Mouth dry, I thought, *Interesting – I would sooner he didn't leave.*

Rekhmire' no longer owns me as a slave. He brought me to Alexandria because he needed to come here himself. Yes, he will help solve the problem of Aldra Videric, but – not, perhaps, personally.

I must look bewildered and stupid, I realised, but I could find no words for this realisation I would have preferred to avoid.

174

The Pharaoh-Queen studied me with a sparrow-like tilt to her head. I thought it an even throw of the dice whether she would accept my silence, or have one of the sandal-hurling outbursts of temper that Egypt seems to permit its female rulers.

'Great Queen.' I wiped my hand over my face. Spots of colour told me I had missed spatters; I doused my fingers in the bowl and wiped water over my skin again. 'I . . . would still wish to help him.'

She gave a decided nod.

'We should talk of the future.' Her features a mask of distaste, she raised her free hand a fraction. 'Elsewhere.'

The nearest slave crossed the room instantly and bowed, giving her a scented cloth. I avoided the slave's eye. Even with the stone surface sluiced down, the stink of the dead slave still hung in this room. If this slave dies of age or sickness here, will he end up opened on a stone table?

'Bakennefi Aa wouldn't mind a look under *my* skin,' I said before I knew I was to be quite so honest.

Queen Ty-ameny frowned at me over her silk kerchief.

'I do hope you're careful about taking food and drink around him . . .'

Rekhmire' entered the chamber just as Queen Ty-ameny of the Five Great Names doubled up, giggling like a schoolgirl.

I folded my arms.

At Rekhmire''s raised brow, Ty-ameny pointed at me, waved a hand weakly in dismissal of the matter, and shot me a glance with more genuine apology than I have ever had from King Rodrigo.

'It's hardly fair,' she murmured. 'I'm Alexandria's queen; how much free interchange can there be between a queen and any other man or woman?'

Before I thought, I said, 'That's what I tell my slave.'

Rekhmire''s rumbled louder comment drowned me out. 'That's why I freed Ilario, cousin.'

The tiny woman smiled wryly. 'Well, no man is going to free me from the throne. And I don't think I would let them. Very well: we need to talk. The matter of Zheng He must be settled soon – before there is more trouble from Carthage.'

16

Pharaoh-Queen Ty-ameny of the Five Great Names sat small and erect, among cushions embroidered in blue and gold with her lineal ancestor Ra the Sun-God of Old Egypt.

The Admiral of the Ocean Sea, at last on shore, sat on her right-hand side, on the ochre marble ledge of the sunken area of her Council chamber, Jian beside him. Rekhmire' was next to Ty-ameny, then I on Rekhmire''s left hand, with half the eunuch bureaucracy beyond me. Zheng He's other officers and Alexandria's sea-captains and army-generals, at the end of the great chamber, shared space with Ty-ameny's natural philosophers and Royal Mathematicians, who kept papers and instruments and charts beside them on the low seat.

The Alexandrines might be old, young, fat, thin, eunuch, or – occasionally – intact male. What they all had in common was an intensity of gaze when it came to Zheng He.

Absently, I began to sketch Ty-ameny on the virgin wax surface of my tablet. She wore a gold mask that included the shape of a beard; less hot, I thought, to tie over her face than the hair-replica. I put the lines of Zheng He in beside her to give scale. She barely came up to his shoulder.

She is the only woman in the room. If you do not count the half of me.

I pushed other concerns out of my mind.

Because if Videric can reach out to harm me in the middle of Ty-ameny's court in Alexandria, I may as well give up now.

In fact, there was little enough said over the next hour that had not been said between Rekhmire' and Admiral Zheng He on the great war-junk. I came to the conclusion that the Admiral wanted to hear it from the mouth of – as he called her – 'the Great Foreign Empress'.

Rekhmire' himself finally caught Ty-ameny's eye, and hauled forward one of the sea-charts.

'In fact, noble Admiral, it is as the Great Queen of the Five Name's captains inform you. That enticing eastward-leading sea there, vast as it appears, will not take you further than Turkish ports close to Aleppo. And if you have maps of the land routes between your home and those cities, you will know that they are still hundreds of leagues distant from it; perhaps thousands.'

And full of Turks and Persians, though Rekhmire' said nothing of that. Ty-ameny might suppose this foreigner ultimately an ally of those more eastern powers.

Zheng He grunted, leaned forward to study the map, and waved Jian's formal polite thanks aside, interrupting his subordinate. 'Yes, I see, but why would I believe?'

Ty-ameny's face behind the mask would be fascinating to draw, I thought regretfully.

Rekhmire' smiled, inclining his head. 'Because if the Black Sea were the way to your home, New Alexandria would be asking you to pay the fee to pass the Bosphorus, great Admiral. As we do with all vessels passing to trade in the Black Sea.'

'And you don't charge us a fee in any case? And send us through and keep silent about—' Zheng He waved a huge hand at the charts. '—this bounded Black Sea of yours?'

Ty-ameny's voice issued from behind the full curved mouth of the golden mask of Ra. 'There is a reasonable chance that you and your ship would afterwards return here.'

Her rich tone showed her definitely amused, to anyone who knew her.

Rekhmire' smoothly added, 'This is the only route into, and out of, the closed sea. Forgive the Great Queen of the Five Names if she doesn't desire to have you and your great ship back here angry at perceived treachery. That would hardly be worth anything we could extort from you now.'

Zheng He slapped his thigh. His officers obediently laughed. I saw a certain relaxation go through Ty-ameny's commanders. Having used up almost all the wax surface of my tablets, I set myself to detailing the embroidery on Zheng He's high collar, and the lines around his eyes and mouth that signified amused satisfaction.

'If closed sea.' He traced the lines of the Black Sea on the Egyptian chart before him – it was meagre with detail, I noted – before moving west to Alexandria and the straits, and the beginning of the Greek islands. 'Is this, you call it "Middle Sea", also closed? But no. Because we came in. And where there is a way in, there is also a way out.'

None of the Pharaoh-Queen's charts showed any of the sea or land west of Crete. That was in no way an accident. Zheng He's ship might navigate back from Alexandria, through the long straits after Marmara, to the Aegean. But after that . . . the natural direction for him would be south and east, but that would only bring him, eventually, to Sidon and Tyre.

'We have not yet,' Zheng He said equably to Ty-ameny's implacable mask, 'begun to discuss the advantages of trade between my land and yours, great Empress.'

Plain as the daylight outside the linen-shaded windows: *Now we merely argue about the price!*

I shifted where I sat, not able to talk to Rekhmire' now he was the main conduit of translation between Zheng He and the Pharaoh-Queen.

It should be possible to find the Straits to the western ocean simply by following along the coast of North Africa, I thought, but not if no man was willing to tell him how it might be done.

I saw instantly what Ty-ameny had to bargain with. Charts, yes, but charts are often inaccurate. What Zheng He will need to get back to the Straits between Iberia and North Africa is a pilot.

Something nagged at the back of my brain. I prodded and scraped my tablets clean, and fell to doodling Horus-eyes while the council continued with every man desiring his say.

Two hours later, there was a pause for wine and light food.

I took Rekhmire''s elbow on pretence of assisting him, and steered him into one of the alcoves, out of earshot of Ty-ameny and her generals socially chatting with Zheng He and Jian and the other foreigners.

Rekhmire' raised a familiar brow at me.

'Would you call this a crisis?' I demanded.

His brows came down, frowning. 'Potential. I think it defused by what we've done—'

'The *arrival* of his ship.' I clamped down on my impatience. 'No kingdom in the Middle Sea has anything to match it. Whatever port sees Zheng He, there'll be panic and crisis. Am I right?'

Rekhmire''s lips parted, very slightly; in any other man it would have been an *ah* of realisation.

I spoke before he could.

'Perhaps, cause enough panic that a King – no matter what difficulties he might seem to be having with his most trusted adviser – would find himself forced to call that man back to court?'

17

I held Rekhmire''s gaze.

'I comprehend,' he murmured. 'If it could be negotiated for Zheng He to sail to *Taraco* . . . '

My mind raced. I glanced back into the chamber, ensuring no eunuch or man of Chin was within hearing distance. 'King Rodrigo could take that as the excuse to bring Videric back from his estate.'

Rekhmire' stood very still, his face intent.

I urged, 'He *would*. If a messenger was sent ahead to explain to him . . . Look at that ship! Do you think any man in Taraco would be surprised if Rodrigo wanted his best adviser back to help him deal with it? Even *Carthage* wouldn't blink at that.'

Rekhmire' clasped his hands over the top of his stick. His intense gazed focused onto me. 'That – would be a beginning.'

My hands sweated. I rubbed them on my linen tunic. 'You think—'

'It would soon become apparent that the Admiral is no threat. The scandal around Videric's name might not be entirely gone. But, yes, as a beginning—' He interrupted himself. 'Carthage! If Carthage was to take the war-junk as an ally of Taraconensis . . . '

'Would that be good or bad?' I asked anxiously.

'Good, if it makes the Lords-Amir cautious about sending legions into Iberia. Bad, if it provokes them into doing that very thing out of panic.'

I found my hand clenching around the wood frame of the wax tablets, cutting into my skin. 'I didn't think of that.'

Rekhmire' stroked his hand down his hairless chin, his eyes narrowing. 'This is worth considering. Many ramifications – many . . . '

His monumental face momentarily split in a warm smile that was all Rekhmire'. And a nod that was pure professional cousin of Ty-ameny.

'I'll speak with the Pharaoh-Queen. It must be discussed through and through. Ty-ameny has no greater wish than you to see war start in Taraconensis, and bring every other kingdom in with it.'

He blinked eyes that caught the linen-sifted light, and shone the colour of brandy.

'It won't be a quick answer, I fear. Between Ty-ameny's councillors and the Admiral's advisers . . . But I'll have an answer. I will. Well done, Ilario.'

I watched him as he limped away towards the Pharaoh-Queen, my stomach fairly tying itself into knots.

True to his word, time passed.

In those occasional hours when I saw him out of council, he desired only to rest his mind, and this seemed to take the form of escorting Onorata and myself (with the German brothers) about Constantinople – 'A city,' as he said, 'where you can walk from Europe to Asia in the space of a mile.'

I did just that, dragging Tottola and Attila along with me in the evening's warmth, taking Onorata under a great paper sunshade from the Chin war-junk. So that I would be able to tell her, when she was old enough, that she had stood in Asian lands.

Which assumes she does not stay here, grow up in Alexandria-in-exile . . .

Both Rekhmire' and the Pharaoh-Queen Ty-ameny showed an interest in my daughter.

The book-buyer, finding me holding her on the room's balcony again one morning, bent over to study her more closely. Onorata was solidly asleep, one closed fist resting up under her fat chins, and I stroked with a forefinger at the dark hair slicked down on her scalp.

Rekhmire' straightened up. 'When do they get interesting?'

'They *what*?'

'Infants. Will she talk soon? Or move around more?'

I raised an eyebrow at him, as much in his own fashion as I could imitate. 'You don't know?'

'I'm a book-buyer, not a nurse!' Half affronted and half amused, he gazed down at me. 'Aren't you supposed to know these things?'

'I was the youngest. I expect Sunilda or Matasuntha could tell you. And I'm a *painter*!'

Tottola strolled in from the anterooms, evidently changing shift on guard duty, and gave the Egyptian a look that clearly inquired *And the thing that's so funny is—?*, without needing a word. He stripped off his mail-shirt and garments, abandoning them for striped linen robes that reminded me painfully sharply of Iberia, nodded respectfully to me, and fell instantly asleep on his palliasse.

Onorata began a grumble in her sleep. Rocking her in the crook of my arm, I discovered she found that motion no substitute for milk.

Rekhmire' offered her a blunt-nailed thumb, with no better success.

I said, 'I'll get Carrasco to make her feed.'

Rekhmire' made himself scarce.

Ty-ameny's interest was the authentic tone of the Alexandrine philosopher. She visited, a day or two after, and leaned forward from among the cushions, studying my child who had fallen asleep on a blanket on the floor.

How I'll ever convince anyone of the hellion she is, when she angelically sleeps in their presence—

'Is she normal?' Ty-ameny asked.

Any other woman, I would have slapped. It was the Alexandrine curiosity in her tone that restrained me, more than her rank. Although that carried its weight.

'It appears so, Aldro. Until she grows up, who can say?'

The small woman nodded, and leaned back.

Without requesting permission, I settled on the goats'-wool blankets beside Onorata.

Rekhmire' remained standing.

Ty-ameny complained almost sulkily, 'You're making my neck ache. Sit down, in Ra's name!'

Rekhmire' bowed as deeply as slaves do. With the help of his stick, he moved as if to seat himself on the stone ledge beyond her.

Her hand closed over his wrist as he passed.

Rekhmire' let her arrest him. I saw in a heart's beat all their history in the glance between them. I felt curiously shut out. Although the ruling of New Alexandria is no concern of mine.

Ty-ameny's cheeks darkened a little, as if the heat of the room flushed her face. She moved her hand to her chin, as if she would stroke the Pharaoh's false beard that she was not wearing today. 'It was a reasonable question!'

'Yes, Great Queen,' Rekhmire' said mildly.

The queen looked at him through narrowed eyes.

Without turning, she said, 'Ilario, I apologise for not asking that in a more tactful manner.'

I bowed, catching how Rekhmire''s face warmed as she spoke.

'Too many people have thought it a reasonable question for me to like it, Great Queen,' I said.

'I believe that was the reason I was just slapped down.' She spoke darkly, looking up at Rekhmire'. 'Isn't that right, cousin?'

'The wisdom of the everlasting Gods is spoken through the mouth of the Pharaoh-Queen.' Rekhmire''s monumental face broke into a smile that made him look twenty. 'Most of the time . . . '

'Stop towering over me, book-buyer. I can still shorten you by a head, any day of the week!'

'Of course, cousin.' Rekhmire''s bow was so elegantly proper that, had I been Ty-ameny, I would have thrown something at him. I saw her small fingers tighten around one of the cushions as she grinned. The large Egyptian moved, seating himself on the bench beside her, and under cover of smoothing out the folds of his linen kilt, shot me a reassuring look.

I envied them their closeness.

'In fact,' Ty-ameny added, with more gravitas than one might expect from a woman with the stature of a twelve-year-old, 'if it would set your mind at ease to have her examined, the best of my Royal Mathematicians and physicians will do so.'

I could manage only 'Thank you', but it must have been clear what I meant.

The next several days had all my attention on my child, who bawled dispiritingly whenever an Alexandrine picked her up, and looked at me as if I were the Frankish version of Judas.

All of them pronounced her normal, but let me know that the extent of their knowledge – 'Without dissection!', Bakennefi Aa cheerily remarked – must be limited.

Slaves continued to bring food to our quarters at regular intervals. I sunk myself into the enjoyment of palace living – since I did not know if I would ever live in a palace again – and on two days when it was too hot to go outside, or do more than lay down on the great bed on the dais in my chamber, I dozed beside Onorata's cradle.

I woke on the third day, bored.

Zheng He, on land, would not have barbarians on his ship while he was not there.

I had itchy fingers, and established myself under a striped awning on another of the palace balconies, with Onorata asleep in a hooded cradle, and a stack of old parchments and a stoppered flask of oak-gall ink.

The striped awning reminded me of Taraco. I began a letter to Honorius, got as far as *Honoured Father*, and the ink dried on my quill while I tried to think of what I could say that would do no harm if someone opened the letter.

'*Father*' is not harmless.

Nor was anything else I could come up with.

I turned the parchment over, shaping the quill with an evilly sharp pen knife that I hadn't been able to resist in Alexandria's main market square, both for its Damascus steel and its beautiful walnut haft, and set about sketching the lines of the aqueduct that came into the palace here. Arches of yellow brick cast shadows across a square. People came and went around the statue of a griffin-like creature on a plinth. A white mongrel dog paused long enough to cock its leg.

The sun arriving overhead, I took Onorata back to our chambers and our own balcony, and set about drawing the great harbour, and the mass of streets going down from here to the massive walls.

It turned into a study of Zheng He's distant warship, but the size of it made the perspective look wrong.

I checked it as mathematically as Masaccio and Leon Battista had ever instructed me, found it correct, and wondered, *What do I do when reality itself seems incredible, even by an accurate description?*

Chin on fist, I stared down absently into the harbour, looking for another subject. I might draw Onorata, if Rekhmire' wasn't already making smart remarks about how many drawings of the child he's expected to make comment on . . .

I began a listless study of another ship moored between Europa and Asia. Dwarfed by comparison with Zheng He's it might be, but the lines interested me – not a war-ship, or a fat-bellied cargo-ship, or a dhow, but a fast light galley with canvas-shrouded arbalests on prow and stern for defence.

My quill-point scritched at the treated surface of the parchment; I made a reasonable attempt at the sterncastle and rudder before I startled, and the pen blotted a great spurt of ink over all.

I have drawn a ship like this before, and when I did – it was a Carthaginian bireme!

'Agatha and Jude!' It was safer to swear by Christian saints in this city, if you were a foreigner. I mopped at the ink with my sleeve, but the thin cotton only absorbed most of the liquid, leaving enough to shroud the carefully-drawn lines.

'That will be the envoy,' Rekhmire' said, an arm's length behind me.

I started again, jerked my wrist, and sent a hooked line of ink through the harbour wall. 'Caius Gaius *Judas*! Stop creeping up on me!'

The tall Egyptian grinned, entirely unrepentant, and bent to stroke a fingertip over Onorata's brow. She wriggled a little, and settled deeper into sleep. Rekhmire' looked up and to the side.

'Shadow will be off this balcony soon. You'll need to take her in.'

'*You* take her in,' I muttered. 'This is the Carthaginian envoy? The one you expected? Why's he here?'

'As far as I know, nothing but a previously-arranged diplomatic visit. Ty-ameny's ministers are running around like drunken piglets,' Rekhmire' observed, in response to my querying look. 'Now the jaws truly bite – Carthage's envoy will expect to see their latest gift on display in the Pharaoh-Queen's throne room. None of the Royal Mathematicians can yet promise it won't do to her as it did to Masaccio. She has a choice of offending Carthage – which we can't afford – *or* afford to have them find *that* out! – or else put herself in danger of murder by the golem.'

The ink had dried on my nib. I scratched it against my thumb, wishing for treated wooden boards on which I could use encaustic wax, or Masaccio's expensive pigments, and try out designs for Honorius's altar-panels.

'No.' I looked up, blinking. 'She doesn't.'

Rekhmire''s brows, stark under his shaved head, dipped down, casting all his face into severe lines.

'If we smash the golem's limbs, or chain it, or immobilise it safely in some way, that would be no less offensive to Carthage—'

I interrupted him before his rising tone could wake Onorata. It was difficult to keep my own voice sufficiently quiet.

'*No*. They don't have to break the damned thing to stop it hurting the Pharaoh-Queen. I know how we can do it. I *know*.'

Rekhmire''s sceptical look had hope badly suppressed under the surface. 'You know?'

I ignored his stress on the initial word.

'I know,' I said. 'Cheese glue.'

18

'Cheese glue?' the Pharaoh-Queen of Alexandria said.

'Cheese glue.'

'*Cheese* glue?'

One of the Royal Mathematicians muttered, 'Cheese *glue?*', in an equally bemused tone.

Rekhmire' smoothly intervened. 'Hear Ilario out, Great Name of Sekhmet; I think you should.'

Ty-ameny's sloe-black eyes darted to his face. Whatever she found there was sufficient to have her not throw me straight out of the Royal apartments.

'Explain,' she demanded grimly.

'Cheese glue's made with limestone and . . . cheese.'

I shuffled a little where I sat, hearing the words as they must sound to her.

'Yes, it *sounds* foolish, but I know this part of my trade! The best kind is cheese that's gone bad. Great Queen, when I was in Rome, Mastro Masaccio had me crumbling cheese and limestone and mixing the glue. You use it to size boards for painting, especially if your board has to be made up of several smaller pieces. When it sets . . . '

In memory I still hear Masaccio's hammer.

'I saw examples twice, in his workshop,' I said, seeing the Alexandrines perk up at the sound of empirical evidence. 'Once of a six-part panel put together before the plague came to Europa, that a man couldn't break with all his strength. The other was more subtle, I think – an older board, that had a funeral portrait on it from Hannibal Barca's time. The wax was gone, and the pigments too, and the wood broken in many places.'

I held finger and thumb a half-inch apart.

'But the glue that had held the wood together, *that* was still intact! Where the worms had eaten the wood all away, the cheese and lime glue stood up alone, rigid, like a framework.'

I took a breath, realising the frown on the Royal Mathematician Bakennefi Aa's face was calculation rather than scorn.

'When it ages, it yellows, but initially it sets clear. Like glass. You would not ever know it was there.' My mouth felt dry. I swallowed. Rekhmire' remained silent where he sat beside me.

Either he desires me to have all the credit for this – or all the blame!

Ty-ameny's frown was now of a different kind, I saw. She asked, 'How would this help us?'

She's willing to consider it!

'The golem's limbs are articulated.' The memory of stone fingers was one I pushed aside almost by habit now. 'Each of the arms, knees, fingers, feet – they're all jointed, by metal gears. If you were to pour prepared glue into the joint mechanisms and let it set . . . '

Ty-ameny blinked as if dazed.

'And no one could see this?' Her black gaze snapped into focus. 'At a distance, say, of – Ahhotep, over there, beside the window. If I am here, and he is there, will he see this has been done?'

I considered it, heart racing, not wanting to seem too sure of myself.

'No,' I said at last. 'Not even if he knew what he was looking for. The joints are brass, they shine. The extra coating will shine the same way.'

The room of advisers was silent for the space of ten heartbeats; Tyameny put her chin in her hand. She gazed unseeing at Rekhmire', silhouetted against the white afternoon heat.

My voice creaked and dropped down into the lower male registers. 'At the very worst, it would give you warning, when the joints move and the glue shatters. There would be time enough to move away. If the cheese glue's allowed time to cure and set – the golem will pull itself to pieces before those joints will move.'

'Bakennefi Aa.' Ty-ameny gave the Royal Mathematician and his cohorts a look that indicated they should – as rapidly as possible – search out sources in the Library. As the three Bakennefi brothers bowed and left, she turned back to me.

'You know how to mix this? The proportions of each; all the ingredients?'

That amount of implied responsibility cut off my breath. My heart pounded in palpable thuds. I swallowed, I hoped imperceptibly, and nodded.

'You mix a batch,' the Pharaoh-Queen said. 'My mathematicians will run tests. But, at the same time – the golem will be treated with your substance, too. Where it stands, beside the royal throne; undertake the treatment there.'

She shot a glance at Rekhmire'.

'Plausible ways can be found to delay the Carthaginian envoy's formal audience for a few more days?'

'He's a diplomat, Great Queen, he'll expect it.'

The corner of her mouth tweaked up, although she nodded solemnly enough. Her gaze switched back to me.

'*Cheese* glue!' she muttered.

19

The envoy of the King-Caliph Ammianus of Carthage was received with the proper amount of ceremony, Pharaoh-Queen Ty-amenhotep giving the impression – as I note Alexandrines like to do – that she condescended to pay respect to a member of a younger and more barbaric civilisation.

Rekhmire', shielding me from the view of the envoy's entourage, murmured, 'If he *does* anything in public, he's a fool.'

The great audience hall had space enough to hide me, veiled and therefore female, among Ty-ameny's advisers. I hoped that if the Carthaginian envoy had been briefed at all, he would be looking for Rekhmire''s scribe, or at best the painter's apprentice from Rome, and not the pregnant woman of Venice.

Apprehension made my mouth dry.

Onorata lay newly-fed and grumpy up in our apartments, with Ramiro Carrasco and the German brothers and a squad of Ty-ameny's Royal Guard in attendance. I didn't trust the Carthaginians not to attempt abduction of my baby. Nor, evidently, did the Pharaoh-Queen.

Brass horns blared.

The crowds at the doors shifted.

I guessed the envoy's party had begun their way up the Thousand Stairs to the Daughter of Ra's palace. In the white heat of afternoon. Surely a calculated insult?

'He may well think that,' Rekhmire' confirmed my suggestion. 'But he's from the Darkness. The sun in the middle of the day addles the brains of any local man fool enough to walk out in it. What it'll do to a man used to twilight, and used to being out in all the hours of the day . . . '

'Any advantage she can get?' I speculated.

The bald man's lip quirked. 'Regrettably the Pharaoh-Queen could not find time in her busy schedule until this hour.'

Constantinople is worse than Taraco at midday. I'd made the mistake of going out drawing in the day's heat once and only once. The lines of silver-point on the treated paper scrawled off into flicks and trailing half-circles; and I had had to be brought home by Carrasco, of all men, and put in a darkened room to be fed cool water in drips.

By the time Carrasco found me, I had rolled under the edge of a cart at the side of the market square's infinite hot expanse. The air shimmered, the heat hit like a hammer, and I had sought out the only tiny piece of visible shade.

Ramiro Carrasco pulled me out by one foot and smugly carried me back to the palace over his shoulder. It might have left him scarlet-faced and gasping, but he evidently thought the moral ascendancy worth it. I felt too grateful to even resent that. If I had been fool enough to take Onorata out with me, she would be dead.

Picturing the unknown envoy, I knew that he would be craving darkness, cool, shade; that his head will throb, and his eyes pain him.

The crowd parted as the horns blasted out a flat raw sound.

Men stood silhouetted against the white sky.

The Carthaginian party moved inside, almost with unseemly haste. Perhaps a dozen men, most of them wearing Carthaginian plate armour – I winced in sympathy for the soldiers – and two in long white robes. The envoy and an aide, I guessed.

They stood for a long moment in the entrance to the throne-hall, long enough for whispers to start.

The taller of the robed men put his hand up to his face.

I realised he was unknotting the length of white gauze cloth he wore tied about his head, over his eyes. His entourage also.

Of course: they're Carthaginians, they must *know* what countries outside the Penitence are like!

His hawk-bearded face uncovered, the taller man bowed to his shorter companion, and signalled to the guards. They walked between impassive lines of the Pharaoh-Queen's Royal Guard, ignoring the ceremonial sarissas that the men held.

The Carthaginian soldiers had empty scabbards at their sides. I guessed there were halberds left at the palace gatehouse, too. They walked as stiffly as men in plate armour in high heat do, and I caught two of them exchanging a word and a grimace, exactly as Honorius's men might have done.

'You stay here,' Rekhmire' murmured. 'I must be beside the Queen, but I want you out of danger.'

I thought him angry that the Pharaoh's ban on armed foreigners in the throne room should extend to Attila and Tottola. And that I had insisted on being present.

'Rekhmire', I'm not *in* danger—'

'I can't protect both of you!'

He did not speak loudly, but the intensity of it stopped me dead.

'If it comes to it,' I said, as steadily as I could, 'don't throw yourself between anybody and a sword. I don't want you to do that.'

Rekhmire''s mouth twisted. He gazed down at the short, stout staff with a silver handle, that he had substituted for his usual crutches. 'You need not worry. It's not likely I'll be able to move fast enough to put myself between Ty-ameny and harm—'

His whisper was grim and somewhat self-mocking; I interrupted it mercilessly. '*Unless* you're right next to her. Don't think I don't know why you want to be at her elbow.'

'I can't be at hers *and* yours.'

His expression was frighteningly raw for a usually composed man.

He looks torn in two, as if he would literally divide himself up to defend both of us – and sell his soul to be the man of quick movement that he was before his injury.

'I'll be safe enough,' I said, indicating my female dress.

He desires to keep me as safe as his Pharaoh-Queen, I realised. As for what that means—

I don't know if he values my knowledge and political usefulness – or if he's as fond of me as he plainly is of Ty-ameny of the Five Great Names, who he treats like a brat of a schoolgirl.

Aiding him the only way I could think of, I said, 'Where am I safest, for you?'

'This side of the throne.' His eyes narrowed at the hulking apparent statue beside the tiny figure of Ty-ameny. 'I don't trust that thing not to come for you, Ilario. Far more likely Carthage intends it for her, but how do we know it doesn't remember you?'

'It doesn't remember anything. It's stone.' I thought of it killing. Nothing with feelings could act that way without *some* emotion showing, if only satisfaction at an order obeyed. 'It's a set of orders, waiting to act on command.'

Rekhmire''s look had something I recognised, eventually, as respect. If he hadn't seen the golem act in Rome, he trusted what I'd observed. That is a responsibility, too.

His hand closed once on my shoulder, and he ambled off, deceptively relaxed, sliding into the group of advisers around Ty-ameny's imperial purple throne.

The Carthaginians would recognise his role, I thought, assuming any of them had been on diplomatic duty for more than a week. But the ability to deter an assassination is also valuable.

Unless they're sure an attack will succeed; so sure that it doesn't matter how many men Ty-ameny has around herself, or how well armed they are, because hands of stone can bat swords aside without a second thought, and stone can smash iron, bone, arm, skull—

'Welcome our visitors,' Ty-ameny said aloud, her voice muffled by the gold mask and braided false beard she wore. Her herald stepped forward, rapped his serpent-staff on the marble steps, and began a lengthy greeting to the lords of Carthage and the representatives of his sublime greatness the King-Caliph of that nation . . .

The herald stuttered a couple of times and looked annoyed with himself. He wanted to be nothing but imperturbable duty, a role rather than a man, I guessed, and not seem as on edge and apprehensive as the rest of us were.

' . . . the Daughter of Sekhmet and the Regent of Ra graciously allows you to present yourself to her.' The herald bowed and stepped back.

The shorter of the two robed men stepped forward, as if they were engaged in a formal dance. Which I supposed, in fact, they were.

Out of respect, the man put back his hood. It left his sun-reddened face exposed to the courtiers, with the white strip of skin where he had covered his eyes with cloth.

His tight expression suggested him aware of the comic tone of his appearance.

The man's features, which would otherwise have been handsome, tugged at my awareness.

Rummaging in one sleeve, I pulled out a folded sheet of paper and a remnant of willow-twig charcoal. The palace laundry could be excused for complaining at me, I reflected, while I looked up and back, up and back, marking the values of the ambassador's face on the paper.

With the tones and shape broadly in place I studied the sketch, while the initial diplomatic niceties droned on. And dabbed at the charcoal, smoothing it to a paler grey where I had drawn his hair in its long single braid.

With pale hair, that suddenly seemed like the white of old age, the face of Hanno Anagastes stared off the paper at me.

Under the drawing, I scrawled, *Younger son of House of Hanno???*, beckoned a page, and sent the boy off with it to Rekhmire'. As I watched him thread his way through the press of bodies, the ambassador's pleasantly resonant baritone rang through the throne room.

'I have a question for the great Pharaoh-Queen. Why do you consort with that ship of demons?'

Ty-ameny must love her ceremonial mask, I thought. No change was visible in her small figure, sitting with her gold sandals neatly together on a footstool set on the throne's step. Without a view of her features, her body was impassive.

The Carthaginian diplomat stirred a little in the silence that followed his words.

Ty-ameny beckoned her herald and spoke briefly into his ear.

The herald straightened and fixed the ambassador with a bland look. 'The Divine Daughter of Ra says her Royal Mathematicians have not yet finished determining what the nature of the ship and its crew may be.'

'It's obvious what they are!'

It was obvious to *me* that the man seized on the excuse of working himself up. He threw off the hand the taller man rested on his arm – which I was willing to bet they'd cooked up between them, back on the Carthaginian bireme.

He wants to be able to shout at Ty-ameny.

My body was suddenly and instantly cold, knowing the reason why he might need to do that.

'Even followers of false gods must be able to recognise the presence of corruption in their midst—'

The Pharaoh-Queen's captain of the guard shifted his gaze, just barely, to catch her orders. She lifted one finger, where her hand lay on the arm of her throne. He stiffened, made no further move and issued no orders, but I saw his nostrils flare.

The pale skin of Rekhmire' caught my eye, in a chiaroscuro against the black robes of the palace guard. Idly, he clasped his hands behind him, leaning back on his stick, standing squarely between Ty-ameny's throne and the stone golem.

He rocked unevenly back and forth on heels and toes as if this were nothing more than another trade delegation, political approach, or other everyday order of government. The Carthaginian man of House Hanno shot him a glance.

He won't care if the golem goes straight through you to get to the Queen.

If I'm wrong, I thought. If this stupid, stupid idea doesn't work – oh, Judas, he does mean to kill her!

The ambassador's voice was rising to a peroration. Ty-ameny leaned one slender elbow on the arm of her throne, chin in hand, as if supremely bored. I obsessively repeated Masaccio's ingredients and method for glue; wondering if a week in the creating and curing could make anything with a tensile strength greater than a spiderweb.

I was on tiptoe, I found, and straining my eyes to stare at the golem. Not a quiver of movement.

The joints glistened in reflected light from the piazza outside, but that could be the polished brass and bronze gears. The finished glue had poured like liquid glass in Milano's factories; poured in and settled around every cog, every spring, every wheel, every plate, every part of the statue that moved.

And that it did move had been confirmed by Ty-amenhotep's orders to it, shouted from thirty yards off, so that it exposed all its limbs and joints to us to anoint.

Alexandrine Constantinople – or the life of Ty-ameny, at least – depends on the tensile strength of glue, once set.

I bit my lip until the sharp pain of bursting skin gave me the taste of blood.

'—consorting against even the tenets of the heretic Frankish church—'

Rekhmire' turned his head as the page tugged on his sleeve. I saw him read the note; his lips moved, saying something to the boy. He returned his gaze to the ambassador, not looking over towards me.

Too professional to seek me out. Too concerned that I may be a target. But I realised I would find it infinitely reassuring to meet his gaze.

'—and it is treachery! Conspiring with slant-eyed demons against the civilised world! Treachery in the highest degree, without even the excuse of necessity of – Saint – Gaius – Judas!'

He hit the saint's Carthaginian and Frankish names heavily, with a hammer's rhythm.

That's *it*! That's the trigger for the golem's orders—

The son of the House of Hanno stared, white showing all around his eyes.

A faint click sounded, below the discreet mutterings of the courtiers about the discourtesy of this diplomat, and speculations as to what Tyameny would do about him. The faintest possible abrasion of metal against metal.

The surface of the stone quivered. Once, twice. And—

Nothing.

Nothing more.

20

The Carthaginian envoy stared at the stone golem.

The stone golem stared sightlessly into the distance, as if the palace walls were transparent to it, and it could see all of the city, the sea, and the walls of Carthage that lay so many weeks of travel to the west.

It still did not move.

I frowned, squinting. Most of the crowd were looking at the ambassador or their Queen; I doubted more than half a dozen of us were looking at the golem.

Nothing.

Holding my breath made my mouth arid as the desert around Carthage, and dread made me feel as cold. Stare as I might, I could see no more vibration in the stone limbs and body.

They *meant* it to kill her!

Rage soared through me, bringing welcome heat. The golem's response, minimal as it was, spoke of all the danger that Carthage's gift would have brought here – a poisoned chalice that the Pharaoh-Queen could not diplomatically set aside; a trap that would have stood statue-like at her side, until the right words from an agent of Carthage sent it into convulsions of violence.

For a moment I could smell an illusion of the carnage that this hall would have suffered; see the pale bodies marked with blood, and Ty-ameny's limbs and head pulled from her body in grotesque parody of a child pulling apart an insect.

'We are pleased to accept the new envoy of Carthage, Hanno Gaiseric.' Ty-ameny spoke up, her tone with something savagely restrained under it. 'And if the King-Caliph will accept a poor gift in recompense for this gift of his—'

Here she gestured at the motionless stone golem.

'—then I have drawings, documents, and divers other things concerning the foreign demons of Chin, which the King-Caliph's scientist-magi may find of interest.'

Hanno Gaiseric tore his gaze away from the golem with evident difficulty.

'The King-Caliph accepts with—' The word seemed to choke him: '—gratitude.'

Forty-eight hours later, Hanno Gaiseric went aboard the bireme and unexpectedly left the grand harbour; Ty-ameny's spies reported the ship heading unerringly and unstoppably back towards Carthage.

An hour after *that*, the Pharaoh-Queen announced Carthage's gift so valuable that it must be installed in the Royal Library. And Rekhmire' came back up to our quarters dusting his hands together, having lent a hand at mortaring the stone blocks and iron bars that irrevocably closed up one of the Library's lowest storage chambers, now buried well below ground-level.

'"Safe".' Ty-ameny shook her head, her unbound hair rippling over her bare shoulders. 'Yes. Yes, but – Carthage desired us to know we cannot engineer what they can. Very well, we have been lessoned . . . '

Even in her private chambers, wearing only a linen wrap in the afternoon heat, she kept the presence of the Pharaoh-Queen. Hanno Gaiseric's attempt at murder seemed only to have energised her. She smiled ferociously at Rekhmire'.

'I think, therefore, it's time to issue a lesson of our own.'

As ever in a court, it may have seemed that we were alone, but as soon as Ty-ameny lifted her hand, slaves and servants came with wine, ivory cups, small crisp biscuits, and a number of leather map-cases. A shaven-headed slave ordered the placing of a low table in the room's sunken-floor area, spread the maps with his own hands, and bowed to his queen as he left.

Each chart was bordered at top and bottom with brass, to keep them from rolling back up; I found myself wondering if there was a use for that in drawing.

Had I been able to pick them up to investigate, I would; in fact, my hands were occupied in sliding under Onorata to check she was still dry. The palace's smallest tyrant having decided she would spend any part of the day out of my company in screaming, I had no option but to bring her with me, and sit as much out of the way as possible.

'Here.' Ty-ameny put her finger on a point on the larger map, glancing at Rekhmire', and then to me.

She beckoned me forward. 'Let me hold the child.'

Reluctantly I got up and moved forward. 'If she wakes, she'll scream, Great Name . . . '

'She won't.'

The Pharaoh-Queen held out her hands, confident enough, I thought. *Of course, I am a fool: she has had three daughters.*

I passed Onorata into the wiry, muscular arms, and watched Ty-ameny smile down at her. The venal thought of a monarch as god-parent to my child came into my mind. But courts are cut-throat: Onorata will be better out of them . . .

'There.' Ty-ameny pointed with her chin. Rekhmire' spread out the largest map.

The Middle Sea, I saw. Or a version of it. The headland on the African coast could only be Carthage, given how close it was to Malta – the furthest edge of the Penitence – and Sardinia and the Italies.

Rekhmire' lifted his head where he sat. After a moment, I realised I was hearing, with him, the creak of slave-wielded fans, loud in the silence. He looked questioningly at the Pharaoh-Queen. Ty-ameny gestured them away.

There have been kings who would merely kill their slaves after, in case they had overheard what they should not.

The last slave left. Heat grew in the palace room, despite the open windows. I could still taste, in the back of my throat, the smell of dead meat. Ty-ameny clucked at my child, and I seated myself beside Rekhmire'.

I thought, not for the first time, *If I had been bought by any other man . . .*

As King Rodrigo's Freak, I was always spared the worst excesses of being owned. My time as Rekhmire''s slave has been far more like Constantinople's bureaucratic model than how life is outside of the courts of power. Compared to Ty-ameny's palace slaves, I have barely been in slavery; compared to the world outside Alexandria – labour, prostitution, either way worked to death – I have been closest to free. I watched the Queen stroke Onorata's bare ankle.

My daughter will never be a slave, no matter what.

'There,' Ty-ameny said, her voice low and even.

Rekhmire', as if his hands were hers, indicated cities on the North African coast, and ports at Sicily, Crete, and Rhodes.

'We'll issue a warning,' she said. 'The golem-*machina* is their opening shot. House Barbas has put this weapon into the King-Caliph's hand . . . I am told.'

She gave a sudden smile, looking from under her kohl-blackened lashes at Rekhmire'. He returned his 'only a book-buyer' expression of innocence. I bit the inside of my lip so as not to laugh aloud. With an inexplicable lift of the heart, I thought, *They are closer to brother and sister than cousins.*

'That being so,' she continued, rocking Onorata gently, 'King-Caliph Ammianus will continue to test us. Rekhmire', how many golem have they?'

'As much as I can now tell, no more than a dozen, we think. Ammianus keeps most, but his chief allies among the Lords-Amir have been given them as gifts.'

Hanno Anagastes, I thought.

I saw tears in his eyes when I gave him the funeral portrait of Hanno Tesha, although I'd had to put the lustrous brown eyes and sleek dark hair of cliché, since that was the only description of the child he could give me. Would he be capable of ordering a golem like the one in his house to kill men as Masaccio was killed?

Given what men do in war, yes. No question.

Rekhmire' leaned back, his fingers absently kneading at the muscles above his knee though the linen kilt. 'It's possible the King-Caliph will gift one to the Turkish Sultan. And to at least one of the Frankish Kings. As far as we know, we're first outside the Bursa-hill itself.'

'A warning.' The Pharaoh-Queen repeated it stubbornly. She darted a glance at me, keen and black, jolting me with the intensity of her attention. 'And here, I think, is where our business intersects.'

'Aldro.' I waited as respectfully as I might, for impatience.

Ty-ameny spoke while she watched my sleeping child. 'Rekhmire' has brought me knowledge of how Taraconensis appears to be unstable, and how your stepfather may be a solution to that.'

There is nothing she has not been told.

But I expected that.

'You have your own reasons for wishing to see Lord Videric in his place at court again.' The gleam in Ty-ameny's black eyes was in part serious, in part amused, and wholly elated. 'Chief among which, I imagine, is not continually anticipating murder.'

I answered the question she had carefully not asked.

'When I trusted Aldro Videric – when I thought he was my father, and a good man – I also thought he was King Rodrigo Sanguerra's necessary right hand. He's still that. Without being a good man.'

I caught a scowl on Rekhmire''s face, briefly wondered if I had spoken amiss, and found the Pharaoh-Queen nodding with approval.

'I had counted on forty years,' she observed, 'and, if I must, will settle for twenty.'

Before Alexandrine Constantinople falls.

It hit me like a falling boulder: in twenty years, my daughter could be twenty. A woman. Those identical baby-features, that have only a suggestion of her grandfather and I in the bones behind the skin, and the colour of her hair, will give way to a face uniquely hers, a mind uniquely hers.

Cold down my spine under the linen tunic, despite the heat of the room, I said, 'I grew up during peace – it guarantees nothing. But I know what war guarantees.'

Ty-ameny pressed her lips together, nodding. She looked like a girl cuddling a small sister.

She sat up, both her arms cradling Onorata, and the change was as sudden and different as the crack of lightning falling from heaven to earth.

'The King-Caliph Ammianus sees fit to send me a warning.' Ty-ameny's eyes glinted. 'It is my intention now to send a warning back!'

She lifted her arms, and I automatically stood and came to take

196

Onorata from her. The Queen of Constantinople knelt down by the map-table, like a beggar-child playing at marbles in the street. I moved to watch over her shoulder.

A little frown making a fold of skin between her brows, Ty-ameny said, 'The Admiral Zheng He and I are debating an agreement. I will loan him a pilot, and charts, to help him regain the ocean sea, and find his fleet, if they're not sunk. My captains suggest it will have been a storm around the West African islands; those are dangerous waters.'

The thought of more war-junks, no matter how few more there might be, made me shudder. Jian thought nothing of his crew numbering five thousand Chin men, as I knew from speaking to him. There are armies in the Frankish lands made up of fewer men than that. If they should decide to conquer a kingdom and stay here . . .

A little too intuitively for my liking, Ty-ameny remarked, 'I think the Admiral truly anxious to get back to his Emperor – this is not the first voyage they've made to foreign waters, and they've found only "barbarians" wherever they sail. Zheng He's words.'

The little smile curved her lip.

'We rank as civilised, having a proper eunuch bureaucracy. Although he cares very little for having a woman and a heathen on the throne. However,' she added briskly, 'he will agree to visit the port of Carthage, on his voyage back to the ocean sea.'

'Carthage?'

She gestured irritably for me to sit down, a moment before I realised that she had no desire to crick her neck looking up. I set Onorata cautiously into her sling around my neck (for which she was almost too large, now) and sat beside Rekhmire'.

'Zheng He will replenish his ship at Carthage,' Ty-ameny said. 'And while there, he will let it be thought that Alexandria has himself and his ship as an ally.'

Rekhmire' smiled: I supposed at my expression.

'For this, the Queen is prepared to lend her best pilot,' he observed cheerfully. 'And Carthage is not to know a pilot is guiding the Admiral *out* of the Middle Sea. For all the King-Caliph knows, the war-junk will be roaming the sea on our behalf indefinitely.'

He exchanged a smile with Ty-ameny.

'A theoretical Zheng He may be a great deal more useful as an ally than a material one, given that he can never change his mind and seek other alliances!'

The Pharaoh-Queen lifted her bare shoulders in a shrug, tracing routes on the blue- and gold-inked map. 'I understand from Admiral Zheng He that his country has contact along the Silk Road with the Rus, the Turk, and the Persians; Carthage is not an important ally for them. He's willing to show himself under our banner.'

She sat back on her heels, glossy hair sliding away to show her face.

197

'And then there is your home, Ilario.'

Head tight with effort, I strained to keep up with her thought. 'Aldro, you think Zheng He should sail to Taraconensis?'

Her thin finger traced a course. 'Taraconensis, before Carthage. I see it thus: it is imperative Carthage has no excuse to send legions into Taraconensis this year. War will begin if that happens, and it will draw all of us in. As the Franks cannot be allowed to think they can invade your northern frontier, so Carthage cannot be allowed to provoke them into an invasion, by putting a Carthaginian Governor into Taraco.'

Her words were only my thoughts spoken aloud, and no more than a natural consequence of the discussion with Rekhmire' – but I felt it all suddenly made more real.

Onorata stirred in her sling; I tried by force of will to quiet my pounding heartbeat.

'Will the Admiral agree to this, Aldro?'

'He sees the desirability of having an Alexandrine pilot.' Her grin was almost brutal. 'And he understands the necessity for trade. There must be some degree of trust – there's little to prevent him from kidnapping my pilot and attempting to leave the Middle Sea on his own. But I think he desires to leave a good name with us, as a civilised man in a world of barbarians.'

Worlds have turned on stranger things. I felt myself dizzy, not only from the humid heat.

Ty-ameny made fists of her hands, like bunches of knucklebones, and stretched; breaking the position to reach out and touch Rekhmire''s arm.

'Admiral Zheng He will also be carrying a humble book-buyer, along with my pilot – which, naturally, will have nothing to do with what impression the Carthaginians gain of relations between Alexandria and Chin.'

Naturally not. I would have answered in the same manner, but I couldn't speak.

'If you agree,' Ty-ameny concluded, looking at me, 'you will go to Taraco with them.'

The unexpected constriction in my throat kept me silent for an embarrassing minute.

I managed, finally, to croak, 'My family owes you a debt.'

Ty-ameny rose in one graceful movement, not putting her hand to the floor. 'Pay me by doing what you would in any case do – have your King Rodrigo Sanguerra summon Pirro Videric back as his first minister.'

The small woman looked at me, and at Rekhmire', in turn.

'This *must* happen. By any means possible.'

Part Three

Herm and Jethou

1

"'*Cào nî zûxian shí bâ dai.*'" I pronounced the sounds as closely to Jian's as I could manage, ignoring the plainly undisguised amusement on his face. Tracing ink deftly onto my paper, I continued in the haphazard mixture of bad North African Latin which Zheng He's crew appeared to have picked up on the West African coast, and scattered words from Alexandrine Egyptian. 'And this means . . . '

"'I am honoured beyond measure to meet you.'"

The small boat rocked, despite a calm that had been absolute enough to becalm the war-junk. I slitted my eyes against morning sunlight and the ship laying a hundred paces off. Easier to trace the marks Jian had made for me to copy.

A dozen or more ink studies lay discarded on the thwarts of the dinghy, careless of sea-water; each a less successful attempt to capture the war-junk with her immensely tall thin sails spread to catch every fraction of breeze.

So far, she did not travel so fast that Commander Jian's men couldn't row us back to her. In fact I thought she might not be moving at all.

'*Cào nî zûxian shí bâ dai* . . . ' I thought I heard a noise from one or other of the Chin men on the rowers' benches, but my suspicions were centred on Jian's far too innocent expression.

Twenty days have given me insight enough into him to read at least the broader emotions. And this game is called 'get the foreign devil into amusing trouble'.

"'Honoured to meet you,'" I mused, and looked at him brightly. 'So this is what I should say to the Admiral when we get back on board? Then I can ask him to reward *you* for teaching me so well.'

Jian's square frame went utterly still for a heartbeat.

He lifted his hand, slapped it down on his thigh, and burst into high-pitched laughter.

Out of the corner of my eye, I caught the rowers slapping each other on the back and wiping their eyes, which I thought was just as well; they showed every sign of rupturing themselves if they'd had to keep quiet much longer.

I smiled at Jian with deliberate innocence, and traced the lines that made up the drawn picture-words of Chin. 'So what does this mean?'

The Chin officer spluttered, waving his hand in plain refusal.

I brandished the paper. 'If I show this around the ship, someone will tell me . . . '

Jian was in the habit of treating me as a court eunuch, but I knew the man smart enough to know it not entirely true. *Yin yang ren!* got whispered sometimes when I passed: an impolite version of 'hermaphrodite'.

I watched Jian tripping himself up on what might be expected behaviour towards a man, or towards a woman, and let him squirm for a minute or two before copying him with a thigh-slap and a laugh.

The noise from our boat would frighten sea-birds away for miles, I thought. When every man aboard found himself permitted to laugh – and for once to laugh at his commanding officer – it was loud.

Jian solved his disciplinary problem by pointing to the youngest of the rowers, and firing off a rapid rattle of words that I knew must translate as '*You* tell her!'

If he'd been Iberian, the boy would have been blushing; he ducked his head and rattled off apologies non-stop.

'Is it rude?' I asked helpfully.

'Yes, Lord Barbarian!'

Ruder than 'barbarian'? I wondered. But none of them seem to think that word is anything more than purely descriptive.

'Is it *very* rude?'

The rest of the crew assured me, over the boy's squirming, that it was extremely rude, not meant for any man except the vilest of enemies, and that the great Lord Admiral would flay my skin off and tan it for a rug if I used it towards him, barbarian ignorance notwithstanding. I'd seen enough casual brutality aboard to not be completely convinced he was joking.

Jian seized my paper, and – with the tip of his tongue sticking out of the corner of his mouth – drew three or four lines that, as I stared hard, resolved themselves into an image. This—

I turned the page a quarter round, attempting to make out what I was seeing. 'Are they doing what I think they're doing?'

'Is rude. It means—' Jian's hand gesture was fairly universal.

'"Fuck"?' I prompted, in several of the languages they might have heard in Constantinople's harbour, and there was an outbreak of nodding and applause.

'Means, "fuck eighteen generations of your ancestors",' Jian exclaimed, and gave me a smile that made a square and ugly face beautiful. 'Not to say to the Admiral, no!'

I smiled and agreed that no, that probably wasn't wise, and the joke was repeated backwards and forwards in the boat until I got them to row me further south simply to put an end to it.

They shipped oars, having turned us into what would have been the direction of the wind, had it not been dead calm. Jian gave an order, which was evidently to stand down. I smoothed a fresh sheet of paper on my drawing board, set it firmly on my knees, and went back to attempting to draw the war-junk well enough that I could paint her at some time in the future. Who could miss the chance to see this ship, from a distance, with nothing else around her?

And somewhere on the ship, I thought, narrowing my eyes against the sunlight off the waves, Rekhmire' is negotiating exactly how long Zheng He will anchor off the shore of Taraco.

Because we can't tell how long it will take to solve this – and I can't blame Zheng He that he wants to be gone. Our wars aren't his concern; he comes from too far away.

And every man I spoke to seemed to take their 'lost fleet' for granted . . .

The wide-bottomed boat rocked. Jian's men ran up a slatted small sail without being ordered, steadying us where we stood, forty leagues out of sight of the North African coast.

There might be enough of a breeze to move our small boat; the war-junk, I saw – even with tier upon tier of slatted sails raised up on its seven main masts, and three smaller masts – remained stationary.

Commander Jian leaned over my shoulder, just as the shift of the boat sent my chalk skidding across the paper. 'That's not very good.'

'*Cào nî zûxian shí bâ dai!*'

Even as it came out of my mouth, I was appalled. He'll truly take offence—

Jian burst into deep, choking laughter.

His crew decided it was worth applause, too; banging their fists on the gunnels. I suspected they had not expected their commander to be told that. Or not by any man who'd get to keep his head afterwards.

'Perhaps I'm not a very good artist,' I said apologetically, and had the idea then of offering Jian paper and chalk of his own.

We passed an hour or two exchanging what we could of technique, hampered by lack of language. Jian's war-junk was mostly a matter of lines, but it was recognisably a war-junk; the fact that he put in islands we had passed above and below the ship, so that he seemed to be drawing everything on one long ribbon, I couldn't talk him out of. Pulling a small version of Leon Battista's perspective frame out of the snapsack, I attempted to show him how it related to what I was drawing on my paper – but I think neither of us understood my explanation.

With the sun descending into my eyes, I settled for adding in a quick sketch of a European cog to give me the scale of the war-junk. There was not, in truth, so much difference between the high poop of a Frankish ship and the curves of the junk's flat stern.

Only in sheer size.

As for how many ship-lengths the war-junk was long . . .

'If it's an inch less than four hundred feet, I'll boil my sandals and eat them!'

Jian looked bemused at my mutter. I was saved from explanation. A faint whooshing noise and a *pop!* was succeeded by a light falling down the sky – one of Zheng He's signal rockets, barely bright enough to show in daylight, but clear enough that Jian gave a grunting sigh and ordered his rowers to their oars.

I had seen much larger rockets in the war-junk's hold. I guessed them launched from some of the arbalest-like machines and tubes on the foredecks. How effective they might be in a sea battle, Ty-ameny's pilot Sebekhotep said he could have no professional opinion on.

But I saw he took note of them all the same.

Jian's crew brought the boat towards what seemed a vast wooden wall, when we got up close, rather than the side of a sea-going ship. I spent time in several languages making it known that if a stupid barbarian used insulting words, it would only be out of ignorance, and no reflection on the officer in question. Jian finally gave me a slap on the shoulder and a sip at his flask of tepid sour wine, taught me the proper pronunciation of 'foreign devil' in his own language, and I thought matters settled reasonably well. It helped that he could be amused by my attempts to scale the ladder to the entry-port of the war-junk.

The scent of salt and deep water faded, replaced by the spices and sandalwood of the junk, always underlying its permanent odour of sweat and cooking. I swung myself inboard.

A hand caught my elbow, steadying me enough that I didn't drop the leather sack of drawings.

Rekhmire', I found; looking up into his sun-flushed face. He glared down with unexpected disapproval.

I thought it best to ask plain and direct. 'What's the matter?'

The Egyptian snorted, with a sour look at the boat on its davits. 'I saw you scrambling down into that, earlier . . . '

Between the steps on the hull's slope, and a rope and wood ladder, 'scramble' is not an inappropriate term, both down and back up.

Rekhmire''s sun-darkened finger indicated the main one of the seven masts, and the platform high in the cross-trees. 'And you've climbed up there.'

The crow's-nest made me dizzy in a more than physical sense.

Gripping hard enough that my nails dug into the wood, I had found myself surrounded at dawn by a vast and chilly circle of sea, green as Venetian glass, with the sun laying stripes across the waves of a crimson so startling I would not have dared to paint it so. The sea turned innocent milky-blue as the sun rose, and I had heard the lookout's cry of a sail, and squinted into the light at the horizon.

The sails of a dhow appeared, blistering white, but not the ship itself –

I saw the tops of the lateen sails first, and then the mid parts, and only as it advanced to us up the slope of the world did the hull become visible.

It was that knowledge that we stand all the time at the crest of an invisible hill that dizzied me. I welcomed the return to the deck, and the illusion that the world is flat.

'Yes.' I drew a sharp, deep breath. 'I have. And?'

'Are you *trying* to leave your child an orphan!'

Silenced thoroughly, it was a moment before I could gather enough wit to say, 'Her grandfather Honorius would care for her, likely better than I could – and she would at least grow up without being watched to see if she turns into a monster!'

Rekhmire''s complexion darkened and reddened. He turned his back on me, knuckles white, swinging his crutch to shift himself down the deck towards the stern cabins.

I am a fool.

Sails towered above me as I ran to catch him up on the tar-spotted deck. Sails themselves taller than palace walls, creaking and swaying, but picking up no breeze. I scrambled after his unexpectedly brisk passage, past mast after mast, slatted shadows falling across the wood underfoot. The deck was hot despite my sandals.

'Rekhmire' – I know you'd climb if you could: you don't desire me to stop because of that?'

He glared at me. 'Of course not.'

Make that 'tactless fool'.

Heat-melted tar dropped from the rigging in hot black roundels. Rekhmire' strode on down the deck without being touched. I dodged one – only to catch another, streaking down the front of my linen tunic with a sharp sting.

Grins came at me from crewmen hauling on ropes or descending from the three main crow's-nests. I did not need to translate their remarks as I followed Rekhmire' into the welcome shade of the cabin.

'I'm sorry!' I blurted.

'"Stupid barbarian"!' Rekhmire' shot a smile over his shoulder, lifted one pointing finger to indicate the crew outside, and assumed an innocence as of one merely translating the words of others.

I stripped the tar-marked tunic off. Grinning in relief, I muttered, 'Fuck eighteen generations of your ancestors, book-buyer!'

I was careful enough to practise my Chin out of earshot of the crew, however much the tar stung.

'I *am* sorry,' I added. 'Where are we? Other than becalmed in Hell?'

Rekhmire' gave me an amused look. 'What have you got against the last eighteen generations of my ancestors in particular? And, becalmed in the Gulf of Sirte, Sebekhotep tells me.'

Passing into the first of the airy and spacious inner cabins we had been allocated – and certainly I had never known of such a thing on a

European ship of any kind – I threw myself flat on the low bed, letting the snapsack fall where it might, and rubbed at the reddened mark the tar left. 'You're not joking, are you? You do know the last eighteen generations of your family!'

'I share my ancestors with Queen Ty-ameny. That helps.' The large Egyptian smiled a little. 'I can trace my ancestors back to the first Cleopatra.'

'I can trace mine back to my father . . . '

He held his hand out: I realised it held an impossibly translucent porcelain cup. I beamed, took it, and drank. The herbal drink was bearable, cold, in this hot weather.

Trace my ancestry back to my father – and to my mother.

My smile died, the thought of Rosamunda still enough to make me cold in my belly.

A further door opened and shut, and cut off the sound of a crying baby.

'Carrasco . . . ' I lifted my head. 'How long?'

He shrugged. 'Not very long.'

I scrambled up, moving through the open door into the next room, and dropped into a crouch by Onorata's cradle. Fed an hour ago, not wet – I checked – and Carrasco had evidently been sitting by the fan that cooled her. I straightened up.

'She's bored,' I guessed. 'Take her to see the goats again.'

We travelled accompanied by two nanny-goats from the *Sekhmet*, their offspring, and a sire, in case we should need more. Onorata appeared to thrive on the warm fresh milk that I fed her, along with Carrasco's gruel. She was, I thought, passably fond of the goats, or at least she pushed herself up on her front with her round arms when I laid her in the straw, and laughed in what sounded like delight, staring at Carrasco or I milking them.

I went back through, to search out a clean tunic, and found Carrasco with his head down and shoulders hunched, as if he could avoid Rekhmire' looking at him. The book-buyer had sat on the wide ledge of the cabin window.

'Carrasco—' I pulled the new tunic on, and realised only in retrospect that I had not been in the least self-conscious exposing my small breasts.

I coloured, despite them now being covered.

'When you were spying,' I said bluntly. 'Did you send word back telling Videric—' *Rosamunda!* '—about being a grandparent?'

'That you were with child, yes.'

He did not say, *After she was born, I was in jail*, but I could read it in the flush that reddened his neck.

Rekhmire' swallowed his own cup of liquid, and spoke as if Carrasco did not exist. 'I've been looking at charts with Sebekhotep.'

Sebekhotep, with the face of a Pharaoh, a lean and wolfish body, and

206

an appetite that could feed four men, had served on Queen Ty-ameny's naval fire-ships as well as commercial cargo ships; I suspected he might not actually need the many portolans and charts he'd come aboard with, to find his way around the Middle Sea. But he behaved as if he did, and I might have, in his place – too spectacularly good a navigator, and Zheng He might just decide he needed to keep this particular barbarian.

I accepted the change of subject. 'How long to Taraco?'

'Once we get a wind? A few days.' Rekhmire' frowned. 'We need to have our plans definitely made . . . '

The deck barely moved beneath me, although I heard the constant creak and slow shift of a becalmed vessel. Above the stern, on the deck that was our roof, I heard one of the bosuns yelling the omnipresent 'Mâshàng!', 'Jump to it!', and a thunder of hurrying feet.

Onorata's yelling shifted up to an irritated scream.

'Take her along to the animal pens,' I directed Carrasco.

He ducked his head in an awkward gesture of respect. I watched him go in and pick her up from the cradle, together with the sail-awning we habitually tied up to shade her. Tottola and Attila sat visible in the far corner, playing at dice. For all the unlikelihood of an attack here, the brothers still slept watch and watch about, except for an hour or so of overlap.

Attila pocketed a string of the odd bronze coins, pierced through with a square hole, that the Chin men used as gambling chips, and stood to buckle on his sword. Approaching Carrasco's shoulder, Attila ignored the man, but hummed in a low bass at my daughter where she stared at him.

A lullaby, I realised after a moment. I couldn't help but smile.

Rekhmire''s gaze followed mine. 'Ah. They're fond of the little one . . . Of course, *they* don't have to wake to feed her three hours before dawn.'

If his expression seemed neutral, I could hear amusement in his voice.

'Remind me never to hire an Alexandrine nurse,' I remarked. 'The Iberians are much superior . . . '

Rekhmire' huffled a suppressed laugh.

Except that *I* can hire nobody.

If not for my father, I would be trying to keep the child on what I could earn as a painter: that thought still wakes me up in the long hours before dawn, in a cold sweat.

Breeding itself out of selfishness, I thought.

Because not only are there sufficient painters of funeral portraits and chapel frescoes in this world that I would be hard put to keep us – it would also mean I must work at that hard enough that I would never have a chance to stop, and learn to improve.

If I had a true mother's instinct, I would not at times hate my child.

Surprisingly enough, the only relief from that fear had come in Alexandria, when in a fit of sleepless volubility I voiced it to Ty-ameny.

207

'Great Sekhmet's claws!' She had shown her white teeth in a grin. 'I hated all of my three! Asenath wouldn't feed; Esemkhebe wouldn't stop, and Peshet was always bawling her head off for me when I needed urgently to sit in council. And then my breasts would leak milk all through the diplomatic meetings.'

Ty-ameny had shaken her head.

'Some mothers only like infants. Perhaps that's why they have more. I didn't *begin* to love mine until they were old enough to move about and talk.'

It made me feel a little less guilty.

I felt a touch on my arm, and returned to myself to find Rekhmire' frowning slightly.

'I had meant to broach this before,' he remarked, apparently idly. 'As an assistant to one of the Royal Library's buyers, you're entitled to a finder's fee, and a small remittance when your work is otherwise satisfactory.'

He indicated other drawings spilling across the low bed. The war-junk, from every angle that I could contrive; including the upper crow's-nests.

'You intend these as studies for a painting, but I doubt you ignorant of the fact that copies will be well-received by Ty-ameny and her philosophers.'

The philosophers having taken thorough advantage of my presence before we left Alexandria, I thought I could speak reasonably well as to their infinite curiosity.

I forced a smile. 'If I copy scrolls you want, yes; pay me a fee. You can have copies of these drawings in any case. It's not like I'm Ty-ameny's cousin . . . '

'Do you despise spies so much then?'

It came as a lightly-voiced question, Rekhmire''s gaze not on me, but directed at Carrasco and Attila's preparations in the far cabin, and Tottola's quiet amusement at the sheer number of things they took with them. The Egyptian spoke as if the answer would mean nothing of any significance.

I said, 'You were born to it. Alexandria's your home. It's not *my* country.'

He seemed unsatisfied.

I got up to hold the main door open, while Carrasco and baby and parasol and escort left the cabins. Not that I mistrust Attila or Tottola, but I knew how little Rekhmire' cared to discuss any business in front of Ramiro Carrasco.

The cabin's floor had been padded in places with some cloth very like a tapestry; it was soft under my feet when I kicked my sandals off. Padding back towards Rekhmire', I observed, 'You want to know if I despise you, for being a spy.'

The Egyptian rapidly smoothed down the folds of his linen kilt. That action was automatic by now: it hid his scars.

Apparently studying the ink-scroll hanging down from one ceiling-beam, he remarked, 'That would be one of the reasons I have never forced you to see what my business is.'

'*Chun zi!*'

His eyebrows climbed up towards his shaven scalp. 'And that would mean?'

'"Moron"!'

'Fascinating.' He took his tablets out of the bag at his belt, and incised a quick note in the wax. If he had been another man, I would have said he was suppressing a grin. 'Why is it you can be impolite in thirteen languages, painter?'

'Probably the people I travel around with, book-buyer!'

The Egyptian snorted.

'Of course,' I added, 'I may not be saying it right. My ear still isn't adjusted to Chin voices.'

'Perhaps,' Rekhmire' agreed. 'But the tone was unmistakable – at least to a foreign barbarian . . . '

He glanced away from me, at the dark wooden beams, and the intricately inlaid chests we had been loaned for our belongings. If he was pleased not to be despised, he was also embarrassed, although it would have been necessary to know him well to be aware of that.

'Listen—' He held up his hand.

For a long moment I heard nothing, only the natural creaking and shifting of a ship, even one this size.

Creaking in rhythm.

I shot to the cabin door and looked up.

Against the hazy sky, all of the sails were belling out, one by one, to catch the wind.

2

On the morning that we passed the Balearic Islands, Onorata taught herself to roll.

I had her on the floor-tapestry that the Chin-men used instead of fur rugs, laying on my belly so I might look her in the eye. She went from staring vaguely in the direction of the ceiling to thrusting with one still-small arm at the floor, and was abruptly over on her front.

We surveyed each other in equal surprise.

She broke out into a crow of laughter.

'Clever!' I wondered if she had wit enough yet to imitate, and if she copied the position of her mother-father. I sat up, thinking to encourage her to roll back the other way.

A fist rapped against the slatted wooden door, the knocking done in a Frankish fashion.

'In!'

A dark-haired figure slunk in from the deck: Ramiro Carrasco de Luis. He shot a wary look over at Tottola, apparently asleep in one corner with his arms and ankles crossed.

'May I speak to you, madonna? Mistress?'

Three months of seeing me in skirts in Venice evidently established me as a woman so firmly in his mind I will not shift it.

I sighed, and reached over to nudge Tottola's boot.

The large man's eyes were already open.

'Will you take her for a while?' I nodded towards the inner room. 'I won't be long. It's probably those *chou ba guai* goats again!'

Tottola's dark expression changed to a grin at that. He scooped an indignant Onorata up and made for the door.

Clearly he thinks Ramiro Carrasco will one day try again to assassinate me.

Well, I was hardly joking when I told Carrasco that, as a slave, I would take care to be trusted for a long time before I killed my master. And then the judges might blame someone else.

The German man-at-arms snorted, ducking under the door lintel to the inner room. Ramiro Carrasco kept quiet, in a manner that told me, if he wasn't yet used to being a slave, he had some idea of what behaviour was expected of him.

I stood, tugging my tunic straight, picking up my leather sack. The tiny inlaid drawers of the Chin furniture ideally suit painting tools. Remembering to clean and put them away is essential, however, and my hellion child had distracted me.

'You can get me a bucket of hot water when you're done . . . '

Ramiro Carrasco stood awkwardly in the middle of the cabin; a life study would show tension in his shoulders and spine.

'What?' I demanded.

'I need to talk to you.' He glanced at the door to the back cabin, that stood ajar, not by accident. I saw him take a breath, expanding his sternum; he scowled to himself.

His feet were bare, dirty, and callused, now. He wore a bleached and dirty tunic, pulled down over a Frankish shirt that hung to his mid-thigh, and his hose were rolled down to his knees in the heat. I saw his sleek black hair had grown down to touch his ears, and was no longer sleek, but breaking out into curled ends. Someone must have given him orders to shave: dark stubble patched his jaw.

His hand came up, fingers hooking under the smooth iron of his collar. In the clear light from the cabin window it was possible to read *::I am owned by Ilario::* engraved in Venetian script.

'Ramiro?'

'I have to . . . ' His head came up.

For a stark heartbeat I wondered, *Should I call Honorius's men?*

Ramiro Carrasco bent down, awkwardly, on one knee and then the next, until he was kneeling in front of me.

'Get up!' I must sound shrill, I realised.

'*Please.*' The Iberian hunched into himself. His face showed a shining pink where the stubble did not grow. His fingers locked into each other. 'Please, I'm begging you – slaves beg, don't they? Please. Ilario - mistress—'

I shot a glance at the inner door; Tottola was not visible. He would be alertly listening. Judging whether to guard Onorata or myself first.

Flushing as red as Carrasco, fully as embarrassed, I hissed, 'Stand up! *What* is this about?'

His head lifted.

I saw a vestige of Ramiro Carrasco de Luis in Venice in the jut of his jaw. His hands shook where he clenched them together. All of his body where he knelt down on the war-junk's deck had a faint shiver to it.

I grabbed him by the shoulders of his tunic and hauled, not caring that I heard fabric tear. All but throwing him up off the deck and onto his feet, I spat out, 'You don't kneel to me!'

He stared wildly.

Too used to thinking of 'Ilaria', with a woman's strength.

I stepped forward and he automatically stepped back, stopping only as his spine came into hard contact with the ship's hull beside the outer door.

211

He blurted out, 'You have to kill me!'

'*What?*'

Attila's voice sounded from the deck outside. 'Need any help?'

I stretched across Carrasco to open the outer door.

The German man-at-arms leaned up against the door-frame, apparently casual. I had seen him draw his blade in a heartbeat from just such a stance.

'What a way to live a life!' I muttered, saw him grin with feral teeth, and nodded politely. 'I'll shout if I need anything.'

Attila returned the nod. I believed he chose to view me a male at such moments: a man, who of course would need little assistance with Carrasco.

I pushed the door closed as Attila placed his back to it.

'Now.' I stared at Ramiro Carrasco without moving away from him. 'What is this?'

He stood as if the hull held him up. 'You have to kill me.'

'*Kill* you?'

In the port's clear light, his skin had an unhealthy shine. Ochre and green, if I had to choose pigments. Lines cut deeply into his face, and could have been dehydration, or pain, or fear, or all those things.

I shook my head, and pointed at a low stool. 'Sit.'

Ramiro Carrasco looked uncertain. I recognised that. The slave does not sit before the master.

I am doing you no favours, if you ever pass to another master, I reflected.

The unlikelihood of that circumstance made me feel a little better. I indicated the stool again. 'Do as I say.'

He collapsed onto the lacquered and padded stool as if his legs folded up under him. His eyes did not leave my face.

'Why would I *kill* you?' Exasperation sharpened my voice to high tenor; I dragged it downward. 'Carrasco. If I *wanted* you dead, I wouldn't have bought you in Venice!'

He began slowly to rub his hands over his arms. For all the heat, I could see the fine black hairs at his wrists standing up on gooseflesh.

'This ship is going to Taraconensis.'

No question in his tone. Keeping any rumour from a ship's crew is a lost cause, but Carrasco in any case might know the Balearic coasts by sight.

He raised his head. Luminous eyes showed rawly accessible pain, hatred, fear. 'You *have* to kill me. Because otherwise I'll betray you.'

I could not doubt the shaking honesty in his tone.

'Why would you tell me about it?'

'So that you can order your men – if I'm within Lord Videric's reach—' Ramiro Carrasco stuttered over the Aldra's name. 'He'll *find out* that I'm here. Once we sail into Taraco . . . He'll threaten my family. He'll offer me what he can give me, but he'll threaten them, and he owns them!'

He spoke in Iberian, clearly forgetting in his desperation that Attila and Tottola were both the other side of thin doors. He made fists of his hands, clenching them so hard that his nails must break the skin in a minute.

'What can Videric *offer* you?' I hesitated. 'You wouldn't trust him to offer you freedom?'

Ramiro's mouth curved a little, only at one side. I recall that ironic smile from Venice, when this dishevelled man was Federico's sleek secretary.

I do not expect to feel empathy for the man who would have killed me—

'Freedom after a fashion.' Carrasco shrugged. 'He'll offer me a quick death.'

I stared.

'He'll offer to keep my family safe,' he said, 'and he'll offer to give me what *I'd* promise, if I were him – a quick execution, to spare me the judicial torture of a slave, or being left to die after some ambush with my guts hanging out.'

He bit at his lip, and rose awkwardly to his feet as if he could not bear to be sitting while I stood. We were much of a height.

Slaves on their own – as, among foreigners like these Chin-men – have no acquaintance to confide in. Only too much time to think.

This is what Ramiro Carrasco has been thinking, over the cradle of my child.

'You want *me* to order your death, instead?'

His face crumpled in a way an adult man's should not.

'I want you to save my family! If I'm dead, then there's no reason for him to harm them!'

I cut him short with a cruel truth. 'Videric may make an example of them. To convince the men he uses as spies *after* you.'

Ramiro Carrasco wiped a hand over his face. He sweated now, but not from the humid heat. Bitterness and desperation sounded in his voice. 'I'm already your slave. One day you'll punish me for assaulting you in Venice. Why not make it now? I'll *beg* for punishment. But you have to keep me away from Taraco—'

'Christus! No. Stop embarrassing yourself!'

I wanted to shake him. I dared not touch him.

Because he is my slave, and no man can stop me if I whip the skin off his back.

Or if I kill him.

Ramiro Carrasco looked at me with sheer desperation. 'I *accept* I am your slave. In God's name, do something, because I can't!'

A man cannot be watched all day, every day.

If Ramiro Carrasco de Luis feels driven enough by this to kill himself, what will drive him is the contrast between the free man of Venice and the slave. There is no action he can take against the situation he is in. I have cause to know how fear is strongest then.

Carrasco let out a sound that was both sigh and groan. With one ragged swift movement, he drove his fist against the wooden wall: a loud crack echoed around the cabin.

'No—' I waved Attila away as the blond man-at-arms swung the door open again. 'Leave us!'

The door clicked shut.

I held my hand out. 'Let me see that.'

Carrasco's fingers felt cold in mine. Blood welled out of the scrapes on his knuckles.

Manipulating the joints with my thumbs got a suppressed grunt out of him, but I felt no unusual movement of bone under my pressure.

I wish I might get the flayed image of the Royal Mathematicians' autopsy from my mind to paper. I do not desire to know what the living flesh is like under the skin. Or how easily a man may be flayed alive, rather than dead.

But the truth is, my charcoal drawings of hands have been better since then.

Ramiro Carrasco muttered, 'What can a slave say to a master that's honest? You're right. Send me off to be beaten; have done with it!'

'So you can jump over the ship's rail?'

'No!'

He trod on my words far too quickly.

I pushed his hand back towards him. He flexed it, looking down; unkempt black hair falling into his eyes.

He did not look at me. 'Perhaps I *wish* you to believe I would do that.'

Men take their most stupid actions in such undecided passionate states.

'Sit.' I pointed at the low stool.

Returning to my sack for paper and a stub of charcoal, I saw in peripheral vision how he sank slowly down onto the stool again, never taking his eyes off me.

Long experience as a slave has me used to judging men, sometimes even accurately. But I read neither souls nor minds; I doubted I could read in him whether he was honest or not, with me or with himself.

I may know better after this.

I pulled up a second stool, sat down, and began sketching, with paper and board across my knee.

Sitting for me was calming him, I realised.

It's a familiar routine.

'Videric can threaten you again.'

'Yes.' The light didn't alter on his luminous brown eyes.

'He may have imprisoned your family as hostages by now.'

Eyes moving from his face to the paper, I knew him aware of that. I need not say Videric may also have sent in his soldiers to fire and burn the villages. A man can drive his serfs off his own estates, if he wishes. Or kill them. No one speaks for them; in law they're property.

'I know so little.' Ramiro shifted, meeting my eyes. 'And I was of the same kind as your Alexandrine – in possession of every fact and rumour.'

My chalk discovered the lines of frustration, anger, passion.

'I could have *killed* you in Venice! If.' He stopped dead.

I finished. 'If you could have brought yourself to do it.'

He glared as if I had deeply insulted him. 'You think I couldn't kill you?'

'I think you're the first man in your family to have a choice at anything except digging dirt – and you chose the university of Barcelona and training as a lawyer, not going for a soldier, like most farmer's sons.'

I watched the pupils of his eyes widen.

'I think Videric saw a man who could be blackmailed, and made a bad error of judgement about what he could be blackmailed into. A man who studies the law isn't necessarily the best choice for a casual murderer.' I sketched the slackened flesh around his jaw. 'Which leaves you caught with nowhere to go. Not the best situation.'

He visibly struggled, and at last managed, 'You're not as rash as you seem, are you?'

'Possibly you mean "not as stupid as I look"? I don't have to tell you – a slave studies people. When anyone can do anything to you, you learn to look.'

Ramiro Carrasco shot *me* a look, that I thought for the first time was not solely directed at 'Madonna Ilaria'.

I remarked, 'Only you would blush because I *don't* think you're a murderer.'

Having reduced him to silenced confusion, I used the charcoal to darken in the masses of his hair.

'You will have heard—' Because it could not be otherwise, travelling with us. '—that we intend Videric to return to court, in his old rank and position. If we succeed, that makes us safe.' I caught his eye. 'All of us.'

Abruptly his face creased. He gave me a look of sardonic scorn.

'You think if Lord Videric's back in power, he won't make damn sure to clear up every loose end? That he'll let you run around loose, knowing what you know?'

Ramiro Carrasco did not need to add, *And I, with what I know?*

This dread slicing coldly through me is not new. This wakes me at nights – suppose what we plan is not enough?

As calmly as I might, I said, 'You truly don't believe this will succeed.'

Carrasco snorted as if he were a freeman. 'I will not be responsible for the deaths of my family!'

The war-junk slowly tacking, the shift of sunlight altered all the tone and values of his face.

He will have thought what Rekhmire' and I have thought, because Ramiro Carrasco is not stupid. Only at the frayed end of his rope.

'Suppose I strike the rivets out, and take your collar off, and let you run?'

His eyes widened. My fingers rummaged in the sack for a white chalk to make highlights. Only a fool doesn't use what tool there is to hand.

'No!' He got the word out with difficulty. 'The sole reason he hasn't had me killed yet is that it's more difficult to kill both you and I at once!'

'Then we'll continue to make it difficult for him . . . '

Carrasco sat as if stunned.

To have refused your own freedom commits you – as I once discovered – to much.

'Two things,' I said.

I put in the curls of his hair, tumbling over his forehead, and found my skill not great enough to reproduce the confusion in his expression.

'First, Ramiro Carrasco, if I come out of this conversation even *thinking* you might kill yourself, you'll leave this cabin in chains, and you'll stay that way.'

Carrasco sat perfectly still, moving only with the minor movements of the ship. I smudged in the values of his stubble in the sunlight, botched it, and set the board and paper down at my feet.

'Secondly, Onorata will need feeding soon. You do it.'

His face turned so rawly open that it was painful to watch.

He spoke barely above a whisper. 'I don't understand.'

'I made use of you before,' I said, 'on the *Sekhmet*. I trust you, now, not to hurt a child.'

Ramiro Carrasco stared.

I said, 'Yes, there's no honesty between master and slave – but I can't free you yet; as you say, I need to have that threat over Videric. So if you have to trust me, then I have to trust you.'

He sat motionless – and all in a rush put his elbows on his knees and his hands over his face.

I would let you have that privacy. But I need to see.

I reached forward and took his wrists, pulling his hands down.

Ramiro Carrasco stared away, sounding stifled. 'You can't do this! If he demands of me—'

'If I choose to have trust in you—'

Water shone in the creases of skin about his eyes. He wrenched it out word by word: 'If it was a choice – my father – my brothers – I would choose them over your child. You must know that!'

'Then I'll see you won't be put where you have that choice to make.'

He made as if he would say something, struggled, and no word came out.

Rekhmire''s tenor voice abruptly cracked through the silence in the cabin. 'Are you completely mad?'

The Egyptian stood in the cabin doorway.

Ramiro Carrasco sprang to his feet with the quickness of a man who has been whipped for not doing so. His hands tore out of my grip.

I stood, slowly, heart hammering in my chest. 'You were listening?'

The Egyptian snorted. 'And Attila, too!'

Rekhmire''s expression was one I did not recognise. Scorn, I realised finally.

I have never seen him without his self-control—

Rekhmire' limped into the cabin, to the window-port, gazing out as if he did not see the masts and sails. Before I could speak, he swung clumsily around on his heel.

'What is it with you and your waifs and strays, Ilario? First Sulva. Then this . . . spy.'

It would have hurt less, been less surprising, had he walked up and slapped me in the face.

I raised my voice. 'Attila!'

The German put his head around the door.

'Take Ramiro down to the animal pens. He'll milk the goat for the baby.'

I stayed aware of them out of peripheral vision, my gaze locked with Rekhmire''s.

Some of Honorius's authority evidently belonged to me by proxy; Attila did not hesitate, but stepped in, jerking his thumb expressively at Ramiro Carrasco. The slave-secretary moved as if his legs were made of wet paper, stumbling out of the cabin in front of the soldier.

I kicked the door closed behind them. 'Rekhmire'—'

'I apologise.' Rekhmire' wiped his hand over his shaven scalp. 'I know Sulva – is not mine to discuss.'

Sitting abruptly down on the low chair behind me, I caught a brush under my sandal and heard it crack.

I no longer look at the badly executed paintings I made of Sulva Paziathe. The shape of her face is marked out by my guilt.

Rekhmire' slid off his reed and linen headband, running the woven length of it through his fingers. He snorted. '*Carrasco,* on the other hand—'

'We need to trust him.'

'*Trust?*' Rekhmire' limped across the cabin and stood before me. The short stick let him walk only with a swivelling limp.

This close, he smelled of the Alexandrine spices kept in his clothes chest, and that different male sweat I had become used to in Constantinople.

'You can't trust a slave. You should know this.'

I glared. 'We need him on our side, or Videric will have him back, one way or another!'

It was not necessary to add that, spending months in our company, Carrasco will have learned too much of what we plan to do.

Exasperated, Rekhmire' snapped, 'You know there's no trust between slave and master!'

'No.' I pushed the stool back squarely onto all its legs, and found myself reaching out to the Egyptian's large hands. 'But sometimes it begins there.'

A dark ruddy colour showed on his neck, growing to stain him at cheek and brow.

It took me a moment to realise that I saw Rekhmire' blushing.

'I – that is – well—' He opened his hands to me as if we had done it a hundred times before.

His grip felt warm and strong.

'*Some* slaves,' he muttered, remarkably apologetically.

I couldn't help a cheerful barb in return. 'I might rescue Ramiro Carrasco de Luis; you needn't act as if I'm about to marry him!'

'Just as well, I think.' Rekhmire' stared at our hands. 'Marrying three times in the same year *might* be considered excessive.'

'This must be why Ty-ameny values your opinion so much, book-buyer – how keenly you see into a matter!'

He snorted.

I released Rekhmire''s hands, stooping to rescue board and tinted paper.

'I'll draw you, too,' I added, 'if you're jealous of that.'

The Egyptian stilled for a moment. He shot me a look. 'I'm transparent to you, evidently.'

Rekhmire' did not smile, but somehow warmth suffused his expression.

'I confess I would be curious to see the results of a sketch. But we should speak with Zheng He first, and settle how long he's prepared to give us at Taraco.'

'Long enough, I hope.' I swept my hair back, tied it with a leather thong, and re-buckled the thin leather belt (all I currently wore of my Iberian clothing) over an Alexandrine tunic.

The ship is surely large enough to cause panic. Is large enough, certainly, that I have felt no fear of the sea while aboard – as if I were not on a ship at all, but a wooden island.

Rekhmire''s head tilted, speculatively. 'I estimate the crew of this ship at between four and a half and five thousand Chin-men.'

'And there are the weapons.'

It was necessary to look up, given the inches of difference in our heights. Three parts of a year together: I read him so much more easily than I do Carrasco.

And now I see we have been thinking on parallel lines these last few days.
'I'm concerned,' I said.

He nodded.

I voiced it, nonetheless. 'However long we're here – how much of a panic there is, when we appear off the coast of Taraco – we need King Rodrigo to recall Videric. And . . . is this going to be enough?'

3

A sound like ripping paper tensed all the muscles of my shoulders and spine.

The rockets of Chin soared up from the launcher into the night sky.

Lights exploded.

'*Kek and Keket!*'

'Amen!'

Rekhmire' put his hand up between his face and the luminous sky and squinted. I rubbed the after-impressions of brilliance out of my eyes; night vision entirely gone. I could make out nothing of the deck, the rigging, the creaking sails, the crawling waves so far beneath the rail.

Seven bright lights sank down towards the blackness that was the coast close to Taraco.

So near and I can see nothing of it!

I left home – for want of a better word – in August, in the sign of Leo, Now the Twins rule the night sky. Two months short of a year. And it feels at the same time no time, and an age. I might have stepped out of the palace yesterday, or in the days of the Caesars and Barcas.

Rekhmire''s arm brushed against mine, his skin warm. 'I can only imagine what the Royal Mathematicians would have done if the Admiral had demonstrated these at Alexandria.'

I grinned. 'Swarmed the ship, I think. If they had to swim to it!'

Anonymous figures jostled me in the dark, the crew moving around to reload the launcher and send another shower of fire into the sky.

'I see no explosion where they land. But there may be some part of the weapon not yet used, if they only signal. I wonder . . . '

The dark shapes of Attila and Tottola were at my shoulder. I could all but feel them speculating if Zheng He would sell the secrets of such weapons.

Not even to the Lion of Castile, I thought.

What I could see now of Admiral Zheng He, stroking his beard in the lightning-coloured illumination, showed a man with the expression of a civilised commander sending out a warning to barbarians.

I turned blindly in the direction of the cabins. 'I imagine King Rodrigo knows we're here by now.'

There had been fishing boats in view since we sighted the Balearic

Islands. If their captains hadn't raised every sail to race to the mainland and be paid for their information, I would be astounded.

King Rodrigo Sanguerra would first hold his few warships in reserve – and now this monstrous vessel cleared the horizon, he would send them up the coast or down it, but certainly out of our way.

I added, 'We should make final plans, as much as we can.'

Rekhmire''s hand gaining support from my shoulder, we steered a way to the war-junk's stern. The cabin held a welcome familiarity in the golden lantern-light, that put gleams of gilding on cabinets and low tables, and soft dark shadows in corners. Scattered Egyptian cushions surrounded one of the tables, on which there were plates of food.

I helped Rekhmire' sit; he swore under his breath – and aloud, as Ramiro Carrasco came out of the inner cabin, Onorata rocking in his arms.

I padded across to touch her warm, dozing face. 'Did the noise wake her?'

'For a while.' His tone was low. 'But she sleeps again, mistress. Master. Ah – shall I take her back to her cradle?'

I stroked Onorata's fine hair, that had grown a wispy matt black. Her eyelids screwed shut; her small sleeping mouth opened in a yawn, and she made contented noises.

Not desiring to miss this moment of her being angelic – since I had quite enough of her other moods – I reached to take her solid small body into my arms. 'I'll settle her. You wait here.'

In the inner room, I put her down infinitely carefully; on her back in the cradle as Ty-ameny's nurses had advised me. I nodded to Tottola and Attila, as Tottola settled himself on his palliasse, and Attila took up his sword to guard the outer doors.

I did not begin my life under armed guard.

And I desire to make certain that she doesn't need to – as soon as ever I can.

Walking back into the main cabin, I encountered raised voices, and snarled, 'Quiet!' in an intense whisper. 'Don't wake her!'

The two men fell silent as I sat by the low table. Ramiro Carrasco looked at me from under his shaggy hair, and knelt down beside and behind me.

'You will have him present?' Rekhmire' spoke with the utmost polite mildness.

I would sooner he shouted.

'He was Aldra Videric's man. We need to ask him questions.' I reached for a plate, unsure of what was before me. Stodgy clumps of white stuff, like maggots, nevertheless tasted reasonably bland. I poked among it with my fingers, removing sharp pickles. 'I know you don't trust Ramiro Carrasco—'

Rekhmire' arched a brow, all Alexandrine civility.

I wish I might slap him!

'Very well.' I passed a dirty plate back to Carrasco. 'I'll call you when I need you.'

As the door closed behind Carrasco, Rekhmire' took up a small translucent bowl, eating with a quick-fingered hunger that surprised me. Between bites, he said, 'Tell me reasons why – this ship may not be enough?'

My hunger vanished.

I counted factors off on my fingers.

'The opposition faction at Rodrigo's court are right, in fact. Even if for the wrong reason. Videric *did* endanger the country. He has robbed it of stability. They see that as stemming from the scandal—' I didn't look up at the Egyptian. '—which caused Carthage to be able to slap the King's wrist, and demand that Videric should be set aside as First Minister. I know the nobles of Taraco. Even with the threat of something the size of this war-junk, there'll be some hot-heads who think it's one ship, they can capture it or destroy it.'

Rekhmire' smiled his familiar hidden amusement. It failed to amuse me.

I crossed my legs in the fashion of Carthage, and reached for the wine. 'On the other hand . . . We go ashore, we explain this to Rodrigo, and I promise you the King will find every way possible to make it work! Because *he* will want Aldra Videric back.'

If I could have kept bitterness from my voice, I would have added, *Whether or not Videric tried to kill his freak offspring.*

He remains the man that Rodrigo needs to see standing beside his throne.

'Is this—' I gestured around at the cabin walls, and by implication the vast ship itself. '—enough to make men forget last year's scandal?'

Rekhmire' tipped his bowl towards me in acknowledgement. 'I've asked the Admiral to permit no contact with the land. He'll anchor here offshore. We go in and speak to your King. That way the ship remains an unknown threat, and more persuasive.'

'Zheng He is determined to let no man aboard?'

Attila's voice interrupted, from the shadows by the door. 'Boats will come out; they'll sell fruit, wine, whores if they can. The captain and officers can't watch all their men all the time.'

I put my cup down. 'Then I guarantee that within forty-eight hours, Videric and half the counts and dukes of Rodrigo's court will know about the ship's weapons, and anything else here on board.'

'Don't worry,' Attila reassured. 'Lord Honorius warned us you'd be in danger; we'll see you safe.'

There was a silence, in which I heard Carrasco's movements in the inner cabins, and the wind blew one of the shutters open. Standing and crossing the deck to latch it shut, I caught a face full of the wind off the land.

Instantly, the scents brought back the colonnades of Rodrigo's court. As if I stood there, in the palace that has been home to me from the age of fifteen.

But now I have travelled.

My fingers fumbled the latch; I swore and finally got the shutter fastened.

'Bear this in mind,' I warned. 'It's as likely to be an assassin looking for Carrasco, as one looking for me. We need Carrasco alive.'

In the shadows, I could not see if Attila disapproved, but he nodded obedience.

'Let's not forget the most important weapon in any soldier's arsenal, sir – ma'am.'

It seemed unfair to deprive him of something he'd evidently practised with company after company of armed men. 'And what would that be?'

'Dumb luck!'

I snorted. Even Rekhmire' smiled.

'So. The first move.' I sent a prompting look at the Egyptian.

'Our first move,' Rekhmire' said ponderously, 'is that you do not go ashore.'

I opened my mouth and Rekhmire' snatched two porcelain bowls and a cup off the low table close to me.

I stared at him.

Wine and pickle splashed his fingers.

'Just making sure.' There wasn't a smile on his face, but his eyes were bright.

I glared at the Egyptian – and nearly cracked when Attila, large and impressive as he was, looked frankly bewildered.

'Let's discuss this—' I reached over and recovered my cup from Rekhmire''s hand. '—like sensible and responsible adults.'

He lifted his own bowl, looking at me over the rim.

Catching a deep warmth in his gaze, I could not do otherwise than smile back at him.

'You can distract me as much as you like.' I leaned back on cushions embroidered with Sekhmet's sigils. 'But you need me ashore. King Rodrigo must speak to me. With all possible respect—'

'With complete *dis*respect,' Rekhmire' echoed in a muttered aside that made Attila's grin flash out of the shadows.

'—the King won't trust an Alexandrine spy as far as he could throw you. I don't think you can play the humble book-buyer this time.'

Rekhmire' reached into his robes and pulled out a leather scroll-case. He held it out. I put my bowl down, uncapped the case, unrolled the scroll, and found myself looking at the seal of the Pharaoh-Queen.

'I can play the diplomatic envoy of Ty-ameny of the Five Great

Names.' Rekhmire''s brows lifted towards his shaved scalp. 'I thought you'd assume something of the sort.'

The ancient pictorial script of Alexandria might have declared him envoy from the Moon, but there was a Latin copy also in the scroll case.

'Perhaps,' I said. 'I may have been gone from Taraco some time. But I know how much the east isn't trusted. Unless you outright plan to tell King Rodrigo that your Queen is using Admiral Zheng He to scare the shite out of Carthage—'

'That would be one option.' Rekhmire' took the scroll-case back. 'I do admit, the first approach might be better made by one of King Rodrigo's own subjects. But, Ilario, you're in too much danger. What use is all of this if a hired gang of thugs kills you at Taraco docks?'

'Unless you plan on locking me up with Ramiro, I'm going ashore. I want to see Honorius!'

The Egyptian slowly nodded. 'I understand. Again, it would be safer if the Admiral made an exception, and permitted the Captain-General to come here.'

I wavered. *Onorata is in the next cabin. And I cannot take her ashore with me.* 'Would Zheng He allow that?'

We talked, after one of Jian's officers took a message. I stood at the port for a time, and then paced. Ramiro Carrasco answered Onorata's sleepy cries, and I let him feed her again. I watched candle-light shift and change on men's faces; stretched my spine, and caught a glimmer of grey out in the open air.

'Attila, if I can borrow one of your mail-shirts,' I suggested – Attila being slightly less large around his chest than his brother. 'And wear a helmet. If I carry a sword as the Alexandrine's escort, no one will look at me; you *know* that. No man looks in obvious places.'

Rekhmire' opened his mouth to protest.

And clearly thought better of it.

'Then we must hope there's a way to get a message to Lord Honorius, once we're ashore.'

The cabin door opened. Commander Jian himself came in, meeting my gaze and nodding his head sharply.

'No man to come here,' he managed, in Mediterranean Latin. 'You go ashore now?'

A glimmer of white showed at the oared boat's prow.

Sebekhotep's robes.

The Egyptian pilot must be there for reassurance or curiosity's sake. From what I recall, a six-year-old child could steer a boat to the quay at Taraco.

We docked, and the ground was painfully hard beneath my boots.

How could I have forgotten the air and the light!

Even before dawn, with the east bright but unscarred by the sun, every

224

dew-wet breeze brings the scent and reality of home to me. No brush will capture this.

I raised my head and looked around the quay as Rekhmire' disembarked with appropriate dignity. I might wish to be a guard in more than my clothing, but I was overwhelmed, as if I had not seen the city since childhood. And, at the same time, the ghost-white buildings, and the feather-silhouettes of the fronds of the trees, were as familiar to me as my own skin.

Dawn turned the sea-spray yellow, peach, scarlet; the Alexandrine banner unrolled in yards of blue silk down the offshore wind. I smelled salt, the old Roman drains of Taraco, and the scent of outdoor food-booths already beginning to cook for early workers. Fruit-sellers' cries echoed down the dusty streets.

I turned my head, looking thirty yards in the other direction.

There, where a coastal ship is tied up to the bollard, first catch of fish already unloaded – that's where I walked up the gang-plank of a galley sailing south down the coast to Carthage. Two hours beforehand, my mother attempted to stick a dagger into my stomach.

I thought of the blade, black with poison.

Most poisons that you can daub on metal do less harm than rust. There's always talk in court of such weapons; of poisoned cups, of scent that can poison a pair of gloves . . . In all honesty, more men die of the fever turning their guts out. And more women in childbed.

Tottola's elbow caught me ungently in the kidney.

I shouldered the pennant of Alexandria, becoming an anonymous soldier and banner-bearer. Tottola and Attila were in blue doublets of one shade or another, and scarlet hose. They had not yet replaced their household badges.

If we meet Aldra Videric at the top of this hill with a gang of hired criminals, I thought – or Rodrigo and the royal guard out to arrest us – these men could die around me now.

In which case, I'll step out in front of them, because in either case it's me they want. And wasting a life because of that would be stupid.

I resolved not to mention it to Rekhmire'. *The Egyptian will expect something more sensible from me.*

The same feeling of familiarity and strangeness suffused me on the winding road to the palace. Mountains shone on the horizon, blue glass; but would be yellow rough scrub under the noon sun. Every peak and trough, I remember. Plodding under the shade of palm-feathered branches, bare-footed children shinning up the trunks out of our way; a pavement shoe-maker looking up from his last as we passed him. And the dark eyes of men stopping their work at tavern or shop or household, momentarily and silently taking in the sight of soldiers as we trudged up the steep slope.

The intricacies of the Sanguerra fortress-palace begin with a crenellated gate-house at the bend of the road.

It had been dark when we left the ship. By the time we passed men at guard-house, courtyards, outer and inner baileys, and were allowed into the palace proper, the sun had risen over the sea high enough to make me sweat.

'How much *more* of this!' Tottola fingered under the unfamiliar woollen collar of his winter doublet. (Neither man-at-arms had summer gear with them.) Attila echoed his muttering.

'It's an old palace—'

'Rabbit warren!' Tottola interrupted me, under his breath.

'—and you wouldn't begrudge the King a chance to impress us, would you?'

The tall armoured brothers grinned, instantly, and as instantly looked as unimpressed as it is possible for a man to be.

The King's guards were leading us towards one of the eastern courtyards, I realised. This older part of the palace has Carthaginian influence, from ancient days before they were driven out to Africa. Two altars burned at the foot of a wide flight of steps, servants keeping the flames high, although invisible as the sun reached down to them. Above the steps, a wall of niches and crumbling urns enclosed an open square.

Beyond the wall, poplar trees screened masonry pyramids. My hand recalled painting the desert beyond Carthage. I shivered.

That chill, and the dusty green feathers of the poplars, took me suddenly to Venice's lazaretto islands; I turned my head to look at the walls as we were marched past them – *Before this was a courtyard . . . it was a necropolis.*

I have not ever noticed this before.

Would I notice, if I had not travelled?

Around the crumbled end of the wall, the character changed. We walked over cracked sandstone slabs, with ahead of us the walls of the castle's east wing – a million featureless pale bricks running up to corbels, and battlements, and the terracotta tiles roofing the machicolations. Guards' heads showed as small as grape-pips. The walls towered high enough to block out most of the sky: certainly enough to humble petitioners to a king.

King Rodrigo Sanguerra had his chair of state outdoors, under a striped awning, beside a flight of palace steps with stylised faces carved on their balustrades.

I could not see the King himself over the heads of the surrounding crowd. Most were guards or servants – only a few courtiers would attend an audience beginning this early; Rodrigo held it for common tradesmen and workers, so they might not lose too much of the working day. The guards shepherded us under the far end of the awning. Somewhat shaded by the sun, I lowered the Alexandrine banner so it would not catch on the billows of cloth, and shifted up on my toes, to see if I might see King Rodrigo.

Rekhmire' caught my eye. 'We shall doubtless wait the usual long time; no need to waste it . . . '

I nodded, and set myself to watching inferior courtiers as they came and went, and men and women from the kitchens, in case there might be a face I knew.

Heat bounced back off the stone, and the balustrade's ancient faces changelessly stared.

There!

'Hold this!' I hissed, and shoved my banner into Attila's hand. He caught it, much startled.

I stepped to intercept the path of a man whose broad face had often sat across from me in the royal scriptorium, on those occasions when Rodrigo Sanguerra had employed me for my actual talents.

'Galindus!' Seizing his upper arm, I shifted us into the partial concealment of the flight of steps, where the wall cast a shadow.

I smiled. He frowned, briefly. I saw him abruptly recognise me – more by voice than clothes, as many do.

'Ilario! You're back!'

'Yes and no.' I kept the smile with an effort, threw everything of our acquaintance into my expression, and got my demand out. 'You still hear all the gossip, don't you? Listen, Galindus, tell me this. Lord Licinus Honorius – is he here?'

'What?'

'Licinus Honorius. *Il leone di Castiglia.* Is he at court!'

Seconds dripped past like cold honey. Galindus shot an unmistakably prurient look at the crowd around Rodrigo's chair of state.

'Well . . . ' His voice held the avidity of a man with a piece of choice gossip. My heart thudded until I thought it would tear.

Galindus spoke.

'Well, yes. He's here. Licinus Honorius.'

Honorius is alive.

I had not known how much I feared otherwise, until warmth entered into every frozen blood-vessel in my body.

'Honorius is at court? In the palace?'

Galindus looked left and right, his long dark hair whipping with the jerky movement. He glanced above us, at the steps, for secrecy's sake.

'He's here,' Galindus whispered. 'He's in prison.'

4

Attila gripped me about the elbow, hauled me two steps back without so much as an acknowledgement to Galindus, and shoved the pennant's pole into my hands.

'What—'

'*Quiet!*'

One of the court officers, whose face I didn't know, scowled at the both of us, regarding us as men-at-arms who do not know a courtly discipline.

The officer rapped his ivory staff on the stone of the courtyard.

I stepped briskly in beside Rekhmire' as he moved forward, just catching the end of the herald's full-voiced cry:

'—of the city of New Alexandria, known commonly as Constantinople!'

A flutter of women-in-waiting and courtiers stepped back as we approached. Lesser men, according to some: mayors of distant hill-towns, and the captains of Rodrigo Sanguerra's frontier towers. Certainly leaner men. I could see none of the kingdom's more influential and powerful lords.

Is the King hiding us by making us seem unimportant?

A flare of hope seemed almost distant. Numb, I could only think, *But – Honorius!*

Rekhmire' paused before the rank of guards to either side, and for all the chair of state was on a stone dais, he looked down at my King.

With immense dignity, Rekhmire' began to kneel.

I saw the spasm of pain he suppressed.

Immediately I knelt, still clasping the banner pole. That put my shoulder where he could reach it. Large fingers bit deep into my muscles, hard enough that I thought he would still lose balance and sprawl.

The Egyptian thumped down on one knee beside me.

'*Rekhmire'!*' I bowed my head low enough that no man would see my mouth. 'My *father*! He's alive!'

Rekhmire' shot me a startled look – at why I sounded angry, I realised – and had time to do no more than raise his head as King Rodrigo, fifth of that name, looked up from his gilded chair, and leaned forward to speak graciously.

Blood thundering in my ears cut off the formalities.

Have you put my father in prison? Who *else* could be responsible!

The linen of the awning softened the sun's light. More white than dark showed now in Rodrigo's wiry short-cut beard. His eyes, under thick brows, might be bloodshot in the corners, but I could still feel the force of his personality, blazing from them.

It occurred to me, belatedly. The King will be frighteningly angry that no man apparently trusts him to hold his kingdom without Aldra Videric at his side.

But even King Rodrigo Sanguerra knows there's no fighting men's opinions. Whether they're right or wrong.

Rekhmire' rose, with equal effort, his weight almost pushing me down onto the sandstone paving.

King Rodrigo signalled his guards to step back, and his servants to pour wine; let his gaze imperceptibly stray while he continued to speak with the representative of New Alexandria, and stopped midway through a sentence.

'Master Envoy . . . '

Rekhmire' bowed his head. 'Ah. We thought this safer, Exalted One.'

Rodrigo Sanguerra Coverrubias stared at me.

A year ago, I thought, I could not have held your gaze so long.

'I freed you, hermaphrodite.'

I passed Rekhmire''s banner to Tottola and knelt down as one does before kings. 'Yes, Your Majesty.'

'And then you repay me as you did. Not well.'

Biting down on rage allowed me to control my voice. 'Is it well, Majesty, to have put the Lion of Castile into your prison?'

At my elbow, Rekhmire' twitched.

He would have advised me against that, I thought, and momentarily regretted my anger.

No more than a moment. The world is still carmine about me.

Rodrigo Sanguerra leaned back in his gilt chair, steepling his fingers. He gave the impression of choosing his words very carefully.

'Tell me, Ilario, what I *should* have done with Licinus Honorius?'

He did not say 'your father'. I had not the slightest doubt he knew.

Before I could stop choking and get out an answer, King Rodrigo lifted the full force of his gaze to me.

'Here is a lord of my kingdom,' he said, measuredly, 'Aldra Licinus Honorius, whose presence I require at court. I send to inform him. He does not come. I send to *order* him. He delays, says he will come . . . but does not. Meantime, all my other lords – less rich than Licinus Honorius, perhaps, and not "the Lion of Castile", but still noble lords – watch this behaviour . . . and judge how weak I've grown.'

No proper words of objection would form in my dry mouth.

'Therefore,' Rodrigo concluded, leaning back, 'when Aldra Honorius finally *does* deign to obey his King's summons, what do I do? Thank him kindly for his arrival? Ask him how I should have worded my summons, to be better obeyed?'

'Your Majesty—'

'*Yes!*' His hand slapped loudly down on the carved chair's arm. '"Majesty." "King." But only so long as men call me so! Licinus Honorius is a subject of mine. He defied me. He is therefore now serving me – by being an object lesson to any man who might think of doing likewise!'

Rekhmire' stirred, beside me.

It was the pain of his leg, I saw. Nothing in the Egyptian's expression signified dissent.

'It's not justice to put him in prison, Majesty!' I spoke fiercely. 'It's my fault he didn't come. He was helping me. If you put anybody in the dungeon, it should be me.'

Rodrigo Sanguerra briefly smiled.

'I know.' He rested his chin on his fist. The hooded lids of his eyes dipped down – in a way that had always, in the past, signalled covert amusement. 'But my hermaphrodite Fool in prison is hardly an object lesson to the men who covet my throne. Of which there are always some.'

'Sire . . . '

Rodrigo Sanguerra waved his free hand dismissively. 'Aldra Honorius can stay in my dungeons until I'm satisfied every man has realised he's there. *And* that he submits to his King. And then, on payment of a sufficiently large fine, he can find himself at liberty.'

He frowned, his pause unstudied.

'What, did you suppose I was going to execute the Lion of Castile?'

Dizziness made me unable to answer properly.

'You may see him,' King Rodrigo remarked, 'when we're done here. The more visitors, the more mouths to carry the story, after all.'

He smiled at me.

'Are you still free, hermaphrodite?'

What a question. Curtailing a long story, I said, 'Yes, Your Majesty.'

He would be in his late fifties or early sixties, this King of Taraconensis. If I tried to look at him as a stranger would – as Rekhmire' might be doing now – I saw the unforgiving and unwelcoming face of a country mostly composed of mountain, infertile plain, and rocky coast.

Growing up with the land, I know there are valleys that flower at the foothills of the mountains, and rich seas and forests, if a man can find the way to them. Rodrigo had been rumoured a less grave man before his Queen, Cixila, died in giving birth to their dead fourth child.

'Come here.' Rodrigo beckoned, and held out his hand. I moved to kneel on the dais steps, and kissed the cabochon-cut emerald he wore in his massive ouroboros-ring.

For a moment, he rested his hand on my head.

'You come back bringing trouble, Ilario.'

A flood of emotion would have had me in tears like a girl. I waited until it passed. And saw King Rodrigo had, as ever, read everything visible in a man's face.

'We'll break our fast and talk,' he said, glancing around absently for servants – and, on a sudden, looked back at me.

He gestured with his lined hand. 'Rise, Ilario.'

Stiffly, slowly, I stood up.

It is still instinctive in me – not to rise until he gives me direct permission.

'The envoy of Alexandria is best qualified to speak with you, Your Majesty.' I prayed he did not read how rigid I stood, and how much it was out of determination. 'No man knows I'm here, yet; no man will recognise me, dressed like this. May I be excused to visit Lord Honorius in prison?'

I did not suppose Honorius would be in a prison elsewhere than in Taraco. And not in the civil jail down in the city, reserved for men who are not noble. Somewhere in this palace's oubliettes and rat-infested dungeons, thick with the stench of ancient shit and despair . . . *Because if King Rodrigo desires to make an object lesson out of Honorius, he will keep him under his hand.*

Rekhmire''s fingers closed around my biceps. Without seeming to care that he broke protocol in speaking before the King did, he snapped, 'We need you here!'

The flash of Rekhmire''s gaze prompted *Videric!* very plainly.

'You were previously of the opinion I could stay on the ship, Master Rekhmire'. You can bring the introductory matters to my Lord King's attention. I'll continue after I've seen Lord Honorius—'

I bit back the words *my father.*

'—with His Majesty's permission.'

Rekhmire' glared at me, clearly divided between exasperation and a fear that I might throw something.

Observing us, King Rodrigo shifted his chin to his other hand, all the time watching me as closely as a painter does. He allowed silence to return.

Rekhmire' murmured, 'I apologise, Exalted One.'

I echoed him. 'I apologise, sire.'

Underlining that with silence, King Rodrigo did nothing more than observe me from under lowered lids.

'Very well!' He sat up, briskly. 'Master Egyptian, we will have a private audience. Ilario – one hour. And you will not afterwards whine to me that this is too brief!'

Without waiting for an answer, the King beckoned one of his men forward; a lugubrious-faced knight in a forest-green surcoat over Milanese armour.

'The prison, first; then bring Ilario to me in the east tower, when the hour of Terce has struck.'

5

The knight's lugubriosity appeared to be a function merely of his long features. He introduced himself as Safrac de Aguilar, and smiled amiably enough as I halted midway up a flight of sandstone spiral steps.

Four sets of steps serve the floors of the prison tower of the Sanguerra castle. One at each corner of the building. Any one of them enough to leave men breathless.

It was not the constriction of my ribs that made me stop, but a sudden thought.

'Aldra Aguilar, I have no money for a bribe!'

That we were going up, not down, the stairs, told me I was being taken to the governor or overseer – whatever knight King Rodrigo had placed in charge of prisoners, and who therefore kept his chambers at the top of this high square tower. And whose income depends on what prisoners' relatives will pay him for good treatment of a prisoner.

Appalled, I thought, *Nor do I have money to pay a jailer for food, or candles, or clean water, or anything my father will need!*

Safrac de Aguilar gave me a wry smile. 'Your money isn't needed.'

And *that* means?

He gave me no chance to question him, turning his back. I followed the muffled clack of plate armour up the ever-turning stairs. His was not a face I recalled from court life, but the King must think him honest and not prone to gossip.

Or else he wouldn't let the man see Honorius and I together, with kinship written on our faces.

Unless Honorius is not recognisable—

The steps ceased, and I all but fell over de Aguilar's heels. He opened the door set counter-wise into the tower's wall, and gestured for me to pass through.

'Could you lend me money, Aldra?' I persisted.

Safrac de Aguilar sighed, his face giving it the force of extreme misery. 'Just go inside!'

An arrow-slit window opened into the antechamber, spilling bright sunlight onto terracotta tiles. De Aguilar nodded to the guards in royal livery, beckoning them aside and speaking in an undertone. I caught a glimpse of the sea through the narrow slit, far out on the horizon, and wondered, *If I had my babe in my arms, would I be more likely to move a prison governor to sympathy?*

Sharp knocking brought me back to myself. De Aguilar was just lowering his hand from the nail-sprinkled oak door of the inner rooms.

The door opened. A young and curly-haired man put his head out.

I stared. '*Saverico?*'

Safrac de Aguilar said something that did not penetrate the shock of seeing Ensign Saverico in clean green doublet and red hose, with a pewter lion badge sewn to his sleeve.

'Donna Ilario!' He grinned. 'I have your dress, still!'

The door was pushed further open from the inside: a shorter and skinnier man demanded, 'What is it *this* time?', and I recognised his voice before I saw his face – Honorius's Armenian sergeant, Orazi.

The door opened into a wide, well-furnished chamber. On the far side of the room, opposite the door, a window showed the sky to the north. Beneath the window stood a table. The chair on its left had been pushed back – by either Saverico or Orazi, when they came to open the door.

A chess-board stood on the table itself, and in the right-hand chair, Licinus Honorius, *il leone di Castiglia*, lifted his chin from his hand and contemplation of the board, and called without looking towards the door:

'By my calculation, Sergeant, you now owe me Carthage, Alexandria, and a year's dye-trade in Bruges ... Would you rather play me at dice?'

Orazi carries a sword at his side.

The sergeant stepped quickly back across the room, fast enough that I saw why Honorius might keep him as a bodyguard, and moved a bishop. 'Check!' He finished with a jerk of his chin towards us at the door.

Honorius looked. His eyes met mine.

I felt it in a blow to my stomach.

It was as if it took an age for him to rise from the chair.

Safrac de Aguilar murmured something behind me, stepping back with the royal guards; I was dimly aware that the solid oak door closed with them outside.

Honorius opened his mouth, and said nothing.

His cheeks were not sunken in or unshaven, his tunic looked clean; he carried a dagger scabbarded at his right hip.

'*I thought you were in some rat-infested piss-hole!*'

Words ripped out of my throat with the force of a winter storm.

'The King told me you were in *prison*! You're all right! *Why didn't you tell me?*'

Honorius stepped forward, his expression shifting from shock to wonder and solemnity.

I could do nothing but stare.

'Ilario ... '

Honorius broke into a great wide grin, covered the remaining distance in a moment, and threw his arms about me hard enough that I felt my ribs crunch.

'Ilario!'

'*Oof!*' It would have been more than a whisper, if I could have got the breath. And had I not been embracing him equally hard.

Without letting go, Honorius briefly turned his head. 'Saverico, get another goblet out! And the good wine. Tell Berenguer to put the kettle on the fire!'

He stepped back, hands gripping my shoulders, looking me up and down.

'Berenguer won't let me eat prison food,' he added absently, with a nod towards a door I had not noted; this was not one room, but a set of chambers, evidently. 'You're looking well. Have you eaten?'

'Have *I* eaten?'

'There's some beef left from last night, and chicken. And maybe a bit of mutton—'

'*Honorius!*'

I swore in Italian, Alexandrine Latin, and a little of the vocabulary of Chin.

Honorius beamed at me.

'*Mutton?* But you're in prison!' I protested.

My father put his fists on his hips and grinned. 'Yes, I am, aren't I?'

There was a long oak settle beside this room's hearth, a length of red velvet thrown over the back to prevent draughts. I collapsed down onto the wooden seat. 'I don't understand!'

Honorius signalled, without looking, and sat down on the settle beside me. A moment or two later another man-at-arms – I recognised Berenguer's angular features – entered wearing an apron over his doublet, and carrying a tray with wine and bread and cold mutton. He gave me a nod of greeting.

I looked around at the soldiers, as well as my father. 'You could walk right out of here! *Why* are you here?'

Honorius leaned his elbow on the back of the low settle. His hand, holding his wine goblet, just visibly shook. His face glowed, looking at me.

I tried again. '*Why are you in prison?*'

'Because I want to be.'

One should not regard one's own father as if he were stark mad. Except under this kind of provocation. 'Father—'

'Because it's necessary.' Honorius smiled. 'I may be a soldier, but I do understand *some* things about politics. I'm on display.'

Saverico and Orazi both nodded at that. Honorius waved a hand to dismiss them from their attentive stances – which meant they retired to the chess table five feet away, to watch us from there.

'On display,' Honorius repeated, 'and contrite. An object lesson. Soon

235

to be impoverished. Well – comparatively, and for a while. Then all will be well between me and the King—'

'But you're in prison!' I couldn't conquer the enormity of it, even if the rats and dung were absent. 'You've vanished; Rodrigo could have you quietly killed! Why—'

'To keep the stupid from rebelling against their King.' Honorius rubbed his chin. 'Who, come to think of it, is *my* King. I don't like serving under a weak king.'

I saw the truth of it as if someone had flung shutters open to sunlight. I tried not to sound accusatory – and failed. 'Honorius, you *agreed* to this!'

'It's necessary,' he said simply.

Orazi, at the window table, prodded his bishop and grinned.

Words choked themselves in my throat. I put my goblet down before I should spill it.

'And you *didn't let me know!*'

Honorius cocked a brow.

He said nothing of the distance of Constantinople, or the likelihood that I would have been somewhere else by the time letters or messengers arrived. Which saved my pride, if nothing else.

'I wasn't certain this would happen until I got here.' He shrugged. 'One of the possibilities was execution, but you tell me your Rodrigo Sanguerra's a reasonable king, so that didn't seem likely. This didn't surprise me when he ordered it.'

He paused, putting his hand on my shoulder again as if reassuring himself of my solidity.

'Letters can be intercepted. What could I safely say to you?'

'I had the same difficulty in Alexandria . . . ' I watched Orazi passing the castle-piece back and forth between his fingers.

Honorius's grip tightened. 'Why are you here and not in Alexandria? What happened? And how did you get here?'

'Ah.' I craned my chin up to see what was beyond the window, but I had been correct before: it was the mountains and the north. No visible sea. 'Have you heard any gossip about a "devil-ship"?'

Honorius's lips pursed surprisingly delicately; he might have been a disapproving duenna in the Court of Ladies. 'I think you'd better explain.'

I explained.

He sat for a minute or more, after I had done.

Quietly, he asked, 'Is Onorata still with us?'

Relief and chagrin hit me in equal measures. *I should have told him that at once!*

'Oh, she is – in *loud* health.'

Awkward although it might be on the hard wooden seat, I leaned over and embraced my father again.

The lines around his eyes tightened as if he looked into sunlight. 'I didn't realise you'd miss my company, Ilario.'

Since it seemed appropriate to a soldier, and since I might otherwise weep, I said, 'Fucking idiot!'

He wrapped his arm about my shoulder and shook me, as if I were a much younger boy.

It left me sitting forward on the settle; I ran my fingers through my hair, and lifted my head to look into his face. 'If you agreed to prison . . . How long do you stay here?'

'Long enough, I suppose. I dare say I'll hear from the King.'

A frown dented his brows.

'Ilario – I sent no word for you to come home! Whether on a "devil ship" or not! What are you doing here? It can't be safe—'

I summarised it as briskly as I might.

'King Rodrigo will call Aldra Videric back as First Minister,' I concluded, 'now that Admiral Zheng He's ship is here causing panic. Then Videric's back in power, and we need not—'

'Wait, wait.' Honorius sliced the edge of his hand through the air. 'How is this one single ship to cause enough danger to Taraco that the King can justify that? If it had been a *fleet*, now . . . What use are a few hundred men?'

It was a reasonable supposition, given the crews of galleys. A man can hear 'giant ship' without any real conception at the reality of the matter.

'Five thousand men,' I corrected.

'Five – *thousand*.'

I had brought no sketchbook, there being no way of doing that. I called to Berenguer to rescue me a charred stick from the edge of the hearth-fire and, under all their eyes, sketched on the wooden table the lines of a Venetian galley, and the size, beside it, of Zheng He's war-junk.

'Bugger me!' Honorius said.

I left him staring at it and ate the remainder of the mutton, suddenly very hungry; and chewed on fresh bread while Honorius and Orazi had a long and technical argument about the probable effectiveness of a ship with a crew of five thousand men.

After that, Honorius picked scraps off my plate, and kept breaking off from his own words to look at me. I did not know whether to feel embarrassed, or valued, or both.

' . . . sent the rest of my men on with orders to my steward, at the estates,' he finished, licking grease and crumbs off his fingers. 'Get the damn place back in order now the King's promised to withdraw his garrison. I kept young Saverico because he's supposedly intelligent.'

The Ensign grinned.

'And at any rate, young and quick enough to get up and down these stairs when he's ordered. And Berenguer because he cooks. And Sergeant Orazi stayed because I needed a man who could hold a conversation and play chess, or I knew I was like to run mad in the first week. Doing nothing doesn't come easily to me.'

'I can believe that . . . '

Judging by Venice, I thought Orazi's idea of intelligent conversation was likely to be, *Do you remember when we got all of the foot-reserve into the battle-line that time in Navarra?*, but my father is a military man.

'And the Egyptian's here?' Honorius added. 'All's well with you and Rekhmire'?'

'Certainly.'

He looked a little blank at that, but I couldn't identify his reasons.

'And that weasel-assassin you had on a chain: what happened to Carrasco?'

'Actually – he's on the ship, looking after your granddaughter.'

It caught Honorius sufficiently off-balance that he inhaled wine, dropped his wooden goblet, and sprang up to dash the wine-lees off his hose, all the while spluttering in outrage and panic. Orazi gave me a reproachful look.

'Carrasco makes an excellent nurse.' It was more than I could do to restrain a grin, but I stifled it at the realisation that Honorius's panic was genuine. 'It's safe. I wouldn't put Onorata in danger.'

Grumbling, Honorius resumed his seat on the settle.

I looked around at the other three, as well as my father.

'I only landed at dawn today. Has there been gossip or news of Videric or Rosamunda? Oh—' The Rialto came vividly back to me. '—and Federico? Did he chicken out? Has he turned up back here in Taraco?'

Orazi shook his head. 'Nah, not him. Nor his lady wife nor family, neither. I reckon they've gone north like they said.'

Honorius said, 'I confess I think better of him for that.'

'I . . . think I may do, too.'

'As for Videric and Rosamunda—' Honorius gave the men-at-arms a questioning look, and spoke again when none of them did. 'There are no *credible* rumours. They're still on his estates.'

Now I am close enough to be in the same kingdom with Videric, I wonder if the idea is as splendid as it seemed in Venice.

A sideways look at Honorius confirmed the man a mind-reader, at least of his son-daughter.

'No rumours about Carthage, either.' Honorius signalled for more wine. 'But I had reason to be concerned about you, son-daughter, I thought. We heard stories of some "demon" attack on Queen Ty-amenhotep. Was that while you were in her city?'

I steadied my goblet with my other hand as Saverico poured.

'It was the golem.'

Honorius snapped his fingers in irritation. 'I should have guessed *that*. "Demon", indeed. What happened?'

'An envoy from Carthage tried to use the golem to kill the Pharaoh-

Queen.' I found it comforting to lean my shoulder against Honorius's. 'But we stopped it.'

Honorius ran his free hand through his cropped hair, looking queasy. 'Damned if I would have gone near it! Wait – *you* stopped it? Not the Queen's soldiers? You—'

I couldn't help but look innocent in the face of his bluster. 'I had the book-buyer's help . . . '

Honorius narrowed his eyes at me. 'How could you fight a monstrous thing like that?'

I took another swallow, feeling a relaxation that was partly drinking wine on top of too little food, and mostly the relief of Honorius's company.

'Who'd *fight* the thing? We disabled it beforehand. So when the envoy tried, nothing happened.'

'Disabled—'

Four pairs of eyes watched me. Saverico and Berenguer in wonder, Orazi both sceptical and bemused, and my father looking as if he suspected some trick was being played on the Lion of Castile.

'We used . . . A secret weapon.' I bit down on my lower lip and managed not to smile.

'Secret weapon,' Honorius echoed.

'You blew it up!' Saverico yelped excitedly.

Gravely, I said, 'No, I think they would have noticed that.'

Orazi snickered.

'And where did this "secret weapon" come from?' Honorius inquired.

'Out of Masaccio's workshop. Or – the recipe did.'

'"Recipe."' My father's eyes began to narrow. His lip twitched. 'They'd notice Greek Fire, too!'

Berenguer interrupted scornfully. 'What kind of weapon comes out of a painter's workshop?'

Over Saverico's and Orazi's raucous comments, I managed to make myself heard. 'It had lime in it . . . '

Honorius grinned and pounced. 'You burned the damn stone man!'

'No, no burning; not even with quicklime.'

A considerable hubbub arose from the men-at-arms, speculating what weapon might destroy a stone man without leaving signs of this. I paid no attention, watching the creasing of lines about Honorius's eyes.

'A secret weapon,' he speculated aloud, holding back a smile. 'Made out of what you may find in a painter's workshop. Which *you* had knowledge of. Beginning with lime—'

The room's outer door opened. Safrac de Aguilar stood with the royal guard, a regretful expression making his long face even longer.

'My apologies, but it's near on the hour of Terce. We must go.'

I rose from the settle, conscious that Honorius stood up beside me.

'It's not a time to annoy Rodrigo Sanguerra.' I looked up at my father. 'I'll be back later. As soon as I can.'

Honorius nodded soberly, and wrung my hands in a parting grip.

Halfway to the door, he called, 'Quicklime and what else? Give me a clue! What other secret ingredient is there?'

Safrac de Aguilar stepped aside to let me pass. I glanced back over my shoulder, and left the Lion of Castile with a single word.

'Cheese!'

6

By the time we reached the royal appartments, Terce had rung out from the chapel bells. De Aguilar looked apprehensive as he led me into King Rodrigo's council chamber.

King Rodrigo Sanguerra and the envoy of Alexandria both stood, chairs shoved rudely back from the inlaid wood table, shouting at each other in contesting bass and tenor.

I crossed my arms over my chest, and glanced at Aldra Safrac. 'No need to be concerned. If I got up on the table and took all my clothes off, I doubt either one of them would notice.'

Safrac de Aguilar proved to have a thoroughly pleasant laugh.

Neither of the quarrelling men reacted to it.

King Rodrigo Sanguerra sat decisively down in his chair.

'No,' he said. '*No.*'

It was Aldra Safrac's suggestion that the King might wish to break his fast which moved us all into one of the lesser chambers. Smaller, more comfortable, I felt it take the edge off Rodrigo's temper.

If I recall correctly, he was never even-tempered if ill-fed.

It would have been impolite to refuse food myself, so I ate in the King's company again. Rekhmire' copied me for the manners of Taraco. When we were done, King Rodrigo took off his overrobe and stretched out his arms, gazing down from the high window at the inland mountains. The late morning sun cut lined crevasses into his features.

'Your pardon, Majesty,' Rekhmire' said, with an inoffensiveness I envied. 'But will you tell me what does not please you about this?'

Rodrigo turned his back to the sculpted window. To my surprise, he gazed at me.

'I'm glad to see you not murdered,' he observed, 'despite all the trouble you've caused me. So much I can say. For the rest, and this "war-junk" . . . My high council is due to meet at Sext. If I tell them I intend to recall Aldra Videric – on what they will see as a pretext – we shall still be talking this time next month, and still nothing will get done!'

Rekhmire''s brandy-coloured eyes met mine, for the briefest of moments. I read *Not enough* perfectly clearly.

The Egyptian spoke deferentially; only someone who knew him well would have detected the acid quality to his speech.

'Would it speed matters if the foreign ship were to fire on that headland?' He indicated the chamber's other window, which faced south east. 'Just by way of a demonstration?'

Through the stone frame carved with oak leaves and acorns, I saw a coastal view long familiar to me. Roman ruins on a headland, a mile or so away from the city itself; broken-off stout pillars rounded by centuries of rain and frost. I remember taking stolen bottles of wine up there with other slaves, resting on the sun-heated rock, watching lizards dart into crevices.

'Even if it would, I do not permit the suggestion.' King Rodrigo seated himself in the oak chair at the table's head, taking his weight on his wrists like an old man. Even with the little time I had been gone, he seemed older to me.

Or perhaps, until now, I have never entirely stopped seeing the man I saw at fifteen. When he bought and paid for me.

Rodrigo Sanguerra studied me with an intent gaze.

Cao!

It sounded better in Chin.

I realised a little late that the light from the windows clearly illuminated my face. The King nodded as if his suspicions were confirmed.

'I think . . . yes. Ilario, if there is anything to be done here, the representative of New Alexandria and I will do it. You should return to the monstrous ship as soon as you can. If anything's to be made out of this, we need not confuse people over who truly sired you!'

I spoke before Rekhmire' could interject.

'Does it matter, sire? My father's in prison, so no man will see us together. And no one will hear it from me if you desire me to say nothing.'

The King shot a look at me, clearly assessing.

'Rosamunda was your dam, I don't doubt it. But the Lion of Castile has left his imprint all over your face. If that story got out, every man would be calling Lord Videric a cuckold!'

Rodrigo shook his head.

'Bad enough that my boy-girl Court Fool should turn out to be First Minister Videric's child! That was scandal enough! If word gets out that all Pirro Videric is to you is your mother's husband . . . '

He eased back in his chair, chin on fist again, watching me. *I know this of old*, I thought, relaxing a little. He doesn't trust an Alexandrine, but me – me he desires to convince him.

Rodrigo scowled. 'After the accusations made by Carthage, Videric's enemies here in my court can despise him for fathering a freak. With your true parentage known – they would laugh at my lord Videric because his wife had another man's child. Nothing is harder to recover from than laughter.'

Captain-General Honorius might resent being accused of fathering a freak, I thought. But the King would have spoken to my father, and would know that by now.

He's seeing if I can be goaded into unwise speech.

'I need Aldra Pirro Videric back.' Rodrigo's voice was a bass growl. He switched his glare to Rekhmire'. 'I don't believe I need Queen Ty-ameny to tell me this!'

Rekhmire' bowed his head, where he sat on a less-decorated chair; much in the manner that I'd seen him do when being book-buyer to a difficult client. 'It's in the interests of New Alexandria to offer what assistance we can, Majesty. No one wants a war.'

The King's gaze shifted to that window which allowed a view south. '*Carthage* wants war. And I dare say Constantinople and Carthage will at some date contest the future of the Middle Sea – although I take it, from what you say, that this is not yet?'

'The Great Queen fights to ensure it is not.'

The late morning haze had burned off the sea. At the window's edge, it was just possible to see Zheng He's impossibly large ship.

The King looked back towards me.

'You bring me *a* cause. Not a sufficient one to carry it through.'

My stomach plummeted.

Rodrigo Sanguerra shifted his gaze rapidly to Rekhmire'. 'So. What else have you to suggest?'

Refreshments were brought in from time to time, and I noted how certain faces appeared again and again among the servants. Like Safrac de Aguilar, who kept the door, men that King Rodrigo could trust not to spread rumours. When I excused myself to the necessary-room, I investigated long enough to find Attila and Tottola in an antechamber, boasting to the King's household guards.

I stopped long enough to arrange food and drink for them, and to comprehend that – however outrageous their stories – they were not touching on the truth.

'I hope you're getting somewhere in there,' Tottola grumbled. 'St Gaius himself would be bored with this!'

Somewhat out of temper myself, I shook my head. 'They might just as well have sent us back to the ship. If things don't change, I'll put a dress on and have a fit of female hysterics!'

That left the German brothers chuckling.

When Rekhmire' and the King began to circle the discussion of royal and clerical legalities for the third time, I gave in to temptation and pulled a folded sheet of paper out of my leather purse. Smoothing it out on my thigh, I began partial studies with a nub of chalk. The woollen hose were warm for summer, and the mail – where the links sucked on to my torso – breath-snatchingly hot. My knight's training is long enough ago that I had forgotten the breathlessness of wearing any armour in hot weather.

The interwoven strands of linen and reed that made up Rekhmire''s headband provided an interesting challenge to draw. I added the curve of his brow-ridge under it, the kohl-marked line of upper and lower eyelid; sketched the shape of his mouth . . .

Is Rekhmire' waiting until the King has talked himself dry before he introduces some idea of his own? Or have they already talked that through, and is he at a loss?

Talk dragged on for another quarter-hour by the King's water clock. I switched to drawing Rodrigo's hands.

The King's voice broke in on my thoughts. 'Well, it is a curious idea . . . '

Glancing up, I found myself the focus of looks from King Rodrigo and the Egyptian.

My hands were out of sight under the table. Or I hoped so. No matter how well-drawn, a study of a man's hands is unlikely to be well received as the reason why I have no idea what has been suggested.

King Rodrigo lifted his chin from his fist and eased back in the oak chair. He looked at me speculatively. 'Would you consider it?'

I shot a glance which the book-buyer seemed accurately to read as *Help!* The envoy of the Pharaoh-Queen stretched his leg out under the oak table, flinching barely perceptibly. 'Perhaps I could explain to you in more detail, Ilario?'

There was an odd glint in his dark eyes. *Yes: I know: I should have drawn less, and paid more attention!* But between the crucial decisions here, which may affect all my life, and Honorius in prison in another part of the palace, is it any wonder I desire only to lose myself in contour and value?

Rekhmire's large hand gestured towards the window. 'Let us agree that Admiral Zheng He's appearance at Taraco *begins* to be a cause for the recall of Lord Videric, but is not sufficient cause.'

The Egyptian switched his gaze to me.

'Last year's scandal that deposed Videric from his position of first minister was an accusation of attempted murder. That he sent his wife, in fact, to murder you – you until then not known to be Videric and Rosamunda's child. And Carthage took this attempted killing badly.'

Rekhmire' kept a perfectly even expression during his last words.

Had I been closer, I would have kicked his ankle under the table, injured knee or not.

'*And?*' I prompted, robbed of anxiety by minor irritation. Which, I realised, is likely his design.

'And . . . ' Rekhmire' glanced at Rodrigo. 'His Majesty agrees that if the scandal was between Videric and you – then any cure for that scandal must also be between Videric and you.'

Did this arise out of your discussion? I wondered. Some moment I was lost in drawing? Or is this something you concocted aboard ship, and failed to tell me?

I found myself chilled, despite the sun in the room.

'It must be assumed that you and Aldra Videric are father and child.' Rekhmire' directed his dark gaze at me, like a shock of cold water. 'Obviously this would involve some degree of untruth.'

'You mean I have to lie.'

I had not expected to hear myself sound so bitter. This can't be unexpected, after all.

Rekhmire' spoke with the greatest apparent innocence. 'Call it diplomacy.'

The humour – which I doubted any man might read there except for me – faded from the Egyptian's eyes as I failed to respond.

'Continue,' King Rodrigo murmured.

'If it were publicly supposed that there had been a *mistake*.'

Rekhmire' emphasised the final word softly.

'If it were discovered that Carthage had been in error, and Lord Videric is *not* responsible for attempted murder. Then that discovery – in addition to negotiating friendly relations with Zheng He – might suffice as a pretext for reappointing him as Taraco's First Minister.'

King Rodrigo grunted. I know that rumble of old. 'Don't try my patience.' I slid the paper in my lap well out of sight.

I asked, 'How would this happen?'

Rekhmire''s eyes sought the King's, with a brief look at me that might have been apology. 'I had thought – some kind of public ceremony of reconciliation?'

I tasted the word in my mind. *Reconciliation.*

Reconciliation between me and Aldra Videric.

Pah!

The book-buyer continued. 'If Lord Videric and Aldro Rosamunda are greeted, on their return to Taraco, with every mark of friendship from their son-daughter Ilario . . . Majesty, might not your court assume the King-Caliph and Carthage's Lord-Amirs *must* be in error?'

Rodrigo Sanguerra blinked like one of the lizards that haunt ancient stone ruins. 'It would need to appear more than friendship.'

Rekhmire' rested his hands on the table before him, fingertips pressed together. I recognised his stance when closing a deal with some scroll-owner. *Yes, he thought this through on Zheng He's ship—*

Delicately, the Alexandrine spy suggested, 'Some formal ceremony, perhaps?'

The King nodded, thoughtfully. 'Some ceremony. Some formal reconciliation . . . In the cathedral, perhaps? Archbishop Cunigast could oversee it. Enough pageantry, enough piety, and a show of pardon . . . Yes!' Energised, Rodrigo Sanguerra sat upright in his chair. 'Yes: if only because my people greatly *desire* a reason to think that the King-Caliph was mistaken, and should therefore have kept his nose out of our business!'

I saw the shape of it in my mind. Lie and pretend. I braced myself and spoke. 'Your Majesty, yes. Provisionally, I would agree to that.'

Rodrigo snapped his fingers.

Servants entered the room, pouring wine and water again for the three of us. The glasses they brought were delicate blue, with double helixes of red and yellow glass in the stem.

Kek and Keket and Rekhmire''s Holy Eight! Put my father in prison, and then confiscate his export glass!

Light glimmered from my Venetian glass to the tabletop, casting twisted ellipses of light. I lifted it, tilting it in an ironic toast to King Rodrigo. He returned the gesture, his expression closed.

The empty spaces of the cathedral in Taraco have always impressed me. Any noise louder than a whisper echoes from the inside of the vast dome, ivory in colour, featureless as an egg; stark in contrast to the gold, ruby, emerald, and sapphire work encrusting the altars and chapels below. Full of the court and citizens of Taraco, a stunning spectacle; the midday sun falling clear down onto the main altar below.

I thought of standing there. Of Videric's face. Of Rosamunda.

'Wait—'

Rekhmire' and the King were talking: I broke into their relaxed speech more harshly than I meant.

'Your Majesty, I'm sorry. I apologise, but I've just thought – "a show of pardon", you said? Would you formally *forgive* Aldra Videric? How can you, if it's Carthage that's supposed to have made the error? What would you be forgiving him for—'

I broke off. King Rodrigo's stolid dark gaze transfixed me.

The shaking of my hand sent reflections of light across the inlaid geometric wood patterns.

Further down the table, Rekhmire' spoke in a smooth apologetic tenor. 'Ilario, you haven't thought through the implications.'

It was difficult to get words out. 'I haven't?'

'His Majesty is suggesting a family reconciliation, to lead to a political reconciliation. But, yes, you're right: Lord Videric can't be pardoned if he's not the one at fault.'

The glass was hard as stone under my fingertips.

Rekhmire''s voice came again. 'Ilario, it won't be Lord Videric who must publicly apologise.'

Bright concentric circles rippled on the surface of my wine. 'Apologise?'

Rodrigo Sanguerra waved a hand at Rekhmire', his velvet sleeve pulling back to show white linen, and curling black hairs at his wrist. 'Listen to the Alexandrine envoy, Ilario.'

You freed me!

Both of you.

I shifted my gaze from the King to Rekhmire'.

The Egyptian interlaced his fingers, where his hands rested on the table. 'His Majesty needs to make the reputation of Lord Videric spotless. Lord Videric can't appear to have anything to do with a murder. Not if he's to return as First Minister.'

Rodrigo's gaze weighed me. 'Therefore, Ilario, it was not an attempted murder.'

I remember, less than a year ago, taking my first manumission papers from that creased hand. He unlocked the collar from my neck with his own fingers.

And this is the man who has worked twenty-five years in harness, if not in collar, with Videric. And whose own reputation, at the moment, is therefore suspect.

Rekhmire' spoke again. 'Ilario, it would be you. If the attempted murder is redefined as a mistake, then you would have to speak publicly. You would need to apologise to Lord Videric, because you allowed the Lord-Amir in Carthage to reach a wrong conclusion. And it won't be difficult to have it credited – men are usefully prone to believing slaves are foolish.'

I will not disgrace myself by throwing this wine in the Egyptian's face.

Rekhmire''s wide shoulders lifted in a minute shrug. 'You might say, for example, that you were attacked by criminals in Carthage. You were rescued by the Lady Rosamunda. Judge Hanno Agastes wrongly mistook her rescue for an attack. And you . . . were too afraid of punishment, when Carthage mistook her actions, to speak up and tell the truth. But now—'

Sharp pain shot through my hand.

Fine curved splinters of glass stood out of my skin.

I opened my palm, not yet wincing at the hot fire of the cuts. Only the stem of the glass was whole. Wine puddled on the table, spattered surprisingly far.

The King silently signalled for his servants to clear the mess.

I felt as if my neck creaked stiffly as I looked up at Rekhmire'. 'You've thought this through.'

And said no word to me.

Rekhmire''s fingers slid apart from each other: his large hands made fists. He met my gaze fearlessly. 'Yes, I've thought! You need to apologise, Ilario—'

'*I* did nothing wrong!'

'Apologise for not speaking up when Carthage drew an erroneous conclusion, thus causing the downfall of your father Lord Videric.'

The Egyptian's gaze was implacable, and Rodrigo Sanguerra sat back, letting him speak.

247

'You would beg Lord Videric's pardon for being coward enough not to speak at the time. And for being timid enough to run from Carthage afterwards, and not come back to Taraco to set matters right until now.'

Rekhmire"'s round chin came up: he stared at me challengingly.

I picked the larger of the glass splinters from my palm. None had gone deep enough to scar, but there was a surprising quantity of blood.

If Honorius hears of this, no possible concern about politics will stop him from protesting!

'Apologise.' I could barely get the word out without stuttering. 'Lie and beg pardon. From Videric.'

King Rodrigo Sanguerra nodded, speaking for the first time in long minutes. 'Yes.'

In the city's cathedral, in front of four, five, perhaps six thousand people.

People that I know.

I desired more than anything to walk out. One shake of my hand, to scatter loose and bloody fragments across the delicate wood patterns; then I might push my way past Safrac de Aguilar and out—

But if I run through the passages of this castle, I will only meet more people that I know.

'You want me to claim that I lied. That I ran away. That I was too afraid to come back and tell the truth. You want me to say this in front of every prominent citizen and nobleman of Taraconensis.'

I found a kerchief in my leather purse. When I wrapped it about my hand, it turned scarlet through the bleached cloth.

'You know that if I say this in public, it doesn't matter what the truth is – I can't rewrite it, after. *That's* the story that will spread out and be believed.'

'Yes,' King Rodrigo Sanguerra said.

I did not look at Rekhmire'. I looked at the king who had owned me. 'No.'

7

Since too many eyes were watching every boat on the way out and back to Zheng He's great floating wooden island, His Majesty Rodrigo Sanguerra Coverrubias changed his decree, and said that his guests should live ashore for the time being, quietly out of the way, in an obscure part of the palace's south wing.

Rekhmire''s hand clamped on my elbow the moment we passed through the doors and were alone.

'Ilario, listen to me!'

'*Now* you talk to me? You should have done that before!'

I threw him off with a vicious movement, caught from the corner of my eye how he stumbled, and swung around fast enough to catch hold of him, preventing him falling.

Not strong enough to hold up his weight, I found the two of us taking staggering round steps as if we danced; until the room's wall caught me squarely between the shoulder-blades, and both of us leaned up against the other, gasping and panting.

I felt the taut expansion of his shoulder and arm muscles; had a moment to think, *Walking with crutches has begun to alter the shape of his body*, and then his other hand got a grip on his staff, and he pushed himself back from me and the wall.

He swayed but stayed on his feet. '*What* should I have spoken to you about?'

These chambers were higher up than Honorius's prison, I registered, and less well-appointed. But airy and light: Onorata would be content here.

I ignored his question. 'I'm risking this disguise once more. Tottola and I will bring Onorata and Carrasco ashore this evening at dusk. Is this my chamber, or yours?'

'They have given me the choice of rooms opposite,' Rekhmire' got out, sounding as if he choked. '*What have I not told you?*'

The exertion had not sapped my explosive temper: I had all I could do to rein it in. I desired to throw anything that would break. Instead, I faced the Egyptian, stabbing a finger towards the open windows, where Taraco drowned in the afternoon's white heat.

'This is not Carthage!' I yanked at the leather laces tying closed the neck of Attila's mail-shirt, but it made me no less heated. 'This isn't

Rome! Or Venice! Or Alexandria! What happens to me here happens in front of people I *know*!'

There are few ways to be got out of a mail-shirt with dignity. A thousand riveted metal rings form a net that cling to the body. Pulling one's shirt off upwards only results in yanking at chin, ears, and capturing hanks of hair to pull out.

The Egyptian was tall enough that he might have held the mail-shirt's shoulders still while I eased myself down out of it, but I felt absolutely no inclination to ask his help.

I copied remembered instructions from my master-at-arms, bending over and putting my hands flat on the floor. I shook myself until the armour's own weight inverted it, and brought it sliding smoothly down over my torso, shoulders, arms and head.

The mail-shirt thudded to the floorboards at my wrists as a small bundle of metal.

I straightened up, gasping with relief, kicked at it, and all but fell over with dizziness.

In the voice of a man who has lost his breath again, Rekhmire' observed, 'A sight I wouldn't have missed for the world . . . '

'*I will not look like a liar and a coward in front of the court I grew up in!*'

The Egyptian's amusement vanished. 'I would not laugh at you—'

There was a joint-stool by the couch: I kicked it the length of the panelled chamber.

'I will not look like a liar and a coward in front of *Videric*!'

Tottola was engaged at the outer door in conversation; I thought it might be with members of the royal guard. I had no hope of understanding a word with rage deafening me.

'Ilario.' Rekhmire' put out his hand: I stepped back.

'Videric made my mother try to kill me. I'll stand in the same room with him, but – claim this never happened? That I've *lied*?'

Rekhmire' grabbed my upper arms, staring down the inch or two difference in our heights.

'And you didn't plan your story well enough,' I said bitterly. 'Videric allowed his *child* to be abandoned and sold! To live here at court as Rodrigo's tame freak. How will *that* reform him in men's eyes?'

Rekhmire''s intent gaze made my heart hammer; I felt a pulse beating in my throat. His mouth quirked, in something like amazement.

'Oh . . . I can devise an answer for that, too. Say that Videric, as your father, wanted you to have a good life at court – but he knew you would suffer prejudice as a hermaphrodite. As the King's possession, no man could ever harm you.'

Rekhmire''s expression was sardonic.

'And if you lived anonymously, court factions could never use you to discredit the King or your father . . . Suppose we say, on Videric's behalf, that coming to court as the King's Freak is the only way you could have lived here as yourself? Not having to pretend to be either wholly a man or wholly a woman.'

Rekhmire''s fingers gradually loosened their grip.

I would have bruises, I realised absently. 'And why was I a slave?'

'Oh, that was *your* idea.'

I blinked.

'When you thought of coming to court, you were afraid you'd hear too much in royal company. You wanted to keep it confidential. If you were King Rodrigo's property, no man could ever ask you to bear witness against the King or your father.'

The surface of my eyes felt dry: now I found I couldn't blink. 'Is there more?'

Rekhmire' snorted. 'What could be more clear? Lord Videric has always had Ilario's best interests at heart. He wanted you safe from gossip and conspiracy and harm – and to be able to live openly as the hermaphrodite you are. Which you did. Until you were foolish enough to run away from some quarrel in Carthage . . . '

Tearing my gaze from his caused me to shake. To have such an interpretation of the facts, and to have it be so far from the truth – and so plausible.

I walked numbly to the window, not seeing the brightness beyond the rippling folds of draped linen, or smelling the sea. 'How long did it take you to cook *this* up?'

There was an audible sigh behind me.

'Ilario . . . I considered all aspects of the matter, from when it was raised at home in the city, all through our journey. Men here are *ripe* for belief. Don't assume only soldiers and courtiers can see that Carthage wants to send the legions in.'

Rekhmire''s voice came closer.

'This is an excuse and a pretext. In other words, it's what we wanted, to allow Aldra Videric back. Ilario's falsely-accused and dutiful father comes back to Taraco as First Minister. What does it matter what you have to say?'

My breath came short. 'It matters because he tried to kill me.'

'This is just pride!'

I spun about, and nearly collided with Rekhmire' directly behind me.

I glared up at him. 'It is not *pride*. I was all but killed in childbed because of Videric. *Onorata* would have died. Videric is the man who sent my mother to kill me in Carthage, and because of him, she was willing to do it!'

Anger's heat stifled me more than wearing the mail-shirt. I wrenched the laces of my doublet undone, pulled at the neck of my shirt, and sank down on the room's bed. My scant baggage was there: I dug in it so that I might go barefoot and in my Alexandrine tunic again. At least until I must return to the ship for Onorata.

I stopped with the linen tunic in my hands. It still smelled of Zheng He's ship.

'Don't ask me to do this. Would you let them brand *you* a liar? This would become the truth, for the rest of my life. And Honorius's. And Onorata's.' I winced. *'They'll say Videric is her grandfather.'*

The Egyptian frowned, seeming to turn inward to where that clever mind devised infinite complicated stratagems.

'If Onorata stays in these chambers, there's little enough to connect her with Videric. You'll dress as a man, I assume? Who would think you connected with a baby?'

That obvious, and it never occurred to me. And Honorius's soldiers would act as our servants, so less gossip will spread.

Rekhmire' observed, 'That answers the problem in the short term.'

'You haven't some long-term plan involving her, too? You surprise me!'

Rekhmire' supported himself on his stick, and lowered himself to sit on the edge of the bed. 'What would you have had me do?'

'Tell me!'

'If I have considered this before . . . ' He pulled off his headband and rubbed at his temples. The long curve of his broad back formed a slump. 'It was never certain this would happen. Not certain your King would agree to it, if I suggested it. I said nothing because I would not worry you with the matter, in case it never arose.'

Sheer disgust silenced me.

I leaped up, went to the door, spoke to Attila, and asked him to wake me at dusk. And with that done, I cast myself down fully clothed on the bed as if Rekhmire' were not present, and fell unexpectedly hard into sleep.

He did not wake me before he left for his own rooms.

Ramiro Carrasco and I endured the crossing back from ship to shore, Onorata screaming her displeasure at the boat, the sea-spray, and the palace apartments.

'You owe me a debt of some sort,' I remarked as we entered our chambers. 'As recompense for trying to kill me. What about an honest answer to a question? Forget you're my property. Tell me what you think.'

The secretary-spy hesitated, seeming bewildered. His hand soothed Onorata's back. She made a little fist and rubbed it up and down the arm of his tunic, screaming fit fading down to gulping sobs and then silence.

He made as if to offer her to me and I shook my head. 'The way I feel now . . . '

She'll scream all night if I take her.

Ramiro Carrasco smoothed Onorata's hair back from her pink forehead, as if it helped him to think. There were milk-stains on the shoulder of his tunic. Low and even, he murmured, 'Would this get what you want? Aldra Videric back in the King's service? All of us safe?'

I had debated not telling Carrasco what Rekhmire' had planned. Until I thought, firstly, that he knew so much of my business, a little more would make no difference – and, secondly, that it affects him almost as much as it does me.

I said truthfully, 'I don't know. Suppose it was asked of you? Would you do it? If it meant you were disgraced, here, at home. And there was no changing it, after?'

The secretary-spy gave me as ironic a look as I have ever had from any man.

'Ilaria, mistress, I'm dirt *now*. You bought me because a court in Venice convicted me of attempted murder. I am disgraced.'

'And?'

'If it saved my family?' He looked straight into my face. 'If it even *helped* save my family, I'd crawl over broken glass. Lie. In public; I wouldn't care. I would do anything. You know that: that's why you're a fool to trust me!'

Oddly, that made me smile. 'But I'm the nearest thing to an ally you and your family have, so I *may* not be as stupid as you think.'

He chuckled, the first unmediated mirth I had heard from him since the Doge's prisons. Unexpectedly, his voice softened.

'I understand that this child will have to live with whatever people think of her mother. Father. *Parent*. I understand that.'

He tucked in one edge of Onorata's linen wrap, his finger still showing the remnants of the callus that comes with holding a pen. Over that, it was scarred with the casual brutality that living as a slave entails.

'*I would do anything.*'

Perhaps because I had slept so deeply that afternoon, I could not sleep in the night.

The door of the apartments abruptly opened.

Since I was cleaning the child after her breakfast, and dirty myself because of it, I looked up with a curse, and found myself staring at Rekhmire'.

Not looking at me, I found.

He stared at Ramiro Carrasco de Luis, where the man had just returned from disposing of soiled shit-rags and emptying chamber-pots.

Rekhmire' pointed to the door he had entered by. 'You. Out.'

'Rekhmire'—' I set the wriggling baby on my lap and wiped at its hands.

'You have a visitor, Ilario. One who requires privacy.' The Egyptian looked pointedly at Carrasco.

I indicated the inner door and spoke as evenly to the assassin-nurse as

I could manage. 'Take Onorata through and dress her. Not too warmly. We're taking her up to see Honorius after this.'

'Yes, madonna.'

The Iberian didn't look at Rekhmire' as he walked past within a foot of the larger man.

'And keep your ear away from the door!' Rekhmire' grunted.

I stood up from the bed. 'What in your eight hells do you think you're—'

'I'm leaving the city.' Rekhmire' crossed to a chest I hadn't noticed, and began to recover small items of his own, which he threw into a bag. 'I have an escort from the King. I'm travelling to Lord Videric's estate, to speak with him.'

The book-buyer had his belongings together by the time a man could count a hundred. Half-sentences came into my mind: I couldn't get any of them out.

Going to Videric.

'Are you going to . . . put this suggestion to him?'

The Egyptian only glanced at me.

I wondered how Videric would be now. And Rosamunda. After six or eight months stewing in the provinces, in the winter cold and spring mud and summer heat. Among peasants and serfs, and whatever minor nobility were their neighbours. If their neighbours haven't snubbed them.

Rosamunda will have hated being away from foreign merchants, and Rodrigo's court entertainments. Who's the leader of the Court of Ladies now?

'Rekhmire'.'

He slammed a tiny chest shut with great vehemence. 'No matter your decision – I must talk to the man.'

He turned around, pushed himself on his stick towards the oak inner doors and turned the key in its lock, locking Carrasco and Onorata in. He limped towards the outer door again.

'I will send in your visitor.'

The door closed behind him before I could get a word out.

The room was frighteningly silent without Onorata's noises, without Honorius's voice, or his soldiers', or the Egyptian's. Only Attila and Tottola's tribal dialect in the antechamber made this sound like a human habitation.

Out of nowhere, I thought, *This is the first time in eight months or more that I won't be in Rekhmire''s company.*

The door creaked. I realised I was studying the pattern of grain in the floorboards, and lifted my head.

King Rodrigo Sanguerra stood just inside the closed door.

I sprang to my feet as rapidly as long-inculcated instinct could move me, and dropped down on one knee.

The King smiled crookedly, gesturing for me to rise.

He crossed past me to stare out of the south-facing windows; ran a finger across the sculpted frame's vine leaves, and picked up one of the translucent porcelain dishes that I had brought back from Zheng He's ship.

There was no noise except the singing of laundry women, hundreds of feet below, beating sheets in tubs in a courtyard exposed to the sun. My chest hurt. I realised I was holding my breath.

'Majesty.' I let the breath out with a little gasp. 'Is it safe for you to visit us here?'

His hooded eyelids dropped down over his large eyes; I knew it for amusement. It faded. 'King Rodrigo Sanguerra isn't here. But the slave Ilario's old owner is.'

'I was freed again. In Rome.' My mouth was dry. 'I won't do what you ask.'

Rodrigo didn't sit down. His habitual slow pace carried him from the windows to the shuttered cupboards that lined the walls, and to the dais on which the bed stood with its hangings closed, and the middle of the bare floor.

Rodrigo Sanguerra said, 'I owe you an apology.'

I could not have imagined this as something he would ever say.

I bit back suspicion. 'Majesty?'

'I won't lie.'

He turned on his heel, looking at me with a glint in his dark eyes. Rodrigo's strong features took the window's light, and I ached to draw him.

He added, 'I owe you an apology for owning you – or, for not freeing you before I did. But I won't lie: I'm more sorry that my ownership of you has come back to bite me . . . '

He walked to stand in front of me. You did not commonly notice, until he was in the (admittedly rich) doublet and hose and cap of any courtier, rather than cloak and crown of the King, that he was not a particularly tall man. I doubted him a hand taller than I. But whatever his stature, he contrived to give the impression of looking down at a man.

'Ilario . . . I know an apology doesn't matter to you—'

'It does!'

The reply startled out of me.

I blushed.

I shook my head, as if I could clear from it the shock of seeing Rodrigo Sanguerra here in these shabby rooms. And the wrench of all the old affection between us. Because affection is possible between master and slave, no matter how distorted.

I stared at Rodrigo. 'But I still won't do what you're— what's being asked of me. I can't. I shouldn't. Not for my sake. Not for my daughter's sake.'

And not for my father's, though I have not yet spoken to Honorius.

Rodrigo Sanguerra slowly shook his head. His presence seemed to fill the room. He came to the throne before I was born; there was white in his beard now. I wondered if he had summoned the Crown Prince back, some time between last year and now, or whether Prince Thorismund was still in the north fighting against Franks.

'You have recognised old friends here,' King Rodrigo said mildly.

Familiar faces among the men on the quayside at the chandlers' shops, and in the long market between the docks and the palace, and in the livery of King Rodrigo at the palace gates . . .

'Yes, Majesty.'

He lifted a blunt-fingered hand, pointing at the window. 'And you know, because you must in the past have ridden over, every mile between here and the mountains.'

'Yes, I've loved this place,' I gritted. 'You want me to make it so that I and Onorata can't come back here without disgrace.'

There would be layer upon layer of thoughts beneath what he actually said; I knew him of old. When he first bought me as a cocky fifteen-year-old, I thought a king would have too many affairs of state to be concerned with what his slave got up to. He sent me to the cane often enough to disabuse me of that very quickly. A king must at least try to think of everything.

Rodrigo looked directly at me. 'Ilario. Will you go through with making a public apology, if Aldra Videric will consent to it?'

Consent!

I stared at Rodrigo Sanguerra. If he asks 'will you do this for me?', I'll spit in his face.

'No. I won't do it. And if you order me, because you're my King – I still won't do it.' I held his gaze. 'I'm not looking for an *excuse* to give consent.'

'No, I see that.'

Rodrigo Sanguerra moved restlessly, walking to the window again, and turning on his heel and walking back.

'A king is a steward of his country.'

I shrugged. 'Slaves don't have a country.'

Rodrigo gazed down at me without acknowledging that. 'Steward. Not a Dictator or Tyrant, as the ancient Greeks had it, to hold everything his private property. Do you understand, a steward? To keep the peace? And to leave that peace to the next generation?'

I thought of Onorata, behind the door with Ramiro Carrasco.

'I understand.' I bit my lip. 'No. The answer is no. I won't have her grow up regarded as dirt because of what I'm supposed to have done. I won't lie!'

The King of Taraconensis knelt down on the bare dusty floor.

I gaped; I must have looked like a gaffed fish.

Rodrigo Sanguerra had moved stiffly getting down on his knees, and he knelt as if the bare boards hurt his bones. His spine was ramrod-stiff; his chin jutted up. I could only stare.

'I can't give you this in public.' His voice sounded low but not particularly quiet. 'Not the way you would wish it. I'm a king: I can't shake my people's confidence in me that way. But I will give you all the humiliation you wish of me, here in private. I once owned you. Ilario, I beg you to do this thing.'

Ilario, close your mouth, I thought.

And did.

'I beg you, on my knees. If you desire an apology for anything that occurred while I owned you, you have only to speak. I kiss your hands and feet and I beg you to go before the people and lie.'

Blood rose up in my face, I could feel it. When Ramiro Carrasco had knelt, the embarrassment was painful enough. This – *Oh, this is only impossible!*

'You can't do this, Majesty!'

'I came here to you to do this.' Rodrigo's dark eyes unwaveringly held my gaze. 'My life's work is tottering. The peace will fail. Carthage will send in legions. If fighting won't serve me, I'll grovel at any man's feet if it stops that.'

'Why don't you put me in prison? There are still torturers here, aren't there? Why don't you force me?'

'Will you make it necessary?'

In another man it would have been an implied threat. With Rodrigo (as I have long had cause to know), it is merely honesty.

He shook his head, as if at an afterthought, red lips quirking in his dark beard. 'And besides, penitence is rarely convincing and true, brought about by those means!'

I stared down at him, starkly disbelieving. Amazed.

There is nothing you will not do to save your home, I thought.

Or to set me an example.

The room, heating in the early sun, held a mere breath of air passing through from the south windows. I stood in hose and shirt and unlaced doublet; I must be stinking of sweat and my child, in no condition to see polite company.

The older man, much my senior, knelt on the hard boards in front of me and waited.

I thought of the long-ago morning when Father Felix had brought me into King Rodrigo's breakfast chamber, to listen to courtiers discussing the hermaphrodite's wedding night with a woman.

Now the King's shoulders were tense under the mole-black velvet of his doublet, sewn everywhere with the flower and serpent of Taraconensis. If I sketched him, I realised, I would have to dig deep to uncover those emotions behind the forced calm.

But they are there.

Bitterly, I said, 'I couldn't teach you what humiliation is, Majesty.'

Looking into those darkest of brown eyes, I thought of Ramiro Carrasco – and realised, in that moment, that Rodrigo Sanguerra of Taraconensis has no more idea of what to expect as a slave than Ramiro Carrasco had. And that, as with Ramiro, this is not the key of the matter.

'You're on your knees to me, Majesty.'

'Yes.' He didn't flush, but the lines in his face altered.

'Begging me.'

'Yes.'

'Because . . . ' I took a deep breath. 'Because you want me to see what you'll do for Taraco. And then – you want me to do the same thing.'

His shoulders went back as if he were one of Honorius's soldiers on parade. It was only in the rigidity of his spine that I could see how much fury, how much outrage, he suppressed in himself.

'What you have to do will be humiliating, yes.' He lifted his gaze, for the first time coming within a hair's breadth of true appeal. 'And I beg, the King begs you: humiliate yourself, in front of your enemy, because I need you to. We need you to.'

I went to speak and he interrupted.

'This is the country in which you were born a bastard, raised and sold and treated as a slave: I understand this—'

'You don't, Majesty.'

He hesitated for the first time. 'No. But there are people here, all the same. Some you know. Most you never will. And I ask you: do it for them. I don't ask you to do it for me. I may be many things, but I am not quite such a fool as that.'

He permitted me to stand in silence, then, watching him. Looking at the King of Taraco, down on his knees to a slave, a freed slave.

It moves me that he'll do this for the people here.

It moved me still more that I could read, in the lines of his body and face, quite how much he feared being made to grovel by someone too young, too spiteful, too unwise not to break another human being.

'Majesty, do you think I'm risking making you into an enemy because I want some petty apology?'

The fear left him.

I read in his face that he knew that, whether I agreed or not, I would not make a king perform the same tricks as a King's Freak.

I fell on my knees in front of him, as I have so often in my life, but never when he himself was kneeling before me. He reached out to take my hands. His grip was strong, but I felt him shaking. Kings are not treated so; undefeated kings, off the field of battle, do not expect to find themselves on their knees.

'Forgive me, Majesty!'

'You ask me? When a slave must have so many justified grudges against his master?'

'You never did anything any other man wouldn't have done, sire.'

Rodrigo winced. 'That is the worst condemnation I have ever had, I think.'

'Sire—'

'Help me up, Ilario. My knees aren't what they were as a young man.'

By the amount of weight he rested on my arm and shoulder when he had to rely on his right knee, he was correct in that.

'I'm sorry I did not treat you better.' His expression was still a touch that of a man speaking to a child or a hound, but less so than I had ever known him. 'Ilario, if you wish, I will implore you every day now. Do this. Please.'

'Stop.' I was still holding his arm, I found. Bewildered, I didn't release it. There were still the muscles of a knight and warrior under the velvet. 'Majesty, please. Do you think I can't see what's at stake?'

'Well then—'

'I'm not only afraid for myself.'

Finally I brought myself to let go of his arm, and look at the face I knew so well.

'I have a child. I have a father. There are others . . . And I know this won't be enough. Not for Videric. Majesty, he sent men to Italy to kill me – I don't know any *fewer* of his secrets now than I did then! If I go through some ceremony of reconciliation, then in a few months, or a few years, Lord Videric will come after me, and kill me. And he'll kill or disgrace or otherwise destroy all of us who know what did happen at Carthage. He'll kill Onorata. He'll kill Captain-General Honorius.'

I did not mention to my King that Rekhmire' and Ramiro Carrasco, Attila and Tottola, and all of Honorius's household guard, would be Videric's targets too. I don't deceive myself that they're of high enough rank for him to care as more than a point of principle.

I held Rodrigo's gaze. 'Taking up his place as your First Minister won't make Lord Videric safe again, Majesty. Not in his eyes—'

'Wait.' Rodrigo held up his scarred hand.

The bushy dark brows came down in a frown.

'While I grant that panic might, in the past, have forced Videric into errors – I know the man! He's worked beside me for twenty-five years. If his King commands him to treat you with all respect and civility, then he will do it. There can be no doubt of that.'

I looked at Rodrigo's expression of certainty.

And one day, one day there'll be bandits, or thieves, or robbers on the road, or pirates who swoop down on a ship, and leave no one they find alive or recognisable.

But this man is Videric's friend. And quite naturally, he won't believe that.

Rodrigo Sanguerra gave me a curt nod.

'Ilario. I'll call on you again tomorrow.'

8

Honorius and Sergeant Orazi were deep in discussion when I arrived at their chambers, debating how the Chin ship's rocket-arbalests and pottery grenadoes might be used in an Iberian army, should Zheng He ever be persuaded to part with any, or part with the plans for them.

'Which I doubt,' Honorius concluded rapidly, a broad grin spreading over his face. He reached out for Onorata with prison-pale hands.

Orazi and Saverico and even Berenguer allowed themselves to be brought to admit the child had grown bigger, and more active; and Honorius's men-at-arms exchanged grins over his head as he put her on a wolf-skin rug at his feet.

My child cooed and laughed, and thwacked her grandfather's toes with her fists.

'She'll be a quick one when she's grown,' Honorius observed. He gave Ramiro Carrasco a thoughtful stare, and directed Berenguer to take the man into the kitchens and feed him.

'Then,' the Lion of Castile added, 'you might feel inclined to tell me what has you worse concerned than yesterday?'

'God preserve me from mercenary commanders with a keen nose!' I could make little amusement sound in my voice.

Orazi took himself to the door, to engage the King's guards in conversation; Saverico appeared no older than fourteen as he sat down on the wolf-skin to prevent a wide-eyed Onorata eating two bone dice and a chess-man; and I detailed the actions of King Rodrigo to my father.

It took me while the sun rose a finger's width up the morning sky. I turned my head fifty times in the hour expecting Rekhmire' to walk in through the door.

' . . . And the King says he will come to me again. Until I agree, evidently.'

Expectant, I tensed for Honorius's bellowing rage.

Honorius presented me with his lean profile as he gazed towards the window. He rubbed a hand through cropped hair in which the sun showed more grey than when we had stood in Venice.

In a level tone, he said, 'I see why King Rodrigo suggests this.'

I sat perfectly still.

I wish I might ask Rekhmire' his opinion of this.

I wish Rekhmire' were not absent from Taraco now with the last word between us an angry one.

'If you were Videric,' I demanded. 'If you went through with this *farce* for public consumption, would you leave Ilario, and Honorius, and Rekhmire', and Onorata, alive afterwards?'

'I'd think it would look suspicious for those people to *die*, son-daughter.'

'So perhaps he'd wait a while—'

Honorius bent over and picked Onorata up from the wolf-skin. She bubbled happily, and pulled at the laces on Honorius's doublet with all ten fingers splayed. He hoisted her, with a grin, as if he tested her weight.

'She's thriving.' The grin became a beam. Honorius stood and tucked her into the crook of his arm, tickled with a forefinger, and was rewarded with a gurgle.

'There might not be war here yet,' he added quietly, continuing to smile down at her. 'But Carthage will most certainly send in legions and a governor this year, if nothing happens to prevent it. The fourteenth Utica and the sixth Leptis Parva, with Hanno Anagastes or the current head of House Barbas, would be my guess.'

That he could put names and legionary insignia to these fears didn't surprise me, but added to the knot in my stomach.

'Under guise of protecting us against the Franks, you understand.' Honorius looked quickly away from Onorata, as if some other memory had filled his mind. He walked to the window. 'You don't want to see what happens in Aragon and Leon and Castile happening here.'

The window-ledge might be several feet wide, but I was relieved he did not sit Onorata down on it, there being no bars. I leaned my elbows on cool stone and stared down.

'You think I ought to do this.'

'Because I can think of nothing else!'

The diminishing perspective looking directly down the castle's wall made me dizzy. I resolved to draw it some day, and lifted my head. Just visible over the castle's outer walls, grassy slopes lay speckled yellow like lizards under the heat. All Taraco's white houses and colonnades were busy with men and traffic, before they would become deserted under the noon sun. Ochre earth and lapis-blue haze in the distance . . .

'You think I should lie and beg Videric's pardon in public!'

'If you or the Egyptian have a better idea, I'll hear it!'

Onorata began to grizzle.

I shushed her, gently, and Honorius jiggled her a very little, giving her one of the gloves from his belt to chew on. She gummed enthusiastically and wetly at the fingers of it.

'Revolting child,' my father observed besottedly.

I caught Carrasco's voice in the kitchens, evidently in conversation with Berenguer.

'Ask Videric's assassin,' I said. 'He's under threat, and his family too. He'd drown men like kittens in a bucket if it kept his mother and father and brothers safe and *I know how he feels!*'

With considerable asperity, Honorius snapped, 'I am fifty years old: I have fought in all the major fields of the last thirty years of the Crusades; I can take care of myself!'

'And Onorata? Can she?'

I let Onorata grip my thumb. She smiled at me, or I thought she did.

Honorius made a sound I couldn't identify, and when I looked at him, he merely hitched her in his arms again, and carried her back to the rug, and set her down on it.

He sounded exasperated, even in a whisper.

'We need Videric back as the King's minister! This is what we came here for! We came here to have that bastard Videric owe us his job.'

He didn't take his eyes from the baby, even as he growled at me.

'I won't tell you to risk Onorata, you know that! But this is a dangerous world, there are thieves and pirates out there who *aren't* Videric's hired killers. We need to be prepared to protect her in any case. As for me . . . Ilario, I won't allow you to make an excuse out of me.'

The prison appartments rang with the sudden silence.

I felt heat rising in my face.

Because my father, it seems, is undergoing a formal imprisonment by King Rodrigo Sanguerra that – despite its purely political nature – is at some level a profound humiliation for Licinus Honorius. And Honorius suffers it because he wants the country secure.

'Perhaps I need no excuse,' I said. 'You'll be able to live in Taraco. If I do this, I doubt Onorata and I will – because Videric will insist that I leave.'

'Would you not seek an apprenticeship with a master painter somewhere, in any case?' Honorius shrugged, with every appearance of being casual. 'A lot may change in seven years.'

Yes, and my father is a fifty-year-old man: at the end of seven years, he may not be alive.

The day passed: twenty-four hours going by in not much more than a century or two. True to his word, Rodrigo Sanguerra came to my rooms privately, hooded in a linen cloak against discovery; and true to his word, he got down on his knees on the floor.

If anything it was the more excruciatingly embarrassing this second time, when we both knew what would happen.

When I failed to persuade him to stand up – and only just managed to reject the idea of hauling him up bodily – I sat down on my arse beside my King, on the bare floorboards, and put my head in my hands.

'I've been round this trail over and over, sire. Yes: I'll look a fool. I'll be branded a coward and a weakling. And . . . I'll be putting my family at the mercy of a man who wants me dead. I no longer know which is the most essential matter; which might be an excuse for any other. I can't think it through! I just know there are too many reasons why I shouldn't do this.'

King Rodrigo rested his hands on his thighs, sitting back on his heels, and then reached out to take hold of my jaw and turn me to face him.

'King's Freak,' he said softly, and then: 'The King begs you. I beg you.'

'Don't!'

'Don't make me, then.' His crooked smile was the same one that had always signalled a paternal warmth between us, in those rare moments that we had left position and power out of the equation.

I said, 'You've seen my baby.'

His smile flashed in his beard. 'The miraculous child! Yes. Although I suppose they all are. Any miracle that common will tend to be discounted.'

If I gave him a jaundiced look, he took it well.

I said, 'You want me to think about the children in Taraconensis if war comes.'

He gave a shrug, with bulky shoulders; and winced at kneeling on the hard wood. 'Of course. I want you to think about anything that speaks to my side of the argument!'

I might prove my own case, of what truly happened – but that wouldn't help bring Aldra Videric back as your adviser . . .

I sat with my elbows on my knees, and thrust my fingers through my hair

It would begin to prove the true story if I used Ramiro Carrasco de Luis as a witness. The confused emotions of guilt, gratitude, hatred, and attraction that he felt towards his hermaphrodite rescuer would make him speak.

I might make King Rodrigo believe in the extent of Videric's guilt.

But I should not seek to do that. Since he needs to retain that shred of trust to work with the man.

'Do I have to swallow the "forgiveness" of a man who sent people after me to kill me?'

The King of Taraconensis gave me the quirk-lipped look that I have known as long as I have known him. 'Ilario, I assure you, abasement becomes quite natural after a while . . . '

'It does?'

'No.'

I couldn't have painted Rodrigo's expression; the gleam in his dark eyes that was amusement, grief, anger, and self-mockery; all together.

'No,' Rodrigo Sanguerra repeated. 'And you're not my enemy. In fact, you bear a surprisingly small grudge against your King. I don't envy you on your knees before a man who hates you. But . . . '

263

He put one hand down, to begin to rise; I leapt up and offered hand and arm.

'You're wrong about the grudge, sire.'

'Am I?'

'All that's in the past. I can't carry it now.'

'Ah.' He made fists of his hands as he stood there, stretched his arms out, and I heard tendons and ligaments crack. 'I think I'm wearing you down. If I come tomorrow, who knows what you'll say?'

If there was an hour during the night when I slept, I didn't know about it.

The water clock marked what would have been watches on Frankish and Iberian ships, and were hours of prayer here. After a while I got up and dressed, and, when the time came, fed Onorata with the warm goat's milk that Ramiro Carrasco deftly obtained.

If we had both been slaves, I would have teased him with how a lawyer felt about being skilled in milking goats. As it was, I left him to resume his sleep.

Onorata rarely woke more than once in the night, now. I almost regretted that, leaning at the window and watching moonlight mimic the earlier sun on distant crawling waves. I could have done with somewhat to keep me occupied.

In all honesty, had it been a night in Carthage or Rome or Venice, I would have contrived some accident to wake up Rekhmire', just so that I could talk to the Egyptian.

I squinted out at the black featureless immensity that was the land-mass of Taraco. Wondering how long the mules would take to Aldra Videric's estates, and how riding was treating his knee.

It's possible to become surprisingly accustomed to someone's company, I concluded, and went back to wrestle with Iberian wolf-skin bed-covers, and lay awake until dawn.

Honorius liking Onorata's company, and I not knowing how long I would be here for him to have it, I spent more time in the prison than in my own quarters.

I sat on the wide ledge, one leg hanging down inside the room. From this acute angle, I might just see the sea in the north-east. Sun flashed like hammered gold. From this high citadel I could watch Zheng He's ship tacking slowly up and down the coast – showing its sheer dimensions off to Taraconensis' smaller towns, and bringing their knights and mayors hot-foot to Taraco and the King's presence.

Rodrigo Sanguerra had abandoned kneeling, and that morning had sat with me in my rooms with an air of relaxation. As if, despite what he must attempt to persuade me into, this time was a pleasant relief from court politics.

Now I recall why he kept his hermaphrodite slave . . .

Where the sun fell on the sea, it was bright enough to make eyes sting and water.

King Rodrigo had said, *Panic is spreading very well.* Up here, it's too high to see what men and women do when the dragon-painted ship threatens them; too far off to hear screams, or shouts of anger, or see whether any man is hurt.

I pushed myself back into the room, off the sill, and leaned on the back of the settle, watching with Honorius as Onorata tugged at the wolf's pelt. She might have been wriggling forward on her belly, or only wriggling by accident.

'This plan of the King's,' I began.

The door of the prison opened; royal guards strode in, Rodrigo Sanguerra behind them. Honorius sprang to his feet. I crouched to pick up Onorata, and put her into Saverico's arms, the young ensign being nearest me.

Honorius nodded and Carrasco and the three men-at-arms retired to the kitchens. He bowed his head to his King. 'Majesty?'

Rodrigo Sanguerra waved a hand to dismiss his escort. They filed out. Absently, he seated himself on the oak settle, gesturing that we might sit too if we so chose.

'You have knowledge of the Alexandrine envoy,' he observed. 'I thought I might therefore ask you questions, confidentially.'

'What?' I managed intelligently.

The King ignored me, passing a sheet of parchment to Honorius.

'Is this in his own hand?'

'His scribe would know better.' Honorius held it out to me.

It was signed *Rekhmire'* and a Pharaonic pictogram, as he had signed letters he had had me write.

I read it out. '"I find it compelling to stay with the Aldra Videric at his estate for some time longer. Perhaps a week or a month. His hospitality is overwhelming, and he desires me to stay for the hunting."'

'Is it genuine?' Rodrigo demanded impatiently.

Compelling. Overwhelming.

'Yes. He wrote it, Majesty. But . . . ' I tried to catch Honorius's eye.

Noblemen die of hunting accidents, horses and beasts are dangerous pastimes. But they die also of conspiracy or ambush and are reported as 'hunting accidents'. I saw Honorius recognised my thought.

He frowned. 'It *could* be true. The damned book-buyer – sorry, Majesty; I mean Master Rekhmire'. He might have decided he needs time enough there to persuade Lord Videric into seeing things his way . . . '

The words trailed off into the heated air of the chamber.

The King raised a bushy eyebrow. 'Ilario?'

My hands clenched into fists. 'Yes, it's *possible* – but also possible it's a flat lie! I think – Videric has decided to hold the Alexandrine envoy as a hostage.'

The King looked very close to startled. 'No. No, I think not. The Videric that I know is not a fool! If Master Rekhmire' has conveyed what we do here, Pirro must think he has only to wait for me to recall him. He would also know that Taraconensis can't afford to harm the representative of Queen Ty-ameny.'

I took several steps, pacing about the room, arms wrapped around my body. For all the heat, I was cold.

'Alexandria would only hear it was a hunting accident. Impossible to prove it wasn't.'

'Ilario, really—' King Rodrigo sighed, as I have known him sigh before. 'You allow your fear and hatred to distort your judgement. My lord Videric is not fool enough to allow harm to come to the Egyptian.'

Insight hit me as if it were a bolt from a crossbow.

I all but bit my tongue as the realisation struck.

'No.' I stepped forward, putting my hand on Honorius's shoulder, willing him to understand. 'No, that's right. I am misjudging him. Videric's not that stupid.'

'Then—'

'*Rosamunda is.*'

9

The King scowled, but I ignored him; aware I was gripping Honorius's shoulder hard enough that my fingers must hurt. He would have bruises. I felt as if I needed to urge the clarity of this truth into his body and blood.

My father frowned.

Thinking of . . . his Rosamunda? The woman who would have run away from her husband, until she was offered a choice between material comfort and my father's love?

The woman who twice, in Taraco and in Carthage, came close to killing her son-daughter?

Honorius's frown deepened. 'It's not in Aldro Rosamunda's interests to harm the book-buyer. She'll want her husband made First Minister again.'

'She won't think that far!'

The house of Hanno Anagastes came back to me: Rosamunda's expression behind her frozen eyes.

'Rekhmire' *ruined* her. You didn't see her face in Carthage!'

The frown became a scowl. Honorius absently reached up and peeled my fingers from the ball of his shoulder, and gripped my hand in his. 'She'd end up the wife of an exile if she did this. Or Videric would divorce her!'

'Rosamunda has a queue of rich and powerful men who'd marry her on the spot if she were divorced by Videric—'

Abruptly, I was silenced by the look that flashed across his face.

No way to apologise in front of King Rodrigo without enabling him to guess why Honorius would need an apology.

King Rodrigo slowly nodded. 'The Queen of the Court of Ladies? Yes . . . There are always men willing to take beauty and ignore the reputation that comes with it. Can you think Aldro Rosamunda honestly possessed of such a hatred against the Alexandrine—'

I interrupted a king. 'Can you ask me to bet Rekhmire''s life on the chance that she's more greedy than she is vindictive?'

I let go of Honorius's hands and glared at Rodrigo Sanguerra.

'Majesty, how soon can you talk to the bishops?'

King Rodrigo blinked, caught for once wrong-footed. 'The bishops?'

'This ceremony – reconciliation – apology – "ceremony of peace" –

penitence. Whatever you call it! How soon can it be arranged? How long will it take to summon Aldra Videric and get the bishops into the cathedral? Let's get this started before that lunatic woman does something to harm Rekhmire'!'

The King of Taraco looked at blankly at the Captain-General of Leon and Castile. My father smiled.

I found my face heating. I rubbed my hands across my cheeks.

More cautiously, Honorius inquired, 'Ilario . . . You do know what this involves?'

'Yes. I'm happy to eat dirt as publicly as required! Satisfied?'

A broad grin spread over Honorius's face, despite his evident best efforts to suppress it.

Rodrigo looked self-possessed; I couldn't read what else might be hiding under that efficient expression. 'Very well. The King's household guard may accompany the return message to Aldra Videric – in what strength would you suggest, Ilario?'

'I want him protected. Well protected.'

'Wise.' King Rodrigo stood, dropped a curt nod at Honorius and strode towards the door, barely waiting for us to rise. 'I'll send a full company. The more of the King's Guard, the more honour, after all.'

He broke out into a smile just before the door shut on his heels.

Honorius looked at me.

He said nothing.

'What!' I protested.

The retired Captain-General of Castile and Leon glanced over his shoulder at Saverico, as the men-at-arms came back into the room, and gestured for the young ensign to bring him Onorata.

Hefting the child into his arms, Honorius murmured, 'Taken you long enough to realise . . . '

Orazi smirked.

I swore. 'I'm not – I don't – there isn't – *cao!*'

Honorius pulled me into an embrace gentle only because of the child he also held.

'Rosamunda won't cause his death – because the damn book-buyer isn't stupid. Don't worry for him. Do what you have to do, Ilario. And I'll stand with you, if I have to disguise myself with a sack over my head!'

I spluttered out an uncertain laugh.

'That's better.' Honorius put one hand on the nape of my neck and shook me gently. 'I swear, in all my years as a soldier, I've learned how to tell rash men and fools from the rest – and Rekhmire' is neither.'

He paused. Smiled.

'Your judgement isn't so bad, son-daughter.'

There was no sensible reply to make, I thought.

And Honorius's grip felt surprisingly reassuring, even if his conclusions were self-evidently mistaken.

'Let's get this over with,' I said.

The initial part of the ceremony took three days.

If something excruciatingly humiliating can be boring, I thought, this is.

On the first day I knelt outside the church door as one of the *flentes*, those who weep; dressed only in a shirt, and formally asking the men and woman who went in to Mass to pray for me, and to intercede with God on my behalf. On the second day I was allowed into the narthex of the cathedral as one of the *audientes*, the hearers, and knelt on the cold mosaic floor behind the catechumens until the end of the sermon – not listening very much to what Bishop Ermanaric said, in fact, but lost in the sensation of chill stone under my shins, and trying to work out (in the slanting light from the ogee windows) what were the differences between these pale stones and the glass mosaics of Venice and Constantinople.

On the third day a different bishop, Heldefredus, preached about pardoning those who had sinned, and I took my place as one of the *genuflectentes*, kneeling between the cathedral door and the ambo, dizzy because of a whole day's fast, and speaking only to implore the procession of priests as they walked past me:

'Pray for me, a sinner!'

Again, I was taken out before the Mass was celebrated.

Videric was not present. Nor Rekhmire'.

Honorius let me know himself forbidden to come, and offered his presence all the same. I sent Orazi back with strict instructions to keep the Lion of Castile caged.

Let this not cause any more trouble than it has to!

King Rodrigo sent his household guard to assist in bringing me the plain meats that the bishops had allowed in my penitential cell on the first and second days.

Sergeant Orazi, scowling, told me each day in bad Alexandrine – incomprehensible to the junior priests who oversaw us – that none of our expected visitors had ridden into Taraco yet. And in the language of Taraconensis added that Onorata was well, and possibly missing me. Not knowing young babies, the sergeant said, he found it difficult to tell.

On the night of the first fast I didn't see any of the guard, since no man was to bring me food, and the bishops' priests evidently thought themselves capable of providing fresh water.

There was no candle or lantern in the hermit's cell built outside, up against the cathedral walls. I took advantage of what daylight there was left coming through the door-grate to take the smuggled paper and chalk out from under the thin straw palliasse.

I drew faces. Odoin, who'd been a lieutenant in Rodrigo's royal guard when I left, and now had his promotion to captain. Hunulf, and Winguric; who had worked with me in the scriptorium, and Galindus, of course.

I appreciated that they didn't visit, since every other man or woman I might know from nine years in Rodrigo's palace crowded close to satisfy their urge to stare at me.

The sheet of paper was not large. I drew faces in miniature. Egica, who taught me Latin and letters at sixteen, when it became apparent that Federico's hired tutor had been cheap for a reason. Egica's face was more lined, his nose more covered in red broken veins, in this last year; I could smell spirits on him when he stumbled past me, one hand outstretched as if he would have ruffled my hair in passing.

More men greeted me with shuttered faces. Less than a year, and I am ignored by those I have diced with and trained with in arms, and women-gossips with whom I debated what colours one might put together in embroidered tapestries . . . even young children whose parents had been passing friendly to the King's Freak –

The light was definitely gone.

I crumpled the paper up into a compressed ball in my hand, and crammed it under the palliasse.

This is not the Empty Chair, or the Most Serene, or the city of the Pharaoh in exile. This is not Carthage – *Although I am under a penitence of sorts*, I found myself thinking, and smiled crookedly in the dark.

It was the kind of irony Ramiro Carrasco would have liked, when he was a sardonic lawyer and not a slave.

They ought at least to send Carrasco to me here, a time or two; it would cheer him up to see me in sackcloth and ashes . . .

A voice outside the studded oak door of the hermit's cell said, 'Ilario?'

Yellow light glinted through the iron grate set into the door. An oil-lamp or a candle; oil by the smell.

The voice was for one dumb-struck moment strange to me, and then—

'*Father Felix?*'

'May I come in? They've sent me to instruct you.'

'Yes.' I said it before I thought. 'Yes, of course, Father!'

He had to duck almost double to get under the low lintel. The builders had left a ledge against the far wall, where the masonry was set deep; Father Felix put his lantern on the earthen floor with a muttered prayer, swept his green robes around him, and seated himself. He gazed directly at me.

He looks no different, I thought.

It only seems a decade since I left Taraco; in reality it is only ten or eleven months.

Father Felix's copper-brown features showed as strong as ever, illuminated under his hood; his astonishing pale grey eyes looked through me as much as they ever used to.

'The bishop wishes me to prepare you for the fourth and fifth stations of the exomologesis.' He leaned forward, and his fingers felt warm against my forehead as he brushed my hair back. 'Ilario, are you all right?'

'I haven't practised fasting this year, so I'm unused to it.' I could only stare at him. 'Father . . . '

No man had ever known Father Felix's name outside the church, or his origins; all he would tell me was that he had travelled from beyond the lands of the Turk, beyond the Caucasus mountains. Seeing him with new eyes, I suddenly wondered if he would know more of Zheng He's land than the rest of us.

When this is done, I will persuade him to take word to Honorius, and bring news back to me.

'Tertullian,' Father Felix said, in a measured tone.

The black pupils in his grey eyes expanded in the dim lantern light.

'Tertullian instructs us that exomologesis is the discipline which obliges a man to prostrate and humiliate himself, so as to draw down God's mercy. You've performed three of the stations. Tomorrow, you take your place as one of the *substrati*, as Gregory Thaumaturgus defines it; prostrating yourself where you were kneeling today. The bishop will lay his hand on you and bless you. The day after tomorrow, on the final day, you'll act as one of the *consistentes*, and be allowed to be present to hear Mass. Then you come forward to the altar, recite a psalm and litany, and beg forgiveness of the man you've wronged.'

My stomach rolled over.

Father Felix continued, 'The King and the bishops and this man you have offended will hold a *concilium*, there and then, to determine if you deserve re-admission and pardon. And if so, you will be led around the cathedral carrying a lighted candle, prayers will be said, and you will be given public absolution. And the kiss of peace, by Aldra Videric.'

His voice altered on the last word.

'Felix . . . ' I sought desperately for words. For some reason Rekhmire''s prayer-box came into my mind's eye: I wondered if he was praying to Kek and Amunet and the rest of the Eight tonight, in Videric's provincial fortress. 'Should I do this?'

Felix's robes were coarse homespun wool, dyed the colour of hedge-weeds. I suspected they were the same robes he had worn when I left last year, faded through many washings. His dark hands were the hands of a workman, if you looked at them apart from the rest of him.

'If your desire for pardon is in any way not genuine, I would need to inform the bishops.' He held my gaze with more ease than most men. 'Tomorrow they'll smear wood-ash on your forehead, and dress you in coarse yellow linen. If you're not truly penitent, that's no more than a play-actor's costume. You can't insult God that way.'

I read the implied *And I won't allow it* without difficulty, knowing Father Felix as long as I have.

It never occurred to me – that as well as begging pardon of my stepfather Videric, I might have to mean it!

I delayed directly answering. 'Aldra Videric will be there on the last day?'

'Lord Videric arrived tonight. He will be in the cathedral tomorrow, as well as on the last day.'

Did he have an Egyptian spy with him!

No way to ask that question.

I drew up my knees where I sat on the thin mattress. The chill of the earth permeated through the straw. Linking my arms around my shins, I was at least grateful that the penitential shirt came down far enough to cover me to the knees.

I said, 'I very much want to ask pardon of Videric.'

Since that was true, I hoped it would sound true. Even if the reason for it isn't what Felix would think of as the correct one.

I shifted as my empty belly rumbled, and watched Father Felix's expression. 'I have a child, Father.'

Slowly, he smiled. It altered his face beyond belief. 'God has blessed you, then.'

'I'm still what I was. A man's body and a woman's body. Will the church re-admit a hermaphrodite?'

I had been five or six when it occurred to me that the rags the peasants tied on bushes at sacred wells and springs didn't alter their lives in any perceptible way. Valdamerca kept me in the women's section of the church at our estate, and I paid attention after that, and concluded this was much the same business as well-fairies and forest ghosts. The two-year-long argument over whether I could be permitted to attend Mass with King Rodrigo's household, therefore, had both taken me by surprise and completely bewildered me.

I suspected Felix knew that. He had argued fiercely for me to take communion. If a God as kind as the one Felix believed in had existed in this world, I would have resented the debate about my soul considerably more.

He ignored my question. 'Is your desire for pardon genuine?'

'Yes, Father.'

'You have done wrong, you have caused great wrong, to the Aldra Videric, and you humbly wish him to pardon you?'

The night felt cool, after the heat of the day, but my cheeks were hot. Father Felix watched me blush, himself apparently unmoved.

'You have to let me do this!' I said.

'Perjure yourself in court if you wish, Ilario, but not before God's face. And not before the altar in this church.'

Reaching out for his long-fingered hand, I knelt up on the straw mattress.

'Father, you go back and tell the bishops that this is right. If you don't, my family are in danger, the King is in danger, Carthage will take control of this country, and I guarantee that we'll be in a war with the Franks within two years. If God doesn't want towns burned and men slaughtered and women raped, then God will let me lay at Videric's feet and beg his pardon!'

Father Felix's hand felt cool. His skin glowed a dark hue on the back, where I could see tendons shifting under the skin. A pale gold for the creased palm.

Slowly, he brought his other hand up to grip mine.

It had not occurred to me before I left Taraco that Father Felix stands a head shorter than I do, and is wiry rather than strong. If I had Honorius's grasp of military necessity, I might put my hand around Felix's throat until he choked into unconsciousness, and claim the old man had a fit.

But even Honorius knows I have no ability to do that.

'Do you want me to lie to God, Ilario?'

'No, just to His bishops!'

Father Felix's lips formed a firm line.

I knew he would be thinking, with that keen mind of his; what I couldn't predict was how differently he might value things, having the faith in his God that he did.

'Rodrigo knows of this,' he mused.

'Yes.'

'If His Majesty hasn't informed the bishops, he presumably trusts in your – quite genuine penitence – to convince them.' Felix's pale eyes flickered a gaze at me, and then he resumed staring at our interlocked hands. 'Well . . . pride is a sin. And I shouldn't be proud enough to think I know better than the men of God in *concilium*. If God objects to you, Ilario, I think He's quite capable of making that plain to them at the appropriate time.'

He squeezed my hand and let it go, his knuckles like a bagful of jack-stones.

'Have you done anything you're ashamed of while you've been away, Ilario?'

'Yes.' My face was hot again, I found.

'Then I suggest you use this as an opportunity to ask God to forgive you for those things. Do you wish to confess them to me?'

The secrecy of the confessional might have been broken in the past, but not by men such as Father Felix.

I knelt on the packed earth floor and let him take me through antiphons and responses.

He gave me a searching look, as if I were both taller and older than he had expected. 'And what is it you're ashamed of?'

Dutifully, I said, 'I gave way to the lusts of the flesh, Father.'

'And you are sorry?'

His pale gaze made me shift a little, then. I reached for a pat lie, and could only find honesty. 'It brought me my child. So . . . I don't regret it.'

'Then what is it you do feel shame over?'

Masaccio's death. Paying money to own Ramiro Carrasco de Luis, and enjoying the power that gave me over the man. Exulting in the talent that made Masaccio call me in to paint the golem – although that could not be directly mentioned. I spoke in general terms of pride.

'And I've taken too much money from my – family.' I changed the word from *father* at the last moment. 'I owe a debt there—'

'Families should support each other.' Felix looked a little puzzled, as well he might, supposing that I must be talking about the absent Federico and Valdamerca. 'You would do the same for them, wouldn't you?'

I thought of the unlikelihood of the retired Captain-General of Castile needing support from me, and smiled. 'Yes. Of course.'

'The man you own as a slave: he attempted to kill you?'

'Yes, Father.'

'And you have forgiven him.'

'I trust him not to do it again,' I said grimly, and caught a slight smile on Father Felix's face. The *perigrinati christus* never smiled often. I must have looked puzzled.

'Has this man atoned, in your eyes?' Father Felix asked.

'I . . . Yes.' It startled me to find that true.

'Then it was not wrong to have bought him. Although you should free him as soon as possible. No matter what the law and the Old Testament say, I cannot believe that owning a man is good and right.'

The situation that kept Ramiro Carrasco in his collar couldn't be explained, and I didn't try. I talked to Father Felix of minor sins, finding more comfort in his voice and presence than in anything he might be saying. It was not until the lantern had almost burned out of oil, and he asked me for the last time if I had sins unconfessed, that something burst out of me:

'Is it a sin to hate your father and mother?'

Father Felix steepled his fingers on his chest, looked me up and down, and slowly shook his head – not answering my question, I saw, but in a general negation.

'The scriptures would say so.'

'What would you say? Father Felix?'

'I'd say I don't have answers for you, Ilario. Much as you always wished to believe I might. Is it wrong?'

274

I thought of Videric, my mother's husband, whom I will have to see tomorrow. And keep silent about so much.

I thought of Rosamunda, my mother – whose presence or absence I haven't asked after, because how can I bear either? The thought that she could see me subjected to this, or the thought that she could stay away?

I looked up from the floor at Father Felix. Eyes adjusted to the almost-dark, I could see every line of his sixty-year-old face. I desired desperately to paint him in the style of the New Art: recognisably Felix, *perigrinati christus* of Taraconensis.

'It's wrong.' I shrugged, half desperate. 'It's corrosive. Like sublimates in an alchemist's workshop. I only feel contempt for him. I hate her so much that it'll burn me away.'

He didn't ask me for names. 'And are you guiltless towards these people, yourself?'

This time I shook my head in confusion. 'You know I can't be, Father.'

'Spend your time in the cathedral meditating on that, then. I believe, as I believe in God Himself, that this will be of more use to your soul than any amount of grovelling in ashes.'

Even qualified relief went through me and lightened me, as if my body could float. I answered his small smile with one of my own.

'I have to do the grovelling in any case. But I'll take your advice, Father. Will you be present?'

He looked up from preparing to give me blessing, if not absolution. 'That's as you prefer. My duties don't compel me to it, but they don't keep me from it, either.'

'Don't come.' I couldn't make myself say anything less honest. 'Neither day. It'll be easier for me if I don't have to speak knowing you're there – and I do have to do this.'

Father Felix nodded.

'I think I understand why. Bless you, Ilario. Here. Take these.'

He stooped and picked up the lantern, muttering a little as the streaming heat caught his fingers, and got it into a safe grip.

His other hand, in the dark, pushed at me half a dozen sheets of folded blank paper, that recognisably came from the scriptorium, and two broken ends of chalks.

Videric wasn't there on the fourth day.

Nor Rosamunda.

Nor Rekhmire'.

10

Slaves are used to being on their knees in the presence of other men. But this is different – is intended, primarily rather than secondarily, to be humiliating.

Humbling, I thought. Ashes are no dirtier than a woman gets cleaning out hearths all day. I've worn coarser shirts working with King Rodrigo's horses in the royal stables. And wearing a shift that only comes down to mid-thigh, when I know every eye in the cathedral watches me to see if they can see a cock and balls under the hem, or women's nipples and breasts through the weave . . . That's not so different from some days at court, here.

But it *is* different.

My face burned: half of it shame, and half rage at the sheer injustice.

A decision must have been made that to keep me from my child for five nights was cruel. Attila and Tottola brought her to the hermit's cell beforehand for a very few minutes, in the hour when other men would break their fasts. She whimpered. I touched her warm skin, murmured in her ear, and found her unharmed and well cared for.

The two soldiers had four priests with them, solemn faced, not permitting any word to be spoken; not even a greeting and a farewell. Tottola smiled at me. Attila looked intense.

I put my hands inside Onorata's linen shirt and blanket to find out why she grizzled, and encountered the hard nub of folded paper.

There was enough light when they left with her for me to puzzle out the words – the scribe's hand of Ramiro Carrasco. But my father Honorius's unmistakable irascible tone:

'The damn book-buyer's back. Persuaded me I can't be there tomorrow. He says, Chances are, anyway, you'll have more parents there than you know what to do with.'

This is supposed to humble, I thought. *But how can it do anything except make a man proud?*

Being at the centre of all this attention, as the sinner is.

Polyphonic voices echoed out from the great heights of the cathedral roof; like bells, organs, great waterfalls of sound. The reverberations struck me under the breastbone. I trembled. If I had had to walk, I might have fallen down. But I was directed to crawl.

Five thousand people lined the road to the cathedral doors. I could see through the great arched opening that the cathedral was full. Keeping myself conscious of lines of legs, lines of bodies, tonal mass of heads, I might reduce all to their component parts, I need not see them as men and women of the court, who know, or know of, the King's hermaphrodite Ilario.

The mosaic floor was hard under my hands and knees. One drum, tapped by a royal page walking behind me, kept to a rhythm. I crawled under the shadow of the great receding arches of the door, passing from under the gazes of the stone saints in their round-arched niches.

Not out of sight of the crowds. Their voices rumbled behind me, loud enough for me to hear even over the thunder of the choirs.

Scent is the most familiar thing, and sound next. The great horns blazing out anthems, echoing down the long aisles of the cathedral – how many times have I stood at the back, near this door, watching the King in procession to the altar? How many times have I smelled the flowers and dust on these ancient tiles: stags, bulls, boar, star maps, ships, all shaped out of tiny squares of coloured stone?

The wind whisked dust through the open door behind me and I pressed my chin down, staring at the floor, and praying that my shirt wouldn't blow up over my arse.

Bad enough to be crawling up the centre aisle, under the eye of every man.

Bad enough to know the women are up above, behind pierced stone screens, staring down with their hands over their mouths, frantic with enjoyment of the scandal.

For a second I pictured this from their perspective: looking down the great open space of the ochre-walled cathedral, all the spaces between the striped red pillars crowded elbow-to-elbow with Rodrigo Sanguerra's courtiers. Lines of priests in their green robes keeping the centre aisle clear. And there, on that wide empty paving, the lone small figure on hands and knees, creeping slowly, so slowly, forward . . .

All I could see were priests' sandals and the hems of green robes embroidered with gold oak leaves. I didn't lift my head to look higher. It cannot possibly be further to the lectern and the altar—

A hand touched my hair.

'Here,' Bishop Heldefredus's voice said above me, and his fingers pushed me to the side.

Light fell down in green and blue and scarlet and gold, patching the floor, drowning out the colours of the mosaic. The great Briar Cross stood in front of the coloured glass window, all the red glass centred about it, so the light fell over the altar like the Unspilled Blood of Christus Imperator, and the birth-blood of His Mother.

I didn't look higher than the bare feet of the Emperor tied to the Tree. I couldn't lift my head; I shook.

'We are brought here to witness reconciliation,' Heldefredus's voice called out, above my bowed head. 'Which is a holy state, belonging to God, and we will first pray for God's guidance.'

The antiphonal response thundered back.

My eyes were running; I blinked furiously to be able to see. The bishop's hand pressed down on my shoulder. *Yes, I remember—*

The stone floor between the altar and the lectern felt bare and cold, no different from when Bishop Heldefredus had led me here this morning to instruct me. Except that then the cathedral had been empty, open doors letting in slanting sunlight, and silence, and the smell of the sea. Not packed with sweating men, all in court clothes, all with their eyes on me.

I stood up on legs like water, saw my knees had bled onto the hem of my shirt, and stumbled two steps. I fell on the stone floor and pitched forward, caught myself on my hands, and lowered myself down, my arms before me as the bishop had directed.

Prostration is moral and mental, as well as physical, but it is also practical. Laying face down while Heldefredus mounted the lectern and began to preach over my prone body, I could lean my forehead against the muscles of my arms, and ease a little of the pain from the cold floor. The shirt they'd given me was long enough to be decent, if I stayed still. But it was thin. I felt every line of the mosaic, every shiver of the cold marble and basalt.

I shut the congregation out of my thoughts. Telling myself: This is only the cathedral I have attended since the age of fifteen: there is no one here to watch me—

Quieter than the preaching bishop could hear, one of the royal guards standing over me murmured, 'Bet his cock's cold down there.'

The answer from his companion came in the tone of a man being self-congratulatorily clever. 'Bet her tits are!'

I knew if I looked up, I wouldn't see anything but impassive expressions. By the voices, these are men whom I have known by name, to speak to when we passed in palace corridors . . .

Heldefredus stopped speaking.

As the second bishop, Ermanaric, climbed up to the lectern, I followed my instructions and pushed myself up and back, so that I was on my knees.

Aldra Pirro Videric met my gaze.

The packed faces in the body of the church vanished.

I turned my head swiftly away from him. Looking up—

I caught a movement. A dark silhouette, behind the fragile fretwork of stone that hides the women's congregation from the sight of the men.

My mother, Rosamunda.

Without seeing her face, without seeing the colour of her gown, without more than the hint of an outline – I know her.

For a heart's beat I was back in Carthage, on the great dock below the

Bursa-hill, under the brown twilight of the Penitence. Following Rekhmire' onto a ship. Looking back past Honorius and his then-unknown household guard as they embarked with us. Hoping that, even then – even though I knew she had gone back to Taraco in disgrace weeks ago – even then she might still come after me to make her apology.

No, not an apology, I thought, peering up at the stone screen with my neck aching. Sadder than that. If she had only come to take me into her arms, I would have imagined the apology without her needing to speak it.

And imagination would have been all it would be.

'Ilario!'

Heldefredus's whisper brought my head jerking back down.

Aldra Videric stared at me, his face impassive. Knowing him, I could see in his eyes that my turning to Rosamunda first had angered him almost to the point of losing that perfect control.

The stiff embroidered robes of the archbishop swept between me and my stepfather. I found myself staring at viridian silk, fine white lawn, and the ends of a stole crusted with gold thread and embroidered with Eagle, Boar, Oak-leaf, and *gladius hispaniensis*. Because this was an archbishop, the sword blade was sewn in silver thread.

A sweaty hand lay heavily on my head and I heard the blessing ring out.

'Penitent,' he added, removing the hand. With an effort I looked up at Archbishop Cunigast. Thought of sermons slept through in short winter days when the King has coal-braziers brought into his chapel in this cathedral, and it is necessary to break the ice on the holy water in the font.

The heated June afternoon swept back over me. I blinked, hardly able to hold Cunigast's gaze.

'Penitent, do you truly desire to make restitution?'

'Yes, my lord.' My voice broke from alto to baritone and back. I heard a flutter of amusement behind me.

Scarlet, I kept my gaze fixed on the folds of the archbishop's robes. Folds in cloth: an elementary difficulty for the novice painter.

'You will be prepared,' Cunigast said, and stepped away in a swirl of bullion thread and silk.

In the order of service it read *Prepare him* or *Prepare her*. Neither fitted me.

Two priests in plain green robes stepped smartly up beside me; one pulled my hair up and snipped briskly away at it with scissors; the other lathered soap and warm water in a silver bowl, and followed his brother, shaving away the trimmed hair. I shut my eyes as soapy water trickled down my forehead, soaking the front of my shirt.

A cloth dabbed across my closed eyes.

'Thank you.' I acknowledged the priest, forgetting I wasn't to speak, and he bobbed his head awkwardly, eyes wide.

If he's a day over sixteen, I'm Videric's natural son!

Eyes clear of soap, I had no excuse not to look in the direction of the altar while a third bishop, whom I didn't know, blessed me, and flicked consecrated water over me.

Am I blessed or exorcised? I wondered, and gave up to focus on Videric.

He seems – no different.

I suppose I had expected him to look older, or tired. Or more impressive, perhaps. Either less frightening than the Videric of my mind who had sent Ramiro Carrasco and others to kill me, or else more so.

No . . .

Four chairs had been set up below the altar, on the widest step. Black polished oak, with pointed Gothic arches cut into the woodwork, and finials crowning their high backs. The seats were boxes; the sides fretwork open enough to make a pattern by showing the coloured robes of each man. The King, Rodrigo Sanguerra, with the gold Roman laurels of one of the Ancient Kingdoms winding around his brow. The archbishop, in forest green and silver. One chair empty – *Aldro Rosamunda will not be permitted to sit down here in the main body of the church next to her husband, even today.*

And, in the chair nearest me, Videric.

A burly, fair-haired man, blue eyes half closed against the light pouring down from the highest ogee windows. His legs were encased in mirror-bright steel: sabatons on his feet, greaves and chausses covering shin and thigh. Over that, a striped blue and white livery coat covered all of his breastplate; all of his armour but his gorget and haut-pieces; and above that he was bare-headed. He wore Rodrigo Sanguerra's badge on the breast of his livery coat over his heart, and he had had himself shaven and his beard clipped down to a fine gold shadow. Nobleman; knight; a man entirely fitted to be first minister to a king.

His chin rested on his hand. His eyes were fixed on me.

My skin crawled. I felt worse than naked.

I rubbed my palm nervously over my scalp, feeling the tufts of hair the boy priests had missed. One single layer of cloth kept my body from the prurient interest of the court behind me. Videric . . .

Looks clear through me.

One of the bishops began to repeat the Penitential Psalms, his voice echoing confidently through the vast spaces of the church.

I allowed myself one glance back into the body of the cathedral, as if I looked up at the lectern above me and eased an ache in my neck.

No man that I could take to be a tall shaven-headed Egyptian.

Is he here? Would Honorius try to reassure me with a lie?

As if I put my hand back onto hot metal, I looked in the direction that I was supposed to. At the chairs. At my King and the churchman Cunigast. The empty chair . . . If I look at that, I thought, perhaps I need not look at Videric until the end; until I have to.

I must look.

Aldro Pirro Videric, eyes still slitted against the light, continued to rest his chin on the heel of his hand. The bulk of his body and shoulders filled the space the chair allowed him. There was a smudge of pale dust on the boot sole under one sabaton. He would have ridden down from the palace with King Rodrigo this morning, not trudged here like the townsmen outside, or some of the poorer courtiers in the cathedral.

I let myself meet his gaze.

His attention struck me like a physical shock.

How in the name of the eight gods am I going to sound convincing!

Panic flooded me. Tension weakened the muscles of my knees, or I might have sprung up and turned to run out of the building. This man, this man with absolute control over himself—

Fountains flashing in the palace's enclosed courtyards, Videric's sandals rapping on the tiles as he strode down the corridor, and his concerned tone as he glanced at me: *She wants to speak to you. I don't know why. Be kind to her.*

I met his eyes, deliberately, and stared him down.

She wanted to see me because you ordered her to kill me.

You ordered *her* to make friends with me. Long ago. So that she could be there if it became necessary to kill me.

Videric's mouth moved, lip curving up a small amount. He gave me a measuring smile.

Every muscle in my body tensed. I saw it as clearly as if I lay anatomised on a slab in Alexandria's Royal Library: the pull of tendon, the contraction and swelling of muscle, the support of bone.

I am four yards away from his chair, and once again they have forgotten that the King's master-at-arms trained me as a knight.

I am swift enough to cover the distance, snatch Videric's dagger out of that tooled leather sheath, and have the blade down between his collar and his gorget into his heart before any man can stop me.

Videric, his gaze on me, gave a little shrug with his brows, as if disappointed that I had not responded to his smile.

Momentarily I shut my eyes.

Sharp anger flooded through me; washed me away like an undertow of the sea. I bit the inside of my lip until I tasted blood, and opened my eyes and looked at him again.

The ex-First Minister Videric stared amiably back at me.

He truly desires to be Rodrigo's First Minister again. Therefore, I think – he doesn't taunt me. Videric truly thinks that if he smiles, I will assume him a friend.

It took my breath.

The pale lines that being in the sun had put at the corners of his eyes creased. Videric's chin dipped infinitesimally, on his fist. I know him well enough to read what he intends to convey: *Courage!*

'Courage . . . ' I breathed out.

A silence swept through the hot cathedral.

No man moved.

Videric shifted and sat upright in the chair of state. He turned to speak to the King.

'Sire, it will not be justice if my wife is not here to witness Ilario's penitence. I realise where we are – but she is willing to come veiled.'

His words fell like stones into water, in the great crowded building.

Glancing back at the pierced stone screen, I wasn't surprised to see the silhouette gone. Videric would not ask such a question unless he knew the answer. I barely bothered listening to Archbishop Cunigast explain just why God would make a merciful exception in the interests of justice.

Rosamunda walked out from the narthex, behind the altar, and walked past me to sit in the empty chair.

Her scent caught in the back of my throat.

Gold wire made a miniature moon-horn of her head-dress, and the veil that hung down was of the finest flax, perfectly translucent. I gazed at her curling black hair, and full warm lips, and did not let myself look her in the eye.

If I face her, I will not be able to do this.

Heldefredus's narrow hand bit into my shoulder, fingertips curling to catch me under the edge of my collarbone. 'Now, Ilario.'

A tingle shot down my arm. Not pain. Enough sensation to remind me what I must now do.

I stood up, took three paces forward, dropped down on my knees as the bishop had rehearsed me, and looked directly up at Videric where he sat on the chair above me.

The position placed me equally carefully. The slanting beam of light from the altar window shone down, illuminating me so that every man, every woman, in this building can see the broad shoulders and wide hips of the one who is man *and* woman.

And therefore not a man, and not a woman.

I knelt, my spine stiff, my head up.

'I beg for your pardon.' Tension cracked my voice again: deep one moment and falsetto the next. 'Aldra Pirro Videric, I humbly beg your forgiveness.'

Videric stood up, both hands momentarily gripping the arms of his chair.

The sun shone off his armour and livery surcoat. Steel and blue and white . . . With the sun so bright on him, the thinning of his hair was hidden, and the incipient rounding of his jaw lost.

A shame, I thought. It made him more human to me. Something in him might touch me if I thought him just a man of Honorius's age, subject to piles and insomnia and stomach-ache when he ate spices that hadn't troubled him if he ate them at twenty.

Rosamunda stood up, resting her hand on her husband's arm, flax linen gloves showing the delicate rose-pink of her fingers against the steel of his vambrace.

Get away from me!

I forced myself not to shout it aloud.

The humiliation of this is that I am still, after a year, afraid of them both.

The stone was hard under my knees. Through Rosamunda's veil I saw the shape of spite and pleasure on her face. Only I was close enough to see.

I stumbled over the words Bishop Heldefredus had rehearsed me in.

'Aldra Videric, I beseech you humbly to intercede on my behalf. With God and with His Majesty, for their, for their forgiveness. I swear to do as I have done these past days: to prostrate and humiliate myself, to lie in sackcloth and ashes, to clothe my body in rags and plunge my soul in sorrow—'

Videric took a step forward.

I had not expected it.

A shiver went through me; I thought it must be visible at least to the closest row of men watching.

'And, and.' I found my place in the words again. 'To correct my soul by harsh treatment of myself. And by prayer, and fasting. And whole days and nights together to weep and seek your forgiveness. I cast myself at your feet, who I have wronged.'

I couldn't look up at Rosamunda, close as she was. I stared at Videric's face as if he were a rope thrown to a drowning man.

'I swear to atone, I for this reason fall on my knees before you.' I licked at dry lips, conscious that the words were absorbed by the air. They should echo back, and it was fear that softened what I spoke. 'And I beg you to lead me to absolution if you see fit.'

He smiled.

Confident, all his weight back on his heels, not even glancing behind at the archbishop and the king. They will have discussed this beforehand.

He held out his right hand.

'I acknowledge you,' he said. 'Child of my wife's body—'

The intake of breath was audible through the cathedral.

They hear it as formal poetics, I realised, staring up at him. *Not as the literal truth.*

Another hand extended itself into my vision. Pale, smooth, clothed in transparent linen.

Rosamunda's voice rang like a soprano bell. 'I acknowledge you and pardon you, Ilario. Rise now and come with me.'

Videric's hand was hot and dry; he gripped my wrist as if I had been a young man in the knights' training halls, and his effort would have brought me to my feet even without my own.

My mother's hand lay bonelessly in mine and I couldn't look at her.

They led me forward, one on either side, to the archbishop at the main altar.

Cunigast lit a candle, and at last my hands were free.

I reached out and took hold of the cool wax. *Rather that than Rosamunda's waxen skin.* The yellow flame danced, all but invisible in sunlight.

The archbishop raised his voice. 'The penitent will join us in the celebration of Mass, and then the public absolution will be given.'

Videric put his hands on my shoulders and kissed me on either cheek with the brusque efficiency of a courtier.

Rosamunda lifted her veil with both hands, looking at me with those green eyes that I see in the mirror.

She stood on her toes to press her lips softly against mine.

As Archbishop Cunigast proclaimed the kiss of peace I fell down on my knees in front of the altar and didn't move.

Celebration of Mass went on around me – Rosamunda being hustled off back up to the women's area of the cathedral – and I didn't stand up; could not stand up. The back of my throat filled with bile. It took every ounce of concentration not to spit it across the ancient mosaics.

King Rodrigo Sanguerra moved to stand at my right hand side when the Mass ended. Videric stayed on my left. I caught Rodrigo's eye, and he nodded, briefly.

I turned about, facing the congregation between the two men.

I knelt again and begged pardon of both, and both men helped me rise. The kiss of absolution from Pirro Videric burned my forehead as if it had been painted there with alchemists' acid.

Every yard of the walk around the nave of the cathedral sank into my memory: every curious or avid or disgusted face that I passed. The candle shook, and hot wax spilled over my fingers, the momentary pains anchoring me in myself.

If I'm pale, they'll take it for humiliation and grief and gladness.

It was four hours before it was over.

Rodrigo Sanguerra held a banquet in the castle, with Aldra Videric and I at the high table.

I slid away before the sun touched the horizon, on the excuse of changing into the clean shirt and hose and doublet that Father Felix brought for me – and slipped out of the palace with a nod to the guards.

I sprinted through Taraco's streets, boots thumping up squirts of dry dust. Assuming that Honorius my father does not lie; assuming that Rekhmire' *is* here—

A silk dragon-banner unrolled on the wind at the quay. I saw Commander Jian sitting in the stern of one of the Chin boats, among his oarsmen. He lifted his hand in a Frankish gesture of greeting he must have learned since their ship entered the Middle Sea.

A cloaked figure stood on the quay beside them.

Behind that cloaked man, another man; standing with bare chest and head, the reddening sun shining on his shaven scalp and white linen kilt.

I staggered up to them and caught Honorius's hand; he pulled me into a hard embrace, and released me, staring into my face, and pushing me at the Egyptian.

As if I had done it a hundred times before, I put my arms tightly around Rekhmire', felt him grip me and run his fingers over my cropped scalp, and fell down on my knees in the dust.

My father held my shoulders, and Rekhmire' leaned over and steadied my head, and I vomited up bitter bile, time after time, into the harbour, until I was shaking, sore-throated, and empty.

It took me a time to be willing to let go of either man. The quick setting of the sun had given way to blue dusk, I found; blackening into night.

Honorius wore his brigandine, I noted as I lifted my head from his shoulder; an anonymous armour that any guard might wear, or a poor knight.

'All's well,' my father reassured, as if he might read my thoughts. 'His Majesty told me to come down here and meet the book-buyer. I won't be arrested again if I keep to my curfew.'

Rodrigo asked him for his parole, I realised.

Little enough chance Honorius will ever break it.

I caught sight of Orazi and Tottola in the shadows of the nearer warehouses; the German lifted his hand in acknowledgement.

'Master Rekhmire' . . . ' I strove for formality, and finally persuaded myself to look up at the Egyptian. His arm still lay heavily about my shoulder.

Rekhmire' signalled with his other hand. One of Jian's men handed up a snapsack.

'Zheng He sailed south at the King's request, and picked me up further down the Via Augusta,' Rekhmire' observed, dark eyes hidden by shadow. Even so, I could see the corners crease. 'For some odd reason I didn't desire to ride to Taraco in the company of Aldro Rosamunda . . . '

Dryly, I said, 'I wonder why.'

My supposition was exactly right!

'Were you in the cathedral?' I added.

I felt the Egyptian shrug, rather than saw it.

'Forgive me: I didn't desire to see it. I would have throttled the insolent barbarian.'

It was unclear whether he meant Videric, King Rodrigo, or any other man; the true accent of Alexandria reminded me that we are all barbarians in that city's eyes.

A scent of pitch and a flare of light let me know that Orazi had fired a torch. Honorius glanced at the stars on the horizon.

'We should get back.' He glanced at me, and at the book-buyer, and I thought I saw him smile.

Rekhmire' kept his arm over my shoulder, using me as well as his stick to propel himself along at a reasonable rate. The torchlight showed irregularities in the ground; his concentration was on those.

'No hunting accidents?' I observed.

He smiled without looking at me, giving him a profile that might well have appeared in one of Ty-ameny's bas-reliefs.

'That depends on your definition of "accident".' He scowled, mood changing. 'And hunting. The wild boar on Aldra Videric's estate are tame enough that they come to a whistle. It's not sport.'

The rising white light brought Sulva clearly into my mind's eye, the massive wild boar attentive to her aulos flute. I thought suddenly, *I should have confessed to Father Felix that I regret how badly I treated Sulva Paziathe.*

'I had crossbow bolts sent too close to me for my liking,' Rekhmire' observed, shooting a glance up at the Sanguerra castle's black bulk. 'If I had thought of myself as a hunter rather than prey, I might have come back more battered even than I went.'

He means his knee, I realised.

Before I could say anything rational or comforting, I saw other torches approaching us down the dock steps.

Honorius and Orazi exchanged a wordless look.

Only two torches, and – I squinted, now the night had fully fallen; the moon was not yet bright – only three men visible. Two guards, and one man who dressed like a knight.

'I have a message for you!' the leading figure called.

Under the flickering yellow light, I recognised his lugubrious features.

'That's Safrac de Aguilar – King Rodrigo trusts him,' I muttered briskly to Honorius.

We were four or five men to three, in any case – and I wondered when it had become natural for me to think that way in my home city.

Aldra de Aguilar evidently recognised Honorius in the torchlight. His voice became much less loud. 'Greetings, my lord. The King desires to see you, urgently.'

Honorius nodded and fell in beside the Iberian knight. I registered Tottola bringing up the rear, eyes scanning the darkness of the town as we made our way through black streets.

There should be words to say to Rekhmire', but for the moment, I could find none of them; I merely enjoyed his presence, and the assistance I could lend him.

King Rodrigo Sanguerra sat in his private chambers, the night wind blowing the scent of the city through the rooms, along with a firefly or two. He sat with his head down over a clutch of maps, not lifting it when his page announced us, but only waving a hand to gesture that we should be allowed in.

Not having been given permission to sit, I spent my energies in being a prop to the book-buyer, whose injury clearly – to my eyes, at least – pained him.

The King pushed a map aside and leaned back. Hooded black eyes surveyed us all, settling at last on Licinus Honorius.

Rodrigo Sanguerra beamed.

'Aldra Honorius,' he said. 'I'm pleased to have released you from confinement. If you will, I have a task that you may do for your King.'

My father's expression said *You do?*, but his voice smoothly managed, 'Yes, Your Majesty?'

'Yes.' King Rodrigo looked at Rekhmire', and at me, and back at Honorius. 'You're going to Carthage.'

11

'I'm doing *what?*' Honorius didn't give his King the chance to do so much as draw breath. '*Carthage!* Sire! You suspected me of conspiring with Carthage! Wanting to take your place as Carthage's governor! And now you *want* me to go there?'

His incredulity could have burst eardrums. I opened my mouth, a suggestion forming in my mind. King Rodrigo signalled forcefully for us to sit down at the table.

I loaned Rekhmire' my arm. 'But you're going to Carthage, in any case? For Ty-ameny?'

Rodrigo Sanguerra caught my low-voiced comment.

'If I understand it correctly . . . ' He pushed maps back as his page brought wine, and took a glass of Falernian. 'The Pharaoh-Queen desires you to go to Carthage, Master Rekhmire', to instruct the King-Caliph that the devil-ship is now your ally, and they should be duly alarmed?'

Rekhmire' inclined his head in agreement.

The King sipped at his wine. 'I had occasion to speak with the foreign Admiral, over the rendezvous to bring you back to Taraco. A very amiable man in many ways.'

I bit my tongue, managing not to tactlessly ask what my King and Zheng He might have in common – or what they might have discussed.

'In any case,' Rodrigo Sanguerra turned to Honorius, 'I desire you to travel to Carthage on the devil-ship, and do precisely the same thing.'

Honorius's eyebrows went up.

'Claim to be the Chin's allies, as well?'

'Claim them to be *our* allies,' Rodrigo corrected.

His hooded eyes watched my father, with a combination of amusement and judgement.

'I desire you to travel as my kingdom's Captain-General,' he added.

Honorius pushed his hand across his face, wiping sweat out of his eyes, and downed his wine in one swallow. 'If I wanted to stay a captain, I'd have stayed in Castile!'

'If I wanted a war, I'd appoint a Captain-General who wanted to fight!'

Rekhmire' broke out in a light tenor laugh. My father and the King stared at him. He shook his head apologetically.

'Pardon me, Your Majesty. What else would you wish Aldra Honorius to convey, officially, to the King-Caliph? Perhaps the news that First Minister Videric has recovered from his illness and resumed his position at court?'

Rodrigo watched the book-buyer for a moment.

He smiled.

'An excellent idea.'

'Oh, I see where this is going . . . ' Honorius's moroseness was not particularly convincing.

I nodded agreement. 'So do I!'

King Rodrigo Sanguerra linked his fingers on the maps of the Hesperides, and showed me his teeth. 'You tell us then, Ilario.'

Rekhmire''s look informed me I might have kept my big mouth shut with more advantage; Honorius merely beamed proudly. *The King may as well know his Freak has a mind*, I thought.

'You want Lord Honorius as Captain-General because every Frankish kingdom will be afraid to fight him,' I said. 'Even if all he ever does is stay on his estate and breed war-horses! You want him to go to Carthage as your Captain-General because that would make it very difficult for him to ally himself with Carthage. Especially if he's the one who tells King-Caliph Ammianus that Aldra Videric is back – the King-Caliph won't be pleased with whoever brings him that message!'

I did not add, *It nails Licinus Honorius's colours to your mast*, because no man at the table appeared to need that confirmation.

Rodrigo grinned like a boy.

'I should have sent you away before, Ilario. You've learned much.'

I've learned to be wary of compliments from powerful rulers . . .

'You understand, Ilario,' King Rodrigo added, 'that I need to send you away again. For a year or two, until there's no scandal attached to the resemblance between you and Licinus Honorius.'

That might mean anything from two years to 'don't come back until Pirro Videric is dead', but I saw I had no current choice, and nodded.

'I have business in Carthage, too,' I added, 'if you won't think it suspicious, sire. It's personal and to do with being a painter.'

King Rodrigo nodded absently. Most of his attention was on Honorius, which I had counted on. *At least I have my place on Zheng He's ship.*

Rekhmire' gave me a sideways look, but had to abandon the query when Rodrigo Sanguerra beckoned the page to fill his wine glass and addressed the Egyptian again.

'As I understand it, your Queen desires you and Pilot Sebekhotep to return at some time to Constantinople?'

'The Admiral will put into Gades,' Rekhmire' volunteered. 'That would be the nearest friendly port from which we could return to Alexandria.'

Rodrigo thoughtfully nodded. I wondered if he perceived that Admiral Zheng He would leave the Middle Sea.

I know the man: certainly he's thinking of *some*thing!

'Captain-General Honorius, you may return via Gades, or otherwise, depending on how long your business takes in Carthage.' King Rodrigo saluted him lightly with the wine glass. 'But I'm ahead of myself. Licinus Honorius. Will you accept this position at my court?'

My father caught my eye, and I glimpsed a grin. Almost demurely, for such a battle-hardened man, he murmured, 'Yes, sire. Of course.'

'Very well.' Rodrigo thrust a map across the table at him. 'When the celebrations attendant on Ilario's penitence and Videric's return are over, you may leave.'

Admiral Zheng He appeared to have no objection to my presence continuing on board his ship.

'We leave here in a . . . week?' He glanced at Sebekhotep, who nodded. 'A week. You may come.'

The Admiral cut off my thanks with a sharp gesture. A glance passed between him and Commander Jian.

'The sailors say you're good luck,' Jian ventured. With another look at Zheng He, he added, 'They find a eunuch clerk comforting, and familiar. It's what they take you to be. But that is not quite correct, is it?'

The Admiral signalled for wine. At Zheng He's gesture, I sat down again. One of the Admiral's clerks dodged in, with paper, brush, and ink-block on his wooden case. Commander Jian looked at me questioningly.

I suppose an explanation is a reasonable price for a voyage.

I regarded the Chin Admiral, and managed not to smile. 'Not a eunuch, my lord, no . . . '

Silverpoint is delicate, but I needed to give what I drew more body. If I had little enough left in the way of pigments now, I could still use tinted paper as a mid tone, and the earths for dark values, and white lead for highlights.

I ground burnt sienna as fine as Masaccio had ever taught me, and prepared with charcoal studies done by observation at Rodrigo's court. Although the majority of my images came from that hour in the cathedral, when I would have sworn I noticed nothing around me.

I used egg tempera, on a lime board to which I had applied gesso, and painted more quickly and with more skill than I had since Rome.

No, I thought, looking at the monochrome shapes taking on mass and depth. *Better than I ever have before.*

Father Felix came to my quarters, far too casually and often, until he was happy that I had no inclination to throw myself in the harbour, or off the castle's highest tower.

'Lies are poison,' he remarked at one point. And followed that up, later the same day, with, 'You're not welcome at the King's court.'

I had taken a walk along the battlements with him, the air being cooler on the castle walls. I took my gaze from the mountains of the north, just visible in this morning's impossibly clear aerial perspective.

There was no spite in Father Felix's tone.

'No,' I agreed. 'Not welcome.'

'A year or two, perhaps. But not yet.'

'I'll miss you, Father.'

His smile was white in his dark face, and startlingly beautiful. 'And I you. Where are you going?'

'Firstly,' I said, 'if I can, to the King's banquet at the week's end. And after that, on board a ship.'

'The second is wise. The first . . . ' Father Felix shook his head.

'I've been absolved,' I said. 'I can go anywhere I please.'

It took a week longer than Zheng He's estimate for the war-junk to be fully provisioned and the holds loaded up. That didn't displease me. It took that long for the paint to properly dry

The last of the celebratory banquets was lit by pages in Classical costumes holding torches, in the great gardens of the Sanguerra palace.

The last of the sun's red faded swiftly over the western mountains. I walked down between the fountains and into the garden, a painted board wrapped in a cloth and carried under my arm.

Rekhmire' drifted out of the crowd, Orazi and Saverico behind him. Honorius, stuck now on board Zheng He's ship, appeared to have determined to send men who would pick up gossip.

I looked up to meet the Egyptian's black gaze. He turned to limp with me through the throng of courtiers. Someone played a mandolin, under the vines. With every man speaking, it was loud enough that we might have discussed any matter without danger of eavesdroppers.

The book-buyer appeared to have nothing he wanted to say.

Similarly at a loss, I asked, 'How many days will it take us to Carthage?' and cursed myself for trivial chatter.

'A handful.' Rekhmire' narrowed his eyes at the Taracon courtiers. His expression suddenly turned sour. 'Would your journey to Carthage have somewhat to do with needing to keep your "wet-nurse" out of Taraco at the moment?'

I shook my head. 'You really don't like Ramiro, do you?'

'I like your nursemaid well enough. I'd like him better if he were somewhere else.'

'I won't tempt Videric to tidy up what he might see as loose ends. So, yes, I'm taking the "nursemaid" with us. Honorius says Onorata would miss him.'

'She's not old enough to know faces!'

'She grizzled enough when *you* were gone.'

The shock on his face was enough to make me smile.

'I didn't think the Little Wise One liked me,' he muttered.

'She's a sad judge of character.' I grinned at him. 'And now, I regret to say, I must go and be polite to the rest of my family . . .'

Neither Pirro Videric nor Rosamunda appeared to be present.

That, or I could not find them in the crowds.

My place at the banqueting table was well below Rekhmire''s, but above the court musicians, at least. There were enough men I knew casually at the table that I passed a reasonably entertaining evening, although the fireflies and other mites and pismires gave me no better an opinion than I have ever had of dining out of doors.

The formal toasts finished. King Rodrigo Sanguerra caught my eye, and beckoned me. I left my seat and walked up to the high table.

Since I was in male clothing, I bowed. 'Sire. Lady Rosamunda. Aldra Videric.'

The torchlight glinted on Videric's fair hair, and on a face superficially friendly. He smiled up at me from where he sat at the King's right hand.

He will be good for Taraconensis.

That doesn't mean I have to like him.

No man will ever bring him to judgement for sending Ramiro Carrasco de Luis to kill me. And there'll never be justice for the Carrasco and de Luis families; for the threat that has hung over them all this time, and to some degree always will.

More honestly – no man will ever hurt him for hurting me.

'I have a gift, Aldra Videric,' I said, bringing out the cloth-covered board. 'It's not valuable, and I have little enough talent, but I grew to know some of the New Art in the Italies, and I've made you this.'

King Rodrigo Sanguerra watched me, eyes dark in the candle-light, sipping from his gold goblet. Not far down the high table, Rekhmire' gazed at me with the imbecilic amiability that diplomatic envoys are supposed to assume at social events. Knowing both men as I did, I could feel how keenly I was watched.

Rosamunda, on the King's left, sipped from a silver goblet studded with sapphires, that she had evidently chosen to go with her white sarcenet and sapphire velvet gown. Her hair had no grey, her face no wrinkles; she had the kind of beauty that is unnatural because so perfect. I found myself rubbing one hand across my doublet over my belly, thinking, *She must have the lines of childbirth there at least!*

But even so it will not be this disfiguring scar.

Videric's wide, capable-looking hands took the package from me and unwrapped the cloth with deft care.

He stared.

Rosamunda leaned a little back in her chair to see.

She flashed a smile at me.

'Why, that's very well painted, Ilario! And thank you for the compliment.'

I bowed as men do. 'It was the least I could do, Aldro.'

Videric gazed down at the board, tilting it to catch the light of the torches.

I made drawings, the night after I paid for my absolution at the cathedral. Searched my memory, sketched studies, and then reached for pigments to put things down as accurately and as truthfully as I could.

Looking now, I saw things I would change if I had it to do again. Technical imperfections abound.

But I have managed to paint irrevocably one aspect of the truth.

The monochrome images of Videric and Rosamunda, my once-father and my mother, gleamed in the soft torchlight. Painted as lord and lady, they were seated side by side in high-backed wooden chairs. Both wore the court clothing of this year of Our Lord 1429; and through the arched window behind them, the forts and rivers and mountains of Taraconensis shone in miniature.

The image of Rosamunda gazed out at the world, every aspect of her beauty on show, her hands clasped modestly in her lap. Videric's painted hands clasped the carved ends of the chair-arms. He looks, not at us, but at her. She, beauty; and he, power.

'This is wonderful.' Videric tilted the board further. 'Sire, will you excuse me if I take it closer to the light? Ilario, will you explain your technique to me here?'

It was done smoothly enough that Rosamunda noticed nothing.

Rodrigo must know that Videric could simply summon a torch-bearer closer to us!

The King waved dispassionate permission. He deliberately turned back to converse with Rekhmire'.

The Egyptian's gaze followed me as I walked over to Videric, where he held the portraits up to the torch's gilding illumination.

I stood beside Pirro Videric in silence.

Videric's tone was almost absent-minded. 'I've studied the New Art. It's an interesting concept: to draw what is. Heresy, perhaps. Only God can judge what truly *is*. But this is a . . . different kind of representation to those I've seen before.'

I'd wondered what Videric found to keep him interested in his exile.

Did you think you could find me by studying this art?

In all likelihood, yes.

His gaze was riveted on the images.

I thought the distortions of perspective might confuse him. Or the individuality of the faces and lack of symbols remove all the meaning.

Evidently not.

Videric lifted his chin, looking me challengingly in the eye. 'You know I will hang this privately? Where no other man can see it?'

'Not all men will see the same thing in it, Aldra Videric.'

'Oh, I think they will.' He tilted the painted board the other way.

It had already lasted longer than I thought; I had imagined he might throw it in one of the bonfires.

He mused aloud. 'There she is . . . Discovered. Disclosed, for any man to see. Who she is. What she is.'

He looked up at me.

'Shallow. Cruel. Greedy.'

It felt sharp as a punch in the gut.

I had no expectation of him being so honest!

Pirro Videric reached a fingertip towards his own painted face, but did not touch the surface. 'You've painted me as an unhappy man.'

'You love her. Rosamunda. My mother.'

He gave me a small smile. 'Yes. I do.'

If I could paint that smile to keep it with me always, I would count myself lucky and need no other revenge.

Even the remants of the smile slipped from his face. 'I will do anything to keep her. One day, perhaps, you will understand why. It's curious – you spent five days with the Church lying yourself black in the face. But this painting is one of the most truthful things I've ever seen.'

Videric's hands gripped the wood tightly enough that I heard it creak. I watched him.

He lowered his gaze to the limewood again. This surface where I have used gesso and pigment, wood and egg-yolk, to paint this man who – over the course of twenty-five years and against all odds – has fought to keep this woman with him.

His figure faces her: you can see his passion for her.

And you can see the woman who could abandon the lover who fathered her child. Abandon her baby in the snow. All to stay with the man who is rich and powerful – *while* he is rich and powerful. She looks out at the world, and does not see him there.

I took up the cloth Videric had dropped, folded it, and handed it to him.

And took up the remaining weapon left to me.

I said, 'You know she'll never love you.'

Videric looked at me. 'I know.'

12

Dragon pennants rippled ahead of us, unrolling down the wind.

I couldn't count how many of them I saw on the seven masts – dozens, perhaps a hundred. Chin men scrambled up the yards to release the sails. Wind strengthening behind us bellied out the cloth.

Zheng He's massive ship tacked around in a final curve that let us see all the coast of Taraco submerged in morning mist. And all the distant mountain peaks, west and north.

And the host of tiny cogs and galleys that, at King Rodrigo Sanguerra's insistence, escorted the war-junk south down the coast, until the land borders of Taraconensis were left behind.

Squinting at the land, I could make out dust on the Via Augusta, that ancient road that runs from the Frankish lands down to the straits that open the Atlantic. Clouds of dust.

The King and his court riding out, as a compliment to such far-travelled men as Zheng He and his officers, to bid them farewell.

The rail almost imperceptibly shivered under my hand. Deep waters darkened under our prow.

Honorius stood beside me, his hands clasped behind his back. On my other side, Rekhmire' wore Onorata's sling, and held her cautiously, gazing with a puzzled look into her tiny and messy features – possibly trying to deduce if she indeed recognised him.

I whipped out a kerchief to wipe her nose, and spent some time pointing out to my child the chief landmarks of Taraconensis as we left them behind, and naming the different parts of the war-junk in Chin.

'Ilario . . . ' Rekhmire' removed his hand from under the sling, examined it, and put it back. 'She's five months old!'

'It's never too early to start . . . '

Honorius choked off a laugh, and stepped aside to confer with Orazi. I knew more than half of the men-at-arms he had chosen to accompany the Captain-General of Taraconensis to Carthage: acquainted with them from Venice and Rome. The others were veterans of having His Majesty's royal guard garrisoned on Honorius's estate; the evenings were rife with exaggerated tales, each trying to out-do the other.

'Ilario.' Rekhmire''s eyes slitted against the brilliance. He stepped out of the way of two of Jian's sailors sprinting past. 'Do you see something? There, ahead?'

I looked into the shining mist of the horizon, and rubbed my dazzled eyes. 'Not a damn thing!'

I had not yet got over the relief of seeing Rekhmire' returned safe from Videric's estates. I would have said this to him, if not for the fact that he hardly ever spoke to me now.

He says more to Onorata . . .

I checked the ties on her tiny hood, and she yawned in my face. 'Charming child!'

Rekhmire' gave me a look of the greatest apparent innocence. 'Should I risk saying I know how she feels?'

'Not unless you want your shins kicked! Except that I suppose I can't while you have her – is that why you volunteered to carry the baby sling?'

The Egyptian made an unsuccessful attempt at appearing wounded. 'I should be wary of complaining about boredom,' he added, seeing me failing to be moved. 'That usually serves to call up sea-serpents and comets and acts of the gods . . . '

'I can do without any of those!'

I found I must step back out of another running man's way—
Jian himself.

'What . . . ?' Squinting after the Chin commander, I found myself looking south, into sun and brilliant mist – and dark protuberances that could not be the Balearic Islands. *Not unless we've sailed infinitely faster than I thought we could!*

Rekhmire' closed both his large hands protectively around Onorata.

Honorius appeared at the rail again, beside me. 'What is it?'

'I don't know. There are no reefs—'

I saw Carrasco come up from below, talking quite companionably with Berenguer and Tottola. The German man-at-arms suddenly seized Ramiro Carrasco's shoulder and pointed forward.

I turned and leaned forward over the rail, as if straining those few inches further forward would let me see what Tottola saw. Honorius's fingers clenched over the back of my belt.

The dark protuberances resolved a very little more out of the haze.

'Not islands . . . ' I whispered.

Rekhmire' choked out an obscene oath.

Honorius said, 'Ships.'

My father's eyes narrowed as he stared into the bright south. I felt the harsh luminosity bring tears running out of my own eyes.

But I see masts, stacked masts, narrow and impossibly high . . .

Zheng He's war-junk actually *leaned*. Every sail set, I saw, craning back to look overhead.

Feet thundered; I heard orders screamed at high pitch; the bows slowly tacked across.

'Two. Five. Eight. Ten.' Rekhmire' clasped my daughter against him with one hand and shaded his eyes with the other. 'Captain-General. How is my count?'

Honorius gazed south with eyes that have been too long used to looking into hostile distance. He mouthed numbers. I blinked, and looked back.

I will never paint that fire and light! I thought. The delicacy of water-drops with light shattered through them into colour, white foam at the foot of the prows—They swelled into existence on the morning sea, appearing out of the haze, unmistakable in their silhouette.

More than ten. More than twenty. More than fifty.

A signal rocket soared up and broke apart with a piercing shriek.

'What,' Honorius said carefully, his gaze on the southern waters, 'are those?'

My neck felt cramped and cold in the stiff wind. I couldn't stop staring. 'I think – that's the Admiral's lost fleet.'

The nearest one was close enough that I could see a green dragon-face painted on the flat prow.

Raising his voice over the shouting, and banging of signal rockets, Honorius protested, 'There can't be two hundred of them!'

I reached out my arms as Rekhmire' slid the sling's straps around me, and I cuddled my screaming child into my shoulder, putting hands over her ears against the noise.

'Of course there can't be two hundred! Who has two hundred ships like this? Half of them must be a mirage!'

Two Chin crewmen all but knocked me flying; I let Rekhmire' use his solid large body, and his stick, to shelter me across to the companionway.

Ramiro Carrasco climbed down in front of me, sheltering me all the way to the cabins.

A quarter of an hour later, when the noise was very nearly as loud in the cabin as it was outside, Rekhmire' limped in through the door.

'Not two hundred.'

'I knew it!' I made the final fold of cloth and picked Onorata up, her clouts changed for fresh cloth. 'I knew there couldn't be two hundred. How many are there?'

Rekhmire' sat down hard on a carved chair.

'One hundred and eighty-three.'

13

An uncomfortable four hours passed.

From the main deck, I witnessed men, obviously the captains of their war-junks, rowed to Zheng He's flagship. The sound of celebratory drums and conches made my ears numb.

The Armenian sergeant, Orazi, gave voice to every man's fear. Shooting a suspicious glance at the Admiral's cabin, he demanded, 'Where's the bastard going to take this fleet *now*?'

At the end of several hours the captains were rowed back; the towering ships set their sails, and began the long process of tacking for a wind.

Rekhmire' yanked with fingers and teeth at a strip of leather, which I saw he had tied round and over the ferrule of one of his crutches, for a better grip on the deck. He moved his mouth, as if at the taste.

'I dare not calculate the number of men Zheng He has here,' he observed. 'I will, however, see what course we're on . . . '

He stayed absent long enough for Honorius to entertain himself in speculating which kingdoms of the Middle Sea the Chin Admiral might now invade and conquer, if he so desired.

When Rekhmire' returned, he merely shrugged at us.

'By the compass, our course is set *sirocco levante*.'

Even recalling Onorata's lullaby, I looked momentarily blank.

'East south-east,' Rekhmire' said. 'And since compasses don't lie, I judge us to be on the course that will take us past the Balearic Islands and Sardinia, to Carthage. It appears the Admiral is a man of his word.'

The Chin rockets appeared much brighter under the Penitence, in Carthage's harbour. Soaring up in arcs, bursting in showers and fountains, they dimmed the aurora's curtains of light.

Down in the lower stern cabins, with only the small window-ports unshuttered for air, I found the drums and gongs and cymbals muted. But not by much. Even small round drums, wider than they are tall, shake the air when thousands of men sling them at their waists and beat them with hands and sticks.

Onorata lay on her back asleep, but only because she had screamed herself into exhaustion.

Somewhat sourly, Rekhmire' muttered, 'Zheng He won't be talking to

298

King-Caliph Ammianus for some time yet – since the man's likely stone-deaf!'

Honorius stuck his head out of the small port, gazing down the hull – so much larger than any other vessel in Carthage's port. His voice came back muffled. 'If Zheng He was a normal man, he'd be dead drunk!'

I took my father's point. More of the Admiral's junior captains had flocked aboard the war-junk. Two in particular appeared his friends: they called him 'Ma' instead of 'Zheng He', and I saw much male back-thumping and extremely rapid speech going on, before the general noise forced me to retire below.

Rekhmire' rubbed at his knee-joint. 'Apparently their religion doesn't allow drunkenness.'

He glanced away as I caught his eye.

The Egyptian is nervous.

Perhaps Ty-ameny's briefing for what he must say to the King-Caliph Ammianus?

Honorius, pulling on his furred demi-gown, spoke a little apologetically. 'I'd take you with me to the King-Caliph's audience if I could, Ilario.'

Does he read my mind?

I couldn't help but smile.

'As far as I can tell,' I said, stroking at the soft curls sweat-stuck to Onorata's ear, 'there's you, Admiral Black-Eyes, and the book-buyer here, all going up the Bursa-hill to tell the King-Caliph the same thing. "Look at those ships down in the harbour – now keep your nose clean!"'

Honorius chuckled.

'I'd like to see your performance,' I said. 'But King Rodrigo would skin me if I don't keep my face away from your company in public.'

My father held his arms out while Saverico buttoned the pleated demi-gown and arranged his flower-and-serpent-stamped leather belt. Chin awkwardly up as his collar was straightened, Honorius spoke loud enough to be heard over the drums.

'If you go into Carthage, take my men. If you don't need to go, stay on board.'

The din of drums and conches did not die down. I thought it would not until Zheng He and his officers and captains had made their way up to the King-Caliph's palace. And perhaps not even then.

I caught Rekhmire' watching me.

I said, 'I intend to send Ramiro Carrasco out, to find a rooming-house.'

I saw illumination dawn on Honorius's face that was not from the Chin fireworks.

'Even if it's only the once,' I finished, 'I want Onorata to meet her father.'

★

299

Honorius and Rekhmire' accompanied the Admiral up to the Bursa-hill numerous times over the next few days.

I claimed I would wait until they had space in their political business to accompany me to Marcomir's house.

Truthfully, my guts crawled with chills.

Honorius spent thirty years wanting a child he couldn't have. He would have loved anything, I sometimes think. And if he had been shocked by the idea of having an hermaphrodite offspring, he did all his thinking about that between Taraco and Carthage, before he ever met me.

Marcomir, though . . .

Marcomir never struck me as wanting children.

Brief as our acquaintance was.

'Ready?' Rekhmire' questioned.

He wore a simple white tunic, for much the same reason that Honorius – with sighs of relief – was allowing Saverico to buckle him into a blue velvet-fronted brigandine. A book-buyer and a soldier would pass unnoticed in Carthage's streets.

Especially with the city full of Chin strangers, to be studied, and stolen from, and seduced.

I checked, for the fourth or fifth time, that nothing essential was being left in the ship's cabin. That Onorata's clothing was clean, and her sling buckled firmly over my shoulders.

To Honorius, but with an eye on Rekhmire', I said, 'We should bring Ramiro Carrasco.'

Carrasco's expression was unexpectedly optimistic. Before either man could rebuke him, he said, 'Because I'm a lawyer?'

It had not occurred to me.

But he's right: a man trained in the university might serve us well.

'Yes. But also,' I added, 'you're a slave.'

Ramiro Carrasco rubbed his hand through his hair, dishevelling it thoroughly. 'Why do you need a slave, madonna? Master?'

I surveyed Onorata's belongings again by eye. Honorius's experiences with a mercenary baggage train are nothing once one needs to take a young baby out.

'Apart from general baggage-carrying? I don't want Marcomir to think I'm asking for money. If I own a slave, I'm not poor.' I shot a wry look at Honorius. 'Even if the money's yours.'

'We're family, brat!'

It cheered me.

'And,' I said, 'Marcomir might also think this is for revenge. Ramiro, you need not tell him what you did. But if necessary, you can tell him I forgave you a crime.'

And Marcomir did nothing to me that I didn't desire.

300

Ramiro Carrasco stared at the cabin floor. 'Madonna, if you wish, I'll tell him I tried to kill you.'

Any man who didn't know him would not have seen what the honesty cost.

'You can be the judge of whether he needs to hear that.'

Carrasco looked down at his hands. The cabin was dimly lit by oil-lamps, but I thought his skin showed a flush. He stuttered, seeming acutely conscious of the presence of Rekhmire' and Honorius. 'I don't know why you would forgive me!'

'Because since we left Venice, you've been completely trustworthy.'

He looked startled. 'I—That could be a ruse!'

'There are a hundred ways a slave can get back at a master. I know. Believe me. You didn't try any of them.'

Carrasco ducked his head, almost flinching.

If a man ever did good by stealth, or tried to atone without any other man actually *noticing* . . . that would be Ramiro Carrasco de Luis.

Atonement brought the cathedral and Father Felix to mind. I thought suddenly, *I wish I had confessed myself sorry over Sulva Paziathe!*

I did worse to Sulva, and I will never find her to atone for it – when people like the Paziathe disappear, they do it effectively, because lives depend on it.

If I can't pay a debt where it belongs, I must pay it where I may.

Carrasco picked up the sack with Onorata's clothes, toys, and food. As the Alexandrine and my father put on their cloaks, he ventured, 'Onorata's going to be hungry when she wakes up. She wouldn't eat, with all the noise.'

I rested my fingers briefly against her brow, not merely to see if she was feverish, but because her warm skin is a touch like no other. 'I'll feed her when we get there; I doubt they'll mind.'

The baby opened pale blue eyes, coughed, cooed, and loudly choked out, '*Mee-roh!*'

Honorius stared at my baby.

Rekhmire' opened his mouth, as if he would say something, and firmly shut it again.

Carrasco and I stared at each other.

'Did she *say* something? No,' I corrected myself, 'it's too early, surely. Surely? *What* did she say?'

Carrasco brushed the back of his fingers against her cheek.

If she was cool, I saw, he was hot as fire, his skin flushed now from neck to hairline.

He muttered, 'She's said that once or twice before. I . . . think it's what she calls me.'

'Calls . . . '

Ramiro. 'Miro.

'The first word my baby says is *your name?*'

301

He flinched.

In an unexpectedly peace-making tone, my father observed, 'It might equally have been my name. Or the sergeant's. Or the book-buyer's. Or yours, Ilario.'

'This child has too damn many fathers!'

And not a mother among them.

I sighed, shook my head, and hefted my child in her sling.

'Let's go and find another of them . . . '

A hollow moan shuddered through the air.

Outside the immediate area of the port, Carthage's windowless houses and steep, narrow streets resounded to it as if they were the body of a drum.

Impossibly, the sound came from a shell – although larger than any shell should be. Earlier, Jian had given me the spiral conch to hold in my hands and draw.

He all but laughed himself into an apoplexy when I attempted to blow it. All I did was go red-faced and watery-eyed, failing to get the merest squeak or fart out of the thing.

The alien sound echoed out again under the black midday sky.

The street stood deserted.

Because every man and woman in Carthage who could reach the docks crowded down there, I admitted. The novelty has not yet worn off. I could see dark lines of heads silhouetted against the naphtha illuminations of the quayside. And crowds of the King-Caliph's subjects stood up on their flat roofs, and tried to count the number of huge sailed war-junks cruising in the vicinity of the city.

Zheng He quartered a number of ships further down the gulf, I learned from Rekhmire' and Jian. Partly for logistical reasons, and partly because Zheng He had smiled, in a very civil manner, and set about demonstrating Alexandria's apparent new allies to every North African city for fifty miles around.

Almost inaudibly under the conch's racket, a brass horn blared to mark the first hour of the afternoon.

That used to mark my break for a meal, here.

I shot a look at Honorius, his face made sombre in the naphtha street-lights' glare. Light glinted off Orazi and Berenguer's steel sallets where they flanked him.

The narrow streets, cut into steps more often than not, gave Rekhmire' the most trouble. He drove himself forward, cursing under his breath, and I guessed his knee-joint would be inflamed tomorrow.

'Here.' Ramiro Carrasco pointed.

He stopped by a heavy iron door, set deep into the granite wall of a four-storey house. The iron surface showed featureless except for one keyhole.

No way to knock. No windows opening onto the street. They would be on the inside walls, opening into a central courtyard.

'All looks the same to me!' Honorius grunted, squinting up at the brown and gold aurora as if the midday Penitence sky could give him directions.

No point in asking any Carthaginian, I reflected. In the current excitement, Carthaginian Visigoths weren't interested in talking to any stranger who wasn't a man of Chin.

Surveying the iron door, I remarked, 'I don't recognise it.' I added a swift gloss: 'Carthage was new to me!'

I have no desire to tell my father how I stumbled up these stepped narrow streets in Marcomir's company, in a blind haze of arousal.

Since I had stout leather sandals on, I fetched the door a hefty kick. It juddered in the frame.

I raised my voice in case we were overheard. 'We can come back if they're out now—'

I caught the faint grate of metal against stone.

The door swung in, opening into darkness. The street's naphtha-light was not bright enough to show me who stood there. Between that and the sunless day-sky of the Penitence above, I could barely make out that it was a man who stood there.

'Forget your key?' His voice cut off.

The dim figure turned into a black silhouette, as a lamp shone behind him.

Yellow light swelled and swung on the clay walls, and a silver-haired woman walked up behind the man in the doorway. She held up the lamp, her eyes squeezed into slits. I recognised the hawk-nose.

'Donata!'

Now I could see the man. Lean, muscled, dark-haired, middle height. He has left nothing of his face in Onorata.

Marcomir frowned. He might not remember me well, either, I realised. *It was once, and a year ago.*

And these Alexandrine robes might make him think me male or female, according to his assumptions.

'Marcomir?'

He stared at me, finally grunting an assent.

I took a firmer grip on Onorata, cradled in the crook of my right arm. 'Marcomir. This is your daughter. Her name is Onorata.'

Ramiro must have mentioned armed men to him. Marcomir showed no overt reaction to Honorius and his soldiers.

He has not changed so much, in a year. Dark hair curling only a little lower on his neck, and his off-duty tunic cut in a different fashion.

Marcomir met my eyes, and looked away. It was normal human embarrassment I saw on his face.

I said, 'May we come in?'

He thrust his hand through his hair, looked around at each of us, and finally back at the baby in her miniature linen shift and coif.

'Yes . . . '

Donata echoed him. 'Yes, come in.'

He led us through into the inner part of the house.

Donata's face seemed to have strain scored more deeply into her lined skin. But that might just be this present situation.

Above us, feet thundered up and down the narrow stairs. Other occupants, I speculated, listening to the echoing noise.

It's still a rooming-house.

Lamp-light guided us through to the back, into the kitchen that overlooked a central courtyard. Donata caught my gaze as she set the lamp down on the low basalt table. It was no more than a shaped stone block. I recognised the stove, the table crowded with Roman-style pots, hanging onions; even the silver water ladle . . .

In the hoarse dialect that I thought was from Leptis Magna, or one of the other Carthaginian settlements, Donata broke the silence.

'One-Eye said you got a good master out of it.' She nodded at Ramiro Carrasco. 'If you've got slaves of your own, I guess he was right.'

There are no good masters!

A window stood open, into the communal courtyard. The shutters were ajar. Scents of fish and junipers and sewage came in on the early afternoon wind. It vividly brought back to me One-Eye's cells, Rekhmire''s hired house, the tophet.

I sat down on one of the long benches built into the kitchen wall. Onorata woke and began squirming gently in my lap. 'How did you know One-Eye sold me?'

'Oh, my son spoke to him, in the tavern? Afterwards? We always wanted to know people went somewhere comfortable.'

Comfortable.

The choice was between screaming or saying nothing. I doubted I might truly explain to this mother and son what happened to their guests. I still wake in dreams, cold sweat down my spine, as Rekhmire' turns away and does not throw his purse to One-Eye.

'My lord! Sit down, sit down!' Donata flurried around Honorius, ignoring his soldiers in much the same way that she ignored my slave. She put a Samian jug full of wine on the kitchen table, along with pottery cups that seemed remarkably crude after Jian's porcelain.

I caught her eye.

She flushed, defiantly poured out wine, and drunk her cup down in one.

Marcomir ignored her, sitting down on the ledge beside me. He stared at Onorata. 'Is this the . . . How did you – how did we— She's tiny.'

Donata glanced over, hawk-swift and analytic.

'Premature.' She registered my surprise. 'Seven-month baby?'

'Yes. How do you . . . ?'

'I saw enough of them dead at that age.' She shrugged. 'Never could keep a babe in my womb long enough until Marcomir, here. And look how that turned out!'

Her humour was rough teasing, but in any case Marcomir was oblivious. He gently smoothed the curls of black hair that poked up from under Onorata's linen coif. She turned her head and appeared to stare at him.

Rekhmire' thumped down onto the bench, rubbing his knee. I was vaguely aware that Honorius put his hand under Donata's elbow, steering her to sit down. He began to speak quietly to her.

Orazi stationed Berenguer at the door, he himself leaning on the windowsill. A jerk of his head summoned Carrasco.

There is a choice between security and privacy. The Armenian sergeant will give as much of the latter as he safely can.

Marcomir put his finger next to Onorata's hand, and examined the nails. Hers were identical to his, but so very small.

'Got into trouble about selling you, Ilario,' he murmured, quietly enough that Onorata rummaged herself back into a light doze, leaning against me.

'You did?' I stroked her cheek. Fed and changed and allowed to sleep – but for not too long – would usually mean she woke now in a good temper.

'Spoke to One-Eye, like she said.'

He jerked his head, indicating Donata, who stood to pour more wine for Honorius.

'Few weeks later, my boss down at the Hall, he calls me in. He says it doesn't look good if merchants and visitors to Carthage vanish. Not a hard slap on the wrist, but . . . the customs job keeps us. So I said no, of course not, wouldn't happen again. Even if it meant things would be a bit tight.'

He does think I intend to ask him for money.

Onorata screwed up nose and eyes and yawned.

Marcomir shook his head in wonder. He grinned up at me suddenly, and sat back.

'I *said* we were doing people favours! Look at you. One-Eye said your owner was a hard son of a bitch when it came to a bargain, even if he was good-looking. But I guess you got away from him?'

I deliberately refused to look in Rekhmire''s direction. 'My master freed me.'

Marcomir thrust a hand through his hair again. 'What do you want from me?'

I registered Donata's quick frown.

Donata stayed alert to her son's reactions, even though she was deep in conversation with my father. I wondered briefly how much Onorata might take after her, in the future; this . . . grandmother.

As much as Rosamunda is, Donata is Onorata's grandmother.

I pictured the queen of the Court of Ladies and Donata in the same room – or rather, failed to picture it.

'I can't keep a child on my wages.' Marcomir opened a long-fingered hand in my direction. 'But you're dressed well enough, and so's the babe, and you're free, so I suppose that's not what you want anyway. Is she truly mine?'

'You don't remember?'

The light from the clay lamp gave everything a golden cast, transmuting his flush from something pink by sunlight into something bruise-coloured.

'I follow in the Roman tradition,' he said, standing on his dignity. 'A boy or an older man, for true companionship. And a woman for marriage one day, I suppose we must have . . . with what you are . . . ' He shrugged again. 'It's not like I intended to – to—'

'That's my father over there: spare me the detailed explanations!'

The Carthaginian customs officer looked over at the retired Captain-General of the House of Trastamara.

Marcomir turned quickly back to me, being unfamiliar with that particular poker-face that in Honorius indicates the holding back of a belly-laugh.

'If it's not money,' Marcomir persisted, 'then what is it you want? *Oh*. I understand. You want Carthaginian citizenship for her! Through her father.'

We have had this conversation before!

Perceiving Honorius about to fume and swear, I said, 'No citizenship. That's not the issue.'

Marcomir's black eyes glinted in the light from the lamps. Bent over, Onorata evidently had him fascinated. He shook his head.

'I'd never thought of being a father!' He suddenly sat up. 'You're a hermaphrodite: are you sure you didn't do it yourself?'

Berenguer's jaw dropped. Orazi muttered at him, under his breath: 'That one was worthy of you!'

It startled me that I liked Marcomir's appalling honesty.

At least he acknowledges openly what I am.

I snorted. 'I'm a hermaphrodite, not a contortionist!'

I was suddenly faced by the backs of three brigandines: Orazi's shoulders shaking, and Berenguer evidently not daring to look at his Captain-General.

Marcomir only looked bewildered. 'Why did you bring her, then? Can I – can I hold her?'

'Sit closer to me.'

His thigh was warm against mine; I could feel the tension of his muscles. I eased Onorata from my lap to his, keeping my hands curved around her hip and the back of her head until she was safely settled.

Catching his glance, I explained, 'Not all men know how to handle babies.'

I did not add what would have been true: *I learned most of what I know from a failed assassin and a squad of soldiers . . .*

Marcomir held the sleeping form of my child.

I remember his long fingers, and his cool hands.

I remember the conception of this child.

Outside this room, I had seen narrow steps. They would lead to an upstairs room: Marcomir's clothes tossed absently on the floor. Blankets of striped wool spread over a truckle bed too small for two, but possible when one sleeps intertwined, knee socketing home behind knee; buttocks tucked into crotch . . .

I miss the warmth of sleeping with someone else.

In Taraco, I had a bed to myself in the hermit's cell; that was different to sleeping in a bundle with Rodrigo Sanguerra's other slaves. Sleeping communally has its disadvantages – not least any other slaves attempting what Marcomir and I had engaged in while not properly awake. But it has its comforts too.

I flushed and looked away, seeking the window for light, but finding only the brown darkness of the Penitence.

Because when I imagine the warmth of a body next to my skin, I don't think of Marcomir now. Or Sulva. Or Leon Battista; or even Ty-ameny, beautiful as the small woman is.

After some considerable reflection, I don't think of Ramiro Carrasco, either.

Marcomir stroked Onorata's temple very lightly. I wondered how long before she would wake up, cry for the brightly-dyed wooden blocks that Tottola had carved as toys for her, demand feeding, and in general cease to look like a sculpted angel in a chapel.

I felt a little shy. 'I thought you would want to know about her.'

'I'm glad I know.'

More clumsily, but with a willingness to be gentle, Marcomir guided her sleep-limp body back into my lap.

'I can't take her. Even if she was a son, I couldn't.'

I winced.

Harsher than I otherwise would have been, I snapped, 'I don't want you to!'

Donata sprang up. She bustled over to where we sat, and peered down into Onorata's pink, creased face. 'Just as well you got free of that Egyptian who bought you – he would have drowned her for you like a kitten!'

Caught between wanting to cry with laughter, and merely wanting to cry, I only shook my head.

'Oh, he would. And men are always happy if a girl or a cripple goes to the tophet.' The shadow of some old bitterness crossed her face. She seated herself on the other side of her son, leaning in to look at Onorata. 'Is she all right?'

'As much as we can know.'

As much as the Alexandrine physicians can swear to.

Donata reached out to touch Onorata's cheek. 'I know we didn't treat you too well when you were here last. If there's anything we can do . . . '

Without looking at Honorius, I said, 'I think a father, a good father, is one of the best things a child can have. If she had his friendship, that would be all I would ask.'

I found myself looking at the top of Marcomir's head as he gazed down at Onorata's black lashes, and the fingers of her clenched fist. Hesitantly, he put his hand over her hand, hiding half her arm in the shadow of his fingers.

It came to me that a man who works for the city's customs is probably used to looking keenly at things. Marcomir's examination of her might show him resemblances that I couldn't see.

Honorius's deep voice said, 'There'll be a place you can send word to. You can see her if you want to.'

It was Donata who said, 'Thank you,' in a creakingly graceless voice that was moving in its honesty.

Marcomir's finger absently brushed Onorata's forehead, and she opened blue eyes.

He stopped.

I saw they were looking at each other.

He moved his finger, watched her gaze follow it, and smiled at her.

'If the worst happens,' I said abruptly. 'If I and all my family die and she's left alone, I want her to have a father.'

Marcomir's head came up. I saw in his eyes that expectation of poverty, disease, accident, and war that slaves and poor men have. Wealth protects. But even then, not wholly.

His smile slipped slowly away. 'I couldn't pay for her keep.'

'Could you let her die of hunger?'

'I – no; I could not.'

A knock sounded on the room door. Donata glared, and went to the door, opening it a crack, and beginning a long and rambling quarrel with a man clearly a tenant.

Marcomir spoke under their rapid argument. 'It wouldn't be any use sending her to me. Mother's old. In a few years I'll be keeping both of us. There isn't money or room for a child as well.'

'I don't doubt you.'

'Wait . . . ' The Carthaginian glanced around, momentarily frowning. He got up and went to a small tin chest, pushed back on the highest niche by the shelves.

He lifted something out of it and came back to me.

I thought for a moment it was a pair of wax tablets, the two wooden shutters clapped together. But it was small, no larger than the palm of my hand, and the wooden shutters opened out from the centre. I had both hands busy with Onorata. Marcomir folded the shutters back.

'Look.' He cupped it in his hands. 'This isn't much, but, I don't know, maybe you could sell it, buy her something nice with the money?'

The tiny portrait of a girl's head had been cut from a much larger work, clearly, and glued onto the wooden backing. Or it might have been an androgynous young man: the halo backing the head and the rich trappings on the clothes could indicate a saint or angel.

'Thought it was real gold, when I saw it – gold leaf?' Marcomir's forefinger traced the line of the halo, and the gold embroidery on the front of the robe. 'But someone's just painted it to look like gold.'

He sounded more than a little disgusted.

Donata slammed the door on the argument from outside, with a curt dismissal. She stomped back across the room, shot a glance at what was in Marcomir's hands, and folded her lips together severely.

'I'll take it!' I said hastily. 'I'll tell her it was her father's gift.'

Marcomir nodded, with a smile.

Onorata made a small querulous sound, swiping her open hand at him. I had no time to point out that she missed holding onto his finger. The signs of storm began to show: she screwed up her eyes, and began to square her mouth and grizzle.

'I should take her back to the ship.' I jiggled her on my knee, easier to do now that she could hold her head up, but she wasn't mollified. The grizzle turned into a full-throated bawl, and began to work up to a scream.

At these moments, I look around for someone to hand her back to. Honorius only smiled at me.

I freed one hand to take the tiny shuttered portrait, slipped it inside my robe, and mouthed emphatically to Marcomir over Onorata's open-mouthed yelling. 'Remember, she's your daughter! You can always see her, when it's possible—'

'I'm sorry we sold you!' he blurted out. 'Can you forgive me, like you have the assassin?'

Onorata chose that moment to hiccup and draw breath, producing as absolute a silence as could be wished.

Marcomir's face turned as hot as mine felt.

'Things could have turned out worse,' I muttered – caught Honorius's eye, and grinned. 'Much worse!'

Marcomir smiled openly.

His black pupils dilated in the lamp-light. I felt myself shiver, skin prickling. Not difficult at all to remember, now, how arousal sparked between us.

Donata, muttering, stopped in front of Honorius, and threw her hands up with a sharp exclamation.

'We'll send you something!' she announced.

Honorius bemusedly looked down at the poorly-dressed elderly woman. '"Send" . . . '

'Every month or so. We can scrape a few ducats together. I know—' She cut him off. 'That you don't need it. I know that.'

Orazi and Ramiro Carrasco exchanged an inaudible word. Honorius nodded.

I ignored the yammering in my mind that said, *They're too poor, she's too old, it's hardly fair – and it certainly won't be honest—*

There are times to keep silent.

Donata sniffed, looking pointedly at Honorius. 'The brat doesn't have just one grandparent.'

Marcomir's daughter began to scream in the way that I knew from experience she would be happy to keep up for hours.

Donata reached down, picked her off my lap with astonishing dexterity, and put Onorata face-down over her skinny hip.

The crying cut off. Onorata hiccuped in surprise.

Donata shifted her weight, just enough to keep a rhythm.

My child began to giggle.

After a few moments, the old woman brought Onorata upright again, her strong skinny hand at the back of the baby's head. Donata sat Onorata straddling the same hip. She pursed her lips.

'You need a nurse!'

I was too busy staring at my Judas of a child, along with the others in the room. 'What?'

Donata seemed entirely unconcerned to be asking awkward questions. 'How in Tanit's name will *you* raise her?'

The room fell silent.

I had not planned to open this subject with Honorius yet.

The Captain-General's gaze pinned me.

'My problem . . . ' I reached out for Onorata's hand. ' . . . Is that I'm in exile from Taraco. I don't want to bring her up like a gypsy.'

The hawk-faced woman nodded. 'Oh, you can take 'em anywhere when they're this size, if they're not weaklings. But when they walk and talk, that's different!'

Rekhmire' leaned forward, his tenor voice cutting through the noise.

'There is Alexandria. Constantinople. I know Queen Ty-ameny would stand as godmother to the child.'

Marcomir's eyes widened.

'And she might also,' Rekhmire' concluded, 'be able to offer you employment as a scribe.'

Donata interrupted before I could say a word, her hands clasping protectively around Onorata. 'If the child's in Constantinople, we'll never see it!'

Honorius growled, 'Neither will I!'

Marcomir's head turned as if he watched a tourney.

Nothing showed him concerned about the outcome. *He has no fatherly feeling for her,* I realised.

Donata thrust Onorata at me, her hands cutting sharp chopping gestures in the air as she harangued Honorius.

Donata has turned into a grandmother . . .

'I will be away for short times on diplomatic missions!' Honorius's battle-loud voice drowned her out. 'But otherwise on my estate, where Ilario has a home always – and *I* can raise Onorata!'

Marcomir shook beside me. He was laughing, I realised.

'The old guy's men-at-arms can have bets about whether she'll grow up girl or boy!' he snickered.

Donata made a long arm and thwacked her son's ear; Berenguer (it surprised me to note) ambled across the room and loomed threateningly over Marcomir.

I met Honorius's gaze.

'I would have suggested this later,' I said, 'but it might be better for Onorata if you formally adopted her.'

The room went quiet. Honorius seemed to be waiting.

I said, 'All the while my name is attached to her, people will be waiting for her to grow up a monster.'

Honorius looked thoughtful.

'If I do,' he said after a moment, 'no one in our family will ever lie to her about her mother-father. She's my grandchild: she'll need in any case to know what political secrets are. But within the boundaries of my estate, she would be your child, and my grandchild.'

I could not speak.

'In any case,' Honorius's face took on an intent look, 'this all depends on what you intend to do when you leave Carthage, Ilario.'

Rekhmire' glanced at me; so did the Carthaginian mother and son; Carrasco and Berenguer and Orazi stared with varying degrees of curiosity and concern.

'Yes,' I said. 'And – I don't know.'

14

In the end there is no choice, I thought.

Even if she believes I abandon her.

Sunlight slid across the cabin floor as the war-junk tacked across the Gulf of Gades. I sat with neither charcoal nor paper, imprinting Onorata's face onto my memory.

Honorius will travel up the Via Augusta to Taraco, after he has completed the King's business in Gades, and take Onorata with him. She'll be as safe as life allows on his estates. And I will visit, secretly, even before King Rodrigo lifts what is, to all intents, my exile.

But Honorius will see her take her first step. And she will call for 'Miro before she calls for me.

The salt wind and bright sun made my reddened eyes sore.

Rekhmire' glanced up from where he was seated on one of the great hatch-covers. The shadows of sails and masts fell across his face. 'Are you well?'

The polished wood felt hot under my bare legs as I sat down beside the Egyptian.

'If it was the wrong decision, I wouldn't be able to weep for an hour and get it out of my system.'

He gave me a dubious look.

'Taking a baby on roads and ships and who-knows-where.' I shrugged, squinting up at the web of ropes against the sky. 'She's been so *lucky*. Not to die.'

In peripheral vision, I saw him nod.

I followed the lines of taut rope up to a clear sky, seeing blue shadows in the hollow of white sails, and the tapering lines of masts.

Bare feet pounded past, Zheng He's crew leaping for the rigging and swarming up. I tilted my head back, watching them jump, climb; agile and sure; taking in sails and letting others spring free . . .

The hatch-cover hit me squarely between the shoulder -blades.

I looked up at Rekhmire'.

'Perspective. Sometimes it's no man's friend.'

Rekhmire' wordlessly held out a hand, I interlocked fingers, and the world swooped around me as I came swiftly upright.

The Egyptian went back to massaging at his knee, where he had it in the sun.

The sun glittered a trail of fire and sparks off the long rolling waves. Zheng He's ship cut aloof through a swell that would have sunk a smaller ship. *We will make Gades itself before Sext.*

I took Marcomir's fragment of painted wood out of my belt-purse. 'Look at this.'

The Egyptian sat back, taking it carefully into his hands. 'That is not done by the encaustic wax technique?'

'No, but it must be close to it. It's not egg tempera.'

Chin's ink-drawing fascinated me, in the way that Alexandria's architecture did. *But they are both a dead end, in the face of this.* I pointed. Where the scrap of canvas had been glued onto the wooden background, much of the paintwork was spoiled. What was left was still enough to take my breath away, as unbelievable as the first time I saw it in Marcomir's hands.

'I think it's done by pigment and *oil* . . . '

The white face of a girl, or perhaps a male saint, the eyelids modelled subtly to make the downward gaze natural. Most of the hair and neck were gone. There was still a fraction of green cloth at the shoulder, the depths of the folds apple-coloured.

The highlights were the colour of new spring leaves.

And the graduation of colour between them . . .

I didn't dare touch a finger to it, ruined as it was. 'It's blended. See how seamlessly that's done? Those shadows aren't muddy; they're not coloured pigments mixed with black! It's . . . transparent colour. Done on a prepared white canvas, and with so *many* glazes . . . I've seen linseed oils used with pigments before, but not to give effects like this!'

Rekhmire' tilted the wooden shutters. 'It resembles gold more than gold leaf does!'

'One of the things Leon wrote – gold leaf will shine back dark and flat. A skilled paint should be able to *mimic* all the effects of light. Better painted gold than gold leaf painted on.'

The Egyptian slowly nodded. 'Where did Master Marcomir acquire it?'

It had been an awkward conversation, as it always is when one accuses a man of theft.

'As far as I can make out, they had a court painter staying over from Duke Philip's lands in Burgundy – the Duke sent him out to paint possible brides, but he sailed to Carthage to see the light under the Penitence. As for what part of the Burgundian lands . . . ' I shrugged.

'Ty-ameny would be happy to get reports from Bruges,' Rekhmire' observed, as if the matter were of no great interest to him.

He added, 'Burgundy is becoming one of the richest kingdoms of the Franks, and therefore likely to have a greater influence as times goes on.'

I found myself in a mood for taking no prisoners. 'Rekhmire' – can you still spy with your knee permanently injured?'

He did not look at me, but gazed down at the backs of his hands, spreading the fingers as wide as tendons will allow. 'You know the strangest thing? It makes me feel less than a man. Which, from a eunuch . . .'

His snort of amusement sounded bitter.

I persisted. 'But you can still work for Ty-ameny?'

He looked puzzled. 'Oh yes.'

I turned the wooden fragment about in my hands. 'The idea of staying seven years in one place, even in a workshop . . . Do you know, I think I begin to understand why you like travelling around? But could I paint something like this without masters teaching me their secrets? Which they won't, if I'm *not* an apprentice.'

Rekhmire' took my wrist and turned the painted surface to the light. 'There might be treatises like Leon Battista's. You learned from that.'

'That's true. But . . .'

Feet scurried on the deck. I glanced up to see Ramiro Carrasco duck past in something between fear and respect on his way to the cabins.

He barely looked at me. All his wariness was for Rekhmire'.

I don't believe the book-buyer would take up beating him!

In a tone of controlled sarcasm, Rekhmire' remarked, 'Suppose you travel as one of the Queen's book-buyers, while Captain Honorius brings up Onorata – you won't be able to take your pet slave with you if he's back in Taraco changing nappies.'

The Egyptian added something under his breath that a creak of masts and sails prevented me hearing clearly.

I thought it was, *Or do you think* he'll *give you brats as well?*

I covered the image carefully, closing the wooden flap down, and put it back into my purse.

'Rekhmire'—'

Tread carefully, I reminded myself.

No man is at his best in pain, and Carthage's Bursa-hill had not been kind to the Egyptian's body.

'If I do take Carrasco, it will be to keep him safe from Videric. But I do think it would be better if he could live on Honorius's estate – assuming he wants to. Onorata could still see him, then.'

Rekhmire' snorted. 'Don't know why you don't *marry* the damn prick!'

My temper went wherever tempers go.

'Because, like *so many people*, it never appears to have occurred to him to *ask me!*'

Some of Jian's crewmen jumped back, making a wide berth around the hatch-cover. Rekhmire' sat upright, fingers motionless on his knee, staring at me with a wide-eyed shock.

He dropped his gaze and muttered sullenly, 'It was the first thing I asked you – if you wanted a slave-contract to include bed.'

I would have said something, *anything!*, had I control of my wits or my mouth.

Evidently I had neither.

I stared at him.

Rekhmire' returned to gazing at the backs of his hands. 'You weren't interested. As you told me.'

'Not then. I thought it would be two freaks together because they had no other choice—'

He interrupted, his voice a squeak. '"Not then"?'

'Ah—'

My turn to look away. I stared over the rail at the approaching coast of Gades.

'Then again, I've been married twice this year . . . '

'"*Not then*"?' Rekhmire' all but bellowed. 'What do you mean, "not then"? When did it change? Did it change? Why didn't you tell me!'

He glared at me, surprisingly ruffled and breathless for such a large man.

I said, 'If I can put up with you when you're sick in bed in Venice, I've probably seen all your worse qualities . . . '

Rekhmire' looked thoroughly overthrown. 'That discouraged you.'

'I wasn't even *thinking*, at that time—!' I shook my head. 'I'm just saying. You with a bad temper because you're in pain. Nothing of it's a surprise.'

Rekhmire' lurched up, manhandling himself off the hatch-cover and striding to the port rail. He stared out at white spray. I watched the line of his back.

Without turning round, Rekhmire' said, 'The difference is that now I have to *prove* to Ty-ameny that I can do my job.'

I was appalled. 'She'd *dismiss* you over this?'

He laughed, turning to face me, showing me a broad smile. 'Sacred Eight, no! But if she thinks I'm having problems, she'll have me back in Alexandria at a bureaucrat's desk, before you can say "Royal Library"! She wants me *safe*. She'd make everything as comfortable for me as she could. But I . . . '

'Want to be here, doing this,' I completed.

I sat up, cross-legged; shifted again; and got up to walk to the rail beside him. For all the distraction, I couldn't bite back the remaining words in my mind.

'Yes, I'd noticed how close you and Ty-ameny are! She does *know* what you're like after a month in one place?'

His eyes slitted. A little defensively, he said, 'She's like a sister. And furthermore, I would be *perfectly capable* of working at home in the city!'

'Hope she doesn't mind her crockery thrown at people's heads . . . '

The Egyptian narrowed his eyes still further at me. 'Pot. Kettle. Black!'

I would not have laughed if I could have prevented it. Unfortunately, that and his expression reduced me to breathlessness.

'In any case,' he said, a while after my recovery, 'when I say I can offer you Ty-ameny's patronage as a cousin – you may not be aware, precisely, of what it would involve for you.'

He put a stress on the last word that stopped me telling him, *Yes, I understood the book-buyers' trade thank you very much.*

'I mean it would be offered in respect of your particular talents. As with the Admiral's ship at Alexandria harbour.'

Slowly, I said, 'You mean Queen Ty-ameny is offering me the chance to . . . go somewhere and *draw* things?'

'And paint them.' Rekhmire' raised a brow. 'Many places.'

'And be paid for this.'

'It is a very modest amount of money—'

'*Sign me up!*' I bounced on the deck, feeling all of fourteen. 'That's just what I want to do!'

The Egyptian smiled. Not as brightly as I had expected. I caught a glimpse of something bitter-sweet in his expression.

I paused.

'I suppose,' I said, 'before I go wandering around on my own, I'd need some training?'

Rekhmire' looked at me.

'A mentor?' I said. 'Someone more experienced? Someone who, for example, has been doing this for a long—'

'YES! I'll do it!'

I grinned up at the panting book-buyer.

'Did I say I was going to ask you? Maybe I should ask Ty-ameny to decide who she'd recommend—'

He had been reduced to speechlessness, I saw.

'—since she threatened to pull my intestines out of my body,' I added, 'if I ever did anything to hurt you.'

Rekhmire' stared at me.

'What?'

'When we were in the Library one time—'

'The – *interfering little brat!*'

He was too far away, I decided. I took the few steps that crossed the distance between us, on uncertain legs, and stood at the rail by his side.

'Actually . . . ' I surveyed the Gulf of Gades. 'It was Ty-ameny who made me realise that I'd miss you, if you went off somewhere else.'

'You would?'

Frightened as I was, I heard myself sound very definite. 'Yes, I would.'

'Oh.' He sat back. 'Good.'

'Rekhmire'—'

'Good. I suppose that in that case I can stop worrying that you're going to notice I've been *following you around for a year now!*'

All the crew for fifteen feet around briefly turned to stare at the mad barbarian. Rekhmire' gasped in a breath.

I watched his broad chest move.

'Really?' I said. 'All year?'

'I don't know *what* gave Ty-ameny the idea that you're in any way intelligent!'

'No, nor do I.'

I gave way to a temptation of long standing, and leaned my shoulder up against his. His skin felt heated, soft. *Prickling, like silk rubbed over amber.*

He didn't move away.

I shifted, pushing my way into the gap between his arm and his ribs. Rekhmire' beamed and put his arm around me.

'Ilario!'

The voice spoke behind me without giving me any warning so I might move. I turned my head, looked down the deck, and found myself staring directly at Honorius.

Rekhmire' did not so much as twitch beside me – because, I realised from peripheral vision, he appeared to be in a blind panic.

Honorius let out an explosive sigh.

'Oh, thank *God*! It's about damn time!'

I managed to turn my head back and look up at Rekhmire'.

He gazed down at me, lips moving a little, as if he would have formed words if he could.

The Captain-General of Taraconensis snorted and turned his back, stalking away down the deck of the war-junk.

His mutter was perfectly audible.

' . . . Been expecting this since *Rome* . . . !'

We looked at each other.

Rekhmire' gave me his gravest expression. 'I suppose we'd better not disappoint him.'

I was too weak for laughter. I leaned against the warmth of his bare chest. He was not so much taller than I, and he smelled wonderful. 'Only if it's what you want. You know what I am.'

'You know what *I* am. Some things are less – urgent for me than for other men.' He moved his other arm, to enclose me, and I felt the weight as he leaned his smooth cheek against my temple. 'I can't give you children, either. But I can cherish the one you have.'

As long as we have her, I thought, melancholy in the midst of this happiness. What is valuable is always fragile.

The sea rocked us as we sat together on the hatch-cover, playing the game that lovers play of 'when did you first notice?', 'when did you first feel . . . ?'.

It was a long time before I moved, and then it was to get up and go to the ship's rail. I shaded my eyes as the war-junk opened the harbour of Gades.

'Something isn't right.'

Rekhmire' shoved himself to his feet and thumped across the deck to stand beside me.

The myriad other war-junks of Zheng He's fleet kept station astern across the Gulf of Gades – impossibly large under the brilliant sun; impossibly and spikily graceful.

At least a dozen European and North African ships out of Carthage were, out of apparent sheer curiosity, attempting to keep up with us. Frankish cogs, Venetian galleys . . . The wooden rail jammed hard under my ribs as I leaned out, looking toward our stern.

A cog flying the colours of Genoa tacked across the war-junk's wake, bowsprit jutting high out of the blue-grey waves – just as high as the top of our rudder. Their deck was a cliff's depth below me.

Sounding unusually confused, Rekhmire' murmured, 'What ought I to see?'

I pointed at the departing Genoese ship – and the other vessels sailing towards us from the entrance to the harbour.

'*That* isn't right,' I protested. 'It doesn't matter if they've heard rumours. This is Zheng He's giant devil-ship in the flesh – *and* his fleet! Why isn't Gades in a panic?'

15

'There's the answer.' I balanced uneasily, a knee on the boat's prow, and studied the quay of Gades ahead.

Under the banners, a group of men stood, evidently waiting to greet the Captain-General of Taraconensis. The tall man in Carthaginian robes would be the Governor. Beside him . . .

'That's Safrac de Aguilar.' I sat back beside Honorius, avoiding falling by a fraction. 'The man beside *him* is Videric.'

A muscle clenched at the hinge of Honorius's jaw.

'Is it so?'

He spent a moment adjusting his heavy sea-cloak over his demi-gown. With his temper bridled, he added, 'The King told me to return by way of Gades, and as a courtesy inform the Governor that the Admiral's ships have no ill intentions towards him – being our allies.'

The same method of wiping one's enemy's face in it as Rodrigo Sanguerra had ordered for Carthage, evidently.

'Therefore,' Honorius gritted, 'I should very much like to know what Pirro Videric is doing here!'

Wind caught the banners, rolling them out on the wind. I recognised the Sanguerra colours, as well as Videric's personal banner.

'The King trusts de Aguilar, for what *that's* worth.'

Honorius set his jaw and didn't speak.

I clung to the boat's side, wishing I might talk to Rekhmire' – who travelled with the other men in the second boat. Neither Honorius nor Orazi were willing to speculate. I concentrated, impatiently, on reaching the quay, and on not being sick.

Videric stepped forward out of the crowd as soon as Honorius finished his formal greetings to the Governor of Gades.

'King Rodrigo was uncertain when you'd complete your business in Carthage. Whether it would be done before the Pharaoh-Queen's subjects would be put ashore at Gades.' Videric smiled, his fair hair and open expression making him appear very guileless. 'The King sent me here in case you should miss the day.'

Of all the odd things I have seen in the last twelve months, my stepfather Videric walking amiably beside my natural father Honorius, towards the Governor of Gades' palace, must be the most remarkable of all.

'I see where you get your glass-throwing habits from,' the book-buyer remarked.

I winced at a crash from the opulent chambers the Governor had provided for Captain-General Honorius.

Tottola, idly leaning up against the archway, grinned and pulled the curtain aside for me to pass through.

Honorius halted, halfway through pulling off the fur-trimmed demi-gown, and fixed me with a glare. '*Your* stepfather!'

He threw his boot at my head.

I caught it neatly, since there had been no real force behind it, and returned it to him with a grin. 'I've had masters who threw so much harder and better than that . . . '

It evidently defused the remains of his bad temper. He ruffled my hair, reducing it to a haystack.

'I wish you'd gone through none of that.' He perked up. 'But are you sure you wouldn't like to see your stepfather challenged to a duel? I'm sure Rodrigo-damned-Sanguerra doesn't need his First Minister *that* badly . . . '

'Court politics.' I shrugged. 'Videric gets the glory of telling the Lord-Amir here in charge of Gades that no, he needn't worry, the devil-ships are just passing allies of Taraconensis . . . '

'I had Carthage. I suppose I can forgive him stealing Gades out from under me!'

Honorius's buoyant mood returned too readily for a man who would play court politics seriously. *But then,* I thought, *he'd likely rather be back on his estate, waiting for his mares to foal.*

'And another damn banquet tonight,' Honorius added, yanking at the strings of his shirt. 'I imagine I'll stay several days. Ilario, have you decided where you'll go from here?'

My face may have been a little hot as I glanced at the Egyptian. 'We haven't had time to discuss it, really . . . '

My father has very eloquent eyebrows, when he chooses.

I sighed. 'I suppose I ought to stay out of the way of the banquet, since you're there. How I suffer . . . '

'How *I* suffer,' Honorius snorted.

Voices at the arched doorway interrupted him. I turned, as he did, to find the German man-at-arms escorting a well-dressed Iberian into the Captain-General's room.

The Lord Pirro Videric gave me a tight smile.

'Lord Honorius. Ilario – I saw you at the dock. This may be unwise. I know you are only exiled from Taraconensis. But would it not be wiser if you left Iberia altogether?'

I was close enough to tread heavily on Honorius's foot.

'The First Minister is only looking out for King Rodrigo's interests.' I held Videric's pale gaze. 'And of course, he's correct. Aldra Videric, Gades *is* a seaport. I'll be gone by tomorrow.'

Rekhmire' made his excuses to leave the banquet early, and joined me in my room while I ate what I had managed to talk the kitchen staff out of.

'You eat better than *I* do.' He picked an olive off my plate. 'And your temper has certainly improved.'

I ignored that provoking compliment. 'I would have preferred to leave Gades by land ... The Via Augusta starts here. Or ends here. Depending on your perspective.'

I doubted I could rely on Zheng He's fleet to transport me, now Sebekhotep and Rekhmire' had come ashore. An attempt to bribe Commander Jian with two charcoal studies, one of him in profile and one full-face, had only resulted in him cheerfully remarking, 'Keeps the demons away!' as he brandished the papers.

Or at least, I think he said that. My acquaintance with the languages of Chin is still spotty.

Rekhmire' took a seat at the window, gazing out over the city of Gades. 'The Via Augusta? You'd need no ship at all. You could walk all the way back across Iberia to Taraco, to Marseilles, to Genoa, to Italy ... '

I saved him a last olive on my dish. 'What, am I not even allowed a mule to ride?'

'You have enough donkeys with you as it is.'

I couldn't help a smile. 'Oh, cruel!'

'Perhaps I'm wrong.' The Egyptian mimicked thought. 'Lord Honorius's men are quick-witted, for soldiers. Perhaps it's only the lawyer—'

The small weight of the olive made it very satisfactory to lob.

The Egyptian picked it up off the tiles, showing no inclination to eat it.

'But truly,' he said, as if it had been what we discussed. 'You'll let Pirro Videric force your hand, and leave tomorrow?'

When I would have succumbed to temper, now I might cross the room and press my fingers and palms against the large muscles of the Egyptian's neck. I found the touch of silk-warm skin both calmed and aroused.

'If I have to leave Honorius and Onorata, a quick farewell is at least quick, and not long drawn out and painful.'

'Then you need only decide where we are to go.'

'I will. Not now.' I looked up at the window, and the velvet moon. 'I think, since it seems I'll see so little of Gades, I should take this opportunity.'

Going out by way of the elegant marble entrance, we met up with Honorius's men, mingling with the governor's off-duty guards, and with Aldra Safrac de Aguilar.

The dark man's long face metamorphosed to a smile. And since he claimed he knew Gades well, having been here before, I thought it wise enough to let him show us its society.

I heard none of Aldra Videric's secrets, nor anything useful to Honorius, but I did discover the potency of the local wine.

The times when I have trusted any court far enough to get drunk are remarkably few. My previous experience of hangovers in Taraco was due to wine being forced on the King's Freak for the amusement of others.

Still, the buttery-hatch to the Governor's kitchens stood open, and the feeling of sitting in company in the Great Hall and dulling my morning headache with small beer and oatmeal porridge was not unpleasant. I found myself with elbows on the stained yellow linen of the trestle tables, talking casually with those of Honorius's men I knew less well.

Gades seems provincial, after Rome, Venice, Alexandria . . .

That evidence of my own snobbery made me chuckle out loud, and bury myself in my mug of nettle beer while conversations went on around me.

A hand fell on my shoulder. 'Ilario!'

Momentarily lost in studying the walls – considering how much more modern tapestries or even frescoes would look than the red-and-ochre chevrons painted on the stonework – I almost overturned the trestle table and bench as I pushed myself up and away.

'Ilario, no!' A man held up his hands. He wore a green demi-gown, and had only a dagger at his belt. 'No harm intended!'

'Safrac.' My grip on the leather and metal of my dagger's hilt pressed hard enough to turn skin white. It took me three tries to get the point back into the mouth of the scabbard, and sheathe the blade.

Safrac de Aguilar's dark eyes smiled, the rest of his face returning to customary melancholy. 'I was warned how unwise it is to disturb you. Forgive me: you don't always look like a knight. But you're late! Your mother's already left for the meeting.'

'My mother?'

I would be shocked, were I not bewildered.

Rosamunda is here with Videric?

Picking up the leather mug of nettle beer and draining it covered how a nervous shiver went through me, just at the mention of that woman. I tried not to sound as bewildered as I felt. 'What "meeting"? I don't know about any meeting!'

Safrac de Aguilar frowned. 'A few moments ago? I met Aldra Videric, and heard him bidding Aldro Rosamunda hurry, because "Ilario is there already".'

As a slave, I would continue to listen. Or ask apparently innocent leading questions, until I knew what was happening. But I have my freedom.

322

I took hold of Safrac de Aguilar's arm through the fine green velvet. Rodrigo thinks this man honest and incorruptible. *I hope he's correct.*

I lowered my voice below the level of general conversation in the hall. 'Were you *supposed* to overhear this, Safrac? Or was it an accident?'

He gave me the thoughtful look of a man who's been at court many years.

'I think, accidental. To be deliberate . . . It would have needed too much luck. They could hardly know I'd hear that and then encounter you now. You think he intends – what?'

'If I could tell you that, I would.' I found myself frowning. 'Videric never does anything without it being aimed at somebody.'

I see only two options here. And if it isn't me—

'*I* certainly don't know of any meeting,' I said. 'Did Aldro Rosamunda seem to know? Or was it a surprise to her?'

Safrac de Aguilar's brows dipped in concentration, a maze of lines creasing his forehead.

'She knew,' he said finally, giving me a shrewd look. 'Or I believe she did. But . . . You could, perhaps, have been told of this last night, and . . . forgotten during the celebrations?'

Drunk as a fiddler's bitch, they call it. My head did feel as if I'd been drinking the beer they put down in pans for his mastiff, all the night the fiddler plays. Truthfully, it was no large amount unless to an unseasoned drinker. And my head was clear enough last night.

I forget nothing concerning my mother.

I bit at my lip. The small pain helped me focus. 'There's no "meeting". If Rosamunda thinks there is . . . But she's not a fool, she knows there may be agents of Carthage here! Why would she go – Safrac, did either of them say where I was to meet her?'

My thoughts were a tumble of fears: Videric sending Ramiro Carrasco on a murderer's errand to Venice; the Carthaginian agent whose name I never knew dying on Torcello Island; Hanno Anagastes' armed guards surrounding Aldro Rosamunda, putting her under arrest.

Frustrated, I protested, 'There are too many rooms in this palace to search!'

'There's a hall with a fountain,' Safrac de Aguilar emerged from his reverie and interrupted. '*That* was where Aldra Videric said you were waiting for the lady Rosamunda, now.'

The breath went out of my chest, leaving ice and heat. A solid knot of cramped muscle and lung.

The fall of silver water; the ringing fall of steel.

Clear in my mind as that day twelve months ago.

If she expected to meet me – yes, she would go to such a place.

'You know the Egyptian, Rekhmire'?' I barely waited for de Aguilar's assent. 'Go and tell him what you heard. If not him, then Lord Honorius. Tell them – to be cautious.'

Safrac de Aguilar looked alarmed. 'Where will you be, Ilario?'

'Finding this hall with a fountain!'

For all his choked protests, he gave me brisk directions; and strode away from me towards the palace's guest-chambers.

I walked, because running attracts attention. If I ran out of the hall, there are those who would follow. Noblemen's sons, out of curiosity. Guardsmen, wondering what the fuss is about. The women servants who clean, who see everything and everybody.

But a preoccupied fast walk attracts little attention.

I should be thinking – planning—

I don't even know what I expect him to do!

Videric has lied to her.

I don't know *why*.

Breath hissed hot in my lungs. The gangways and stairs of Zheng He's ship had kept me fit. But I'd guessed wrong about the time: it was well past noon. Gades' heat as the sun burns around to the second half of the day is nothing to be sprinting in.

Fifteen minutes at a pounding run, once out of the public eye up corridors and down stairs, wondering if I had mistaken Aguilar's directions – and a stone colonnade opened up in welcome cool.

I slowed to a painful half-trot.

Think. *Think* what you can do—

Twelve months ago I walked another marble-floored corridor, with Aldra Videric; his blue and white linen robe swirling at his heels as he strode.

The sound of a fountain reached me from an open hall ahead.

The sound of a slap, and the flat clatter of a second-rate dagger skittering across the marble floor—

What will he do? Sell her to Carthage's highest bidder, because they think they can make use of her? Then have one of Carrasco's brothers assassinate her on board the ship?

Ridiculous speculations made me feel as if my head would burst.

I could understand if he attacked me. What does he want with her?

And why is it *I* still think I should protect her?

Pain more agonising than the cramp in my ribs came from the immediate realisation.

She wants me to forgive her.

But not for my sake. For hers.

Now that the cathedral penitence means no gossip will ever forget I came out of her womb, she wants to appear magnanimously accepting of her monstrous child.

But she would meet me secretly because, no matter what she pretends in public, she is ashamed of me.

I slowed.

Heat bounced down the white walls from the clerestory windows, high above; a breeze barely penetrated. That was not the only reason I was sweating.

How rash will Rekhmire' say I'm being?

I thought it so clever to show Videric in pigment: 'You love her but she never loved you; never will.' So clever—!

A coldness went through my body and made my hands heavy. My fingers prickled. I thought desperately: No, Videric isn't a stupid man, he will have realised the truth before now. Years ago!

And you were the one who thought it so clever to push his face into it. What might *that* provoke a man to do?

Sound caught my attention.

Movement?

This doorway was a round Roman arch, the keystones white, outlined with gold paint. A beaded curtain hung down across the opening. Kicking off my scandals, I padded over the cool tiles, silencing my breathing.

The beads made an impenetrable barrier until I stood with my nose all but touching them. Vision altered: I saw clearly through their blur into the hall.

The fountains arced silver into the afternoon light, water spilling out of a jug held by a marble nude.

Terracotta pots held plants. The scent of the place was subtle: moist soil, green leaves . . . choked pipes.

I could see the textures of leaves, the patterns of edges; all things for which – before now – I would have reached for my drawing-book. 'Learn to see,' Masaccio said to me, one night in the taverna, his hand sketching flawlessly by candle-light. 'You see too much detail, Ilario. You draw it all. And you give it all the same importance. Look to see what parts of a thing are necessary: show only that.'

Now all I could do was stare through the blurry green and shimmering silver at Videric.

He knelt beside Rosamunda, where she lay supine on the floor.

His hands moved, busy at her mouth. Tying something.

A gag.

Light through the fretwork stone ceiling shone down on pillars and fountain-basins. And glistened off her eyes as she blinked.

Christus Imperator, she's still alive!

Three or four other men stood behind Videric where he knelt. They wore the livery of guards. There were no household badges on arm or cap. Evidently they waited for orders.

Rekhmire' will be behind me, sooner or later.

I swept the bead curtain clattering aside, and strode into the hall.

16

There's no blood.

It was the first thing I noted. No blood; no broken bones protruding through stretched-white skin. A slave learns how to see the crucial things in the first instant.

An absent part of my mind wondered, *Is that what Masaccio meant about an artist's vision?*

Her wrists and ankles were already bound; she squirmed and whimpered in an attempt to get free of Videric's hands. Two red bruises marked the sides of her jaw, where a thumb and forefinger might have gripped her. Nothing more. Her silk robes were rucked up about her knees, but clearly from struggling against being subdued, rather than rape. Sweat beaded across her unlined forehead. She strained against her arms, tied before her; Videric looked up from binding her kerchief into her mouth with silk rope.

Looked directly at me.

One of the other men started forward.

'Wait.' Videric spoke with a quiet intensity that froze the man where he stood.

I stared squarely down at Videric. 'I didn't know how vindictive you could be. But you can let her go now, since you've got me here.'

His face altered. If his control had not been perfect, it would have been a smile. He murmured, 'Nor did *I* know that you thought the world centred upon you.'

'Don't be naive.' I thought it the surest way to shake him. '*Everybody* thinks that.'

Videric turned his head as if I didn't exist. His attention focused on Rosamunda, on the floor. The small choked sound he made would not have carried as far as the guards wearing his livery.

The men were all much similar: Iberian, rather than Visigoth Carthaginian; middle-aged soldiers in doublet and hose, with riding-boots fastened up to their belts, and no surcoat over their mail hauberks. No crest, no coat of arms, no insignia. Nothing to link them to Videric's estates.

The glances between them told me they were his. I have seen similar looks between Honorius and Orazi.

'What's the matter? Do you need four men here to kill me? Can't you do your own murders?'

Videric's expression didn't change. I didn't expect it; he's too good a politician to allow that. But I caught the glance one of the men-at-arms shot at his captain. It wasn't, 'Damn, Ilario knows!' It was, 'You didn't say you were asking *that* of us.'

If he really doesn't want revenge on me, when it's freely offered—

I must have made him desire *her* death.

If he's off-balance, I may find out more. I nodded at the soldiers, speaking with a hope of keeping Videric unsettled. 'Men in a jealous rage don't usually bring four witnesses. If you're not killing my mother, what are you doing to her?'

The Aldra Videric smiled appreciatively. He glanced up and back, at his captain. 'A shame there's not room for two . . . '

The man-at-arms smiled as one does at a lord's joke.

'Whatever you're doing to her—' I kept moving, coming closer to him, and Rosamunda, every moment. '—why *aren't* you doing it to me? I don't believe the – the man who told me about this "meeting" I'm supposedly having with my mother is one of your pawns. But since I'm here . . . why not kill me instead?'

The sun falling through the lattice-patterned ceiling made Videric's fair hair and beard glint. He came lightly up onto his feet, as if he were my age, and shrugged. 'Why *not* you? Honorius. And Alexandria, to a degree. You have powerful friends that make killing you unwise. Even an accident would be suspect.'

'But not for her?' I didn't look down as I reached Rosamunda. The toes of my studded sandals touched the shoulder of her robe. I looked at him across my mother's body. 'She has no powerful friends herself that aren't also your friends. So there's nothing to stop you.'

Videric laughed.

It caught halfway through, as if it snagged on something in his throat.

'I'm not killing her.' The Aldra Videric rubbed the cuff of his robe across his red lips. For the first time in years, he seemed to see me – to see Ilario, rather than the King's slave, or his wife's secret bastard. 'And now you're here, I suppose not you either . . . Not everything is about murder, Ilario.'

He looked at me with sardonic humour, as if he couldn't understand why I didn't smile in return.

The time will come when I don't hear the word 'murder' and see Masaccio's face in front of me, throat crushed in front of my eyes. But not today.

'Is it my fault? Did what I painted make you do this?'

The hall was silent except for the strained, muffled breathing of Rosamunda. And the noises she made in her throat.

I did not need to hear words to know she intended *'Yes: your fault: free me!'*

Videric's captain was a new face since I'd left Taraco; I didn't recognise him, but he had in-country features, and he was a little younger than the other soldiers. Recently promoted, I guessed. He would be a man loyal to Videric, who had been taught to blame me for his lord's initial forced resignation as First Minister.

The captain turned his head towards Aldra Videric, plainly requesting orders. *Kill the intruder? Subdue it?*

For three heartbeats, I was dizzy with the realisation that, had I been a slave still, stepping into this room would have been immediate suicide.

I flinched, momentarily. Two of the men-at-arms exchanged glances, cheered by that. *The hermaphrodite isn't the knight it was trained to be* was plain in their thoughts.

Videric made a gesture with his hand.

The clink and spatter of fountain-water did not drown out boots on the tiles. The men-at-arms went to take up stations at the remaining archways. I might escape if I spun around and dived back the way I came. But I wouldn't bet money.

And I'm not leaving.

Holding Videric's gaze, I sank down on one knee by Rosamunda. Peripheral vision gave me the ability to pull at the knots of her silk gag.

Videric quite deliberately made no move from where he stood. He turned the palms of his hands to me, to emphasise that he held no weapons. I wondered if he knew that it seemed to make him appear defenceless in other ways.

'I wouldn't do that,' he said, 'Wait.'

'"Wait."' I sounded like every speculative, unbelieving courtier I ever met in Rodrigo's court.

'Hear me out, first. Then . . . ' He sighed and shrugged. Not quite 'your folly be on your own head', but something with more sorrow and resignation in than I was used to hearing from my *step*-father.

He'll tell you what you want to hear.

This man who lied, a year ago, about Rosamunda desiring to see me. When it was his own orders that she wait and kill me.

He looks different.

I'd paid attention to him physically, painting him in the new style. Masaccio taught me ratios: the placing of the eye according to the position of ears, jaw, nose. Given Masaccio's emphasis that first a painter needs to see – and wanting to understand him – I had studied my stepfather as lines, planes, shades, edges . . .

As a man, Videric looks older than when I left Taraco, and tired enough that he might not have slept for days.

I said abruptly, 'You painted your face for the cathedral!'

Videric rubbed at his lower lip again. 'It was necessary to look as a

328

man should. Women are not the only ones to mimic health with cosmetic aid.'

I knelt down on the tiles, lifting Rosamunda's head and resting it against my thighs, so that I could support her shoulders with my knees. She stirred, moaning; and looked frantically at me. It felt appalling, unbearable, to see the silk biting into the corners of her lips.

I stroked her soft, braided black hair. The weight of her head was heavy in my lap, and I wondered for a dazed moment if the embroidery on my Alexandrine tunic would leave its pattern embossed in her fine skin.

'Tell me what this is about.' I couldn't keep urgency out of my tone. *If Rekhmire' is following, I need to have heard this first.* 'And – let me untie her wrists. Please. She's hurting, and she can't escape, can she?'

Videric smoothed down the folds of his striped linen robe, his features composed in the look of a thoughtful statesman. I recognised it as a mask he often wore in council. Eventually, after my breath congealed and burned in my chest, he gave a casual nod.

Reaching down, I picked at the bindings where I could reach them while supporting her. She made a pained noise through the gag.

Videric seemed in no hurry.

The Ilario who left Taraco a year ago *would* have run to this meeting without a pause to tell anyone where I'd gone. The same way I left Taraco; the same way I sought out Rosamunda in Carthage.

The silk rope settled into tight, impenetrable knots under my fingertips.

Videric seated himself on the broad marble rim of the fountain beside me. His hand dipped in. He flicked sour water over his neck, cooling himself.

I craned my neck, from where I knelt by his feet.

Videric looked down at me. 'The problem . . . is Carthage.'

17

I stared. And spoke into a silence broken only by the spatter of water on marble:

'Carthage?'

Videric's captain stepped forward from the archway. I had not seen any order pass between him and Videric. The soldier bent over behind me, reaching around to unbuckle the belt from which I hung my dagger. Still holding Videric's gaze, I didn't move. Leather pulled against the fabric of my tunic; I felt the weight of the weapon go missing.

Over the noise of the captain's boots as he stepped back to the door, I repeated, '*Carthage?*'

'I realised, with your painted gift.' Videric tapped his fingers together. 'What it told me . . . is perhaps not as important as what I've told Carthage.'

'I didn't know you were in contact with Carthage—' I stopped.

His smile had the air of sadness that meant I'd missed his point.

'Informed by my *actions*. Last year, you perceive, I had a choice. A scandal comes from Carthage. The First Minister's wife has tried to kill a slave. As my wife, her crimes reflect on me. I might repudiate this woman, put her aside, call her a barren wife, and stay with the King as his First Minister. But . . . that is not what I did.'

My fingers carded the loose hair at the back of my mother's neck, where a braid had come undone. Videric didn't look down at Rosamunda where she lay stiff and recalcitrant against me, the knot of her bindings irretrievably tight.

I wished I had cut her free before I was disarmed. No matter what it might have precipitated.

Videric gazed, his restless pupils following the fall of fountain-jets.

'What did I tell Carthage, by what I *did* do? I told them . . . that this woman is a gate by which any enemy can enter Taraco and break it. Because any enemy who has control of her has control of me. They have only to threaten her.'

'You resigned, left Rodrigo Sanguerra, left us to be at Carthage's mercy if the King-Caliph could manufacture the slightest excuse for sending in the legions . . . '

Videric's blue eyes glimmered in the light reflected up from the fountain basin. The water shone all the shadows on his face into the wrong places. 'And it will be assumed that I will do it again. That whatever threatens my wife, controls *me*. Whether it's to make me abandon my post again, or to guide the King in the way that Carthage wishes him to act.'

I thought of Hanno Anagastes, the King-Caliph, the Amirs for whom Rekhmire' had had me copying scrolls. All of whom assume their sacred right to Iberia.

'But you can't – King Rodrigo could – when they see he trusts you—'

'I've returned to court.' Videric marked off each point on a raised finger. 'My wife is once again Queen of the Court of Ladies. I'm Rodrigo Sanguerra's First Minister, reinstated as if I'd never been away. All despite the rumours that my wife tried to kill my . . . offspring . . . in Carthage.'

Something flinched, in his expression.

I know he hates being thought the father of a monster.

I had not appreciated, until now, quite how humiliating he would find it to make public the other alternative – to have everyone know that his wife had a child by another man, and that it's not she who is barren in this marriage.

Videric continued, 'If she's such a burden, and I *still* keep her, refuse to put her aside and marry again—'

His voice caught in his throat.

I stroked the soft hot skin behind Rosamunda's ear, in apology for speaking as if she weren't present. 'They must know the King will protect her as well as you.'

'Carthage now knows that she *needs* protecting. That is the fatal weakness I showed.'

He narrowed his eyes as if he looked into sunlit distance, rather than the green shadows of the hall.

'The Turks, too . . . Ilario, if any other lord had had his wife threatened, he'd keep her securely behind his own castle walls – and if she died by ambush or assassins, shrug and marry again.'

I wanted to protest it and didn't. If married couples wish it, all of a woman's life can take place in the Court of Ladies, and all of a man's life in the outside world, and their only meeting need be for the begetting of heirs. Few enough men get to see into the women's court, and see how their women's friendships, daughters, their politicking for marriages on behalf of their family name, can become their fulfilling life. And a man who rides, hunts, goes to war, and competes for rank and places of power at court with other noblemen; he doesn't *need* to know his wife, except carnally. Not if he doesn't have some leaning towards companionship that priests and lords never taught him. Men alone together talk as if women are children; women alone together speak as if men are not-very-intelligent animals. For nine years I saw it every day, from both sides.

Videric sighed, finally glancing down at where she lay with her cheek against my thigh. 'If I gave up everything for her once . . . Men will assume that I can be manipulated by any threat to her. And will assume it correctly. That makes me useless to the state. And I can't risk Taraconensis coming as close to disaster as we have this last year.'

It made a perfect and clear shape in my mind.

'I painted the truth. My mother doesn't love you.' I ignored her stir of protest. 'So why, now that you know that—'

'You painted the truth,' he repeated, not looking down at Rosamunda. 'It makes no difference. It never has.'

Because we lie to ourselves, and say it will be different one day.

'It ought to make a difference.'

Lightly, as if he welcomed a distraction from pain, Videric asked, 'Which one of them is it?'

'"Which"?'

'My spy? Or Queen Ty-ameny's spy?' His twist of the lips was very wry, under his moustaches. 'You desire one of them. Tell me which, so that I can make suitable use of the fact.'

For the first time in many years, I felt inclined to smile grimly at my stepfather.

'Perhaps not,' I suggested. 'But are you telling me, even now, with all she's done – Rosamunda—'

'*I* am not the one attempting to comfort the woman who twice tried to kill me.' Videric paused, a frown indenting his forehead. 'Three times.'

The dagger in the hall so like this one. The attempt in Carthage. And the baby left out on stone steps, exposed to the snow of a winter's night. Three times.

Now it was I who could not look down; could only memorise the fine texture of her braids with my fingertips. I felt her warmth, her heartbeat. The skin of her neck had – if only to the touch – the slight slackness of an older woman.

'Lord Barbas, Caliph Ammianus, Lord Hanno.' Videric stirred the moving fountain-water with a fingertip. 'None of them are stupid men. I've watched you observe the Governor's nobles here. I doubt your judgement would be at fault over Carthage – if possibly a little premature. Did you, in honesty, see anything to suggest I'm wrong when I say they will use Rosamunda against me?'

There was no need for me to voice an answer.

'You said you didn't trick her into coming here to kill her?'

'That's correct.' Videric wiped his wet fingers across his forehead. A lizard scuttled past Rosamunda's sandals, skidded, and flicked off behind one of the Roman fern pots.

'Then what *is* this?'

Videric spoke as if I hadn't asked the question.

'I can't put her aside as barren or unfaithful. Or rather, I *can*, but it would not be believed. Some agent of Carthage would kidnap her from her father's estate, or any other noble's castle at which she might be a guest. And then it would be plain how much of a fool I am. Perhaps you paid close attention only to half of what you painted? There is more here than her lack of – affection.'

He shook his head, continuing briskly.

'Rodrigo knows I can't be forced to choose between my country and this woman. The next time I should merely take poisoned wine. So she cannot be abandoned or divorced.'

'That doesn't leave any choices!' A pain went through my chest and stomach at a sudden thought. 'Unless – you've brought her here so she can *watch* you drinking poisoned wine now?'

The Aldra Videric's gaze sharpened enough to let me know I had given myself away. That I have thought of this man as my father for a decade, no matter how distant from me he might have been.

Since perception travels both ways, I could make a good guess that he had at least *considered* dying here. On those nights when a man can't sleep, or properly wake, and can only endlessly measure the walls of his trap.

What tilts the balance too much in his favour is that, as ever, it is the men in this world that I understand. I love my mother, but all the women I know seem to have grown up in cages. I find myself avoiding their company, unless, like Ty-ameny, they are powers in their own right. There's much of me mirrored and reversed in Neferet, that I didn't like to see. I understand how it is that Videric can love Rosamunda and not *know* her.

It is not what I want to be – since half of me *is* woman – but it's what I am.

Videric said quietly, 'No, I haven't come here to kill myself. Despite what men say of it being a coward's act, I think it would be harder than living and enduring the pain.' He hesitated. 'What do you say? You've endured enough, King's Fool. You never hanged yourself or drank poison.'

'I don't have Father Felix's faith.'

Videric nodded. Any other man would have asked if a lack of faith didn't make self-murder easy, since there would be no punishment for it. Videric's ready agreement, I thought, meant he looked at it the same way I do – that this sole and only world is very difficult to leave, no matter what; and that the desire to be dead usually passes into shame-faced appreciation of being alive.

'What will you do? You've left yourself nowhere to go, if anyone who can threaten her can control you. And through you, the King.'

His blue gaze stayed on Rosamunda. 'Do you want her to hear, now? Do you want her to know, while you're present?'

I already knew enough to be a danger to him the minute I stepped through that archway.

'Give me back my knife. She shouldn't be gagged.' I couldn't help my disgust showing.

'Wait until you hear her scream for help. And she may not be permitted that.'

Part of me agreed with him. The part that was half book-buyer by now, I thought, appalled. But the Ilario that lived at Taraco, that knew this woman as a mother – no matter how distant a mother—

'Take it *off*,' I muttered, picking at the knots again and wishing my fingernails were longer. 'It isn't . . . You can't.'

Even I can't bring myself to say 'it isn't fair'.

Fairness and justice can have nothing to do with what I feel for Rosamunda. Or I might be a greater danger to her than Videric is.

The captain of the men-at-arms knelt down beside me and cut the irrevocably knotted silk bonds of her gag. Something he would not do without Videric's orders; none of Videric's soldiers ever would. I looked up to thank my stepfather.

Rosamunda lifted her head from my thigh and rolled away from me, still bound hand and foot, sitting up on the white marble tiles, shaking out her dishevelled hair.

She screamed.

Shatteringly loud, raw-edged, ragged; panicked enough to send ice down my spine. The men-at-arms came to instant readiness, staring around, expecting the King's guardsmen to come running in—

I pushed myself across the cold, smooth stone, grabbed at her shoulder, and pulled her back up against my chest. I clapped my palm over her mouth, pinching her delicate nostrils between my thumb and finger.

Rosamunda's scream choked off into a gasp. Into coughs.

I loosened my grip as she tossed her head, as if she could clear her nose and throat that way – and she screamed again.

My hand felt slick with fluids as I clamped it over her nose and mouth again.

I loosed my grip by stages, cutting her off each time I felt the breath of a sound begin. She strained against me, as if she had forgotten how much stronger than an adult woman I am.

At last she slumped back against me, her chest shaking. I felt the hot tears running over my wrist before I realised she was weeping.

None of the men-at-arms had left their posts at the archways.

I held Videric's gaze. 'You shouldn't make me do this. *I* shouldn't make me do this.'

Videric spoke quietly. 'You might feel that you're a hermaphrodite monster. You grew up in Taraconensis, and you care for it, nonetheless. You wouldn't have humiliated yourself in the cathedral if that wasn't true.'

'I thought it was necessary!'

To my annoyance, I could feel myself hot behind the ears, and in my face; hot and cold with a sick shame at the memory of it.

'I thought it was *all* that was necessary! Now you tell me there's this!'

Videric interlaced his broad fingers and looked down at them. 'I know these things. I know, also, that she's . . . not the only one of us who has tried to murder you. I ask. In this. Will you give me a hearing?'

It's the portrait, I realised.

He wants to talk to me for many reasons, but one is that I'm the only other person who sees the truth of him and her. Who can he talk to about it? Not even King Rodrigo Sanguerra. And . . . Not Rosamunda.

'Mother – Aldro Rosamunda – you'll have to be quiet.' The way I held her was oddly like a mother holding its child. Releasing her, I wiped my hand down my tunic. 'Videric . . . You tell me how you solve the unsolvable.'

There was a look on his face of amusement and gratitude.

I saw the moment when Rosamunda realised it.

'You can't do what he tells you!' Her voice sounded wet and thick; not its usual melodious contralto. 'Ilario! *You can't—*'

I cut her off before her tone could rise. 'I'll hear what he has to say.'

She looked at me as if I were mad enough to be dragged away in sacks and chains and tethered in the lower dungeons, to amuse the courtiers when they visited the moon-touched. 'Videric tried to have you *killed*.'

I shrugged. 'Yes. But it seems to me – men spend their time hurting one another. I feel a woman should be different. A mother. *My* mother—'

Rosamunda smiled with complete spite. 'How long is it since you saw your child, Ilario? Have you seen her today?'

I reckoned the time by the sunlight burning down into the room. Well past Terce.

'I haven't seen Onorata since yesterday.'

Because she's safer with her grandfather. But that has the sound of an excuse. Had I wanted to see her, I need not have slept late.

'Carrasco will be looking after her,' I said briskly. 'He won't expect me. I have no *idea* how to be a mother. If I were inclined to thank Christus Imperator for anything, it's that Honorius knows how to be a father.'

I put out my hand, brushing Rosamunda's cheek.

She leaned into the touch unwillingly; her expression was spite and triumph mixed. And no guilt. Will she never ask herself *why* I need to learn how to mother my child?

The truth came up as inexorable as tidewater; not a surprise to me, but this time inescapable. *No, she'll never ask; it would never occur to her even to wonder.*

I helped Rosamunda to her feet, as young men are trained to do. And seated her on the marble surround of the fountain, arranging the folds of her skirt as ladies-in-waiting are taught. I dipped my kerchief in the cool water and cleaned her face, which she accepted with the air of accepting something usual from a servant.

I found a second clean kerchief and made a damp pad of it, holding it to her forehead. 'You should want to hear this too.'

She closed her eyes, without answering.

Videric's voice broke into my thoughts. I realised I had been standing in front of Rosamunda for several moments, lost in studying her.

'Wait as long as you like,' he said, 'but you won't hear an apology from her.'

'An *apology*? For *screaming*?'

'No.' He looked at me as if I were a fool.

I seated myself slowly beside the spread of her blackthorn-berry-coloured silken skirts. She didn't look at me. One protest about the situation in which she found herself, then – nothing.

With any other woman, I would have guessed that she ignored me out of embarrassment, or even shame. Watching her gaze intent on Videric, I knew Rosamunda saw no one here except the man who she thought had power over her.

Certainly I will never hear, *I'm sorry I tried to kill you in Carthage.*

For her, that's forgotten; gone.

'*You* could shout as loudly as she,' Videric observed. 'This palace is infested with servants: someone would hear you and raise an alarm. So I see no reason not to disclose to you what I'm about to do. Then, if you wish to scream for your friends . . . ' He shrugged. 'Captain.'

The captain directing them, the men-at-arms went out through the archways; nominally out of earshot. If I concentrated, I could hear their boots shifting on the marble tiles.

'He's a trustworthy man,' Videric said, a nod of his head to the departing captain's back, deliberately not mentioning the man's name. 'Like Ramiro Carrasco. But I never like to give a man more information than he ought to hear.'

Trustworthy for the same reason as Carrasco?

I'd trust Orazi or any of Honorius's men. But if I explain why to Videric, he'll regard me as even more of a fool.

'My mother,' I said. 'Your wife. She's an Achilles' heel to you. You can't keep her at court. She won't be safe back on your estates.'

I would have touched Rosamunda's hand to comfort her, if I didn't know from her expression that she would jerk them away.

'You won't murder her.' I brought the word out coolly, ashamed a moment later when Rosamunda's eyes snapped open and she gazed about the hall, rumpled and clearly terrified.

Where is Rekhmire'? Where is my father?

I managed to say, 'This doesn't leave much, Aldra Videric.' I wiped at my sweaty forehead. 'In fact, I don't see that it leaves anything. If you send her away to any branch of her family—'

Like most of the nobles of the Iberian courts, she has relatives in Aragon, Castile, Granada, Catalonia, and the Frankish lands beyond.

'—Carthage *will* track her down. So. Tell me what you have planned.'

Videric nodded slowly. 'Rodrigo is the only other man to know. I don't suppose the King will be in the least surprised to hear that you've found your way into this.'

His smile was oddly poised between sympathy and malice.

'I'm half inclined to tell you all and let *you* decide, Ilario. Unfortunately, since it seems to need both Rodrigo Sanguerra and myself to keep the Carthaginian legions at home, I can't do that.'

'You're not so necessary,' I said coldly. 'If you died, Rodrigo would have another man in your place, performing perfectly well, inside three days.'

Videric smiled. 'But as you, especially, will have discovered – it doesn't matter what the truth is. It matters what people *think* the truth is. Because that's what they act on. In fact, my death may well bring the legions marching up the Via Augusta. So I must hope to be as long-lived as my grandfather . . . '

He got abruptly to his feet, pacing, gazing up at the arcing droplets of water. Stopping in front of both of us, he looked only at Rosamunda.

'I couldn't do anything to harm you. You've always known that.'

She brought her head up with that artificial arch of the neck that allows a woman to look up at a man through her lashes. It was familiar enough that I suspected the court deportment tutor, Dolores, had taught both of us. *Mother and . . . son-daughter.*

She fixed an intense gaze on him. 'Don't do this. Even when I was with Honorius, it was foolishness, infatuation—'

She cut her gaze across to me.

'—and I've been punished.'

I didn't hear what she said next; couldn't decipher the low, intense conviction in her words. It may have been some effort to recall their sexual connection to his mind.

'*I've been punished.*' After all this, this is what I am to you?

A piece on the board to be moved, to convince Videric how remorseful you are towards him.

Why did I imagine anything else? I should know, by now.

Videric's voice interrupted my dazed state. 'Hope dies last.'

He might have been referring to himself, or to me. Or to us both, I thought.

'Perhaps unfortunately,' he added, looking down at Rosamunda, 'this doesn't depend on Honorius, or on Ilario's parentage, or on your infidelity. If it did, I think I might eventually teach myself to hate you.'

Her huge dark eyes brimmed.

I could have told him, even at thirty or forty years younger than he, that hate is no different to love. Not in the intensity. Not in how much it occupies your mind, and wastes your time.

Videric shook his head. 'You're a weapon, Rosamunda. I've been fool enough to show myself besotted with my wife. That makes you a sword at my throat. And whatever the story is here, in Carthage the Lords-Amir *know* that you attempted murder—'

'Because you told me to!'

I winced at the shrill note in Rosamunda's voice. Shrill as when she claimed the same thing about my infant exposure: *He made me.*

'No one ever made you do anything,' I interrupted. 'You just chose whichever was easiest at the time and didn't think of what would happen after.'

Her eye caught the light as she turned to me. She had the blank-eyed gaze of a marble medusa.

'You be quiet, you monster! If it wasn't for you, *none* of this would have happened to me!'

I drew as much of my hard-earned court composure about me as I could, and looked at her without shaking, or weeping. I found voice enough to say, 'If I were in your position, I'd be trying to make an ally of *both* of us – Videric, me. But I don't know if you're too stupid to think of that, or if you just hate me too much.'

She narrowed her eyes, so that the smudge of kohl at the corner of one bled out into the incipient wrinkles there. 'All your fault!'

'You're mistaken,' Videric said gently.

Her face shifted; showed ingratiation and confusion.

He went on: 'You think I have the power here today, and you can sacrifice Ilario to that. But the truth is, *I* have no choice either. I did all I could in coming up with an alternative that Rodrigo preferred to your quiet and immediate execution.'

Rosamunda's eyes and mouth rounded.

She seemed to fall into herself, staring around the hall as if she searched out any way she could run.

'I doubt that's wholly correct.' I didn't trust myself to do more than sit, my hands shook so hard. 'If King Rodrigo knows she can be used to get at you, and knows that without you the legions sail for Taraco . . . He'd have killed Aldro Rosamunda long before now. Except for one thing.'

Videric cocked his head invitingly. Odd, how I had always wished to have him take what I said seriously. *Beware what you wish for.*

'It's truly hard to make a death look like an accident if it isn't,' I said. 'That only happens in bards' tales. And if anybody kills Rosamunda under those circumstances, you'd *know* the King was responsible. And I don't think you two could work together after that, not like you have done. So he loses you anyway.'

I shook my head, trailing fingers in the cold green endlessly disturbed water.

'As usual, you've got things so that you can do exactly as you want. Except . . . that I don't see how you can have what you want. Even if you hide – her – away as well as you can, someone would follow you to her, eventually.'

'I must personally congratulate Queen Ty-ameny, the next time I go on a diplomatic mission to Constantinople.' Videric's smile was wry, and genuine. 'You appear to have had a considerable education in the last twelve months.'

'Some of it in things I never wanted to know.'

It was not something I imagined saying to this man, my father, my stepfather. I saw how he looked at me when he turned. He may even have been a little impressed. I wished I were still the Ilario who could appreciate that.

I said, 'Even if you formally put her aside, nullify the marriage to a barren wife, no one would believe it. Not after you gave up your position at court for her.'

The position second only to the King's.

Not death, not divorce . . . what?

Rosamunda, her chin lifting defiantly, snapped, 'I am *not* barren! Remember the cathedral, lord husband? It may be a monster of a child, but I conceived and bore Ilario! And never anything from you, monster or not!'

She must see how she's affecting him—

I stopped breathing for a second, and caught it again in a rush.

Is it possible she's behaving this way, angering him, so that he doesn't feel so guilty over what it is he has to do? Is she sparing him anguish?

I looked at the lines that anger was starting to pinch permanently into the corners of her mouth. Nothing visible except anger, resentment – and the resentment seemed to be that all this should happen to *her*.

Hope dies last.

She snorted under her breath. 'If it's your doting that's the problem, then . . . I made you love me, Videric. I could make you stop loving me.'

Her sneering grated on me. If I could have got words out at that moment, they would have been, *I am ashamed to be your son-daughter!* Christ the Emperor knows, Videric is a bad enough man, but Rosamunda came close to making me pity him.

'Let me show myself at the Court of Ladies here tomorrow and take a lover,' she said coolly. 'Two or three, perhaps. Gossip will get around quickly enough. Carthage is ruled by *men*. They won't believe you could love me and let me fornicate with soldiers and stable-hands.'

She took my breath away.

More, I thought: 'soldiers and stable-hands' fell too easily off her tongue.

If she hasn't already practised what she advises, she certainly has her eye on particular men she'd like to seduce.

Videric stood with the arc of the fountains behind him, utterly motionless. In ten years I'd never seen him at a loss for words. He stared at Rosamunda in a dazed way, as if he looked into a bright light, and didn't speak.

My hatred for Videric is almost impersonal. What he'd tried to do to me, he would have done to anyone in my position; it didn't matter to him that I was Ilario.

It made it just that much easier to throw a rope to him, as I would have thrown a rope to a drowning enemy.

'That wouldn't succeed,' I said quietly. 'Rosamunda, *look* at him. I know he's a courtier. But no one is going to believe he's unaffected if you take a lover. Do you really think even he can hide that?'

Over Videric's mumbled protest, Rosamunda repeated with casual cruelty, 'I can make him stop loving me.'

'No.' Videric's burly shoulders were back, and his usually bland face tightened from the emotion in him. 'No. You didn't make me love you. You won't make me stop. If it were possible for me to stop . . . I would have done so by now.'

No sound but Videric's sandals on the marble floor as he began to pace again; Rosamunda utterly silent as her head turned back and forth, following him.

'Then tell me how you can make me safe.'

I heard the echo of other demands in that one. Thirty years since he married his child-bride of fifteen; thirty years of *Videric, make it right for me*, and him finding his satisfaction in pleasing this woman.

I should have thrown the portrait in the sea before I let Videric look at it. That, or only showed it to Rosamunda, so she'd know I understood her game. But no, I have to be so damn *clever* . . .

Videric's pale gaze met mine as if he could follow every thought and feeling in me.

Fifty years of experience. *He may as well read minds! What's the difference?* How did I ever imagine I was going to out-plan someone who's been at court longer than I've been alive?

'I'm not putting Rosamunda aside.' Videric spoke to me, but his gaze continued to slide sideways to her. 'The reverse, in fact. What will happen is that Rosamunda is going to apply to me, formally, to end the carnal part of our marriage—'

A choked sound from her bore no resemblance to a word.

'—and permit her to retire to a place of religious contemplation. To a nunnery, or a convent. So that she can purify her soul for the next world, and glorify the Emperor-Messiah with prayer.'

Rosamunda stood, her fists clenched before her straining against her bands. '*How long?*'

It is not unusual for widows, or wives who are known not to be able to bear their husband's rapes and beatings, to apply to the King for permission to retire to a convent. Whether it's an order of educated women, writing scrolls of theology, or whether it requires digging turnips to feed the other sisters and novices, evidently it seems preferable to what they can expect of life in the world.

I asked Rodrigo Sanguerra myself, once; when I was worse than desperate to escape the humiliations of being Court Fool. He made a public theological debate of it, with bishops arguing whether I could be allowed to join a monastery – where I would contaminate the men with the parts of me that were sinful woman – or a nunnery. It collapsed in riot when one of the male courtiers offered the opinion that I would be far too popular in a convent as a nun with a prick.

These days the thought makes me smile, if with an edge. Trust a man to think I would be popular for what so many of those women are escaping from.

'How *long*?' Rosamunda's voice echoed back from the marble walls, over the noise of the fountains.

Videric spoke as if he talked only to me. 'The Aldro Rosamunda will stay at several different convents, to flush out and elude pursuit. These will all be nunneries used to taking court ladies. The civilised establishments where the Mother Superior is often a rich noblewoman in her own right, and music and literature is practised as well as the worship and glorification of God.'

I found myself nodding as if entranced.

'Truthfully,' Videric said, 'I expect the agents of Carthage to have found and investigated every rich convent of that nature within three months of the announcement being made. Before Yule, certainly. There aren't more than twenty establishments that a woman of Rosamunda's rank would find appropriate.'

The water splashed in my palm where I intercepted a fountain-jet. If it smelled of metal pipes, it was nonetheless ice-cold. I dabbed it on my forehead, feeling it run down inside my tunic, over my small breasts, as it dried in my body's heat.

'However.' Videric's spine stiffened, seemingly without his volition. He didn't look in Rosamunda's direction. 'There are hundreds, perhaps thousands, of *ordinary* religious households in Taraco and Aragon and Granada. Small convents, closed to the world; poor nunneries that rely on local charity and the land to support ten or twenty praying Brides of Christ the Emperor. And a woman takes a new name when she enters religious life as a novice. Who's to know one "Sister Maria Regina" in a thousand convents where there are hundreds of Maria Reginas every year?'

Rosamunda repeated in the numb way that Brides tell their Green beads: 'How. Long?'

'They'll search Taraconensis, and Aragon,' Videric observed, 'and likely the smaller kingdoms if they get desperate. But no matter how hard the King-Caliph drives them . . . '

He blinked, as if he saw something far off.

' . . . For all their Crusades, the Franks haven't yet taken the Northern Islands from us. Jersey, Guernsey, Sark; they all have thriving Iberian populations and fishing ports. If you look at the royal maps, you'll see them clearly marked as part of the kingdoms of Aragon and Navarre.'

He paused.

'What you *won't* see, because they're too small, are the other islands of the archipelago. Some are mere rocks.'

Videric finally turned his head to look at Rosamunda.

'Midway between Sark and Guernsey, with twelve leagues of sea between them and the mainland, lies Herm. Herm is a mile and a half long, half a mile wide. It has a fort on it, and a small fishing village, and enough grass to graze milch-cows . . . And a stone's throw away from Herm, across a channel of sea, is the island of Jethou. Jethou is perhaps a third of a mile long; a little less across. It has grass, a few trees. It's no more than a rock. But on Jethou – there is a convent-house. It is a silent order.'

18

I couldn't have interpreted the look in Videric's eyes to save my own life, never mind Rosamunda's.

He said, 'In all honesty, I think Carthage will assume you're dead long before they think to send agents to a sea-swept and forgotten nunnery on the island of Jethou.'

You'll give out publicly that's she dead, I understood.

Rosamunda's blank expression told me she hadn't thought that far. But it would be an obvious next step.

I could paint her at work in the meagre fields, picking stones out of furrows with her bare hands; her nails broken, her skin cracked. Can paint the bare, plain building that will be the nunnery. A master's brush could paint well enough to make you smell sour vegetables and sour bodies; rancid feelings not able to break out in gossip. Silence, isolation, labour. If Videric does ride out to Jethou in five years' time, they will have pushed her well across the line from beauty to middle age.

If Videric's lucky, he'll find he was in love with a clear complexion and lustrous black hair.

And if Rosamunda's lucky, she'll find that, too; and he can declare her dead and marry again, while she returns to the material world under a different name, at least free of the nunnery.

I tried very hard not to enjoy the thought of her future: to hope that Videric does continue to love her, and so she'll stay there for as many years as it's possible to see ahead. Part of me still scrabbled frantically for some way to save her.

'I don't know how long it will last.' Videric's voice was a whisper. 'I think, for as long as Carthage is under King-Caliph Ammianus's rule—'

Rosamunda shouted, 'No!'

'Or until their conflicts with the Turks break into open war; that could be as soon as five years from now—'

For the first time, I saw them look at each other. Stare, as if each could read secrets in the other's so-familiar face.

A little desperately, Videric protested, 'I'll try to visit. To see you, when it's safe. When I can be sure I won't be followed—'

'*No!*' It was no more than a wheeze of breath.

Videric shrugged hopelessly. 'Five years from now is not so long. But even then, your face can't be seen at court again, it would be too dangerous—'

Rosamunda's body shook; I held her up.

Videric took a step forward, eyes all but glowing with his intensity.

'—but you'll be *safe*. Who'd look for the Queen of the Court of Ladies among poor sisters digging their own turnips, and milking goats? Who could recognise you in homespun black, when every other woman is in the same robes? You won't look the same – you'll have a different name – if no one from this court contacts you, Carthage will never stumble across you; you're too far out of the way—'

She stood – and fell forward off the fountain's marble rim, out of my support, her tied ankles tripping her. Her bound hands reached out, seizing Videric's robes.

The striped linen's stitching broke under her weight, and he caught her by the wrists, dragging her upright. She leaned her body against his from belly to chest and brought her mouth up for a kiss.

I saw it as clearly as if I had it at my brush's end: Videric looking into her face.

And if he could have seen anything in her kiss but desperation, neither King nor Carthage could make him send her away.

He didn't slump, but he withdrew into himself, his hand gently easing her cheek away from contact with his chest. He seated her implacably back on the fountain's marble surround.

She glared and twisted around, facing me.

'You bitch, you monster, you – eunuch! This is all your fault!'

I didn't know I would do it until it was done. My hand cracked across her face and my palm was stinging.

She lurched back where she sat, Videric catching her elbow. I forget that I hit so much harder than most women; almost as hard as the man I'm dressed as.

The mark was carmine on her cheek, turning the blue of sloe-berries already, over the bone.

I noticed coldly that I was shaking, as if I stood out in a damp winter gale.

'Tell me again you should have suffocated me at birth!'

'I should have! I tried!'

She flung out the last words like a child throwing any lie out, in the hopes that it will hurt.

'*You're* the child!' The irony would have made me laugh, under other circumstances.

I see it a lot in the Court of Ladies – women never allowed to deal with money, or property, or the decisions of who they'll marry and be with child by. Without experience, and with only rivalries, friendships, cliques, and lovers to occupy themselves, it's no wonder many of them are still twelve years old at the age of forty-five.

And if I were a man, I wouldn't know what goes on in the Ladies' Court, and if I were a woman, I wouldn't have any different experiences to make the comparisons.

This is what I knew, when I carried Onorata and it tried to make me something I'm not – that I may not be a man, but I have no idea how to be a woman.

She lifted her hands and Videric casually took hold of her bound wrist. It was evident she couldn't free herself, from the silk ropes or her husband.

'You were my punishment, Ilario.' The last word was a painful grunt. She momentarily caught her bottom lip between her teeth. 'I've suffered enough, haven't I? You can't take any *more* away from me!'

Paint would put two catch-lights in her eye, at the edge of the pupil and in the body of the white, to show how lustrous and large her eyes are. Paint could make every fold of her silk dress into rich soft fabric, so fine a rough edge of skin could snag it . . .

And if I painted, I thought, I could paint her life on Jethou, too. No longer Queen of the Court of Ladies. Men say all faces look alike in a Bride's wimple and hood. And even though that's not true – Rosamunda will always have the stunning bones that support her flesh and delicate skin – working outdoors on an island, summer and winter, will bring freckles, broken capillaries, the dryness and paper skin that comes with cold.

Rosamunda stared at me as if she had no consciousness that twelve months ago she tried to stab me in the stomach. Which is a slow and painful death, but she knew too little to know that. She struck at the body because, like most not trained as knights, she couldn't bear to strike at the face.

I saw recognition in her, as if the thought passed from my mind directly to hers.

'I couldn't do it,' she said, all the attention of those dark eyes fixed on me. 'You know that. I told you to run. Ilario . . . Videric's not your father; don't side with him. I'm your mother.'

Turning away, I scooped up a double handful of cool water and doused my face. The dazzles left my vision.

'How will you leave Gades?'

I had a sudden absurd vision of Aldra Videric sneaking out through the kitchen in his finest gown, and every servant staring at him.

'As we came.' Videric's eyes looked weary. 'This is a seaport, Ilario, as you told me. My wife will go aboard a ship for Jethou this evening. And tomorrow, I and my men, and one of the waiting-women in Rosamunda's clothing, will ride out of Gades on the Via Augusta for Taraco. As far as any man here is concerned, Aldro Rosamunda visited Gades and returned with me.'

Who would I tell, to prevent this?

Do I desire to prevent this?

Before I could say anything, I heard raised voices outside; Videric stepped to the archway – and stepped back again, as Rekhmire' strode through.

19

Rekhmire', striding in, took it all in an instant; I could see him do it. Lord Videric, armed men, the Lady Rosamunda with her wrists and ankles tied. And I, who was not apparently restrained in any way, nor had any weapons pointed at me.

A sweep of his glance at Videric and I saw he had it. Carthage. Other enemies of the kingdom. And the danger that Rosamunda will be. He looked as if he wanted to smack himself in the forehead.

'Tell me,' I said steadily. 'I will have missed something. Videric will have fooled me somehow, or told me half-truths that don't look like lies. Tell me this doesn't have to happen this way.'

Strain carved lines from Rekhmire''s nose to the corners of his mouth. With his bald head illuminated by the sun from the lattice roof, he looked even more like one of the statues shining in the Alexandrine palaces at Constantinople, for all he had a linen gown swathing him to the ankles to keep off what he referred to as 'this northern cold'.

'I should have seen this!' he murmured, looking from me to Videric.

He stood a head taller than my stepfather, was broader across the chest, and it wasn't until I saw them standing together that I realised Videric was bordering on late middle age.

But he was a decade older than Rosamunda when he married her for her dowry and for love . . .

'I didn't imagine you would involve *Ilario* in this.' Rekhmire' sounded almost uninterested, his expression bland. 'Is this wise?'

For a moment even I thought, *He knew this was going to happen!* And then read him well enough to see how he picked up cues from the people present, and how we were placed.

Videric wiped his hand over his forehead, taking away the beads of sweat that glistened in the sun. 'I didn't "involve" Ilario. Ilario, as you probably know very well by now, has a gift for finding out where he shouldn't be – and then she goes there!'

The last thing I wanted was a sympathetic look between these two men, even if it had been in Rekhmire''s mind to do it.

'He's – exiling her,' I cut in, choosing the best word I could find in that instant.

Rekhmire' looked down at Rosamunda, and gave her a polite nod.

She appeared to have no ability to conceal her emotion in the slightest.

She scowled, recovered the poise that the Queen of the Court of Ladies should have, and looked at him with slit-eyed hatred. 'I should have had my husband's men see to *you* in Carthage.'

I interrupted. 'Did Ramaz's arm heal up?'

Videric's twisted smile was as much an appreciation of that, in his own way, as the straight look of dislike that Rosamunda gave me. Videric waved a hand at the captain of his men-at-arms.

'Well enough,' the captain said grudgingly. He retained a strong western accent; it confirmed my thought that Videric hadn't brought the man to court before now. These will be all recently promoted men, still with everything to show about their devotion to their liege-lord.

I wasn't surprised, therefore, when the commander did no more than answer Videric's implied question; although the man looked at me with a wary respect, combined with that fear of the unnatural, that I tend to get in skirts when men learn I've done man's work. And an Alexandrine tunic is close enough to a women's robe – as Rekhmire' had been kindly informed by the fisher-children running about in the lower town ...

'This is no business of Alexandria's,' Videric said. His glance made insinuations between Rekhmire' and myself. 'Nor any business of yours, Master Rekhmire'. I shall have to ask you to leave, now.'

A clatter of footsteps sounded outside the stone archways; I glimpsed mail and the flash of light from sword-pommels, and Videric's men-at-arms stepped back inside the hall, looking to their captain.

Perhaps twenty other men in mail and breastplates crowded in after them. I recognised Orazi first – Rekhmire' signalled an acknowledgement to him – and then another man pushed his way through.

Honorius.

Like his men, he didn't have his sword drawn. The fountain-jets reflected in the mirror of his breastplate. Nothing marked him out from his men, off-duty as they were, bar the lion's head badge on his left sleeve. He scratched slowly through his cropped salt-and-pepper hair.

'You're her husband,' he said, voice harsh in the echoing hall.

Videric's soldiers were red-faced at being so outnumbered and so easily, but I saw one elbow the other, and I guessed the story of their lord and their lord's wife had gone the rounds after last year in Carthage. Although in what detail, and how accurately, I couldn't guess.

You couldn't tell from Orazi's face, or the others, that anything out of the ordinary was taking place. I thought, *They all know.* But they won't embarrass the Lion of Castile.

Rekhmire' stood as impassive as any carved sandstone, and I thought him thinking furiously.

The lean, soldierly man my father squinted at Rosamunda as if he squinted into a desert wind, abrasive with particles of sand. She didn't take her eyes off him.

I recognised the split-second hesitation, and that look Honorius wore.

This is something I would have two or three times a week, when I was Rodrigo Sanguerra's Freak. The look that at first goes straight through you, not recognising you at all. And a moment later seems to ask, *Why does that person seem to know me?*, and *No, surely, it can't be*; before they greet me with a rush of relief at the recognition – '*Ilario! I didn't know you, dressed as a—*' man or woman, whichever the case might be.

Honorius's hesitation lasted barely longer than it took to draw breath.

With a rush of relief, he exclaimed, 'Rosamunda!'

She went as red as if she'd been slapped.

Queen of the Court of Ladies, yes. Beautiful, poised, glorious: yes. But forty-five isn't twenty.

Is *so* different from twenty, it seems, that an old lover might not recognise that Rosamunda in this woman standing before him.

And two of us knew her well enough to know it had cut her like knives.

Slowly, Honorius said, 'I wouldn't have known you.'

Rosamunda made a little noise, and attempted to hide her bound hands in the silk folds of her skirt. Her fingers were shaking.

'I'm no different,' she whispered.

Honorius made a face, half-smile and half-grimace. 'That might be true.'

She turned her head and looked at Videric.

Not as a wife looks at the husband she's wronged; not as a sophisticated woman of the court looks at her husband in the socially embarrassing presence of an ex-lover. But plainly and simply for reassurance.

Videric stepped up to her and put his hand on her shoulder. Too quietly to be heard but by her and me, he said, 'You look the same as the day you turned twenty. Don't expect anything but malice from this man.'

She half-turned her head, in a gesture that was triply graceful because unstudied, and rested her forehead against the lower part of Videric's chest.

He looked down at her in the same way that a man looks at a wild animal that, for whatever reason, and for however long, trusts him far enough to touch her.

'I ought to horsewhip you,' Honorius ignored my stepfather and growled, taking a step forward. His only attention was for Rosamunda. 'You tried to kill that baby—'

I stepped forward, interposing myself between them, just as Rosamunda cried out in outrage behind me:

'*You* left me with the child!'

'I would have taken you. I would have taken Ilario.' His pain was bewildering to him, you could see it. After so long, he didn't expect to hurt like this.

And if this wasn't the first time in twenty-five years, perhaps he wouldn't.

Honorius shook his head. 'I remember your eyes as brown. They're . . . not.'

'It doesn't matter how many brown-eyed wenches you tumbled,' she snapped. '*You'd* never be the one with a big belly!'

My father looked frankly bewildered, and a little cross. 'Women have been having babies since the world was made. You can manage as well as the others, can't you?'

I raised my voice.

'Father, you didn't call me a whore for having got Onorata. I suppose I'm the only one here who *can* lay down as a man, and then get up with a child in my belly.'

That stopped the shouting.

What am I doing defending Rosamunda?

I saw how it defused something of the tension between them. There were still lines of force in the hall of the fountains, where desperate looks pinned people together: Honorius staring at Rosamunda, Rosamunda pressing her bound hands against Videric's thigh, Rekhmire' crossing the tiled floor and putting his hand on my shoulder.

His flesh was warm, heavy; and at once greeting and warning.

'I never thought I'd see my mother and father together in the same room,' I said.

Rosamunda stirred, a swathe of black hair coiled across her forehead and cheek where it fell down from her crown of braids. Her eyes flicked quickly from side to side. 'Saints and Sacred Beasts! I was *right*. You have only to stand in the same room together, you two. My lord—'

The sudden appeal, turning her head and looking up at Videric, brought home to me as nothing else could that these two have worked together to plot their rise at court.

That for all the people see Videric as necessary to Rodrigo Sanguerra, Rosamunda has performed Christ knows how much of the unattributed work and support. *And now we're sending her away.*

Rekhmire' was my best choice. I touched his arm, drawing his attention. His skin was hot and a little sweaty. I said, 'Find me a way that she doesn't have to go into exile.'

All three of them looked at me: Honorius, Videric, and my mother. Honorius with the long-suffering bad temper that he evidently only just controlled, not leaping in to say, *She birthed you, but that's all; you owe her nothing!* Rosamunda with the same puzzled bad temper with which she'd regarded me in Hanno Anagastes' court.

Only Videric worried me. What he hid under that bland exterior was enough experience to guess more than *I* could about my impulse not to let my sometime-mother be imprisoned on Jethou.

'Why am I to find an answer?' Rekhmire' sounded disgruntled, as well as still out of breath. 'If you're saying what I think, it seems a perfectly reasonable solution. It's not as if an innocent woman is being condemned to captivity.'

Rosamunda interrupted without appearing to notice that the Egyptian spoke. Her eyes were fixed on Honorius. 'You married, didn't you?'

I caught Videric's stifled surprise. I wondered if he was thinking what I was: *I didn't know she'd kept track of Licinus Honorius . . .*

'Who told you that?' Honorius sounded more interested than annoyed.

'After you came back and started to renovate the estate. There was a lot of gossip in the women's court. One of my friends has a cousin who was married to – well, it doesn't matter. But with the property, and their suspicion that you must have brought money back from Castile with you, there were enough of them with available daughters that they needed to know.'

She blinked, as if what took place in the women's court had happened centuries ago, although it couldn't have been more than twelve months.

'Licinus, what did she die of?'

It sounded odd to me to hear him called that. Shifting uncomfortably on the hard floor, I thought, *Why did he never invite me to call him by his personal name?* Or did he think I was more comfortable with 'Honorius'?

Honorius spoke with the reserve I associated with the man. You would not have known he and Rosamunda had been lovers – but then, I doubted they had, in more than the carnal sense.

'Her name was Ximena. You've obviously heard,' he added. 'She died bearing our second child. Our first had died before it could be baptised. This one . . . '

'Took her with it,' Rosamunda completed. She lifted her tied wrists, smoothing her hair out of her pale face with the backs of her hands. 'That would have been me. If I'd left with you. They say you had another wife before this Ximena. Did you kill her too?'

As dryly as a desert wind, Licinus Honorius observed, 'You *are* well informed. I used to know better than to underestimate the Ladies' Tower in any castle . . . No, Sandrine died of low-land sickness. She never carried a child long enough for it to distress her when it passed.'

Rosamunda's expression held a great deal of doubt on that point; I supposed mine might, also. And, to my surprise, Rekhmire' looked as if he would have spoken, under other circumstances.

'Ilario is my only living son or daughter.' Honorius raised a brow, still with his gaze on Rosamunda. 'In fact, both son *and* daughter—'

'And like all men, you wanted an heir. A true son.' Rosamunda looked dissatisfied.

'Not all men,' I said. 'And you of all people should know that! Since you're standing between two men who prove different to that.'

Rosamunda sighed.

For the first time, she looked at me without dislike; only with a tired melancholy that made me truly believe her a handful of years past forty.

'Perhaps,' she said. 'But it doesn't help. Two of you . . . It means nothing, not when everybody else is different. Ilario, *don't let them do this to me.*'

I caught Rekhmire''s glance. With an acknowledging look to my father and my stepfather, I touched Rekhmire''s arm, and drew him closer to the fountain, where the noise of the falling water would obscure what we said if we spoke quietly.

'It's what every man wants,' he said. 'Your enemy, dependent on *your* actions. Ilario . . . don't let it prove too intoxicating. And remember how very much people dislike being done a good turn.'

'I remember helping you with your knee,' I said acidly. 'You *still* owe me for my patience, book-buyer.'

Rekhmire' grinned at me.

I stopped smiling. 'Be honest with me. What is it I'm not seeing? And – is there any alternative, for her? It must have happened before; she can't be the *only* wife any man has ever been vulnerable through.'

'My lord Videric moves in the same circles as royalty, now, since he's as necessary to Taraconensis as people think he is. We're not discussing a minor nobleman and Carthage wheedling out occasional secrets. If she can be adequately threatened, the Fourteenth Augusta and Third Leptis Parva sail for Gades, and come marching up the Via Augusta to Taraco. The King-Caliph's talking of a *reconquista*, now; of taking Iberia back into the Carthaginian Empire . . . Taraconensis wouldn't be their ideal foothold, but it *would* give Carthage a land-border with the Franks. Somewhere to mass their legions, before they send them against Europe. King-Caliph Ammianus and Hanno Anagastes will take advantage of anything to get them through that gate. They won't kill Aldro Rosamunda – she's too valuable as blackmail – but they will take her and hurt her, if they can find her. And then set her free to come back to Aldra Videric, with the knowledge that they'll maim her worse the next time. It's easier to think of someone dying than it is to think of caring for them when they come home with their eyes gouged out, or half their skin flayed away . . . '

The shimmering cold water of the fountain was all that held me from vomiting. Cold, clear, clean. The sick sweat left my forehead after a while. I rested the palms of my hands against the cold marble.

'And we can't guard her?'

'You should know the answer to that, Ilario.'

Any guard that's strong enough to keep her safe is strong enough to make a prisoner out of her. And even if she were in Rodrigo Sanguerra's deepest dungeon, a servant or a slave would know where she was, and could be bribed into telling. Often for what would seem like a ridiculously small sum, if you're not the slave or servant.

352

Faith is a better barrier. Faith will keep Sister Maria Regina shut off from the mundane world, in communities where bribery means nothing. Because anyone who will live willingly on Jethou doesn't want anything the world can offer.

I stepped away from the arch.

Videric bent, cut her bands, and half-lifted his wife to her feet, urging her forward.

Rosamunda looked over her shoulder at me, on her way to the door.

'You don't understand.' She spoke quietly, frowning; I felt for the first time that she was straining to make me understand, rather than justify herself. She said, 'If no one buys you – if you're a slave and you're manumitted – then you're free.'

I was confused. 'Well, yes.'

She smiled. It was sad. 'Odd, that you should have given birth to a child, and still think like a man. Ilario, you're not legally a woman. Your father can't marry you to a man against your will and desires.' She glanced at Honorius. 'For a good match, *or* because he thinks it would be better for you. And if you take a man as a lover, he can't legally put you aside for not having babies as and when he wants them. I know you have none of the legal protections of being a man. You were made a slave as soon as that Valdamerca woman took you off the chapel steps. But if you'd been *all* girl, you would have been a slave as soon as you left my womb. Do you understand that?'

'Not truly.' I couldn't do anything else but be honest. 'Legally, I suppose I'm not a woman.'

'No,' Videric said. 'According to the Kingdom's best lawyers, you are, in fact, a eunuch.'

'*What*—' I began.

'I know.' Videric cut me off. 'It's the nearest definition they *do* have. Ilario . . . I know you don't wish to hear advice from me. I can't say I blame you. But the last thing you want is any legal taint of womanhood about you – trust me, Ilario.'

The look I gave him must have pierced even his hide. He appeared to wince. Or perhaps it was indigestion.

'It would alter your relationship with your father.' His nod at Honorius was civil, if not warm. His gaze travelled to Rekhmire'. 'And your husband, should you marry a man. That knowledge that you have absolute legal power over your wife . . . it follows you everywhere, do you understand me? Everywhere. If she can't say no, her yes is worth very little.'

Caught between sympathy and distaste – for both of them – I countered Videric with a stare very like his own. 'I understand you. All I need do is imagine being a slave whom no man can free.'

'Precisely.' He nodded agreement, as if unaware of any ironies.

Rekhmire' demanded coldly, 'Why were you making such inquiries?'

Videric inclined his head to me.

'You're not female.' He smiled. 'I had the lawyers look into it . . . If I could have you declared female, you would – as my publicly acknowledged child – belong to me.'

Before I could get a word out, Honorius cut in, in a tone like a stonemason sawing marble. 'Ilario is of *my* begetting, and would belong to me.'

Rekhmire', as urbanely as ever, put one monumental hand up. 'My claim pre-dates the court of Taraco – I bought and owned Ilario; Ilario would therefore be mine.'

The only true woman in the room, Rosamunda, looked up and caught my eye. 'I gave birth to you, but there's no way you'd belong to *me!*'

'Christus and St Gaius and Kek and Keket . . . !' I shook my head, even if it did make me feel cold inside. I eyed Videric warily. 'When you say I would belong to you—'

'Your money or property would be mine, if Master Honorius or any other client—' He stressed the word. '—paid for a painting. It would go into my treasury; you couldn't touch it. You would need my permission to travel, if you wished to study under another master. I could order you in what you wear, where you go, what you eat or drink, who you may speak to.' He shrugged. 'And beat you if you disobeyed, despite your being past the age of majority. It's arguable that, as a woman, the male age of majority wouldn't apply to you.'

The silence was one in which I could hear my heartbeat in my ears, deafening me.

Videric gave another shrug. 'But they seem to feel that a *membrum virile*, however small, qualifies you as a male. There's also the rumour that you fathered a child – that bastard that Carrasco acts as nursemaid to. I believe that carried weight with the justices.'

Fathered a child.

I didn't blink.

My mother looked at me. At Rekhmire'. Back at me.

She smiled sadly.

'There are men who don't want the law to apply. But that really doesn't matter, does it? It's the ones who *do* want it that matter, and then it's there for them, in all their dusty old scrolls, and there's no fighting it. Of the girls I went to school with, all but five are dead now. And ten of them died in childbed. The men are on their third wives.'

She studied me with finality.

'I suppose that it doesn't matter if you have the breasts to give suck, and the womb to carry a child – you have a penis. And no matter how small it may be, it may not make you a man, but it makes you *not* a woman.'

'Sadly, that avenue is closed to us.' Videric took Rosamunda's arm. 'And it remains to see what we may do, now.'

20

Rosamunda looked down intently at his hand, not moving forward as directed.

She spread the fingers of both her tethered hands, directing a searching glance at the skin there. Some thought tugged at the corner of her mouth. I could not tell what she felt.

'When I was a girl . . .' She made fists of her hands, regarding them as if their acts entirely surprised her. '. . . I used to keep a knife and cut my skin.'

She turned her head without raising it, and the light caught the surface of her eyes, obliterating iris and pupil, glimmering white in the sun. She was looking at me.

'I always wanted to cut my face,' Rosamunda said plainly. 'Ever since a man put my hand on his belly when I was twelve, and showed me how it made his male organ stand up. But I saw that plain and ugly women had worse marriages, and worse lives. I thought I'd grow up to marry a rich man, and then take lovers as it pleased me.'

She made a kind of snort, as if of amusement, but there was something wrong in the note of it. 'Then I *did* take a lover, and I found out what happened when a man's potent. The birth nearly killed me. The pain . . . And I came so close to child-bed fever. I could have died at the age of twenty. There is a reason I never left with your father, Ilario, although it's not the one he thinks. I realised that if I left and married Honorius, I could expect to conceive every year – perhaps only every two or three years, if I put the child to my own breast. The women's court *talk* about ways to stop conceiving a child, but most of them become big-bellied all the same. And then it's as dangerous to be rid of it as it is to carry and bear it. The brothers and sisters you never had, Ilario; they would have killed me . . . '

Her head came up: she addressed Videric without any pretence or seduction.

'If I'd already been married to you for five years, and it had taken another man to get me pregnant, I thought I'd be safe with you – so I stayed. If Ilario had been an heir, that would have been perfect. You couldn't have asked anything more of me. While there were no children . . . I wanted you to love me. There was nothing else to keep you from putting me aside. Then my father would have married me off to some other, much poorer, man; because *he* at least knows the bull is sometimes as much at fault as the cow. A garden can't grow if the seed is rotten.'

Videric's face was patched carmine and a colour like spoiled milk.

Rosamunda said quietly, 'I never did take another lover, after Honorius, despite what the Court of Ladies may say. It isn't difficult to flirt and seduce and then be uncomprehending at just the right time . . . And I had you, for the marriage bed, and I wasn't afraid of starting a child, and so I . . . began to enjoy it. I *liked* my life. It was perfect. When I saw what my child had grown up to be, I knew I could never have raised Ilario. I did the right thing, staying with you, my lord. If you asked me to do anything, I would have done it – but it's so difficult, knowing he, she, he was my own flesh . . . I *tried*.'

I thought of her voice, muffled among the green leaves whose water supply could keep hundreds of poor men in Taraco from thirst. *'Run!'* And she had let me run.

'I tried,' Rosamunda repeated. Her bound restless hands crept down, pressing against her belly. 'This last year or two, I've bribed the servants to lie when they did the washing and say I still had my regular courses. My mother, she was free of the moon's curse early; she wasn't forty. And my grandmother too. But if you knew there was never a chance of a child, now – I didn't know how you'd act. If you'd change towards me.'

She didn't look at me. Only at Videric.

'It would have been easier to obey you and kill Ilario if I hadn't known I could never give birth again.' She sighed. 'It feels as if I've spent all of my life avoiding pregnancy! But . . . I *did* have a child. Even grown to a man . . . a woman . . . Ilario's still mine. Even if I never fed her, him, at my breast, he's still my son, my daughter. But I . . . did try.'

Videric took in a deep breath through his nostrils. He looked at her, merely looked at her, entirely in silence, until I felt the stone walls might burst apart from the force of that silence.

He spoke, finally.

Gently, he said, 'I wish you'd told me. We might have worked out some other way it could be done. I assumed yours was the only hand I could trust to it, but – it might have been arranged differently.'

'How could I tell you? What man wants to be told he's loved because he's barren?'

Videric nodded thoughtfully. 'Still, we might have done it some other way.'

The stillness broken, I cut in on his words, a cold shiver prickling the hairs at the nape of my neck. 'I don't know what bothers me more – that you can discuss it this calmly, or that you can discuss my *murder* in front of *me*.'

Aldra Videric's smile turned very ironic indeed. 'We're family, Ilario. We need have no secrets from each other.'

Rosamunda ignored his macabre humour. Her gaze on me was

brilliant, and I wished I had my drawing-paper. It would take me a year to uncover the emotions in how she looked at me.

Her mouth twisted. 'At least you can *pass* as a man, Ilario. That's your escape. There's no life for a woman here; it's worse than being a slave.'

As cruelly as I could, I said, 'You would blame it all on something else, Aldro Rosamunda, wouldn't you? It's because you were born a woman; it's because women have no rights in law . . . If you felt that badly about it, what was to stop you running away to Alexandria, say? You might have been raped a couple of times on the way, but Alexandrine women can enter their government and needn't marry.'

I smiled at her, making sure she saw teeth.

'But, thinking about it – this should please you, then: what's to happen. Everybody's equal under the Mother Superior, in a convent-house. And you'll hardly be in danger of conceiving a child on Jethou. It's a shame you didn't think of running away to the Church when you were twelve . . . '

Her complexion blanched. Instinct hadn't led me wrong, I thought; nine years in the court as Rodrigo's Freak gives you an edge for protecting yourself by attacking people in their keenest fears.

I saw that she had wanted to run, but hadn't found the courage.

Or the court sparkled too brightly, and it drew her too strongly. But somewhere in her heart, she still reproaches that girl who has first had her courses, and then marked her arms with blood.

I said, 'You think if I hadn't been born, things would have been different? You think if I hadn't been born a hermaphrodite, none of this would have happened? I think you were set on this course long before *I* was born.'

My voice went up and down the scale, out of control from anger and pain.

'I'll tell you what would have made it *different*.' I stepped right up close, staring down at Rosamunda, and over her shoulder at Videric. 'I'll tell you. If, when I was born – no matter who fathered me – both of you had *acknowledged* me. Yes, I would have grown up a man-woman, but gossip only lasts so long. If you'd acknowledged me as your child, no one could have blackmailed you later. That fear wouldn't have made you think you should kill me. What could anybody have done to you if there hadn't *been* a secret?'

I couldn't speak for a moment.

'I wouldn't have been a slave, or a King's Fool,' I said quietly, 'but those are things that only caused hurt to me. When you think about where you are, *why* things are as they are – think what would have happened if you'd kept me in the family and raised me openly as what I am.'

I walked past Rosamunda and Videric, past Honorius and Rekhmire', my knees shaking. At the arch, I stopped and looked back.

My father and Rekhmire' looked at each other, and walked to join me. I turned to go, and could not.

I looked back at Rosamunda.

This tie will not be undone or cut, not without death, and perhaps not even then. The past informs the present. And all I can do is speak as honestly as I have learned to be.

I said, 'The truth of it is – if I could find any way at all to get you free of this, I would do it. Still. But if I did find a way . . . I wouldn't hope for anything else. Not now. That's gone.'

I stepped back from the archway.

Videric grasped her bound wrists and led Rosamunda past me, and away into the palace.

The fountain rang clearly and bright on the stone, and my mother stumbled, but she never looked back.

Epilogue: Twenty-Four Years After

Rekhmire' spent time in Alexandria afterwards, but never lived there again, and he did not live to see the final fall of that great city in the year 1453, dying a few months before it.

Frankish Europe mourned Alexandrine Constantinople as the last of the Egyptians gone; Carthage was jealous; Mehmet II gloated; I mourned for the men and women I knew there, and for the aged Ty-ameny going out to fire cannon on the walls of Alexandria itself, before the Turkish bombards reduced all to flying splinters of rock. Fragile flesh vaporised, no trace ever found.

Frankish Europe mourned until the tide of manuscripts and books flooded to its shore; then it gobbled up science, medicine, and art in equal greed. Carthage fumed, no trace being found of how Alexandria's mathematicians had disabled their golem. But, since the Turks appeared to build none themselves, Carthage concluded that at least Alexandria had not learned to build what it could break.

Neferet, visiting me after Rekhmire''s funeral, announced herself an importer of books – products of the Royal Library's *machina*, which she sold the length of Italy and France.

When she asked how I would live without Rekhmire', I inquired as to how long it was since she had seen that cardinal's secretary and man of letters, Leon Battista, and we parted with a quarrel that more than twenty years had made familiar.

In the same year, Ramiro Carrasco and I travelled back to Iberia, reaching Taraco a few weeks before Licinus Honorius died falling from an untrained stallion, at the age of seventy-five. He lived long enough to require me to escort Onorata to Italy, and to look at me with boundless love.

Onorata apprenticed herself to a painter in the Empty Chair, and introduced me to men as her brother. I dressed as a male, as I had done with Rekhmire', for one kind of freedom – though dressing as a female gave me the right to kiss Rekhmire' publicly.

Six months after a rumour followed us from Taraco, it became known that I was a hermaphrodite, and Onorata took the Italian name of Rodiani, and asked me not to contact her for a time. I had no need to worry: her friendship with Honorius's soldiers had lasted all through her own childhood – which was at least hermaphrodite in its education and training – so I might always ask Orazi for news of her.

Ramiro Carrasco sought her out before we left the Empty Chair, and never told me what he said, but Onorata came out to say farewell in the public street, and gave me the kiss of kinship within the sight of all men.

North, south, hill, valley: I could wander where I liked, and draw what I might, but the absence of Rekhmire' was an unbearable pain to me.

Carrasco, having studied me for six weeks, chose to remark that eunuchs lived no great long lifetimes, like as not – certainly not while they were employed as book-buyers – and it was possible hermaphrodites need not live too long either, based on that principle.

It should not have eased pain, to hear Carrasco suggest it; it did, however. He knew me, also, after so many years.

'We might go to Carthage again,' he said, one day, out of a sky containing no warning cloud.

I declined. Instead we went north, to Jethou.

I found Rosamunda a keenly sharp abbess, hair white with age, but all six establishments of the Order of St Gaius under her skilled control. She did not manage men – or women, in this case – with the ease of one born to it, but what she had learned with pains and study, she had learned well.

I met her in a cold room, the casement window open to the grey sea, and her black Bride's clothing covered in addition with a fur-lined cloak, where she stood gazing at the implacable, endless sea.

'How did you manage,' I asked, 'when Videric was assassinated, and I answered none of your letters?'

If I hope to see pain made less raw by time, I did not see it on her austere face.

'Find yourself an occupation,' she said harshly.

I found the truth of it as I spoke. 'There is nothing left to do.'

'Then do what you will.' Rosamunda shrugged, under the heavy wool and wolf's fur. 'And remember.'

When I reached Carthage, to speak to Marcomir (Donata long since buried in the Fields of Baal and Tanitta), I found Onorata had been there before me, and I was not welcome.

I ended as I had begun, in Burgundy, in Bruges, in the house in which Rekhmire' had cursed the cold of all northern lands, suffered a week of coughing and wheezing, turned surprised eyes on me as he woke one morning, and died.

'Go back to your family,' I instructed Carrasco.

'Give me my collar again,' he grumbled, 'if you don't believe I'm already *with* my family, here.'

We slept back to back, for comfort in the northern cold, since I did not believe Rekhmire' would begrudge it.

When spring came, I walked the length of Burgundy to Dijon, in the south, and we lived within sight of the Good Philip's castle, and worked on painting panels by open windows, to the thundering of Dijon's water-mills.

And in the Duke's library, while my sight remained keen enough, I ornamented frontispieces for those books of his that were translations of the flood of knowledge to come to Europa after Alexandria fell, while the effect of those printed volumes began to change the world.

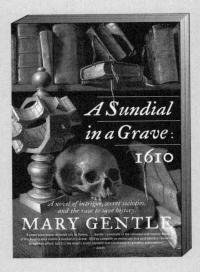